WITH
THESE
WALLS

RICHARD JOHN THORNTON

WITHIN THESE WALLS

Dedicated to enemies we know of.
And enemies yet to be discovered.

A lesson for the innocents.

Those souls generous enough to embrace the entity of the unknown, unwittingly announce their availability as prey to the ruthless individuals that inhabit our world.

The sinister cruelty of the willing mind gives little warning to the kindly. Human nature is capable of the subtlest of horrors…

prologue

Church Drayton. Such a picturesque village.

It reminded me of a seaside hamlet when I first set eyes on it as a child.

White-rendered cottages; decorative greenery; winding narrow roads.

Very much like the towns we'd visited in Devon and Cornwall on our holidays when I was growing up. Just like those tranquil memories, it seemed so peaceful and welcoming.

Having been raised nearby, it always appealed as the place I wished to establish a home for the marriage and family I yearned for. I wanted to raise my own children in that idyllic setting. It was a wondrous location for my husband Robert to retreat to after a hard day working in the hustle and bustle of the city centre.

It seemed perfect in every way.

But life usually has a way of ending those things that seem too good to be true.

Probably because that is exactly the case, most of the time.

That seemingly pristine village concealed a nasty disease. But I suppose a book's cover rarely reveals the true nature of its content.

We've got a new home now. We've worked hard to make it habitable. I think I've recovered from the ordeal, but even though nearly a year has passed since the problems first occurred, I know Robert still harbours thoughts of executing revenge.

And I fully understand why he feels this way.

Once resentment invades your blood stream, it never leaves.

Neither of us have any confidence in people anymore. Our once unquestioned and instinctive faith in fellow man has taken a massive jolt.

Thankfully, my physical scars are almost gone.

But it's the psychological damage that can never be fully repaired.

We go to sleep at night thinking of what happened.

When we wake up the following morning the ghosts still haunt us.

Ironically, Robert and I feel that we are stronger as a couple for all that we endured.

We supported each other when it mattered most.

But it was a terribly upsetting time.

A distressing, difficult induction in the ways that devious people can think and act.

Mind games can hurt you far more than confrontationally threatening behaviour.

Yet, these were people that at one stage I would have trusted with my life. I would have trusted them to guard my children's lives as well.

We were soul mates. Our relationship as neighbours and friends was previously untouched by drama or sorrow.

All in the garden seemed rosy.

Until things began to change.

It crept up slowly at first, but over time the fear enshrouded everything in our family's existence. It rocked us to our very cores. The life we loved so much was taken away from us by pure evil.

A strong word, evil, but I struggle to find a more appropriate one.

That beautiful village I fell in love with now fills me with trepidation even when we pass through in the car to visit my parents.

I cannot hide from my memories. They will stay with me forever.

I think of what we had to what we've got now.

Of course, we still have each other to share our newfound brand of comfort and contentment. That is something that could never be breached - our commitment to each other and to our children.

Though, it's still impossible to look back on events with any semblance of understanding as to why it all went wrong.

And what we did to deserve our fate.

Of all the emotions that arose within me and then subsided with time, it is disbelief that remains my constant companion to this day.

Karen Aspinall
Combined Diary Entries
April; Nineteen-ninety-seven.

one

Twentieth of March; Nineteen-ninety-six. Wednesday.

'Lauren, please fasten your seat belt. Be good for Mummy. A policeman might be watching!'

The little girl eyed her mother mischievously through the rear-view mirror. It was a familiar maternal command that she rarely adhered to in the first instance. Karen Aspinall widened her stare as a final warning for her daughter to oblige.

The reluctant click of the belt buckle ended the issue. Karen continued to observe the youngster with an affectionate smile. Four years of age and already showing signs of being a young rebel.

Karen idly studied her own reflection as she waited for her elder daughter, Chloe, to emerge from the gates of Church Drayton Junior School. Every day Chloe seemed to dawdle until most other pupils had long since vanished. Karen glanced at her watch. Fifteen minutes had passed since the three-thirty bell had sounded. What could take an eight-year-old so long? Most kids couldn't wait to get out of the place.

Back in the mirror, Karen took the chance to scrutinize her rapidly made-up features. Self-analysis wasn't a practice she undertook regularly but being a relatively busy housewife meant those quiet moments outside the school offered a rare chance to study her own image.

Karen was generally pleased by what she saw. She had always liked her classic combination of blue eyes and blond hair. She had always had good skin - at least so her mother used to tell her.

The absence of any real signs of age was comforting. The early indications were that Chloe looked as if she would be a carbon copy of her mother, as opposed to young Lauren, who held the darker impression of her father.

At the age of thirty-one, Karen was still a very attractive woman and was aware of her physical attributes. Slowly puffing out her cheeks, she carefully inspected for blemishes. She pulled at her eyelids to assess the progress of her minimal crow's feet, consoling herself that time was not yet leaving its mark.

Lauren watched her mother's reflection in quiet bemusement before being distracted.

'Mummy! Mummy! There's Chloe!' came the excited cry from the back seat.

Diverting her attention from the mirror, Karen glanced around to see her elder daughter dragging her weary form toward the familiar sight of her mother's red car - that ever-reliable symbol of home time.

Karen lowered her window.

'Come on, slowcoach! Where have you been?'

Chloe did not look overly happy to see her mother and sister in the short distance. In fact, Karen instantly detected that all was definitely not well as her first-born approached.

'Are you okay, love? What's the matter?'

Heaving open the rear passenger door and throwing her duffel bag toward her grinning little sister, Chloe tumbled herself into the seat and yanked the car door shut. Her mother was unimpressed.

'Chloe! I asked you a civil question. Firstly, don't slam my door! Secondly, tell me why you look so unhappy!'

Chloe was not prone to keeping quiet for long. Her attempts to adopt some form of bad mood soon dissipated when she caught Lauren pulling a cross-eyed face to make her laugh - a sibling ploy that rarely failed.

When the grin began to break up the feigned annoyance adorning Chloe's features, Karen realised that nothing serious was at hand.

'Don't tell me. Its boys, isn't it? You've had a row with your boyfriend James again, haven't you?'

The prompt was more than enough encouragement for Chloe to commence her rant.

'I've packed him in! I hate him!'

Karen glimpsed little Lauren's expression of amusement in the mirror before straightening her own features into a semblance of parental sympathy. Lauren put her hand to her mouth as her eyes met with the stern gaze of her mother.

'You know…you're far too young to have man trouble!'

Chloe seemed rather annoyed at her mother's simplistic overview of the situation. Karen relented and ventured to listen to the traumatic events of the school day.

'Okay, okay…what's he done now?'

Chloe stared disapprovingly at her smirking sister before continuing.

'Well, in R.E. we all had to draw a picture of John the Baptist, so I lent my red felt-tip pen to James, and he lent it to Sarah Hughes without asking me first.'

Karen struggled desperately to suppress her desire to laugh.

'So? What's wrong with that? It's kind to share your things with others.'

The expression of woe returned to Chloe's face.

'Yes, but when I got it back it had run out of ink and Sarah had flattened the end! When I told James he said he didn't care! So, I said he *should* care because I was his girlfriend!'

Karen's act of understanding was bearing up rather well despite the clowning frown of her youngest daughter. Her supportive manner continued.

'And what did he say to that, then?'

Chloe again looked sheepishly across toward her gurning sister before replying.

'He said he didn't care about being my boyfriend, either!'

It was all too much for Lauren, who suddenly exploded into a fit of infantile hysteria. Chloe responded instantly by jabbing a loosely clenched fist in her sibling's direction.

Karen opted to end the bout before it began in earnest.

'Oy, young lady! There's no need to hit your sister, is there? It's not her fault! I will buy you a *new* marker pen, okay? And if there's any thumping to be done around here, *I'll* be the one doing it. Okay? Right, now say sorry to Lauren. And put your seat belt on please.'

Now exhibiting a face of thunder, Lauren acknowledged her sister's mumbled apology with a low grunt before folding her arms and staring through the passenger window. With back seat warfare narrowly avoided, Karen started the engine and steered the car out of the school grounds towards the village.

Early spring always encouraged a fine display of seasonal colour around Church Drayton. Trees and shrubs proudly wore sleeves of green, whilst fresh blossom added flashes of pink and yellow. The complementary backdrop of quaintly styled housing completed the scene. Driving was a most pleasurable interlude to Karen Aspinall's daily routine, as opposed to a tiresome chore for the many town dwelling parents that collected their children.

Gliding through the foliage-lined avenues and lanes, Karen flicked on the radio and filled the air with the latest pop sounds, immediately lightening the atmosphere of discontentment that had descended in the rear of the car.

With the music already blasting through the open windows, the girls simultaneously requested an increase in the volume.

'Yeah! We know the words to this one. Quick Mum, turn it up!'

As the car stopped at traffic lights, an old age pensioner could only stand and smile as he observed the young mother and her two daughters singing their heads off as if without a care in the world.

Only when they passed the junction of Benton Road and carried on towards town did the Aspinall girls cease their two-part harmonies and question their mother as to the destination.

'Mum! You've gone past our street, silly!' shouted Chloe.

'Mummy! Where are we going?' enquired Lauren.

Karen changed gear and turned the radio down before responding to the shrieks of puzzlement from her daughters. She checked the rear-view mirror before moving lanes as the dual carriageway beckoned.

'You *know* where we're going.'

The girls still looked dumbfounded as the penny failed to drop.

Karen offered another clue.

'Well, it's *Wednesday*. Where do we *always* go on Wednesdays?'

She watched Chloe and Lauren in the mirror as they frantically forced their memory cogs to turn.

'Lauren…is your belt done up?'

'Yes, Mummy.'

Karen checked the road behind once again before continuing with the guessing game.

'Where do we usually go for tea on Wednesdays?'

Finally, Lauren screamed the correct answer at the top of her tiny voice.

'Grandma's! Of course, we are! Am I right, Mummy? I can't wait to play with Long John!'

Long John was an ageing cockatiel that belonged to Karen's father, Brian. Unfortunately, Lauren's idea of playing with the bird was to poke a pencil at it through the bars of the cage. Not an activity that birds of any kind have affinity to.

Chloe thought it appropriate at that moment to reveal a little secret that even Karen wasn't aware of.

'Yes. But Grandad told you off last week for pulling Long John's tail. That's why he said he's going to put the cage on top of the fridge - so you can't reach it, you bully!'

Karen pretended to be annoyed with Lauren as she shrunk ashamedly before her mother's beady-eyed reflection.

'Oh, he did, *did* he? So *that's* what you do at Grandad's when I'm not there is it? Honestly, Lauren! That's naughty. Long John is very old, you know. You shouldn't torment him.'

Lauren decided to defend her actions.

'Yes, but he pecked me the week before and made my finger bleed.'

'Well, that should be a lesson in itself? If I see you poking Long John tonight, I'll lock you in the cage with him. So there!'

Lauren's argumentative nature was developing nicely.

'Well, I don't think I'd fit in the cage. So there!'

'You would if I chopped you into little pieces! Then Long John could eat you for his tea!' laughed Karen.

The trio were soon into the neighbouring area of Goltham, where Karen's parents had always lived. After navigating a couple of roundabouts and another set of traffic lights, the car was soon pulling into Cobden Terrace where the home of Brian and Jean Hope was situated.

Karen had always appreciated her mother and father being so close. She had never harboured any desire to uproot further from them than was necessary. Especially since the girls had come along. The Hopes doted on their grandchildren and relished every given opportunity to spend time with them.

Jean was in the front garden where she always waited to greet the arrival of her approaching family. Her heart inflated with joy whenever she caught sight of those two inquisitive heads peering through the back windows of the car, soon to evolve into two pairs of frantically waving hands and two beaming smiles.

She rubbed her wizened cheeks before running her hands through greying hair as though adding the finishing touches to her appearance.

No sooner had Karen applied the handbrake than Chloe and Lauren bounded onto the pavement and skipped across the lawn toward their waiting grandmother.

'Grandma! Grandma!'

The shout was united and loud, serving to broaden the delight that dressed Jean Hope's face.

'Hello, my darlings! Lovely to see you both! Hi Kaz, how are you, my love?'

Karen emerged from the driver's side and pushed the door shut. Smirking at her mother, she noticed straight away that her father's transit van was missing from the drive.

'Is Dad not home yet? I thought he only wanted morning work these days.'

Chloe and Lauren clung to their grandmother's s chequered skirt as she replied to her daughter.

'Oh, he's promised to finish a job out at Upton. Some problem with a central heating boiler, I think. He went out at about half past one, so he shouldn't be long I wouldn't have thought.'

The family exchanged kisses as they walked to the back door of the house.

'I thought he was under doctor's orders. His knees won't stand much more of this stupid plumbing lark. He's too old for it now, Mum!'

'I know, I know. But you know your dad. He's made a promise to do this job and that's that. Nothing I say will stop him. Anyway, I bet you'd like a cuppa, wouldn't you love?'

In the kitchen, the girls rummaged through the bottom cupboards for any hidden treats their grandmother may have stashed away.

'Are there any chocolate wafers, Grandma?' asked Lauren excitedly.

'Yes, love. I'm just making a drink for your mum. Go and put the telly on in the front room. Be good girls. I'll bring them through to you in a minute.'

Long John squawked a begrudging welcome at the young visitors as they entered the lounge. Karen's echoing command followed them through.

'And Lauren, leave that bird alone! Or else!'

Lauren affirmed her mother's wishes by peering back around the front room door and offering her zaniest cross-eyed expression. Jean laughed contentedly to herself as she prepared coffee.

'Little darlings. They certainly know how to liven the place up!'

'Little horrors sometimes, mother. Apparently, Lauren's been poking Long John with a stick, hasn't she? Dad is not impressed from what I've heard.'

Jean shook her head and pursed her lips as the kettle finished boiling.

'Oh, take no notice of him. He's as grumpy as that bloody bird these days! Between you and me, I think he wants to pack up work altogether.

Aside from the dodgy knees, he's tired out. I'm hoping the bird croaks it before your father retires, though. I couldn't be doing with them both at home all day. They'd send me mad between them.'

Mother and daughter laughed heartily as they sat at the kitchen table with their drinks.

'So, how are you, Mum? Have you been out this week at all?'

Karen eyed her mother as she sipped her coffee.

'Erm...no. Not that I recall. I'm going to meet Edith and Muriel in the precinct tomorrow for lunch. But that's about it. What about your end? Any news?'

Karen placed her mug on the table and sighed nervously.

'Well, its Robert's final interview today. He'll know tonight whether he's got that promotion to Coventry or not.'

'Oh, my goodness, yes!' Jean exclaimed. 'I'd totally forgotten. You must be so excited! What are you hoping the verdict will be?'

Karen was secretly in two minds about her husband's bid for executive status. Robert was a clever, experienced, and ambitious computer engineer. He had worked hard to attain his current position at Sissons Incorporated. The logical next step was a seat in head office, and he had more than earned the opportunity.

Suited and booted with a company car. It would certainly suit him down to the ground. The only downside was that it would mean living one hundred and fifty miles away in Coventry all week. It was a big move. A big decision for both of them to face. Karen did not yet know how she truly felt about the prospect.

One thing she did know was that she had to support Robert if he took the new role. The increased salary would be most welcome. However, his unavoidable absence from home was not so attractive. No doubt the girls would have a say in things as well.

'To be frank, Mum, I'm not hoping for a decision either way. I'm his wife. If he needs me, I'll be there for him. The decision on the job is his and his alone. I can't hold him back. But I know he wants this move so desperately.'

Jean studied her mug as she pondered another line of enquiry.

'Would you...would you consider ever going with him if he decided that commuting every week was too much?'

'No chance! I *love* Church Drayton. I'm never leaving here. All my family and friends are around me. What on earth would make me want to go to Coventry and leave all this? No, Mum. Don't worry. Wherever Robert decides to go, I'm staying put. I can promise you that much.'

Karen could sense her mother's inner relief as she drained her own mug and set it down again.

She was aware of Jean's understandable fears that she may lose her coveted regular contact with the girls. Similarly, Karen was all too aware of the importance of a grandmother's role. She was a major part of Chloe and Lauren's upbringing, as was her father. Karen never took that fact for granted.

Indeed, Karen Aspinall saw it as a testament to the strength of her marriage that whichever path Robert followed, she would always stay loyal to Church Drayton. There was no reason for anybody to sacrifice any relationships just because of a job promotion.

Jean Hope seemed temporarily appeased and changed the subject.

'How's your neighbour, Evelyn? I haven't seen her for ages!'

Evelyn Chapple had lived next door to Karen and Robert on Benton Road since before the children were born. Her husband Nigel regularly worked abroad for long periods, so naturally, Karen and Evelyn had become close confidantes over the years.

In fact, Karen affectionately regarded Evelyn almost as her second mother, such was the depth of their friendship.

Being nearly twenty years older than Karen, Evelyn had been a major help when the girls were smaller and was always on hand to offer advice or a sympathetic ear. Lauren and Chloe even called her 'Aunty Evelyn' because of the affinity they also felt toward her.

The girls had also filled a void in Evelyn's life, not least because Greg, her one and only son left home several years ago to join the armed forces. For Karen it was a relationship that worked on several levels.

Karen held her standing with the Chapples in high esteem - another arguable reason why she would never consider leaving Church Drayton.

'She's fine, Mum. I haven't seen much of her since the weekend. She popped through the fence on Sunday for a quick chat, but I've hardly seen her all week. No doubt we'll catch up tomorrow. She'll be keen to know how Rob's gone on at work, anyhow.'

Jean felt it appropriate to find out what Evelyn thought of Robert's possible promotion, bearing in mind that she had to deal with the same scenario with Nigel.

'You're lucky to have such a good friend so close by. I can rest easy knowing that help is close at hand should you need it. I suppose she'll know precisely how to cope with becoming a one-parent family.'

Karen seemed a little shocked at her mother's analogy of the situation.

'Mum! That sounds so callous! It's a terrible expression. Robert's not leaving the planet, you know. It's only Coventry. Anyway, Evelyn reckons I'll be fine if he goes. All that time to please myself without a husband to feed and clean up after. Plus, he won't be under my feet. Evelyn says I'll learn to love the single life. Personally, I can't wait.'

Jean Hope quickly realised that she was being teased by her daughter and offered a disapproving stare which was then underlined by a feigned grimace.

'Don't mock your mother, dear. It's not good for your health. And don't listen to *everything* that Evelyn Chapple tells you, either.'

Karen simply laughed and picked up the coffee mugs.

'I'm only joking, Mum. Another drink?'

'Yes, you can do. I bet the girls are hungry, aren't they? I forgot about their chocolate.'

'Good point. I'll just go and check on them.'

Karen approached the lounge to be greeted by an instantly recognisable squawk. She poked her head around the door just in time to catch Lauren with pencil in hand at the side of the cage. With Chloe engaged in the activity on TV, she hadn't noticed her little sister flaunting the rules regarding Long John. Time to nip the game in the bud.

'Er…not a good idea, young Miss Aspinall. What have you been told?'

Lauren almost jumped out of her skin with the shock of being discovered red-handed.

'You are very lucky that it was *me* that caught you and not Grandad! Come into the kitchen and decide what you'd like for your tea.'

Karen marched Lauren out of the room just as her father walked through the back door.

'Grandad! Grandad!'

The four-year-old escaped her mother's light grip and skipped across the floor to greet him.

Lifting his youngest granddaughter into the air, Brian Hope was elated at the warm welcome.

'Hello, trouble. How are you? Are you being a good girl?'

Under the knowing gaze of her mother, Lauren nodded eagerly and kissed her grandfather on the lips. Brian Hope looked at his daughter and smiled.

'You look radiant today, our Karen. Have you been out in the sunshine? You've got a wonderful healthy glow about you!'

It wasn't often that Karen received compliments on her appearance these days, so to get one from her father seemed unusual yet very touching.

'Why thank you, Daddy dear. Busy day?' Karen asked, whilst planting a soft kiss on his cheek.

Brian sighed and removed his jacket.

'Oh, you know, love. Another day, another dollar. What snacks have we got, Jean? I'm peckish!'

With an air of partially feigned sarcasm, Jean looked at her husband in disbelief as he kicked his shoes under the breakfast bar and inserted his feet into a pair of slippers.

'Don't I get a kiss, then? Or aren't maids and cooks privy to such special treatment?'

Brian threw Karen a cheeky knowing wink before complying with the just wishes of his wife.

With Chloe eventually emerging from the front room to complete the throng, the family were finally together. Three generations in a home full of genuine love and affection. As the girls laid the dining table and helped their grandmother, Karen and her father re-located into the front room.

Karen liked to talk to her dad. She found him to be amusing and cruel at times, but reliable and steadfast in his opinions. She always viewed him as being a strong man.

Every inch the father and role model.

As he lowered himself into a chair opposite, she watched him wince with pain as his knees buckled under the weight of his body. Finally, he settled himself down and opened the conversation.

'So, Robert's big day today, isn't it? Has he phoned you at all?'

'No, Dad. His meeting wasn't until two o'clock this afternoon. He's probably still in conference now.'

Brian Hope sensed some unease in his daughter's demeanour.

'You okay, Karen? You look worried. Is it about Rob?'

It was no use trying to hide things from her father. He was far too wise to be fooled by a stiff upper lip. As such, she had only one option - to convey her true feelings to him.

'Actually, I'm scared as to what he's going to tell us when he comes home, Dad. The girls haven't a clue about any of this. I hope they can deal with it. Mind, I don't know if I will be able to cope, never mind those two!'

Brian stared into his daughter's eyes and displayed the conviction and comforting air that Karen had become accustomed to over the years. She needed her father's wisdom and authoritative stance at that moment.

'Listen, love. Robert deserves every chance of success that comes his way. He works hard for you all. He's a fine provider for his family. And he knows you'll be right behind him. I know it's daunting, but you'll all be absolutely fine. Believe me.'

Karen felt only slightly consoled by her father's honesty.

'But it's going to seem so strange him not being at home all week, Dad. That's if he gets the job, of course.'

Brian Hope needed little convincing of his family's strength in facing such a challenge and nodded slowly as he spoke.

'He'll get the job, love. I can feel it in my water. I know it's a big step. But he's big enough to make it. Both of you are.'

As she stared into his kind eyes, Karen listened intently as her father continued with his reassurances.

'Trust me, Karen. You've a wonderful husband and he's got a wonderful wife. You have two adorable children. Nothing can touch any of you. Plus, your mum and I are always around the corner if you need us.'

Brian placed his hand on that of his daughter's. His voice softened, contradicting the harsh, lean look of his features. Karen did not appear overly content about the situation. But he would try and allay her worries, as all loving fathers should do.

As he contemplated a final word, Jean shouted through from the kitchen.

'Come and tell me what you both want to eat!'

Father and daughter rose to their feet and embraced.

Brian whispered into Karen's ear with a comforting smile.

'Be excited my girl, not fearful. After all, there's nothing to fear, is there?'

two

Nervous wasn't the word.

Robert Aspinall glanced at his watch for the umpteenth time that afternoon. Three weeks and several hours of intensive conversation had brought him to this moment of reckoning. Never did he dream that he would ever be in the running for Divisional Operations Manager, let alone have the nerve to edge his way to the last hurrah with the three remaining candidates.

He was the last to be interviewed that day. A process that took approximately three quarters of an hour and came to a promising conclusion exactly forty-two minutes ago.

What the hell was taking them so long? There couldn't be much more to decide upon, could there? They knew his complete company record; previous employment history; schooling and education; aptitude; intelligence and capability, but most importantly, Robert had mastered the art of conveying his hopes and ambitions for a prosperous future with the company.

The other two candidates had been most gracious in their treatment of Robert, and indeed one another. Both had ventured outside for another calming blast of nicotine in the downstairs smoker's compound - thankfully a drug that Robert no longer depended on after quitting several years earlier. However, ex-smokers always say that the cravings still occur from time to time. At that particular moment in the outer office, he would have happily committed murder for a cigarette.

Squinting into the early spring sunshine that streamed into the foyer, Robert's thoughts turned towards his family. The people that were the cornerstones of his life. Despite an unflinching ambition to make it big at Sissons, Robert was aware of his priorities. Images of his loved ones blossomed soothingly into his whirring mind.

He visualised his gorgeous wife Karen, who would have just picked up Chloe from school and they would no doubt be having their tea at her parents' house. Robert loved Brian and Jean also. They had welcomed him into their family from their first meeting all those years ago. Their presence in his life more than compensated for the tragic loss of his own parents when he was just sixteen-years-old.

He felt he owed Karen's family so much.

In time, he would make sure that he showed his appreciation for the vital role they had played in his existence and would hopefully continue to play for the foreseeable future.

However, his attention reverted to the current issue. Back to this consuming vacuum of indecision and prolonged uncertainty. His immediate fate lay in the hands of those unseen souls behind the large oak door.

Suddenly, as if to purposely intrude on this train of thought, that same large oak door swung open to reveal the familiar yet strangely daunting face of Simon Mills, Robert's immediate manager, whose smile revealed neither pleasure nor sympathy.

'Okay, Robert. The jury is back in. Ready when you are.'

Robert's heart was beating like a drum. Flashes of his wife and daughters faces once again zipped through his mind. He had to concentrate, though. It was a time for his full attention to focus on the next few minutes, as opposed to his usual habit of looking forward into the next few months or years.

His hands became clammy - hopefully a condition that would clear up before the throng parted company in a short while. A strong handshake is fatally weakened by moist palms.

Although having spent a large proportion of the afternoon inside that vast grey-looking office, it suddenly loomed threateningly as a place to fear. Robert was now entering the unknown in a room so tediously enclosing. It was not a feeling he was accustomed to.

Then he remembered his colleagues who were still downstairs in the smoke shelter.

'Oh, Simon. Do you want me to go and fetch the other two?'

Simon Mills was assuring and suggestive in his tone. He smirked again as he looked into Robert's eyes.

'No, Rob. No need. We'll call them up next. There's a reason we want to see you first.'

A wave of positive energy encroached upon the arena which rapidly encompassed the whole scene. In an instant, with those few words uttered by his manager, Robert sensed that his dreams were about to be realized.

David Marsden, the second of the three interviewers and full-time personnel director ushered Robert to sit down before addressing him with the decision. For what seemed like the thousandth time that afternoon, Robert nodded, smiled and adjusted his tie in a well-rehearsed sequence.

It may have appeared awkward to the casual observer, but it allowed him to stay relaxed in front of his trio of tormentors.

David Marsden began with his summing up.

'First of all, we would like to thank you for your patience and cooperation in this process. Whilst we know that it can be a stressful exercise, you do need to understand the necessity for depth in this particular interview cycle.'

Robert nodded his head quickly and managed to emit a few words from his increasingly drying throat.

'Yes, David. I understand totally. This is a big hole you're trying to fill. You've got to be sure of getting the right man for the job, haven't you?'

Shit! Robert immediately thought to himself. Did he sound cocky?

Overconfident? Presumptuous? Oh well, too late, now.

David Marsden continued.

'Well, after much deliberation and careful elimination of several other worthy candidates, we believe that we have indeed found our man.'

There was an uncomfortable pause. It only endured for little more than five seconds but seemed like five years. Now what? Who was supposed to speak next? Was the cold silence a coded message for Robert to get out of the office and never come back?

The sweat began to ooze from every pore. His tie suddenly became very constrictive. His shoes became tight. He wished he was at home on the sofa at home with a good book as the aroma of Karen's cooking wafted through the house.

Or perhaps alone up a mountain.

Or on a boat in the middle of the Atlantic.

He wished he was anywhere but sitting in front of these three judges of his curriculum vitae.

The thought fleetingly occurred to Robert Aspinall that he had no right to be in that room and that he would rue the day he ever considered applying for the post of Bloody Divisional Bloody Operations Bloody Manager. He felt small, insignificant, and unworthy of the officials that sat behind the enormous desk across from his own vulnerable and cringing position.

Mike Burton - the company Managing Director, no less - was the third member of the interrogation squad to speak. No doubt to curse Robert's very presence in their company and castigate him for having the brass neck to even think he had the right to associate himself with the vacancy.

Then finally, the pause was ended.

The conjecture and hypothesis could stop. The hiatus mercifully ceased. The misery was finally over as the MD stood to his feet and offered a hand across the table.

'Congratulations, Robert. The job is yours. On behalf of all at the company, well done!'

Robert heard what was said, but it didn't register with his brain for a good while. This was probably because of the reserves his body was utilising to maintain a semblance of control and civility toward his very important inquisitors.

Eventually, his capacity for mental receipt returned and unleashed a flood of delirium.

'Oh my God! You beauty! Oh yes! Jesus Christ! Fan-bloody-tastic! Jesus!'

The trio that had placed him under severe scrutiny for the best part of a month had now relieved him of the binding expectation of disappointment. United in their decision, they smiled as one and in turn each vigorously shook the hand of the newly appointed Divisional Operations Manager.

Robert was overwhelmed with a combination of relief, hysteria, and a degree of gratification that his clammy hands had swiftly dried up.

David Marsden concluded the meeting.

'You know all the basic details of the job, Robert. This envelope contains everything you will need to know about the immediate future. Over the next few days, we will sort out the finer details of the transfer for you and arrange a mutually convenient start date. Please think of all the questions you feel you need to ask, and please feel free to ask them!'

Robert's shaking legs barely supported his weight as his mind strove to take in the news.

'Thank you. Thank you all. I won't let you down.' he beamed.

Mike Burton affirmed Robert's sentiment.

'We *know* you won't, Rob. That's why you've got the job! Congratulations once again. I suppose you'd like to slip off early to go and tell your wife and family?'

Robert's attention re-directed to his loved ones. Karen had told him that very morning that she would support him whatever the result.

Nevertheless, coupled with the injection of euphoria, he felt a sudden surge of trepidation as he bid his colleagues goodbye.

'I'll be back in at nine tomorrow. Possibly with a hangover, but I'll be here!'

The three men laughed and shook his hand once again.

'Feel free to celebrate, Rob. You've earned that right tonight, I'm sure!'

Clasping the large brown envelope containing his future, Robert left the office and maintained an air of silent indifference as he strode past the one-time rival candidates sitting impatiently after their cigarettes.

He eased his way out of the building and manoeuvred his legs in the direction of the car park. The sensation of success was unreal. In the space of a few minutes, he had been transformed from quivering also-ran into accomplished victor.

His heart still beat like a drum, but no longer with anticipation.

Now his very core was throbbing with the thrill of personal achievement.

Slumping into the driver's seat of his silver hatchback, he avidly pulled at the seal of the envelope. The first manual he retrieved was for a selection of cars - company cars. Luxury company cars, that in a couple of weeks' time he would be benefiting from the use of.

Robert sat and laughed to himself as he clenched the steering wheel.

A sudden craving for nicotine ensued once more and was rapidly quashed with will power.

Was this really him?

The new Divisional Operations Manager? Robert Aspinall?

Or was it some cruel joke?

Could he be in a dream brought to him in his sleep by the fairies?

Starting the car for the journey home, he hoped dearly that Karen would both confirm and give approval to his idyllic new status.

three

Karen smiled inwardly as she manoeuvred away from her parents' house and headed back towards Church Drayton. The girls waved frantically and giggled hysterically as they bid farewell to their grandparents through the back window.

Suddenly, the supportive vision of Brian and Jean Hope was gone as Karen hit the main road back through Goltham.

'Come On Lauren. Seat belt, please. You too, Chloe.'

With the car stereo pounding and the three-part harmony quickly back in full flow, the twenty-minute journey back to Benton Road seemed like twenty seconds. Karen eyed the familiar surroundings of the estate. Thoughts of Robert entered her head. She saw that his car was not back as she approached number thirty-nine. Applying the handbrake, she set her car halfway on the pavement before getting out to open the large white wooden gate that led onto to the driveway.

The girls sat patiently for their mother to get back into the car. It was a well-worn drill that both had to learn from a young age. Stay in the car whilst mummy tends the gate. It was safe and simple.

Glancing across as she unlatched it there was no sign of her good friend Evelyn although she must have been home as her large black saloon stood gleaming at the front of the house.

Across the road at number thirty-eight, valued neighbours Colin and Lyndsey Robinson were in their front garden and offered a wave of greeting as the Aspinall ladies finally alighted.

'Hi Karen. You okay girls?' shouted Lyndsey.

As usual, Lauren was the first to be heard with a reply.

'Hello, Mrs. Robinson!' she beamed in response, accompanied by a flap of her arms.

Karen exchanged brief pleasantries with the Robinsons but didn't want to overindulge them by revealing any news. Not that there was any news yet. Over the years, Lyndsey had become notorious around the estate for passing on personal details of her neighbours' lives that really should have been confidential.

Karen was very wary of disclosing anything private that others may find of unwarranted interest.

She closed the gate and proceeded to unlock the front door, noticing the time on her watch displaying nearly twenty past six.

The girls scampered upstairs to play in their bedroom, affording her a few vital moments of solitude. Little did she know that such precious time would be ended abruptly as the familiar sound of Robert's car engine rumbled to a standstill out front.

Karen's stomach lurched as she expectantly re-emerged onto the drive to tend the gate and greet her husband as the evening offered its first signs of dusk. From the corner of her eye, she could detect the Robinsons peering over their privet hedge thirty yards away, no doubt desperately trying to ascertain any information that may get leaked across the street.

Robert felt pensive. Positioning the car behind his wife's he pulled on the hand brake and picked up his briefcase and the envelope off the passenger seat. He was in two minds as to how to tell Karen of the day's developments. Should he look pleased from the outset? Or should he wait for Karen to enquire and play it according to her reaction?

There was little time to formulate a plan, as she stood open-armed as he clambered from behind the steering wheel.

'You got it…didn't you? Tell me, Rob. Don't keep me in suspense any longer. I've been thinking about it all bloody day! Tell me you got the promotion, love.'

Robert was taken aback somewhat by Karen's apparent willingness to hear the news. That morning she seemed rather withdrawn about proceedings. Evidently the prospect had grown on her during the day. Nevertheless, despite his wife's warm welcome, he understood what he was about to say could cause a degree of upset.

Shutting the front door on any prying eyes, he smiled and tightly embraced Karen in the hallway. He whispered into her ear.

'Yes, love. I got it. You are now looking at the new Divisional Operations Manager for Sissons Incorporated.'

Karen put on a convincing act as the lump in her throat expanded. She wanted Robert to be entirely happy with his success and realised that such a situation was only possible if she played along with the supporting role.

Burying her reservations deep down, she held her husband's hand and led him into the kitchen.

The ejecting cork narrowly missed the kitchen light fittings as Karen whooped with joy. Robert's fears were easing by the second as he observed his wife's beautiful smile.

'Bubbly, eh? You must have known before I did!'

Karen handed him a glass and filled it until it overflowed.

'It's not *real* champers, darling. You're not worth that sort of money! Well, not just yet anyway!'

As they laughed, two pairs of feet could be heard racing down the stairs. In an instant, Chloe and Lauren burst into the kitchen and showered their father with hugs and kisses.

'And how are my little angels today? Behaving for Mummy, I trust?'

With her natural comic timing, Lauren answered first.

'Well, *I've* behaved. Chloe fell out with her boyfriend over a felt tip. I've been good though because I didn't poke Long John today!'

Robert was simultaneously bemused and amused by his youngest daughter's outpourings as he lifted her tiny form into the air.

'You're always the good little girl, aren't you? Whiter than white. Little Miss Innocence. Pull me that silly face. Go on, make Daddy giggle.'

With practiced ease, Lauren crossed her eyes and displayed the wild expression to the eager audience. Laughter erupted as husband and wife momentarily gazed into each other's eyes. Another glass of faux champagne would ease his twitching nerves for the announcement to come. The girls retreated up to their rooms for a short while as Karen and Robert discussed the afternoon's events.

*****

Finally, with the ground being stable between man and wife, they agreed it was time to tell the children of their father's move.

'Girls, can you come downstairs to the kitchen for a short while. Daddy wants to talk to you both.'

Reluctantly drawing themselves away from their console game, Lauren and Chloe trooped a weary descent and positioned themselves at the kitchen table where Robert sat with clasped hands and an unwavering frown. Karen situated herself between her daughters and placed an arm around their shoulders.

Chloe showed understandable concern regarding the nature of the summons.

'Are we in trouble, Daddy? I can't think of anything naughty we've done. Is it about Long John?'

Robert took a deep breath before addressing his expectant loved ones.

'No, darling. Long John is fine. This is about us, as a family. Well, about me, really. Something very good has happened to me today at work.'

Again, Chloe's natural curiosity fuelled further questions.

'Have they sacked you, Daddy?'

Robert chuckled at his daughter's earnest query.

'No, Chloe. In fact…just the opposite. I'm…I'm going to have to work away in the week very soon. Daddy's office has been moved. I won't be able to travel back home each night because the journey is too long. I will have to stay away from Monday morning to Friday night each week.'

Silence prevailed as Chloe considered what she had just heard. It was inevitable that Lauren would be too young to truly comprehend the news, but nevertheless she remained quiet and attentive, sensing the temporarily pensive atmosphere in the room.

Chloe looked at her mother for reassurance and understanding.

'Does that mean we won't see Daddy for a long while, then?'

Karen sensed the emotion welling in her eldest offspring and moved rapidly to counter the onset of tears.

'You *will* see him, darling, but not on school nights. But it doesn't matter that much because you'll be in bed by eight o'clock, anyway, won't you? He can still phone us every night. You will both still be able to speak to him every day. But he will be too far away to drive home. He has to remain near his new office in the week.'

Karen gently squeezed the shoulders of her daughters and spotted Chloe wiping a tear from her eye. But to her credit, she held firm and did not weep openly at that point. Even for her tender years she seemed to understand the situation. Yet justifiably, more questions emerged.

'When will you be moving away, Daddy?'

Robert moved position around the table and placed a hand of reassurance on his eldest daughter's cheek.

'I don't know, darling. It hasn't been decided yet. But as soon as I know, you will all know. That's a promise.'

The news had settled around young ears far better than Robert or Karen could have ever expected. They both admired the resilience of their children, although of course it was too early in the scheme of things to rest easily on the matter.

'Could we come and visit you when you leave, Daddy? To see your new office?' pleaded Chloe.

Again, Robert felt his own emotions lurch as he looked into his little girl's eyes.

'I'm not leaving you, darling. I'm just staying away from home for a while. Just on the weekdays.'

Robert looked to Karen for assistance in appeasing his daughter's suspicions. She obliged with calming words.

'Daddy still loves us, Chloe. But this is chance to make us all richer. He's going to be in charge of a lot of people. He's going to be very important at work. We should be happy for Daddy. There's nothing to get upset about.'

Unfortunately, Chloe could no longer stem the flow of emotion and began to cry. Two parents struggled to find any immediate solution to the situation and opted to ride the storm. Chloe eventually composed herself once more and looked to her mother through tear-strewn eyes and frothing lips.

'But I don't *want* Daddy to go away. I want him to stay here with us. Tell him to stay, Mummy. Tell him!'

Karen observed the confused and concerned expression on Lauren's face as she pulled Chloe closer. Lauren smiled and crossed her eyes once more, forcing Karen to smile back.

'Listen, love. We could go and see where Daddy will be working, couldn't we? If you know where he's going to be then it will make things a little easier, won't it?'

Chloe shrugged, nodded, and moved to give her father a hug. It was a tender moment which needed careful handling. Ultimately, the period of juvenile emotion passed by.

Eventually, the girls returned to play upstairs whilst Robert and Karen finished the contents of the champagne bottle.

'Jesus. Thank God for that. I was not looking forward to telling them, Kaz. How do you think it went down?'

Karen eyed the bottom of her glass in contemplation of the imminent future.

'They'll be fine, Rob. They'll soon get used to the idea. I'd be expecting more tears though. But for now, we've done the hard part by setting the seed in their heads. They'll come to terms with things.'

'Yeah...they are wonderful kids. And you're a wonderful woman. Come here.'

Man and wife embraced tightly in the silence of the kitchen.

Karen eyed the view of approaching darkness through the window. Early evening shadows began to smother the scene outside. The dreaded day of reckoning had come, and it would soon be gone. It had brought its good fortune and left the Aspinall family with new aspects in their lives to consider and accommodate.

Karen had been wary of what the day would bring. In hindsight, there was nothing in their lives to find fault with at that moment.

There was nothing to fear.

Her father's words of earlier that afternoon echoed around her conscience as she relaxed in the arms of the man she loved.

The future looked prosperous for the Aspinalls of thirty-nine, Benton Road.

And nobody in the house should have harboured any strand of negativity regarding the times that lay ahead.

four

Spring was now exerting its welcome authority on a daily basis as it eclipsed the last tantrums of a long, dark winter. The radio on the kitchen windowsill blasted out the latest tunes as Karen crouched over the washing machine, pulling damp, clean clothes into a plastic basket.

It was going to be a pleasant relief not to have piles of washing everywhere awaiting their turn for the tumble drier. With warming air and strong seasonal gusts, the burden of laundry duty would be lightened somewhat if the process of drying could be transferred outside.

With Robert long gone to work and the girls at school, Karen was determined to enjoy the temporary solace of a quiet house - at least until she had to fetch Lauren from nursery at dinner time.

Erecting the rotary washing line, she breathed deeply. A plethora of aromas engaged her senses. As she pegged out the clothes, Karen looked around the garden contemplating various jobs that she would need to undertake in the coming weeks.

The grass had started to grow at a rapid rate. The first spring cut was a priority - before it got to knee level. Borders were overgrown and in turn practically begging for a splash of colour from the local garden centre. Shrubs required severe trimming.

Maybe, just maybe, she might convince Robert to help her move the shed to the back of the lawn instead of its somewhat obstructive position along the fence - a task she had set her sights on twelve months earlier and still not yet achieved.

Despite the time of day, a loitering fox warily observed her actions through the hedge bottom before sensing an approaching figure from the adjacent garden. In an undetected flash, the fox was gone, as Evelyn Chapple appeared at the gate in the fence that allowed access between the adjoining properties.

'Morning Karen. You're brave, aren't you? Looks like rain to me. Not a day for hanging washing I shouldn't have thought.'

Recognising the deep, commanding tone of Evelyn's voice, Karen glanced skyward and surveyed the azure sheet above.

It didn't look like rain at all.

'Hi, Evelyn. I'm just glad to be outside in the sunshine, to be honest. It's been ages since I've stood in the garden and appreciated it. How are you?'

'I'm wonderful as you ask. I've just heard some interesting news this morning. So, I've come out to grab you for a coffee so I can tell you all about it! Come on, get the kettle on!'

Unbolting the fence gate from her side, Karen glanced up and caught Evelyn's frowning expression which was strangely underlined with a half-smirk. She was a big woman, not fat, but possessed a large frame for a female. She would often stand and talk with her arms folded. Her mass of dark hair would invariably be arranged into a tumbling mess held together with a single grip at the crown.

One day during the previous summer Karen had just pulled up onto the drive with the girls in the car, as Evelyn stood on the front pavement chewing the neighbourly cud with Lyndsey Robinson. Her manner and stance prompted Karen to bestow a rather cruel nickname for her friend - but one which the girls would remember from that day.

From that moment, Evelyn's secret alter-ego became *Big Chief Crazyhorse,* as she resembled the stereotypical Red Indian tribesman. No doubt, Evelyn Chapple would express differing opinion should the nickname be called out in her earshot.

Nevertheless, the recollection made Karen smile inwardly as her friend walked through into the back garden and closed the gate behind her.

'I can't believe you bolt that gate, Karen. There's no need, you know. You're quite safe around here.'

'Robert prefers it secured. So that it prevents the girls from wandering into your garden.'

With her thick forearms crossed under her ample bosom, Evelyn shuffled behind Karen toward the back door of number thirty-nine and sighed with disbelief.

'Such a worrier, your husband. The girls are perfectly welcome in my home any time. You know that. They're not going to get very far, are they?'

*****

With the kettle boiled and half a chocolate roll sliced onto a plate, the two friends took their positions around the kitchen table. Karen revealed the news about Robert's promotion after a prompting inquiry. Her friend was not taken aback by Robert's success.

In fact, Evelyn Chapple seemed somewhat disgruntled by developments.

'Well, Karen. I knew he'd get the job. That was obvious. But what about the kids? Surely, you can't be happy about them being without their father all week? It's not right!'

Evelyn's viewpoint was slightly puzzling. After all, she had spent much of her married life alone raising a son whilst her husband Nigel worked abroad in property development. Even now, Nigel is only home for three months out of twelve. Karen didn't wish to argue the case, but subtly pointed out the anomaly in Evelyn's opinion.

'When is Nigel due back in England next?'

Evelyn eyed her friend with the merest hint of suspicion before responding.

'Oh, another month or two yet, I think. I'm not entirely sure. I do think you ought to be prepared for some upset from the girls, though. It's not healthy for a family to be led by one parent. I should know. I've got that T-shirt.'

Karen sipped her drink as she watched Evelyn cram a wedge of cake into one cheek. If her friend wanted to persist with this conversation, then Karen would readily comply.

'Rob and I have discussed it with the girls. They understand. I know that more tears will come - probably from me rather than them. But it's for the right reasons. Rob's promotion is the best thing to happen to us for a long time. It could set us up for life. We can relax about things.'

A momentary silence prevailed as Evelyn Chapple carefully selected another slice of the sweet.

'Well, I can tell you Karen that being a single mum is no breeze. There's no one to share the daily burden with. It's a hard slog on your own.'

'But your Greg turned out alright, didn't he?'

A pause ensued as Evelyn chewed vigorously before licking her fingers.

'Time will tell. Time will tell.'

Bemusement shrouded Karen's thoughts. Her friend's appraisal of the situation had gone some way to unhinging the inner contentment she had felt earlier that morning. Outside, the blue sky was beginning to accommodate one or two clouds.

Devouring the last slice of cake, Evelyn again interrupted the peace.

‘Which reminds me. I haven’t told you about *my* news, have I?’

Refilling and switching the kettle back on, Karen returned to her seat and smiled in anticipation of the announcement.

‘Go on then, Evelyn. What have you heard? It’s *good* news judging by the grin on your face!’

Karen’s gaze was met directly with that of her friend. It was a little unnerving. Karen sensed a cold unease about the impending revelation.

‘I’ve had a letter in the post this morning. Our Greg’s coming home soon. Back here to Church Drayton…to live with me.’

Karen deemed it appropriate to act pleased for her friend. She displayed an earnest smile as the strange trepidation of a few seconds earlier quickly dissipated.

‘That’s wonderful, Evelyn. Oh, I’m so pleased for you. You must be ever so excited! How long has he been away?’

Evelyn Chapple fidgeted in her seat whilst contemplating Karen’s innocent query.

‘It would have been eight years this coming September.’

Karen showed genuine interest in the disclosure.

‘Is that it, then? Has he served his time? No more army games?’

Her slight sarcasm was returned with a frosty glare from across the table.

‘He doesn’t play *games*, Karen. He was deadly serious about joining up. It’s not his fault that…well, it doesn’t matter. He’s coming home anyway. The release date is yet to be confirmed.’

It struck Karen as she made two fresh coffees that her friend seemed rather unsettled by the prospective return of her son, but she couldn’t ascertain any reason why. If anything, Evelyn should have been over the moon. She opted to try and maintain a light approach to the subject.

‘I can hardly remember what he looks like. I bet he’s changed into a rugged handsome soldier type. Turned from a boy to a man, eh?’

Evelyn sipped from her mug as she pondered an answer.

‘Yes…I suppose so. It’s been a while since I saw him myself.’

‘How old is Greg now? He must be in his mid-twenties.’ Karen pressed.

Evelyn simply nodded her head and inspected the contents of her mug. For saying she couldn’t wait to tell Karen about her son, the subdued atmosphere that had suddenly developed was perplexing to say the least.

Karen sat quietly and respected the fact that her friend now looked distinctly uncomfortable with the subject at hand.

She gazed beyond the window to see that rain clouds had indeed formed, displacing the wondrous blue sky of only minutes earlier. Then without prompt, Evelyn continued on the theme of her son, taking Karen by surprise.

'He needs a good woman to steady him, Karen. Keep him on the straight and narrow. Keep his feet on the ground and his backside out of trouble.'

Again, the steely stare was cast in Karen's direction. The expression carried a hint of foreboding, as though she were trying to make Karen wary of something. Yet it all seemed too positive a development to be downcast about.

'I'm sure he'll meet someone quickly. These soldier types are pretty popular with the ladies. He'll soon be on someone's leash, all loved up!'

At last, Evelyn offered a smile, albeit seemingly forced. She set her half full mug down on the table and rose to her feet. As she made for the back door, her parting shot was unexpected and abrupt.

'I'd better go. I've things to do.'

The friends strode back down the garden to the fence gate. Karen eyed the scene around her, reminding herself once more of the jobs that needed tending to.

'This back yard needs a facelift, Evelyn. If I can be bothered, that is.'

Big Chief Crazyhorse folded her arms and feigned observation of her own rear lawn.

'My Greg can get himself stuck into some gardening when he comes back. I'll give him the nod to come and sort yours out if you like. It'll keep him occupied with all the spare time he's going to have.'

Karen chuckled as Evelyn opened the gate in the fence and bid her friend good day. Bolting it after her, Karen scanned the sky above once again as slate-coloured clouds gathered at a pace.

Evelyn did not look back as she muttered a parting word.

'Better get that washing back in, Karen. I told you it looked like rain.'

five

Nearly a fortnight had passed since the announcement of the promotion, carrying little in the way of altered routine for the Aspinalls. However, the finer details of Robert's re-posting had now been confirmed and he prepared for his inaugural Monday morning departure to Coventry with hopes high, but heart somewhat heavy.

Four days' notice wasn't much time to prepare for the most important journey of his working life, but Robert was quietly adamant he was doing the right thing. Karen had supported his decision as she had pledged to do, and the girls were putting a brave if slightly confused face on events during the weekend.

The alarm clock whined into life at exactly five am. Robert did not need rousing from slumber, however. He had not slept all night. The obvious benefits and potential consequences of the short-term future raced through his mind, allowing no time for mental or physical relaxation.

Karen had been determined to make the most of her final night with her husband and it was the early hours before their love making eased into a dozed embrace. Robert was not fatigued though. His eyes remained firmly fixed to the ceiling, staring through the murk of the bedroom as he contemplated his decision to leave his loved ones for the new venture.

Switching off the alarm, he sat up in bed as Karen turned over and nuzzled into his midriff. This was mind-numbingly painful. Even though he would be back in his own bed in a few days, he felt like he was deserting his family. He glanced down to his wife as she lay contentedly in his warmth. Robert analysed the silence of the room, then the rest of the house beyond.

He thought of his adored offspring in the adjacent rooms - their juvenile innocence in this matter tearing his soul to shreds. Could he truly leave them alone?

Should he embark on this path into uncertain territory?

Was climbing the ladder worth such personal heartache?

Robert supposed he would never know, until he tried.

'Come on you. You've a busy day ahead. Get that kettle on for me, there's a love.' Karen mumbled into her pillow as she snuggled further into the security of the duvet.

Smiling an unseen, bittersweet smile, Robert climbed out of bed and covered his nakedness with a bath robe before cutting an unsteady path down the stairs. He could still detect the aroma of the scented candles that had illuminated the previous evening's bath that he and Karen had shared like infants. They had laughed, reminisced, and got steadily drunk.

It was like falling in love all over again.

The dreamlike state of bath time and bedtime was now eclipsed by harsh reality - the reality of a long drive to a strange place. Gridlocked motorways; executive decisions. Lonely nights in a hotel with the long phone calls conveying the voices of his wife and daughters to torment him and remind him of what he had left at home.

His home. The loving, happy domesticity that he really did not want to abandon - even for promotion. What had he done by chasing this job? The clock on the kitchen wall showed the time to be twenty past five. In three hours, his daughters would be dressed for school and nursery. They would experience their day and Robert would not be able to see their cherubic features that night.

For the first time, Robert Aspinall would be absent. The sensation induced by such knowledge was most unpleasant. It almost made him feel like vomiting in an effort to rid his palate of the distaste. He loved his wife and children so much. He even felt he was being cruel by having succeeded in achieving his ambitions.

Then an even more disturbing thought flashed through his mind. Would anyone really *notice* his absence to any degree? Was it *really* to his family's detriment that he would be living in bloody Coventry all week? He sincerely hoped not, yet strangely wished it so.

Such emotive thoughts confused his already weary head. Flicking the switch on the kettle, he leaned on the edge of the sink and stared vacantly into the plug hole.

He did not hear Karen pad barefoot into the kitchen to discover him hunched over the draining board. Her croaky morning voice roused him back to attention.

'What have you lost now, Rob? Not one of your new cufflinks, surely? I put them both on the mantelpiece last night. Don't tell me you've dropped it down the drain?'

Turning to face the woman he loved, Robert smirked and observed his wife in the half light. His thoughts were briefly distracted from the day ahead.

She looked fabulous. Even at this early hour.

'You know, Kaz, you really shouldn't walk around the house in that obscenely short nightie. I've got to conserve some energy for the rest of today you know!'

She embraced her man, placing her lips on his as she whispered. And then his hands wandered.

'I'm afraid you can forget about an encore, darling. I think Chloe has just risen from the grave!'

Sure enough, as mother and father listened, tiny footsteps could be heard descending the staircase. A few seconds elapsed before Chloe poked her bedraggled features through the gap in the kitchen door.

'Morning, darling.' Karen beamed. 'Don't worry, Daddy hasn't gone yet! Go back upstairs and try and sleep a while longer. I'll shout you before he goes.'

Chloe looked weary eyed at her father before gaining some assurance on the matter.

'Do you promise to wake me, Mummy?'

'I promise, love. Now off you go.'

Robert felt a stir of emotion welling in his throat. He could not let this moment pass and promptly called his eldest daughter back. Chloe shuffled back across the tiled floor to her parents and looked forlornly up at them both.

'Yes, Daddy?'

Crouching to his knees, Robert Aspinall opened his arms and closed them again around Chloe's unkempt and sleepy form. He closed his eyes as tears fought for an escape route and he squeezed his little girl as much as he dared without hurting her. Karen watched in concerned silence.

For the first time since his promotion had been rubber-stamped, she sensed doubt from her husband. She could see his inner struggle. The understandable turmoil he had hidden so well was now painfully obvious. Subsequently, her own emotions began to churn.

If Robert couldn't handle the situation, what chance did *she* have of holding things together?

Releasing his little girl, he bade Chloe back to bed for an hour or two. Rising to his feet as his daughter obliged, Robert wiped his tears on the sleeve of his robe before falling into the comforting embrace of the woman that loved him.

'This is absolutely shit, Kaz. I *feel* like total shit. I don't know if I'm doing the right thing, now. My heart's tearing itself up. What do I do, Kaz? Tell me.'

It was time for Karen to take the reins and be strong.

She would oversee the house and home for the foreseeable future.

It was appropriate to begin the role now.

'I tell you what you can do. Go and shower. I will cook us a fried breakfast. Then I will wake the girls.'

His moistened gaze locked into that of his wife's.

'Then what? Then what do I do?'

With an air of authority and determination, her expression firmed, and her glare became assured.

'Then, my dear Mister Robert Aspinall…you will go to work!'

*****

Robert eyed the clock as he finished off the remnants of his breakfast.

Nearly seven. He ought to leave the house by eight if he were to make his midday induction meeting. Before that he had to check in to his hotel, which according to instruction was apparently five minutes from Coventry city centre.

'I've packed and double checked your suitcase, Rob. You just need to check your briefcase. I've laid today's suit on the bed. Your other one I've left in its dust jacket.'

Robert admired Karen's lithe form as she scraped congealed lard into the kitchen waste bin. Thankfully, she had now adopted different attire from earlier, which covered far more of her curves and dissuaded him from thoughts of whisking her back to bed.

'You're a fine woman, Mrs. Aspinall. Where would I be without you?'

'Frying your *own* bloody bacon!' she winked in response.

At last, Robert's mood lightened with a hearty chuckle.

'Yes, probably. Okay…better give the girls a nudge, hadn't we?'

*****

Opening the front door on a new era in his career, Robert shook his shoulders as he felt a slight chill edge the late April morning. Packing suitcase, briefcase and spare suit into the car, his thoughts suddenly turned to his new company motor which would be waiting for his collection very soon. This could well be one of his last journeys in the ever-reliable hatchback that had served him through many traffic jams over the past five years.

Now the trappings of success would enable him to procure the use of a brand-new automatic in metallic navy blue. Walnut interior finish. Air conditioning. Heated seats and windscreens. The whole package. A real dog's dinner of a motor car, allegedly.

Closing the rear passenger door, he inhaled a lungful of the shrill air and observed the rising sun over the rooftops. Whilst opening the front gate, he made a point of looking at the dew-covered front lawn and borders, noticing the daffodil bulbs that Karen had planted last year were proudly offering fully bloomed displays.

By strange compulsion, he then glanced across to the black saloon that slept silently on the Chapple's driveway at number forty-one.

Far too big a car for a solitary woman to cruise around in, he always thought. It was like a small tank. Even his own sizable car seemed small in comparison. He smiled inwardly as he read the last three letters of Evelyn Chapple's registration plate.

SCR.

Karen jovially claimed it stood for Secretive Cunning Rodent in reference to the owner. Evelyn would not be impressed with the interpretation. He was pretty sure of that.

Turning back to his own front door Robert felt sure he saw Evelyn's lounge curtains twitch. He stood and stared for a moment or two to try and confirm before re-entering the hallway to bid farewell to his family.

Karen, Chloe, and Lauren. The three people that meant most to Robert Aspinall in the entire world. More important than life. More important than jobs. More important than him, even.

'Drive safely, darling. Ring me, tonight. When you finally get a beer in your hand. We can talk then.'

As the husband bid his wife farewell with a lingering kiss and straining heart, he kneeled to his little girls.

He pulled them tightly to him and whispered in their ears.

'Missing you two, already. Goodbye my darlings. I'll see you on Friday. Be good for Mum. Love you! I'll talk to you both on the phone later.'

Chloe and Lauren attempted to conceal their upset with admiral maturity.

Prolonging the moment would not do anyone any favours. Climbing behind the wheel and buckling up, he waved through the windscreen to his wife and daughters and turned on the ignition.

As he reversed and then steered the car away from number thirty-nine, Benton Road, his family shouted, waved, and cheered. Despite the emotional frailty of everyone at that instant, it was an ultimately upbeat departure.

Few tears, surprisingly.

Multiple earnest smiles.

But time pressed, and Robert did not want to be ensnared in a punctuality issue on his first day.

Keeping the car in second gear all the way down the street, he vigorously gestured to his loved ones, continuing to wave goodbye through the open driver's window, barely keeping an eye on the road as he did so.

The distant, smiling image of his wife at the front gate was the one enduring vision he carried with him for the rest of the day.

*****

Evelyn Chapple had indeed observed the tender ceremony from her covert vantage point behind the lounge curtains. She felt it inappropriate to interrupt the scene outside, although she did wish to speak to Karen.

Keeping her vigil on the activity next door for the following hour, she avidly watched Karen take the girls to school in her car and waited patiently for her return twenty minutes later. No sooner had Karen applied the handbrake, Evelyn pounced on her friend and neighbour, like a spider in its wait for captive prey.

Karen half-smirked as Big Chief Crazyhorse positioned herself in front of her driver door and folded her ample forearms.

'Come on Karen. Get the kettle on! Tell me how it all went this morning. I didn't see much crying! Anyone would think you were glad to see the back of him for a week!'

Karen locked the car and unlocked the front door. If truth be known, she could not be bothered with company at that moment but played along with the charade.

'No, we wanted it to be as pleasurable a send-off as possible. Robert doesn't want to start his new job with us on his mind.'

Slithering toward the front door of number thirty-nine, Evelyn's hooked features broke into a wide, uneven grin.

'Well, now he's gone I can tell you my latest news. I've had confirmation over the weekend that Greg will be home on Friday. Isn't that great? I'm sure he'd love to meet you all. Bet you're dying to get to know him all over again, aren't you, Karen?'

An odd statement, Karen thought.

Even though she was pleased for Evelyn and her son, she had given the matter little consideration since it was first broached a couple of weeks earlier. Why should Evelyn presume her to be so desperate to meet Greg? No doubt Karen wouldn't be seeing much of him anyway. He was never around very often as a teenager from what she could recall.

Karen discreetly rolled her eyes before removing the key from the door.

Evelyn hovered expectantly behind her.

'Let me just tidy up before you come in, Evelyn. The place is a tip. I'll give you a buzz later.'

An expression of dejection befell her friend's features.

'Oh, okay…too busy, are we? The executive's wife hasn't got time for her best mate, anymore? I get it.'

Karen couldn't decide if Evelyn's response was serious or in jest, but nor was she inclined to debate the issue on the front step. Besides which, it was too early in the day, and she was desperate for a bath.

'Don't be so touchy, Evelyn. Just give me a chance to get the house straight. It's been a hectic weekend. We'll talk later, okay?'

Her friend did not answer and turned on her heel. Karen was pleased for her, but nine am on a Monday morning was not the ideal time for a natter. Especially this particular Monday morning.

No sooner had Karen let herself in than the schedule of domestic chores began. Just as Evelyn Chapple entered her own hallway and slammed the front door behind her.

six

'Yes, it is a very weird week. But I'm also relieved that you've settled into the hotel and things are okay up there. I've just put the girls to bed. They'll be happy knowing that you phoned even if they have missed you today.'

'Yes…Mum and Dad are fine, saw them yesterday as usual.'

'I know, it doesn't seem possible that its Friday tomorrow. We can't wait to see you. By the way I've bought a little something to welcome you back to your own bedroom, so you'd better put your foot down tomorrow afternoon!'

'Oh, nothing much. I haven't seen her since Monday morning. Her son's home from the army tomorrow, so no doubt she'll be around shoving him under my nose first chance she gets. I think she's had the funnies with me all week cos I can't be arsed with her at the minute. Too much else going on in my head. Never mind.'

'Yes, my darling…really can't wait…see you tomorrow, bye! Yes, love you – kiss-kiss!'

Karen placed the receiver back in the cradle and stared contentedly into space. The hardest test had seemingly been passed.

Those first few days of solace; of silence; of absence; of the heart growing fonder.

Of boredom, even.

She was now quietly pleased that Robert had chased and attained his promotion. Despite their combined doubt having gathered some momentum recently, her re-affirmed thought process concluded that fortune had blessed them this time.

The tears that Robert had shed on Monday morning had long since been vanquished by a gradual happiness. His introduction to his new duties had apparently been very comprehensive if intensive at times.

Whilst his hotel was one of the most reputable in Coventry, he professed to his wife a painful longing for the familiarity of home.

This was music to Karen's ears. Her husband had flown away and now wished to return to the nest. It was an adage about the truth of love, but Karen rejoiced in its telling philosophy.

A bubbly bath awaited her immersion. Checking that the girls were sleeping soundly, she lit a scented candle to remind her of Robert.

Observing her shapely form in the full-length mirror, Karen dropped her robe on the bathroom floor and sank into the water.

Thoughts of a wondrous reunion occupied her mind as the consoling heat of the tub encouraged a blissful fatigue.

*****

She hated waking up in stone cold bath water. It made her shiver as she dried herself rapidly and dived under the bedclothes. Even more reason to be objectionable to the shrill sound of the alarm clock echoing throughout her bedroom a few hours later.

Seven am. Time to meet and greet a new day. Time to get up and wake the girls for this most special of Fridays. In twelve hours, the family would be together again for the weekend.

For Karen it was a time of genuine euphoria.

The girls seemed particularly lethargic that morning, but it had been a wearing week for everybody. Eventually Karen deposited them in turn to school and nursery before taking a detour to the supermarket to fetch some shopping. Robert would be eating pepper sauce steak tonight.

His favourite meal from his favourite lady.

As she unpacked the carrier bags in the kitchen, the radio emitted the latest chart sounds from the windowsill. It was a blustery day, but bright and unseasonably warm.

Would she risk hanging out some washing? Karen glanced through the kitchen window. Perhaps. Perhaps not.

Movement caught in the corner of her eye re-focused her gaze on the back lawn. She spotted Evelyn at the gate in the fence, peering and pointing into the garden of number thirty-nine. She appeared to be demonstrating the bolts on the gate itself. She was definitely speaking and gesturing to someone who was out of Karen's line of vision behind the shed.

Only when Karen appeared at her back door did her neighbour acknowledge her with a smile and an exaggerated wave. She pointed toward Karen, as though her hidden guest might have wished to take a look. Then in an instant, Evelyn was gone from view.

The kettle had conveniently just boiled when the extremely loud knock at Karen's front door made her jump, sounding just as though someone had put their fist through it.

Karen shuffled through the hallway to greet the caller.

Opening the door revealed two smiling figures.

'Hello, Karen, my love. How are you? So glad you're in. I've brought someone to meet you.'

The shortish yet handsome man standing next to Evelyn flashed his dazzlingly white teeth through a mischievous yet undeniably attractive smile.

Muscular, tanned, brutish, rugged. Greg Chapple looked every inch the soldier, almost filling the width of the doorframe with his toned bulk. The relevance of the call did not register with Karen immediately. She observed her visitors with some curiosity.

'You remember what I told you?' Evelyn gushed.

Karen did remember. Of course, she did. But she had reserved all her enthusiasm for her own family reunion later that day. Staring at the virtual stranger before her, Karen remained in a state of feigned vacancy as her friend eagerly prompted her once again.

'About who was coming home? After all these years?'

Finally, the penny acted as though it had just dropped. Karen Aspinall eagerly placed her hand inside the firm grasp of Greg Chapple.

'I'm so sorry, Greg. Your mum did say you were back today but I'm such a dizzy blonde at times. How are you?'

Karen sensed a sudden wave of unwarranted flirtatiousness that was uncontrollably invigorated for the first time since she could remember.

Greg sensed her feminine responses, smirked knowingly, and observed the bemused yet inviting sight of Karen Aspinall - up and down.

'How do I look?' Greg eventually replied.

A strange introduction thought Karen, but she played along with the supposed frivolity of the moment.

'Well, you look...fine, er...very good, in fact. But er...a lot different. My, yes, how you've changed. All grown up now, eh? The soldier comes home from the front line!'

Karen chuckled at her own inane commentary, but neither Evelyn nor her son offered a visible flicker of humour in response. Karen felt suddenly foolish and opted to dispense with the childish approach, eventually believing it a wiser idea to welcome them both into the house.

Entering the kitchen, Karen could feel Greg's eyes scanning her as she moved passed him.

She did not disclose any discomfort with the situation, but Greg's presence had an instantaneous effect.

He was a new face for Karen to get used to - a new kid on the block.

Someone she felt strangely inclined to get acquainted with, but at that moment as she filled the teapot, she had no idea why she should be reacting so.

The trio placed themselves around the kitchen table as an awkward silence ensued. A silence that Evelyn Chapple did not tolerate for long.

'I've been telling Greg all about you and the girls. How you've been rendered a single mum all week whilst your husband chases the Yankee dollar!'

Karen was a little perturbed by her friend's presumptions, especially by her appraisal of Robert's situation which was entirely inaccurate. Yet Evelyn continued to set her stall out whilst she had the appropriate arena.

'Greg says he'll do your gardening for you. Perhaps even baby-sit if you want to get out for an evening. He could even take *you* out and *I* could baby-sit. That's a better idea!' she cackled.

Karen eyed Evelyn as she continued to carry herself away into her own fantasy world. Greg continued to smile without word across the table. His eyes bore into Karen as though he was reading her every thought. She felt slightly intruded upon, but the enticement was something she was struggling to resist.

He retained his silence as his mother continued with the diatribe.

'Rob won't mind, will he? He'll probably be glad to see you out enjoying yourself. Well, he's not in any position to moan about it anyway, is he?'

Karen felt a need to stop this one-way conversation in its tracks before it led everybody down a path they didn't want to go. Though, at that particular moment, it appeared that both Evelyn and Greg were enjoying the spectacle.

'Just...slow it down will you, Evelyn? Greg's only been in my house five minutes and you're pairing us off together. Aren't you forgetting something? Such as...my husband, for instance?'

Evelyn threw her friend an expression of mild frustration at the mention of Robert.

'Well, he's not going to be here all week, is he? You'll no doubt get lonely, won't you?'

Karen couldn't believe her ears at her friend's uninvited and incredulous whims. Whilst she understood that Evelyn's enthusiasm was perhaps something to admire on occasion, in this context it was ridiculously mis-judged.

However, Evelyn had picked up on the immediate eye contact between Karen and her son. She was not about to discourage their potential friendship by holding back her opinions. Karen, though, opted to change the subject as she placed mugs on the table and perched across from the visitors.

'So, you've finished your army service then, Greg?'

Again, he displayed the wily grin before replying.

'Yes, well...for the moment. I don't know if I'll get re-posted anywhere. I'm not bothered, though. It's good to be home. I've missed Mum. And I know she's missed me. She'll appreciate having me back, I'm sure. I can do all the jobs that she doesn't want to. Do all her dirty work for her...' he grinned, mischievously.

Greg had an immediately infectious charm and evidently doted on his mother. Karen could not deny that much. She was pleased that Evelyn had brought him around so soon but a little wary of her motive. After all, Karen was married with a family. To be seen anywhere near a potentially explosive situation such as this would be wonderful fodder for the gossip brigade of the surrounding estate. Especially the nosy Robinsons living directly across the road.

Then Greg asked a question which effectively removed all caution from Karen's mind.

'I hear you've got *two* daughters, now? I'd like to meet them both. I bet Chloe won't recognise me, anyway. She was barely born when I left home?'

Karen Aspinall became instantly inflated with maternal pride. Greg had referenced her children. She was touched by his consideration and concern - more of which was to come.

'And your husband, Rob? Executive now, eh? Bet he won't know me by sight, either. I'll have to get around to having a few beers with him when he's free. Did you say he's only back at weekends?'

Karen nodded eagerly in response. Greg's interest seemed genuine.

'Yes, that's right. He's based in Coventry, now. Monday to Friday. He's back home tonight, actually. This is his first week away!'

Greg's features evolved once again broadened into a gleaming smile as he pondered a retort.

'Better put our ear plugs in tonight then, eh Kaz?'

A deafening, disbelieving, awkward silence followed, which was soon eclipsed by booms of laughter from Evelyn Chapple.

She quickly changed her tune after catching Karen's stunned expression.

Conveying evidently feigned disgust, she turned to her only son.

'Greg! That's about as rude as you can be! And besides, it's none of your business!'

Greg's eyes never left Karen's as she looked discomfortingly back at him. In truth, despite the interruption to her schedule, she was enjoying the company. Her eventual amusement in the saucy exchange was there for all to see. She no longer saw any reason to conceal her contentment under Greg's scrutiny.

'I know it's rude, mum. The ruder the better, eh Kaz?'

Karen shook her head in mock disapproval as she poured the brewed tea.

'I can see I'm going to have to watch you, Greg Chapple. Bit of a cheeky one, aren't you? How old are you now?'

Again, Greg flashed a taunting smirk that ensnared Karen's attention.

'Have a guess.'

Karen looked across to his mother whose overall response to the conversation was difficult to interpret. She reverted to the question of his age and scanned Greg's sun-browned features.

'Erm…I would say…twenty-five.'

'Spot on!'

Greg watched attentively as Karen's blue eyes widened with her minor success.

'Wow…six years younger than me, then!'

'Yes. I could be your toy-boy…if you wanted!'

More laughter ensued as Evelyn scraped her stool backward along the wooden floor and rose to her feet.

'Come on then, you. Let's not keep Karen from her business.'

'What about your tea?' gasped Karen.

Her friend's tone was strangely intolerant considering she was the one that called round in the first place. Yet again the weird series of exchanges had developed into an abrupt conclusion.

'They'll be plenty of time for chit chat and cups of tea at a later date, I'm quite sure.'

Karen was most perplexed by their sudden exit to say the least, until she noticed the clock on the kitchen wall.

'Shit! I've got to pick Lauren up from nursery at twelve! I don't know where time has gone this morning. I've got ten minutes!'

Escorting her neighbours to the front door, Karen pledged to see Greg again.

'Pop round and see Rob tomorrow if you want. He'd love to meet you again, Greg. You've changed so much from the teenager I can remember of years ago.'

With a slightly wild stare, Greg halted his stride and winked at Karen as his mother wandered with arms folded across the driveway to her own property.

He engaged Karen's full attention with his sapphire blue eyes and spoke in a half whisper.

'Oh yes…I've changed alright. You won't believe how much I've changed. All grown up, now.'

He then waltzed up behind his mother, as both entered the front door of number forty-one door without so much as a goodbye.

seven

'Aunty Judy! Mummy! It's Aunty Judy!'

Chloe hollered through from the hallway to the kitchen as Karen's best friend Judy Simpson was ushered through the front door.

'Happy birthday, Chloe! Are you having a nice day?'

It was a Sunday for a family celebration at thirty-nine, Benton Road, and true to form, the weather had broken. The warm entry of spring had been temporarily halted. Although the sunshine was still soothing when it appeared between the hailstorms and torrential showers.

Judy smiled at Chloe's unbridled excitement as Karen appeared through the kitchen door to greet her best friend.

'Hi Jude. So glad you could come.'

Karen looked at the neatly gift-wrapped parcel under her friend's arm.

'Hope you haven't spoiled her. She's had a fortune spent on her this year. Anyone would think she was eighteen - not nine, for god's sake!'

Judy crouched down to supply a hug and kiss to Chloe.

'She's well worth it, Kaz. Here you are my sweet. Open it. I can see you can't wait.'

The lifelong friends embraced as Chloe scampered off with her prize. Judy was a soul mate to Karen. They had journeyed through school together and she had always remained based in nearby Tenbridge.

Judy's interest in the lives of the Aspinall family was earnest and from the heart.

'How are you all, Kaz? Things okay with you and Rob?'

'Yeah, great. Can't tell you how much I've missed *you*, though, Jude. It's been a lonely few weeks with Robert away. Come on. We're all in here.'

Making her entrance into the living room, Judy was welcomed among the throng and a drink placed conveniently in her hand by the father of the birthday girl. Chloe had wasted little time in ripping off the wrapping paper from her present.

'Wow! My favourite pop group! And new Minnie Mouse pyjamas! Thanks, Aunty Judy! Mum, can I go upstairs and play my new CD?'

'Yes, off you go. Not too loud though. Consider the neighbours! But before you go don't forget to remember who brought you the gifts…'

Chloe sidled up to Judy and shyly planted a kiss on her cheek before retreating upstairs to leave the adults to their own devices.

'So…how's life treating you, Miss Simpson?'

'Oh, can't complain, Rob. I'm still nursing at The Royal Infirmary. I'm also still in my flat. I'm also still *single*! I can't believe Chloe is nine already. Where has the time gone?'

Robert placed his arm around Karen's shoulder and looked at his wife admiringly.

'Don't ask us! I'm just getting my first grey hairs!'

Laughter resumed among the group as Lauren appeared at the lounge door. With only a modicum of reluctance, she jumped up into Judy's arms as though she were her own mother.

Judy kissed her on the lips and squealed with delight as Lauren pulled her cross-eyed expression. In the next instance, Lauren was gone once again, back upstairs to torment her sister and other school friends.

'She is so cute! Looks just like her father, too! How's the job going, Rob? How does it feel to be the boss at last?'

Robert took a large swig of his beer before responding with an exaggerated smile.

'Stressful!'

Judy gestured through the lounge window toward the driveway.

'Err…I wouldn't mind some of that stress if it meant I could have a brand-new motor like yours. What a little runabout *that* is! Is it safe to leave outside on the drive?'

Karen sniggered knowingly.

'Makes my D-reg looked a bit clapped out, doesn't it? I think I'm due an upgrade in transport too!'

Robert nodded as he continued to sip from his can of beer.

'It's safe as houses out there. This is a respectable estate. We don't get any bother around here, you know. We are a very refined community!'

He gestured with an outstretched thumb in the direction of the Chapple's house.

'Especially with the Big Chief being next door. She's a wonderful neighbourhood look-out!' he concluded sarcastically.

Mirth resonated once again as Karen's parents entered the room from the kitchen. Jean Hope had always had a soft spot for Judy ever since she was in Karen's class at school.

'Hello, Jude!' Jean smiled. 'So lovely to see you! It's been ages! You look fabulous! How are your mum and dad?'

Karen rolled her eyes at her friend as the pop music from upstairs began to vibrate through the ceiling. A crescendo compounded by Chloe's party guests dancing in unison to the beat.

'Oh, they are both fine. Still at each other's throats all day long. Still moaning about each other's little ways. But I suppose that's what a forty-year marriage does for a couple. Which reminds me. It's their anniversary soon. A proper house party. Selective invitation only! But *you're* all invited of course! Mind, you two look very happy and contented with each other. It's nice to see for a change! How are you, Brian?'

Karen's father shuffled up beside his wife and placed an arm around Judy's shoulder.

'Apart from a dicky set of knees, I'm fine love, thanks. It's all the rest of the buggers, ain't it?'

Karen seized the chance to whisk her best friend away from the throng for a little privacy.

Retreating to the kitchen they perched at the table and a fresh bottle of wine was duly un-corked.

'Must be three or four months since I saw you last, Kaz. You look lovely. Really fit and glowing. Have you been going back to the gym in the mornings?'

Karen smiled and grabbed at the modicum of extra flesh around her waistline.

'You must be joking! I've not been since…well…before last Christmas.'

'Well, something's keeping you in trim. Look at your figure! I'm insanely jealous! I can see I'm going to have to take you out for a great big lunch. Chips with everything!'

The friends chuckled as Karen topped up their wine glasses. Judy reminded her that she was driving.

'Just a small one for me please, Kaz.'

Karen sensed a query emerging in her friend, which duly arrived after a sip of her drink.

'I take it the Big Chief Rob referred to is her next door? Why *Big Chief*? Is he not a fan, then?'

Karen smirked as she considered her reply.

'It was me and the girls that named her after Big Chief Crazyhorse - because she looks like one!'

Judy smiled and slowly shook her head.

'That's terrible - but funny! How is she these days? Still the local gossip by the sounds of things!'

There was a knock at the door that briefly interrupted the conversation. Karen waved it away with her hand.

'Someone else will get that. Rob's not overly keen on her, but then he never has been. I tell you what though. She's a good friend to me. You just don't tell her what really matters. It's simple. If she doesn't know about it, she can't gossip about it, can she?'

At that moment, Karen's mother poked her head around the kitchen door. Her face donned a slight grimace followed by a forced half-smile.

'You have more visitors, Karen. Mrs. Chapple and son have arrived to see Chloe.'

Judy looked across the table at Karen. They stared at each other as the mutual sense of cheeky amusement displayed itself.

'Sounds like her ears were burning, Miss Aspinall! Shouldn't call people names. It's not nice!' chuckled Judy.

'Shut up, you. You laughed at it. Anyway, her son's just come home from the army.'

Karen pretended to mutter from behind her hand as she continued.

'He's a bit of a dish, actually. He might be on the lookout for a single girl like you! Right up your street. I could put a good word in for you if you want! Mind you he's about three inches shorter than you, too!'

Judy's features creased in mock panic as she reacted to her friend's teasing remarks.

'Don't you bloody dare say anything, you cow! I don't like soldiers, anyway. They can be a bit screwed up when they've done their time. I don't think the army does blokes any favours. Just makes them mental! In my experience, anyway.'

Karen laughed once again and curled her fingers around her mouth as though to conceal her whispers.

'Yes, and you've certainly had some experience, haven't you, girl!'

Greg entered the kitchen, right on cue, just as Judy offered a playful slap to her friend across the table. His distinctive, low tone silenced their banter in an instant.

'Hello ladies! Not fighting over me already, are you?'

Karen stared at the new arrival as he stood proudly in the doorway. She also noticed his tight-fitting t-shirt which displayed a finely honed upper physique.

'You *wish*!' she grinned back at him.

It did not invoke the slightest reaction in Greg, whose interest centred temporarily on the unfamiliar presence of Judy.

Finishing her drink, Karen introduced her best friend to Greg, whose gaze subsequently fixed itself back on Karen. A fact that did not go unnoticed by her as she desperately tried to conceal her mild discomfort. The alcohol was quickly taking effect.

'Pleased to meet you, Greg.'

Judy and Greg shook hands.

'Likewise. Karen never told me she had such a beautiful mate.'

Judy did not respond to his weak attempts at smooth talk.

'Back from the trenches, eh? See any action out there, then?'

Greg eyed Judy sternly as he considered her question.

'Out *where*?'

'Out there, wherever you soldier types go and fight.'

Judy's remarks only served to encourage Greg's penchant for flirtation as he revelled in the company of the two attractive women.

'I intend to see far more action now I'm back home. Besides, the women are a lot better looking over here.'

Karen felt herself blush as the obvious subject of Greg's comments. Although, under the scrutiny of her friend, she wanted the ground to swallow her up. Judy was not ignorant to the blatant interaction and simply stared wide-eyed at the scene playing before her as she forgetfully re-filled her own glass.

The unsettling hiatus in conversation was soon dispatched by Robert, who entered the kitchen and swung open the fridge door.

Karen felt a twinge of unease as her husband stood toe to toe with the young soldier from number forty-one. Thankfully, her mild anguish dissipated as Robert offered a hand of greeting and popped open a can of beer for the neighbour.

Judy continued with her questions.

'Are you staying in Church Drayton for a while, then?'

Again, Greg focused his attention on the gorgeous blonde that sat across the kitchen table, who just happened to be the wife of the man he was standing next to. He smiled at Karen as he responded to the query.

'I don't know how long I'll be around. It depends whether I outstay my welcome, doesn't it?'

Robert closed the fridge door and observed Karen, whose cheeks were a light shade of crimson.

He patted Greg on the shoulder.

'Not much chance of that, mate! Your mum has missed you like mad! Besides, I'm sure you'll make yourself useful around the place. Strong lad like you can do all her jobs for her whilst your dad is away. Here's a birthday drink.'

Robert gestured through the kitchen window.

'You can work your way through *my* job list as well if you like. Plenty in the back garden to be getting on with!'

The men chortled as Greg sampled some lager. He was willingly making Karen more than a little self-conscious, but she seemed receptive enough to the attention.

However, he wasn't prepared to push his luck just yet. After all, he was still practically a stranger to the Aspinalls.

'I'll be on hand to help if I can. I'll always be around. I'm pretty difficult to shake off once I'm settled somewhere.'

A wild scream from the front room diverted everyone's attention from the conversation - much to Karen's relief. Evelyn Chapple's rousing cackle followed Chloe's shouts of excitement as she unwrapped her birthday gift from the neighbours.

Suddenly Lauren bundled her way into the kitchen and announced the cause of the amusement.

'Mummy! Chloe's got Minnie Mouse pyjamas from Aunty Evelyn that are the same as the ones Aunty Judy brought her!'

Karen roused herself from the table and the group made their way back through to the lounge. Greg did not move an inch, forcing Judy, and then Karen to squeeze past him as he hogged the doorway. Karen's emotions whirled as she watched her husband and eldest daughter tease one another before the guests.

She knew instinctively that Judy had picked up on Greg's very obvious attempts to impress. It was ridiculous, yet strangely Karen was not offended at all by the interest. In fact, it was a refreshing change to be the object of attention; to perhaps feel desired.

Robert loved his family. There was doubt about that. But he had been preoccupied with work for weeks.

Regular intimacy with his wife was something that had been placed on the back burner.

Karen suddenly felt womanly in Greg's presence, though of course, she would never openly admit to such a feeling. It was an involuntary response and not of her own choosing.

It was as though he was activating something inside her.

A reaction she could not command; only obey.

She suspected that Judy had already worked out the mutual signals and the inevitable effect they were having. Yet nothing of it made sense to Karen. After all, she barely knew Greg, but something told her that this man was somehow worth getting to know better.

Under oath, she would have to admit to him being on her mind ever since their brief reacquaintance of a couple of weeks earlier.

He was inside her head for reasons she could not grasp.

It was like she had been hit by a bolt from the blue.

In his presence she was a little girl once more.

Vulnerable and wanting.

*****

The lounge was filled with an atmosphere of celebration. Karen's parents were proud to see their family so happy and apparently prosperous.

Robert and Judy chatted about each other's work and future plans, whilst Chloe and Lauren and Chloe's three schoolfriends revelled in the attention from their captive audience, although blowing out the candles on the cake almost caused World War Three.

Wine and beer flowed freely as the afternoon sunshine decided to make fleeting appearances in and around the hail.

Yet clouds were always imminent.

Nobody detected the signs of the downturn that was about to ensue.

Evelyn Chapple stood with a wine glass in her hand at the back of the room, contented and silent as she observed her son and neighbour playfully banter with one another across the crowded lounge.

Their exchanges were harmless to the casual observer, yet to her, most telling.

As far as Evelyn was concerned, her son needed a woman in his life. She would not stand in fate's way should that particular lady be in that room at that very moment, not five yards from where he stood.

Evelyn covertly watched her friend's eyes light up in response to Greg's mixed repertoire of practised and natural charm. She observed with growing inner satisfaction, the beaming smiles on both faces.

Greg was a striking young man with a glint in his eye and a persuasive manner.

Karen was an undoubtedly stunning woman and most suitable company for a wayward son and sometime ex-soldier.

She also viewed Karen Aspinall as possibly lonely, whilst certainly now alone for most of the time.

A woman who was potentially susceptible to suggestion and possibly willing to oblige temptation.

*****

With the evening passing far sooner than most would have preferred, it was time for the party to end. The Hopes departed with a loving wave and a word or two of congratulations for their granddaughter. Chloe's school friends that had been invited were duly collected by their parents.

Evelyn and Greg bid farewell and moved to stand on their own driveway as a belatedly low sun dropped behind distant rooftops. Judy had been careful not to drink over her limit, though the impish giggles that emitted from the porch-way of number thirty-nine would have the passer-by believing otherwise.

Karen hugged her friend tightly.

'Ring me, Jude. We'll have lunch. Soon, okay?'

'Okay, Kaz. I've still got the receipt for the pyjamas. And behave yourself. You know what I mean?'

'Oh no don't worry about that. Chloe will get through both pairs quickly. And don't worry about the other thing, either. You little shit stirrer…never changed, have you?'

Judy offered Karen a cheeky wink and a chuckle as she climbed behind the steering wheel of her white three-door parked on the front. Again, Karen found herself blushing and waved her friend away with a comically rude gesture.

Evelyn Chapple sighed as she bestowed her silent, secret blessing upon the afternoon's events. Opening her own front door before bidding her farewells to the Aspinalls, she felt a welcome vigour regain momentum inside her core.

‘Goodnight, all. Come on Greg. Inside, lad.’

Greg Chapple exchanged one last glance with Karen before both turned to go their separate ways. The celebration of Chloe’s ninth birthday had been a vibrant success.

Karen entered the kitchen and viewed the three empty wine bottles on the table which suggested it was time for something a little less potent. The clock on the wall displayed a time of nearly eight o’clock.

‘Rob. Do you want a coffee? My head’s spinning.’

Robert crept up behind Karen and placed his arms around her waist.

Nuzzling into her neck, he told his wife that he loved her.

‘Yes, coffee please. I’d better prepare my things for tomorrow’s drive. Bring it upstairs will you, love?’

Soon embraced in one other, man and wife slept soundly in their consoling, mutual warmth.

Although beyond that realm of inner fulfilment, out in the concealing night sky, cold black clouds continued to gather with menacing efficiency.

eight

'To be quite honest, Judy, I'm looking forward to September.'

Karen sipped her coke through a straw whilst eyeing Lauren, who scribbled with a crayon beside her. Judy looked surprised at her friend's unexpected confession. Karen expanded as she gestured to her youngest daughter.

'Well, she'll be starting infant school. I'll get full days to myself instead of working everything around dinner time. I think Lauren will appreciate the change of routine as well. Besides, after the six weeks' holiday I'll deserve a break, anyway!'

Judy smiled as the waitress appeared. The sunshine gleamed through the windows of the pizza restaurant causing her to squint at the enquiring young lady with the notebook and pencil.

The friends glanced to one another before Judy confirmed the table's requests.

'I think we'll have two adult's buffets and one small cheese and tomato special, please.'

Lauren's attention suddenly diverted from the clown's face she was inscribing with red wax. She smiled at the thought of impending lunch before resuming with the colouring. Karen grinned back at her daughter as the server thanked them.

Judy gestured toward the waitress as she walked away.

'Don't you think that dress is a little tight, Kaz? Look at how its hugging her backside!'

'Judy! She might have heard you! Don't be so cruel.'

Karen again placed her lips around her drinking straw to hide a smile as Judy giggled to herself and covered her mouth with her hand.

'I know, I'm terrible! It's pure jealousy though, you know! Simply because my arse is *massive*. Though, I'm sure that she's a size twelve and still cramming herself into a size ten!'

Karen shook her head once more as her friend jibed.

Lauren looked up briefly and showed her mother how the clown was progressing.

'Look at her, Kaz! Doesn't seem five minutes since she was in your belly! Little darling!'

Karen was thankful to have Judy around again.

Her routine had developed a monotonous edge and a semblance of a social life was most welcome. In recent weeks, excitement had been in scarce supply for Karen Aspinall. Judy concurred without prompt.

'This is really nice, Kaz. Just like old times, eh?'

Karen simply nodded. She knew just what her friend meant. In their younger days they would while the hours away in café windows, looking at the characters that would pass by outside.

The days before marriages and jobs; before mortgages and families.

Carefree days.

Yet looking back, despite the laughs, those days were also somewhat aimless.

Karen would not willingly admit it, but she was secretly pleased to have found her niche in life. Unlike Judy, who had drifted through the mangle of university and seemingly emerged no different for the experience. Nursing was a most admirable vocation of course. But she was still the schoolgirl who constantly wanted mischief. Growing up was something that Judy Simpson always appeared to be afraid of.

It was one of the things that Karen liked about her. Judy's immaturity was a wonderful facet. It brought relief to every situation.

She was also honest as the day was long.

'You're very fortunate, Karen. When I came to Chloe's party the other week, I could tell that you are in such a happy family. I couldn't see that Rob's new placement has had any adverse effect on things at all. How do you feel about it? You never really said.'

New placement? Well, Karen supposed it was a new placement of sorts. But it was also a genuine promotion, albeit with drawbacks.

Certainly not in the financial sense, but in terms of Karen's growing sense of isolation from real life. Robert had moved on and satisfied his whims to a degree. Karen was yearning slightly for the same.

'I suppose I've remained where I've always been. The ever-loving, reliable housewife bringing up her kids and adhering to domesticity. But I think I might like to return to work once the girls are old enough to sort themselves. A few years yet, eh?' chuckled Karen.

It wasn't so much a case of missing Robert in the week. More a situation of how to fill her time without him to cater for. Karen desperately needed a distraction or two.

Something to regain the inner spark that had seemed to have long since extinguished itself.

Her diverting train of thought was interrupted by Judy's earnest comments.

'Rob's lucky to have a woman like you, Kaz. I don't think I'd be very happy at being deserted all week with two little ones.'

Karen mulled over her friend's words. What was it about this word *desertion*? Why did people assume that Robert had abandoned his family? It was an unsavoury turn of phrase and did not register easily. Robert hadn't deserted anybody. Nobody was suffering consequences of his actions. His promotion wasn't to the detriment of his family's unity.

Was it?

Then again, maybe Karen ought to analyse her life from the outside in for a change. Perhaps she would see things differently from another vantage point? Maybe a third-party opinion was the inspiration she needed to create some thrills in her existence.

'Rob's doing everything for the right reasons, Jude. He's looking after us. Following his dreams - whilst keeping the wolf well away from the door, of course!'

Judy guffawed at her friend's modest reference to his salary.

'Come off it, Kaz! Rob's just chopped his banger in for a fantastic model! You must be bloody rolling in it, girl!'

Karen was equally peeved and amused by her friend's assumptions.

'Money is nice, yes. But it isn't everything, Judy. Besides, the car comes with the job. It's not ours. But yeah…you know…we are okay…moneywise…I suppose…I've never really thought about it.'

'I wouldn't know, Kaz. I've been skint and raggedy all my life! Must be great to be a kept woman, though!' she chuckled.

The ice in Karen's drink made her wince with shock.

'You don't think I married for security reasons, do you? A bit of an old-fashioned approach, isn't it? Women rule the roost now, you know!'

Judy smiled and hid shyly behind her cup.

'Well, I certainly rule my roost…there's only me there! No, I'm only teasing. But you tell me, Kaz. What's more important in life these days than a few quid in the bank? Those that claim money doesn't matter are usually loaded to the eyeballs. The irony of it all is that those who don't have to worry about money do nothing *but* worry about it.'

Whilst entering the debate half-heartedly, Karen didn't feel inclined to end the argument with a failure to agree.

She had a corner to fight - for every bored housewife in the land.

'Health is more important than money. Friends are more important than money. Family is more important than money.'

Judy chortled as she played with her drinking straw.

'Ah, yes. Friends.'

Karen didn't understand the inference of Judy's reply and grappled for her to expand.

'What is that supposed to mean? Why say it as though it's not that important? We're the best of friends, aren't we?'

Judy looked sternly at Karen across the table.

'Of course we are, Kaz. Always and forever. But, come off it! Those dummies that you live next door to. Do you honestly regard *them* as your friends? Or the nosy sods from across the road? Are *they* really your mates?'

Self-scrutiny and analysis of her life was something Karen was becoming accustomed to of late. She was feeling slightly bullied by Judy's comments, yet there was a strand of common sense among her opinions.

Confusion over such issues was another aspect of her well-being that Karen seemed to be confronted with on a more regular basis these days.

The moment was interrupted by the appearance of the waitress at the table with Lauren's pizza, which she duly placed before her. Whilst Karen cut the pizza into smaller morsels, Judy filled two plates at the buffet cart.

Once all three were seated and eating the conversation resumed.

Karen was intrigued by Judy's appraisal of matters.

'Do you not think that the Robinsons across the road are my friends then, Jude?'

A forkful of coleslaw temporarily prevented a coherent answer, so Judy widened her eyes and shook her head. Karen picked up a breadstick and pondered her next move.

'What about next door, then? The Chapples have been very kind to me over the years. Surely that must count for something?'

Judy swallowed her food and took another sip of her drink.

Strangely, she looked around the room before replying, as though wary of potential listeners.

'The Chapples will be friendly to you so long as it suits *them*. I don't trust them. I never have. I don't know why. Believe me, Kaz. When they're ready, they'll drop you like a stone. Mark my words. And that goes for the interfering bleeders across the road, too.'

Karen was becoming distinctly bemused by Judy's opinion of the close neighbours on Benton Road. Yet something in what she was saying struck a chord. An indefinable, yet vaguely recognisable moral was ringing true. Karen could not attach any relevance to the signal at that moment.

Still, she instinctively tried to assuage Judy's rather negative viewpoint.

'But Evelyn's been like a grandmother to the girls. Isn't that a sign of friendship? Someone to rely on when in need? People who are there for you, no matter what?'

Judy crunched a celery stick whilst offering a knowing nod of the head.

'I'd have tried to believe you, Kaz...until the other day when I saw her at your house with her *wonderful* son. That was just mental.'

Karen's slight feelings of confused anger were now eclipsed by a sense of curiosity.

'Greg? Why, what has he ever done to anyone? I hardly know him myself, really. He went straight into the army after school. He seems sociable enough, though...or am I imagining things again?'

The atmosphere between the two was becoming rather pensive, as though a cosy room had suddenly been invaded by a cold draught.

The unease was tempered by Judy's biggest smile.

'Oh yes, Kaz. He's sociable alright. *Extremely* friendly!'

Karen sensed mischief once again, as though she was being teased in true Judy Simpson-style.

'Come on Jude! Don't talk in riddles. Either he's okay or he's not. Make up your mind for Christ's sake!'

Judy began to giggle.

'Don't tell for one single minute that me you didn't notice, Karen! I can't believe how naive you are at times!'

Karen's voice raised in exasperation as she let her cutlery fall heavily to the table, causing Lauren to stare at her for a second or two.

'Notice *what*, Judy? Notice bloody *what*?'

Judy nearly fell off her chair as her laughter exploded around the restaurant. Lauren continued eating contentedly as her mother awaited some clue to solving Judy's charade.

Finally, her friend regained some composure before unveiling her assessment.

'Don't get so aggravated, girl! It's not my fault he fancies the *knickers* off you, is it?'

Whilst desperately trying to conceal her acknowledgment of Judy's theory on the issue, Karen successfully managed to keep a straight face.

'What are you talking about?'

Judy brought her head closer to Karen's across the table to afford her voice a whispered tone.

'He fancies you like *mad*, Kaz! His eyes were all over you! Anyone within fifty yards could see it! I can't believe Rob hasn't noticed.'

Karen could not truthfully deny her friend's conclusions, but nor could she admit to them being somewhere near the mark.

Suddenly, her memory of being briefly excited in Greg's presence was replaced by a sense of discomfort at the very same situation being noticed by a third party.

The conversation had suddenly become twisted and irritating.

'Absolute *rubbish*! You're seeing things, Judy. You're mad! He *can't* fancy me. He's hardly set eyes on me since coming home! Rubbish! Are you sure there's no vodka in that coke you're drinking?'

Again, Judy's amused guffaws filled the room.

'Well, I'm telling you it's true! And I'll tell you something else, girl! His mother knows it as well!'

Karen was now reaching a point of slightly feigned dismay

'Jesus, Jude. Change the subject, will you? You're putting me off my dinner!'

With a mocking expression of remorse, Judy held up both hands as she chewed.

'Okay, okay. Don't take it from me, then. But believe me you'll have to watch him - and his overbearing mother!'

The debate intensified once again as Karen hit back.

'Evelyn Chapple? Overbearing? I don't think so! Her husband Nigel has treated her like a bloody doormat over the years!'

Judy's features adopted a serious expression once again.

'That's what she *likes* you to think. Bet she says she's had it tough, doesn't she? All that time on her own bringing up baby. I bet she shoved her opinion on Rob's promotion under your nose without you asking.'

For once in the conversation, Karen found her friend's astuteness truly fascinating.

'She hasn't had it easy, Jude. She's spent most of her married life alone with Nigel working abroad.'

Judy stared directly at her friend to reply with a question.

'Did you ever stop to ask yourself *why* they decided to live like that?'

The waitress approached once again to enquire as to everybody's satisfaction with their meals.

Lauren looked up from her plate and smiled with lips encrusted in tomato sauce. The waitress crouched down to talk to her.

'I think you deserve a balloon, young lady. Which colour would you like?'

The youngster responded wide-eyed with pleasure.

'Erm…red, please. Like Mummy's car.'

Returning with the balloon of choice, the waitress departed the table once more.

Judy commented on her dress once more.

'She is possibly even a *fourteen*! But the skirt is definitely a *ten*!'

Despite the distracting interlude which raised a chuckle from both women once again, Karen sensed that the exchange regarding the Chapples was not yet over and sought some further answers from Judy.

'Okay! Why the hell would Greg fancy me, then? Go on. Tell me that, know-all.'

Judy loved to wind her favourite companion up.

Karen was being tempted by every morsel of bait.

'Well, for a start, you're an attractive blond with blue eyes. Secondly, he makes you laugh without even trying. Thirdly, he wears tight clothes that show off his muscles. I worked all this out in thirty seconds' flat. Don't tell me you haven't yet picked up on his vibes?'

Of course, Karen's problem now was that she knew exactly what Judy meant. Her friend's feminine interpretations were spot on. It was because of this knowledge that she had fought to avoid Greg in passing for the previous two weeks. He didn't particularly make her feel uneasy - far from it - but it was certainly a liaison she wished to evade and not encourage.

Yes, the mutual signals were already evident and obvious.

But opening herself up to such interplay was potentially disastrous.

Karen had hoped that nobody had noticed her silliness in his company.

But Judy Simpson misses nothing.

His hanging, inviting stare; her willingness to respond to his attentions.

Obviously, it was female genetic instinct to be able to spot a fawning male.

If the undeniable truth be known, Judy had been beaten to it in her recognition of the symptoms. It had taken Karen awhile to feel the heat of attraction. Nor did Judy understand the depth of the impact that Greg's mere appearance had on Karen Aspinall. Yet Karen must keep up the pretence. She should continue to put on the act of denial, for the benefit of everyone concerned.

Judy broke the thought process with another pertinent query.

'Why did he leave the army, Kaz? Do you know?'

An unprecedented question, if a perfectly reasonable one.

One to which Karen did not possess a satisfactory answer.

'I never got told why, Jude. I never asked. I suppose because he'd done his time? I don't know how it works in these circles.'

Judy screwed her features inquisitively.

'But he only joined a few years ago, didn't he? I remember his mother boasting about him becoming a sergeant major or something equally regal. Army Majors last longer than a few years, Kaz!'

Suddenly the subject was becoming rather uninspiring.

'I really don't know, Judy. Anyway, it's not that important, is it?'

Karen cleared her plate and again placed the cutlery down with a clatter. She wasn't so much disgruntled with her friend's persistence, but Karen hadn't travelled into Tenbridge to discuss the failings of her neighbours.

Yet Judy still did not relent in her assessment of the inmates of number forty-one.

'His mother is going to push him on to you, Kaz. I bet you any money on it.'

Karen's patience threshold had finally been broken.

'Right, are we going shopping or what? I've got about two hours before I have to pick Chloe up. And I'm bored with chatting about the Chapples.'

Judy stood up and removed money from her purse to pay the bill.

'I'm sorry, Kaz. I can see that I've got on your nerves. I'm just showing concern, that's all. I'm telling it the way I see it. *That's* what real friends are for. Just be careful. That's all I'm saying. I don't trust them. They're *too* nice. The whole thing is *too* clammy. I don't like it.'

A momentary lapse in the debate allowed Karen time to apply some refining make-up in the toilet. Lauren pulled her cross-eyed face in the mirror causing her mother to laugh.

'You'll stop like that if the wind changes, young lady.'

Lauren offered her mother a look of pure innocence before responding.

'It makes Greg laugh, Mummy. He told me so.'

'*Bloody Greg*! Don't you start on me as well! Christ Almighty! I've got enough on with your Aunty Judy!'

The threesome re-convened outside the restaurant.

'Thanks for dinner, Jude. My treat next time.'

Judy pointed to the sky.

'No problem. I think we'll need brollies by the looks of that lot up there.'

Karen knelt and fastened the top buttons of Lauren's pink cardigan. Her red balloon bobbled excitedly against the increasingly grey shroud above and its merry dance made her giggle as the group advanced toward the precinct.

Judy felt a pang of guilt for enforcing opinions upon her friend. Though whilst a seemingly harmless exchange at the outset, she felt justified in telling Karen how she felt. Judy knew that Karen was taking on board everything she had said. That much placated her for the moment.

'Oh. By the way. Next week! It's my parents' fortieth wedding anniversary party. Remember? You've got to come. Bring the girls! Your parents are invited as well. Next Thursday, I think. You can make it, can't you? They want to do a barbeque if the weather behaves. I know April's a bit early for al fresco dining, but it could be nice.'

Karen held Lauren's hand as they approached the pelican crossing against a whirring backdrop of lunchtime traffic.

'Of course, we'll come. Rob can't make it, obviously. But I'll look forward to it.'

The green man appeared with an accompanying series of shrill bleeps, announcing the way across the road to be safe.

'Come on, Lauren. Let's see if we can find a dress for Aunty Judy to fit into. We might struggle after all that pizza she's guzzled! And keep hold of that balloon or it will be gone!'

*****

The trio merged with the expansive congregation of city dwellers and disappeared through the large glass doors of the main shopping centre for some well-earned retail therapy.

As they vanished among a thousand others, a concealed lone figure stood in distant observation.

He watched, contemplated, and judged the situation, before walking off in the opposite direction.

High above, the black heavens opened, unleashing a torrent on the vulnerable forms below.

nine

The time on the dashboard clock registered nearly twenty to four. The red motor car spun at a pace into the school grounds. A little late, but then shopping with Judy Simpson was usually a protracted affair and rarely went to schedule.

Despite arriving a few minutes after the bell for home time, Karen scanned the school entrance to see that there was still no sign of Chloe. Releasing her seat belt, she quickly scrutinised her features in the rear-view mirror and briefly observed her daughter.

She noticed that Lauren looked a little tired as she gazed forlornly through the rear passenger window. City shopping trips were testing enough for Karen, let alone an infant. Thankfully, it was not an everyday occurrence, though today did seem like a particularly long day for some reason.

Despite the downpours, the sun had maintained its running battle and now blazed impressively through the sunroof creating considerable warmth inside the car. Karen turned the ignition key a notch and switched on the fans to cool things off.

Finally, Chloe emerged at the main door chatting to her renewed friend, Sarah Hughes. Lauren suddenly became animated at the sight of her elder sister and sat up in her seat, pointing avidly through the glass.

Karen sounded the car horn in mild frustration and sighed in relief.

'Hooray! She's been with her friends all bloody day! What can there be left to talk about at home time?'

Lauren peeked at her mother's frosty reflection and smiled.

'Mummy. Does this mean we can go to the swings now?'

Damn it! Karen thought to herself. Lauren remembered. But then, kids always hold mothers to promises, don't they? It was solemn pledge made hours ago at the breakfast table, but Karen's youngest had evidently retained it firmly at the forefront of her mind.

Well, it was only a run around to the local park for an hour. Karen should welcome the chance for both girls to use up the remnants of any energy supply they might have left. She couldn't truthfully be bothered, but she would not disappoint her daughters.

A promise was a promise, even for weary mums.

Although she attempted a slightly dissuasive tactic just to chance her arm.

'Are you sure you want to go to the swings, Lauren? They might be wet with all the showers we've had.'

Lauren gazed grumpily into the bright seasonal sunshine and nodded her head vigorously.

That was the answer, then.

They were going to the park.

Karen resigned herself to silent submission as Chloe finally dragged herself toward the car and crashed into the seat behind her mother. An affirming clang of the door aroused Karen's fatigued frustration once more.

'How many times, Chloe? Don't slam my door!'

'Sorry, Mum. Forgot again.'

'Okay. Both of you fasten your seatbelts.'

Karen started the engine and surveyed her girls in the mirror.

'Okay. The park then, is it?'

A joint cheer of approval was accompanied by a crunching of gears and another heavy sigh. Karen just wanted to collapse in her armchair with a coffee, but her girls deserved the chance to go and play.

Normally Robert would have taken them at the weekend but that was out of the question these days as he seemed to be bringing more work home with him every Friday.

Time with his daughters did not seem to be a priority anymore but she supposed that the extra workload was part of his new territory, now.

As was the custom, the radio was employed at full volume and dozy minds were invigorated with pop music. The trio sang in harmony all the way to Greenacres, which was the nearest recreation ground to Church Drayton.

It was a picturesque scene as the car swung into the designated gravel parking area which was surrounded by tall poplar trees. No sooner had Karen applied the handbrake than Chloe and Lauren had released themselves from their seatbelts and scampered away from the vehicle.

Karen could not help but smile as she watched her daughters sprint along the pathway toward the distant playground. She closed all the doors of the car and activated the central locking. A shrill gust of cool air made her shiver as she strolled on after the girls.

'Not too far in front, you two! Hey...slow down!'

Chloe and Lauren quickly became coloured specks against the backdrop of foliage. Karen could hear Lauren giggling, which in turn induced an inner feeling of intensive maternal love. The park had been a regular attraction for the Aspinall family over the years.

A mother need not concern herself in this place of solace.

Karen watched the girls enter the main playground through the safety gate which swung slowly shut behind them with a spring-loaded whine. One or two other families had already descended on the area, making the most of the returning sunshine. It looked like being a pleasant evening, despite the unpredictable rain of earlier.

From the corner of her eye as she perched on a seat, Karen noticed a lone jogger through the tree line in the adjacent section of parkland. She made a brief mental note of his toned, tanned legs and assured rhythm. The sort of things any woman would notice about a male in running shorts.

Then a chord of familiarity struck. She realised she recognised the guy. His physical traits looked like someone of her recent acquaintance. He drew closer as Karen searched her memory banks. Then the jogger emerged through the trees and revealed somebody that she knew, alright.

'Greg?' Karen muttered under her breath.

The runner slowed to a trot no more than twenty meters from where she sat. He looked in Karen's direction and waved. The smile was cute and boyish, but he was every inch the man as he strode up in t-shirt and shorts. Karen emitted an involuntary smile in response.

She felt almost pleased to see him.

'Greg! It *is* you! What a coincidence!'

He drew close so she could see the hint of perspiration on his limbs and forehead. He had triggered that weird sensation in her once again. His hand resting on her shoulder would ordinarily have been unwelcomed, yet it made her feel instantly at ease.

'Hi-ya, Kaz! Fancy seeing you here!'

Karen tried desperately to avert her gaze from Greg's muscular form. What's more, he sensed her struggle in doing so. He had immediately exerted a primitive, almost whimsical control over her reactions. It was uncanny.

Commanding, yet very inviting.

He exuded a dominating yet pleasurable presence.

Her mindset suddenly took on that of a schoolgirl.

Simultaneous waves of curiosity and infatuation raced through her conscience as she buckled slightly.

'I didn't know you ran.'

She noticed that he didn't seem out of breath as she stood to her feet, and they walked toward the playground.

'Oh, yeah. Got to keep fit in this day and age, haven't you?'

Karen's gaze flitted with his as they approached the gate to the swings area. Greg's concentration seemed to be elsewhere for a moment or two, as though he was struggling to summon the next part of the conversation. Karen relieved him of the trouble.

'I promised I'd bring them here after school. Now the sun's come out I haven't got much of an excuse, have I?'

Greg watched the girls as they clambered up and down the slides and climbing frames.

'They're good kids aren't they. No trouble at all.'

An odd comment, Karen thought. But a complementary one, nonetheless.

'Well, I have to do my bit in the week with Rob being away. Plus, it keeps them away from the TV, just for a while anyway.'

The pair entered the playground and re-positioned themselves on one of the empty benches. Chloe and Lauren quickly spotted Greg and on leaving the swings, raced over to greet him.

'Hi girls. Having a good time?' he grinned.

Chloe was particularly enthusiastic about seeing her neighbour and proceeded to describe her next performance on the slide. Lauren was a little more wary of the man sitting next to her mother and kept a watchful eye on the conversation.

Her silence did not go unnoticed for long.

'You haven't got much to say for yourself, little one? Did you have a good time shopping?'

Greg's comment seemed a most natural query.

It certainly did not strike Karen as out of the ordinary. Not until Lauren responded in the forthright manner that all children seem to do when listening to their elders.

'How do *you* know we were shopping? Were you spying on us?'

Greg fidgeted in his seat and immediately glanced at Karen in expectation of some inevitable scrutiny.

His momentary discomfort was quickly appeased by her reply.

'That's a bit rude, Lauren. Perhaps Greg was shopping, too.'

Greg was quick to recover with his intersection.

'Yes. I had to nip into town for something at dinner.'

Karen observed the younger man as he engaged with her daughter.

'I saw you with your mum and her friend Judy across the market square. I was too far away to shout you. You were going the opposite way, anyhow.'

Lauren eyed him suspiciously before turning on her heel and re-joining her sister at the slides.

Greg chuckled to himself.

'She doesn't miss a trick, does she? Did you buy anything nice in town, Kaz?'

Karen sat back on the bench and crossed her legs.

'No. Just window shopped mainly. Judy - that's the friend you met on Chloe's birthday - well it's her parents' wedding anniversary party next Thursday. She was just eyeing up some dresses for the occasion.'

Greg's attention diverted from the playground at the mention of the imminent gathering.

'Oh. I suppose you'll be going too, then?'

Yet again his response seemed a little awry. It was as though he was carrying a slight objection to the situation. This fleeting thought passed through Karen's mind but did not stir any further undue response in her.

'Well, yes. The whole family is invited. I've been friends with Judy since school. We're best pals. It's a barbeque, I think. No doubt I'll be looking for a new outfit this time next week. I'll have to see what's in my wardrobe that still fits me, first.'

The silence that followed gave time for Greg to ponder the situation. His next statement was possibly a little forward. But Karen did not see anything negative in the offer.

'Kaz…as Rob's away…I…I don't mind coming with you. Just for some company…you know. If you wanted me to come with you, that is.'

Karen looked calmly into the eyes of the man sitting beside her. She hardly knew him, but so far, she liked what she had discovered.

He seemed genuine enough. Karen felt flattered by his concerns.

'It's very sweet of you to offer, Greg. But there's no need. Honestly. Besides, Rob might come home on the Thursday so he can attend. I haven't spoken to him yet.'

Greg tried a more persuasive tactic.

'Well, I'd really like to come with you if he can't make it. It would be my pleasure.'

His sincerity was extremely affecting as the assault on her senses continued.

His follow-up statement really took her by surprise.

'I'd love to take you out, Kaz.'

Despite the similarity of age, Karen suddenly felt like an old woman being pursued by a schoolboy with a crush. She also began to consider what others would make of the scenario.

Especially her daughters.

And of course, Judy's preconceptions of the scenario instantly leapt to the forefront of her thinking.

'You make it sound like a date! Really, Greg, there's no need. Thank you, but honestly, no.'

Greg moved closer and stared into Karen.

She felt slightly pressured by his proximity, but also enamoured by the attention. Her resistance was breaking slightly as he commandeered the argument.

'I insist. Please. Let me take you to Judy's party. There's no need for you to go alone.'

Karen was equally overwhelmed and confused. She burst out laughing to relive the sudden onset of tension.

'You don't take no for an answer, do you Mister Chapple?'

He continued to gaze into her and on smelling victory, offered her a mischievous and enrapturing smile.

'Well, you haven't *definitely* said *no* yet, have you?'

Yet again Karen laughed out loud causing Lauren and Chloe to glance over. She continued to consider the proposition. It was only a family party after all. She was sure Judy wouldn't mind.

A bit of harmless fun.

A one-off night out.

Karen couldn't honestly justify a refusal.

In fact, she was now privately quite enticed by the prospect.

'Okay, okay. You win. You can come. Though God only knows why you want to. You'll be bored rigid!'

Greg's stare remained unmoved, his face offering not a flicker of emotion as he issued a stirring declaration.

'I'll never get bored while I've got you to play with.'

With that, he rose to his feet and began to do some stretching exercises for Karen's benefit. Again, she sat and covertly admired his physique.

Was there more than a grain of truth in what Judy had said earlier?

Karen's mind whirred with anticipation. Did this man that she hardly knew earnestly find her so attractive? He was persistent in the chase - that was evident enough.

To quote his own phrase, he was going to take some shaking off.

Still, all in the name of fun, she supposed.

'Come on girls, we're going. Do you want a lift home, Greg?'

He began to jump up and down on the spot before her.

He was an amusing character.

Entertaining and infectious.

Different.

'Will you stand still for a minute, Greg! You're making me dizzy! Now, do you want a ride home, or not?'

'No thanks. I'll run it. I'll be seeing you around.'

With that, Greg sprinted off into the distance, through the tree line and beyond. Karen gazed fondly after him until he vanished from view.

She did not sense the approach of her daughters.

'What are you smiling at, Mummy? enquired Chloe.

Karen hadn't even realised she was sporting a grin from ear to ear.

It was something that the girls questioned immediately.

'Oh, nothing. Just Greg. He makes me laugh.'

The trio made their way back to the car as late afternoon sunshine bathed the footpath. Lauren lagged behind as Chloe pursued the subject of Karen's new friend.

'He must be nice, Mummy. I haven't seen you smile that much for ages!'

A sad, inciteful truth. But her eldest daughter was probably right.

Karen did not encourage the conversation further. She ushered the girls into the car and drove home.

During the previous half hour, her thoughts had subconsciously centred on the renewed acquaintance with her neighbour at number forty-one.

Karen suddenly felt like somebody else.

Somebody special.

Somebody that mattered.

More than a wife.

More than a mother.

She felt like a woman again.

It was a sensation that she was beginning to enjoy.

An inner feeling that she had long forgotten and one that she was ready and prepared to embrace in its long overdue return.

Yet, there was an undeniably reckless element to events that she would wilfully acknowledge.

It was simply a matter of whether to heed the warning signs.

ten

'Give Judy's parents my best wishes. I'm sorry I can't be there with you, darling. I'm sure Greg will look after you. I can rest easily tonight knowing that you're all in good hands. See you tomorrow. Bye.'

'Goodbye, love. See you soon.'

Karen replaced the receiver and resumed cosmetic duties upstairs in front of the bathroom mirror. It comforted her to know that all in Robert's world was fine. His daily calls were a welcome respite from the monotony of home.

Only tonight, he had put her a little behind schedule.

Quickly applying foundation, Karen fingered a small blemish on her lower lip.

'*Shit!* Hope that isn't a cold sore coming!' she mumbled to her reflection.

Applying some lip gloss, she did not sense Chloe's presence at the bathroom door behind her.

'Mummy…I can't find my black shiny shoes. Do you know where they are?'

'Er…it's been a while since I've seen them. Try under your bed, love. If not there, then in the bottom of your wardrobe. Is Lauren ready? I need to do your hair.'

'Yes, she's not very happy, though.'

Finally, Karen ceased with the cosmetic operation and turned to her eldest daughter with concern.

'Why, what have you been arguing about now?'

A grimace of indignation befell Chloe's features as she swayed in the doorway.

'It's not *me* she's annoyed with, Mummy. It's *you.*' declared Chloe.

Karen's eyes widened with curiosity.

'Why? What have I done to her?'

'She wanted to talk to Daddy, but you put the phone down.'

Karen sighed with relief that nothing more serious was at hand.

'Oh, well…we haven't got time tonight. It's six-thirty, now. Greg will be here in a minute. We were supposed to be at the party for six. She can talk to him tomorrow night when he comes home, can't she?'

Chloe did not seem appeased by her mother's reasoned excuses.

'But it's not the *same*, Mummy. We like to say hello to him *every* night.'

Karen's tone became laced with frustration as she gestured with her forefinger.

'Look, I haven't got time for this now. Go and find your shoes and tell Lauren to hurry up and cheer up, or she can stop here on her own for the evening.'

Following her daughter along the landing, Karen entered her bedroom and pulled on her favourite black party dress. Smoothing herself down in the long pine mirror, she observed her legs and bottom, considering the possibility that she may have put some weight on over the winter. It had been a while since she had donned the dress. She studied the effect of the low crop around the chest and the hem cut just above the knee. Stylish, she thought. Not too tarty, but flashy enough to attract admiring glances.

Judy called it Karen's man-trapping outfit when she first saw her in it. That certainly wasn't the purpose for wearing it this evening, although Karen was feeling rather adventurous at the prospect of being escorted to the party by her handsome neighbour.

Karen pulled a brush through her hair as she wandered into Lauren's bedroom.

'Are you ready, love? Sorry about Daddy, but we're in a hurry tonight.'

A glum-looking stare and a slow nod of the head was the only response from her younger daughter.

'Chloe? You got those shoes, yet?'

Chloe bounced through the bedroom doorway adorning a pair of patent leather buckled slip-ons. Her beaming smile put Karen's mind at rest.

'Well, at least one of you is in a good mood. Go and sit in the lounge and wait for me, both of you. There's good girls. I'll come and sort your hair when I've done mine.'

Back in the bathroom, Karen studied herself once again, as though to erase any last-minute imperfections. Satisfied that there were none visible, she scampered back to her bedroom mirror and patted down her dress one last time before slipping her feet into a pair of black suede heels.

Even by her own silent admission, she looked good.

Better than she had looked for weeks.

Yet her feelings of anticipation were unwarranted. It wasn't even her party.

Though, something inside her was fighting for attention.

A need for some womanly satisfaction. A long-held desire to be noticed all over again. Instinct deemed that tonight would be that night.

A loud knock at the front door signalled her heart to beat ten times faster. Karen felt suddenly nervous as Chloe raced into the hallway and greeted the caller.

Once again Karen checked her appearance and listened for her daughter's shout, which duly came echoing up the stairs.

'Mummy! It's Greg and Big Ch…I mean Aunty Evelyn!'

Karen suppressed her desire to chuckle at Chloe's near faux pas.

Okay, Karen thought.

Time for the big reveal.

Yet, this was crazy. Who was she trying to impress? Herself? Somebody else? And more to the point, *why*? It was only a poxy house party. Not a parade through the streets of Milan. Karen swiftly grappled for a rational cause of her apprehension and its accompanying sense of inner euphoria.

Why should she feel so invigorated about this non-occasion?

Taking several deep breaths, Karen checked her image in the mirror one last time before making the descent.

Floating down the stairway like the princess of the ball, she immediately made eye contact with Greg. He stood open-mouthed in the doorway as his mother hovered outside.

Karen instantly knew she had made the desired impact.

He was literally gobsmacked. Totally speechless.

And he looked very attractive as well.

She observed the crisp white shirt that exhibited his deep suntan.

Black, pin-striped trousers draped over brown leather shoes. The aroma of aftershave hung in the air, which Karen found intoxicating. It had been ages since she had smelled aftershave on a man. Robert never used it. The scent was a most welcome diversion from the ordinariness that she had always known.

Meeting at the bottom step, Karen exchanged smiles with Greg as he summoned a response to the wondrous vision that had appeared before him.

‘Christ! You look bloody lovely!’

Karen offered a childish giggle and covered her mouth in mild embarrassment.

‘Why thank you, kind sir. You don’t scrub up half bad yourself, Mister Chapple.’

Chloe and Lauren peered around the lounge door as the scene unfolded before them. They looked at each other and grinned before retreating out of view.

‘No, I mean it, Kaz. You look incredible. Here, I brought these as a token of my appreciation for tonight.’

A bouquet of fully bloomed daffodils honed into view from behind Greg’s back.

‘Mum said these were your favourite flower. There’s plenty about this time of year.’

Karen’s eyes expanded into the purest blue and again she showed her amusement.

‘Oh, you big softy! Appreciation of *what*, though? I haven’t done anything to deserve them, have I?’

The coy exchange was disturbed by the sound of Evelyn Chapple’s barking address.

‘For letting him go out with you, Karen, of course. We’re very thankful. Aren’t we, Greg? He’s promised to be a good boy.’

Greg grinned and whispered in Karen’s ear.

‘I’m not too hot on keeping promises, though. I might turn out to be a very *bad* boy. You never know!’

Karen felt herself blush.

‘I think I’ll take the risk. You seem worth it.’ she replied in a hushed, playful tone.

Karen turned on her heel and strode to the lounge doorway. She could almost feel Greg’s stare boring into the back of her. She could sense his eyes all over her figure. It was a liberating sensation.

The like of which she had long since forgotten.

‘Let me quickly do your hair, Lauren. You look like a scarecrow!’

Chloe laughed out loud, resulting in a glare of condemnation from her little sister. Greg and Evelyn watched as Karen put the finishing touches to the girls.

‘I don’t mind driving, Kaz. If you don’t mind, that is? Mum says I can have the keys to her car if you fancy a drink or two?’

Karen looked up from the tangled head of her youngest daughter. She was genuinely touched by Greg's consideration.

'What about *you*? Don't you fancy a drink tonight, Greg?'

'Not bothered, Kaz. Just happy to be taking you out. That'll be enough stimulation for me!'

The pair tittered like children as Evelyn feigned her disapproval.

'Greg - not in front of the little ones! Don't be so coarse!'

'Brilliant! I'll get myself stinking drunk then!' chuckled Karen.

'Fine by me. I'll get you home whatever.' beamed Greg.

Karen was now beginning to relish the evening ahead.

'You'll have to watch me when I'm tipsy, though. I'm all over the shop!'

With the house locked up the group made their way around to the large black saloon parked on the driveway at number forty-one.

Karen observed the number plate.

SCR.

Secretive. Cunning. Rodent.

She smirked inwardly as she climbed into the front passenger seat and made sure the girls were safely belted up behind her.

'Mummy, it smells funny in Aunty Evelyn's car.' Chloe observed, oblivious to the fact that the owner was well within earshot.

'It's only because you're not used to it. It's just different to mine. That's all!'

Evelyn stood at the bonnet with her arms folded in customary authoritarian pose, watching her son strap himself in behind the wheel.

Again, Karen was overwhelmed by the potent aroma of Greg's balm.

Chloe was not so impressed, however.

'Mummy, Greg's perfume stinks, doesn't it?'

Karen could not help but fall into a fit of hysterics at her daughter's comical observations. Greg offered a wincing smile but did not reply as he started the engine and found reverse gear.

'Where is the party at?' Greg asked, staring suggestively at Karen.

'This side of Tenbridge. I'll navigate!' she giggled.

Evelyn Chapple continued to stare after her car as it cruised up Benton Road and on through the distant T-junction.

Whilst she would claim it to be an innocent oversight, under scrutiny she would actively defend her son should his passengers discover that he had in fact been banned from driving for a series of dangerous offences over the years.

Still, his passengers were intent on having a good time.

And Greg would not wish to disappoint.

And in similar vein, Evelyn would not want to be the one to spoil the evening with such trivia.

In her view, what the passengers did not know, would surely not hurt them.

Without any iota of change in her expression, Evelyn Chapple stared into the space that her car had just vacated, before returning inside to the hallway of number forty-one.

*****

'Hoo-bloody-ray!' Judy shouted sarcastically as she opened the front door to her parents' house. 'I thought you'd never get here! Come on in! Hi girls! Hi…er, *Greg*.'

Judy's combination of surprise and her perhaps inevitable instant disapproval of Greg's uninvited presence were blindingly obvious to him as he entered from the porch-way.

Once she had ushered the late arrivals inside, Judy began to silently fume at her best friend's inconsiderate presumption.

After all that had been said, Karen plainly didn't want to listen.

Judy closed the door as the hellos and re-acquaintances ensued in the lounge.

'Just in time as usual, Karen!' shouted Judy's mother across the room carrying a welcoming smile.

Shirley Simpson appeared to be intoxicated by the lively atmosphere as well as the alcohol, but Karen was genuinely pleased to see her as they embraced.

'You look delectable, Karen darling. It must be over a year since I saw you. And there's the children, bless them. Hello, darlings! You two lovelies okay? You both look very smart in your dresses!'

Both Chloe and Lauren appeared to be stuck for words for once and simply stared shyly at Judy's mother.

'Yes, Shirley. Everything's fine, thank you. We're all really good.' confirmed Karen.

'And how's Robert? How's the job?'

'Oh…he's making the most of his new opportunity. He sends his apologies for tonight. You're a day too early with the party! He's not home until tomorrow.'

'Well…we thought about holding it on this coming Saturday but tonight's the actual night but Hey-Ho…it can't be helped.'

Karen scanned the occupants of the room to locate her own parents.

'Are my folks not here yet, Shirley?'

'Yes. On the back lawn, dear. I'll give them a shout.'

'No! It's okay. I'll find them eventually.'

At that point Greg made his way through the throng and offered a hand of greeting to Judy's mother. She seemed taken aback by the handsome stranger, but her reserve quickly dissipated as he effortlessly let his charm work its magic.

'Congratulations, Mrs. Simpson. Forty years is a long time. You are to be commended. You'd have got less in prison for shooting him though, you know!'

Shirley laughed heartily as she turned to Karen for an introduction.

'And who is this fine-looking specimen of a man I see before me?'

Narrowly avoiding a glare of scorn from Judy, Karen smiled at her escort.

'This is Greg. Evelyn's son. You know, Evelyn…from next door to me?'

Shirley Simpson beamed as she shook Greg's hand.

'A pleasure, Greg. Glad to see that you're looking after her this evening. She's a bugger for the wine you know!'

Judy very reluctantly observed the spectacle of civility play out before retreating to the kitchen to refill her glass.

Tonight was certainly not the night for re-opening the debate with her best friend. But it was blindingly obvious to Judy that common sense was not currently prevailing in the world of Karen Aspinall.

*****

The party flowed as did the drink and the guests mingled contentedly. Chloe and Lauren soon found the company of Judy's niece and nephew as Karen and Greg spent the evening entwined in conversation with various familiar faces from her past and present.

Judy did her best to avoid the subject, but her patience was wearing thinner by the passing minute.

With Karen's intake of wine serving to increase the volume of her laughter, Judy was struggling to maintain the pretence of acceptance.

In turn, Greg seemed happy to supply the stream of gags if Karen was ever ready with the appreciative responses.

Judy bided her time, which eventually came as Greg made his way to the toilet.

At last, the friends came face to face.

It quickly became evident that Karen was more than a little under the influence.

She hadn't even picked up on the negative vibe coming from her life-long chum.

'I thought you were avoiding me, Jude! Here, top my glass up for me, there's a good girl!'

Judy shook her head and grimaced with disapproval.

'You piss head! Don't you think you've had enough already? And what the fucking hell is *he* doing here? *I* don't recall asking him! I know my parents bloody *didn't*!'

Karen offered an expression of indignation on Greg's behalf.

'If you mean my friend Greg…he wanted to come. He needs to mix a bit, Jude. He's harmless. Plus, he's driving. Hence, I'm getting sloshed!'

Judy leaned in towards Karen's swaying form and whispered.

'I've told you what I think about this, Kaz. If you don't want to listen to me then it's entirely up to you. Just…don't look so happy to be with him. Two and two can sometimes make five to some people, you know.'

Karen offered her mouth to Judy's ear in reply.

'He's just a friend who's a bit lonely, that's all. We're not doing anything wrong. It's all innocent, Jude. Come on. Relax. Let's party! Where's my Ma and Pa, anyway?'

Greg reappeared and followed Karen to the patio where she introduced him to Brian and Jean.

'Mum and Dad. This is Greg. Evelyn's son. The last time you saw him was when Chloe was born, I think!'

Her parents obliged with civility but were more concerned with the fact that Karen had felt the need to bring him at all.

'In the army, weren't you, son?' enquired Brian, eyeing his daughter's companion with more than a degree of suspicion.

Greg seemed a little discomforted by the subject and shuffled his weight from foot to foot as he searched for an answer to Brian Hope's genuine if unwelcome inquisition.

'Yes, for a time. Not for me, though.'

'Oh? Why's that then? Strapping lad like you! Tailor made for the forces I'd have thought.'

Karen kissed her mother on the cheek.

She sensed Greg's unease regarding her father's interest and strove to change the conversation. A few minutes later, Karen bid her parents a temporary goodbye as they opted to depart the scene.

Jean offer their excuses.

'We've had enough anyway, love. Your dad's struggling with his knees having been at work again today. We were only coming for an hour to say hello. See you next week. Give our love to the girls. I think they're off playing somewhere down the garden. Bye, Greg. See you soon!'

Karen soon forgot about her parents as they bid farewell to the hosts and made their way to the front door. She was in the throes of enjoying herself and was determined to make the most of her sober companion's attention.

Stuff what everybody else thought.

At that moment in time, the opinions of others mattered very little.

*****

Stumbling from the Simpsons' front doorway, Karen was twice saved from a headlong fall by Greg's alertness and speed of response. Chloe and Lauren found it amusing to watch their mother stagger across the road to the waiting car. To see her inebriated was an untypical spectacle to say the least.

Judy was secretly glad to see the back of the group as she ushered them out. She dreaded to think what things must have looked like to the rest of the guests. Most of them knew Robert and would have been surprised and likely disapproving of his wife's behaviour. But on the other hand, if Robert were around then Karen would have remained relatively sober, anyway.

Still, the evening passed without undue incident, and everybody had a good time. Despite her overriding reservations about him, Judy could not deny that Greg had been the ultimate gentlemen and was very adept at making Karen laugh.

'Thank you, Aunty Judy!' hollered the girls as they clambered into the back seats of the large, black saloon.

'Yes…brilliant fuddle, girly! Thank your parents, for me. I think I'm going to feel a bit rough in the morning!' Karen squawked.

Greg smiled as he belted her in and closed the door on her hysterical, waving form.

'Don't worry, Judy. I'll get them home safe. I haven't touched a drop.'

Judy considered his words for a second or two as her feelings towards him softened slightly.

'Thank you, Greg. It's nice to know *someone's* in control of things this evening.'

The saloon roared into life and cruised up the road as its passengers smiled and gestured through the darkened windows.

Judy's thoughts became confused as the vision of her best friend disappeared around the corner and into the night.

In turn, she was again struck with bolts of disapproval at the potential perception of Karen's social liaison with her neighbour.

The game being played between them could carry real consequence.

As she returned to the remains of the party, her troubled thoughts briefly transported her to a place of bleak foreboding.

She sincerely hoped that Karen would not be drawn there, too.

eleven

It had taken the best part of the following day for Karen to shake off her worst hangover for years. The symptoms had varied from a lurching stomach accompanied by a thumping skull and had now diminished somewhat to a mild pain in the head and a rampant need for water.

The shopping trolley seemed to have a life of its own as Karen skated it around the aisles of the supermarket, giving Lauren in the child seat a thrillingly unpredictable ride of laughter.

The thought briefly occurred to Karen that she must surely have been driving illegally when she took the girls to nursery and school that morning, but it was a distant memory now and mattered little.

The intensity of the pain in and around her eyes indicated that the party at Judy's parents must have been a success, although she couldn't remember leaving the celebration or indeed arriving back home.

She woke up in bed fully clothed bar her shoes and Greg had apparently asked the girls to don their pyjamas and go to sleep. He had then proceeded to lock the front door to number thirty-nine and dropped the keys back through the letterbox.

Greg had been the perfect chaperone and Karen could not deny that she had enjoyed her best night out for months - soon to be followed by her worst morning.

A gesture of thanks for Greg's company the previous evening would not go amiss.

Karen scanned the shelves in the confectionary aisle to take him back a little gift of appreciation.

Although the trip to the supermarket with a hangover would be a non-starter under normal circumstances, Karen had nothing edible in the cupboards and Robert would home later that evening expecting his steak dinner. It had become the custom for him to sit down on a Friday night with a well-done piece of rump in front of him.

The double entendre made Karen smile as she selected a large bar of chocolate for Greg.

'Are you feeling better yet, Mummy?' Lauren enquired at the checkout queue.

'Yes, love. A little bit.'

Finally, Karen paid for her groceries and checked the large clock at the back wall of the shop.

Three fifteen. It would soon be time to fetch Chloe, who would no doubt be excited at the thought of her father's return.

With the carrier bags in the boot and Lauren safely belted into the back seat, Karen turned the ignition key. The engine refused to fire up. Karen waggled the gear stick and tried again.

As the starter motor remained unresponsive, the thought implanted itself into her head that she may have a problem. Again and again, Karen tried in vain to encourage the engine into life. But to no avail.

Then she thought of Chloe waiting alone at the school gate and slight panic set in.

'Lauren, we're going to have to go back into the shop and make a phone call.'

Rather confused and understandably tired after the previous night, Lauren merely yawned and followed her mother's orders. She watched quietly as Karen led them both to the public phone booth and punched in a number.

She was mightily relieved to hear that the intended recipient of the call was at home.

'Hello? Evelyn? Hi, it's Karen. I'm in a bit of a pickle. I'm at the supermarket and the car won't start. I'll have to phone the garage and wait for a mechanic. You couldn't nip to school and meet Chloe for me, could you?'

Lauren observed her mother's features as they evolved from maternal worry into a relieved smile.

'Brilliant, Evelyn. Thanks ever such a lot. I shouldn't be long. See you in a little while.'

*****

Chloe Aspinall waited with her friend Sarah Hughes at the school gates. She had always been told to stay there if there was no sign of her mother's familiar red car.

She couldn't recall the last time her mother had failed to materialize at home time. But Chloe was not unduly concerned. It would afford her chance to discuss the latest school heart throb with Sarah or debate the confusing nature of the morning's maths lesson.

It was a good fifteen minutes after the final bell had droned before Sarah's mother opted to offer Chloe a ride home.

'I'd better not, Mrs. Hughes. My mum will come soon.'

Janet Hughes was not convinced and remained on the side of caution.

'Well, I'm going to stay with you. Just in case.'

Chloe looked at Mrs. Hughes a little perplexed.

'Just in case what, Mrs. Hughes?'

'Just in case she doesn't make it to fetch you.'

A further ten minutes endured before Chloe spotted a familiar figure bounding into the school grounds. He waved as he approached the waiting trio. Chloe immediately recognised the young man who appeared to have arrived on foot. The sweat on his forehead was visible and he sounded out of breath. She waved back at him whilst tugging frantically on Sarah's school jumper.

'Hi Greg! Sarah, this is Greg. He's our neighbour. He's Mummy's new friend.'

Sarah glanced up to her mother, who seemed equally bemused.

With his reassuring smile that Chloe had become recently accustomed to, Greg placed both hands on her shoulders.

'I'm sorry I'm late, Chloe. Your mum's car's broken down. She's asked me to take you home instead. She won't be long, though.'

Janet Hughes had little option but to allow Chloe's appointed escort the benefit of the doubt as she watched them walk out of the school grounds hand in hand.

With the brief emergency now over, the pair cut a slow path back to Benton Road. Chloe was immediately comforted by Greg's presence. Since meeting him just a few weeks earlier, she had looked upon Greg as someone to depend upon. The fact that her mother trusted him was enough for her to follow suit. It was pleasant having him around with her father away all week.

In record fashion, Greg had wittingly established himself as a reliable role mode.

In her eyes, if he made her mother laugh, then he was a good guy. Besides which, it would be a pleasant change to be walked home. All her friends would no doubt want to know about him on Monday if Sarah performed her usual role of school gossip.

Greg and Chloe were bathed in sunshine as they made their way slowly through the tree-lined village and toward the local newsagents.

'Would you like some sweets, Chloe?'

Her eyes lit up at the thought of such an unexpected treat.

'Yes, please, Greg. Can I choose?'

Greg held open the door of the shop for the youngster to enter.

'Of course. Anything you want, Chloe.'

Indulging in her chocolate bar moments later, Chloe happily bounced along beside her temporary guardian.

'What do you think could be wrong with Mummy's car, Greg?'

He glanced down to meet the little girl's gaze before diverting his attention back to the path in front.

'I don't really know. Hopefully it'll be nothing too complicated. She was hoping to get it fixed tonight.'

Like any inquisitive child, Chloe had harboured certain basic questions regarding Greg's recent friendship with the family. Kids saw everything and missed nothing. Even if they couldn't understand the significance of what they were witnessing.

However, Chloe's queries were direct and to the point.

'Greg, do you like Mummy?'

He smiled, pleased that she had noticed. His stride and expression did not falter as he considered an appropriate response.

'Yes. Your mum is a lovely lady. She's a good friend to my mum, too. She's very special.'

Chloe digested the reply as she gnawed at her chocolate bar.

Her next question was perhaps a little more delicate in nature and required a more shrouded answer.

'Greg…are you Mummy's boyfriend while Daddy's at work?'

The question was music to Greg Chapple's ears.

He smiled broadly whilst digesting Chloe's innocent query, but also for the fact that she had observed the natural and harmless rapport that he had quickly developed with Karen.

Whilst not prepared to admit to his feelings, especially to a nine-year-old, Greg was content in the knowledge that he had quickly exerted some influence over the situation.

He had obviously made the right impression on the right people.

Nevertheless, he was uncertain how to respond to the youngster, especially considering that the one demanding the answers was so integral to matters.

Ultimately, Greg opted for an easy way out and turned the question on its head.

'Why? Would you like me to be your mummy's boyfriend, Chloe?'

She did not give a reply as she pondered the consequences of giving the wrong one. Even for her tender years, for once this was a conversation that she wished she hadn't started.

Instead, she continued munching on her chocolate and stared ahead as the junction to Benton Road appeared in the distance.

'Not far now, Greg!' she giggled.

'No, Chloe. It won't be long, now.'

*****

Karen watched the mechanic withdraw from under the bonnet and finger his chin with an oily digit. He looked at her as though being confronted with the most difficult repair imaginable.

Karen's thoughts were centred mainly on her daughter being collected from school until she observed the expression of curiosity on the mechanic's face. Then the prime concern became financial.

'Oh, no. Don't tell me. You've got to tow it away to the garage. It's an expensive job, right?'

The man in the overalls smiled and scratched his head.

'I've fixed it, love. There's no problem with the car. More of a puzzle, really.'

Still reeling from the surprise, Karen was suddenly intrigued and pressed for him to explain.

'What? So…the car will start, now?'

'Yes, love. The battery leads had come away from the terminals. That's all. It's sorted. I just can't understand how they could have disconnected themselves. I've never seen it before. Still, there's no problem. That's the main thing isn't it.'

Karen reached into the front passenger foot well for her handbag and delved into her purse. Offering the repairman a crisp ten-pound note, she thanked him for his urgent response.

'Very kind of you, love. I'll have a pint then. If you insist. Thank you. Just keep an eye under the bonnet, though. But there's no wear and tear on the couplings and they are tightened again now. Should be okay. I'll wait though to make sure you drive off okay.''

*****

Driving home, Karen thought of Chloe once again as the increasingly high sun beat relentlessly from a clear blue sky. The booming car radio announced her arrival at Benton Road, as did the rather speedy approach to the driveway. Swinging the front gate open, Karen noticed that Lauren had nodded off in her seat. No doubt still in recovery from last night.

Positioning the car on the drive, Karen looked in her rear-view mirror to see that Evelyn had already appeared from nowhere and was closing the front gate behind her.

There was no sign of Chloe, causing her a moment or two of distress as she applied the handbrake.

'Everything okay, Karen? You get it fixed, alright?'

Karen pulled Lauren from the back of the car and cradled her up into her arms.

'Yes. Just the battery playing up. Did you pick Chloe up for me?'

Evelyn smiled and curled a forefinger in her direction.

'Come here and have a look at this!'

Karen was led next door, through the hallway and into the kitchen of number forty-one. Evelyn pointed toward the back garden whilst displaying the zaniest of grins.

'Look at that. You'd think they were father and daughter.'

Karen peered through the half-drawn kitchen curtains towards the scene in the Chapple's rear yard. Chloe and Greg were playing football together. The former wore a huge smile as she kicked the leather ball toward Greg, who proceeded to dive around like a demented goalkeeper.

More giggles emitted from Karen's eldest as she scampered about the grass in her school uniform.

It was a scene that brought welcome relief to Karen, but she could not understand why Evelyn seemed so overly enthusiastic about things.

'Thanks, Evelyn. You saved my bacon today.'

Big Chief Crazyhorse closed her eyes and shook her head. She folded her arms and pursed her lips before gesturing to her son.

'*He* saved your bacon today, Karen. Greg collected her from school for you. He wanted to. As thanks for last night. He tells me that you two had a very good time. I'm so pleased for him, Karen. It's just what our Greg needs. A good steady woman to look after him.'

Karen was taken aback by her friend's fantastical appraisal of the situation. It was only a family party. It was only a pickup from school. Anyonc would think that Greg and Karen had enjoyed a first date as a budding couple.

Evelyn's relentless smirk suddenly made Karen uncomfortable.

The unwarranted presumptions about her and Greg were baffling.

It was perhaps all said in earnest, but Karen's thoughts transferred to what Judy had said at some point in the recent past.

On more than one occasion.

She's pushing Greg onto you. The mother is behind it.

It seemed a ridiculous summary at the time and Karen paid it no mind. Yet there and then in the Chapple's kitchen, the evidence was unavoidable. Evelyn's overtly enthusiastic reactions to things so relatively trivial were slightly unsettling.

No one had saved a life. No one had split the atom.

It was a favour.

A neighbourly rescue in an hour of need.

There was nothing to analyse. There was nothing more to be said on the issue, aside from thank you.

Karen ushered herself into an exit.

'Well, I'd better get back home and unpack the shopping. The frozen stuff will be thawed out now. Rob will be home soon enough.'

Karen noticed the steel in the eye of her friend and neighbour as Evelyn fixed a glare at her.

'I've closed your front gate. I didn't know you wanted it left open for Robert. You didn't say.'

'I didn't. No. I'm sorry. It doesn't matter.'

Karen stopped herself.

Why was she apologizing?

'It's no problem. I'll open it again when he arrives.'

Evelyn re-directed her gaze towards the scene through the window.

'Aren't you going to thank my son for fetching your daughter? I think you should.'

The atmosphere had turned rather formal and unreasonably tense.

'Of course. I've brought him a little present for last night. I'll have to find it and pop it back round to him later this evening.'

As if by the flick of a switch, Evelyn's eyes lit up once again.

'A present? For my Greg? Oh, he'll love that! Wonderful!'

Again, Evelyn Chapple's reaction seemed forced and unduly exaggerated.

As though Karen was offering a vast sum of money as a reward.

'Calm down, Evelyn. It's only a bar of chocolate.'

Once more Evelyn focused her attention directly to Karen and her tone sounded unusually stark.

'Greg will appreciate any kind offer. He likes to feel that he's valued. You know what I mean? He wouldn't like to think you were taking him for granted.'

Yet again Evelyn had confounded her friend with her choice of words.

The instantaneous shift in mood was bizarre.

'What? No one is being taken for granted, Evelyn. Like I said...I haven't forgotten what he's done for me today.'

Greg's mother leaned in close to whisper.

'Or last night. Don't forget last night.'

Karen now felt herself becoming agitated at Evelyn's persistent fawning over her son. Last night was at Greg's insistence. He wasn't even invited to the blessed party! Why was his mother so determined to put a false slant on such menial events?

Her train of thought was interrupted by Chloe's excited voice at the back door.

'Mummy! Mummy! I'm alright, look! Greg picked me up from school! I'm okay!'

Lauren yawned as her elder sister's voice roused her from slumber. Karen shuffled down the step and placed her youngest daughter on the ground. As she stood up, she felt a hand on her back. Greg stood behind her, carrying a look of immense satisfaction.

'Hi, Kaz. Sort the car out?'

Karen felt suddenly nervous in his presence. Evelyn's odd manner had unexpectedly placed her on guard about being acquainted with her son. Yet Greg quickly diminished Karen's reservations about their friendship, simply by the sound of his voice.

'Yes. Thirty seconds it was all fixed. Thanks for fetching Chloe. You're a hero. I'll bring your prize round later.'

Greg flashed his winning smile, further lightening the mood with his easy charm.

At ease once more, Karen and the girls returned home to await the arrival of her husband. It had been an eventful end to the week. It was ironic that Karen now longed for a semblance of normality in her routine.

Although strangely enough, she had recently begun to forget what normality had previously entailed.

*****

'He's your real knight in shining armour this week isn't he! I'll go round now and take him some cans as well.'

Robert Aspinall enthused about Greg's contribution to the comings and goings at number thirty-nine.

'Are you coming with me, Kaz?'

Karen sat hunched on the settee in front of her favourite soap opera. She pretended not to hear her husband, when in fact his words pulsed through her core. She had seen enough of the Chapples for one week.

Her instincts were telling her to maintain a discreet distance for the foreseeable future.

She had found Evelyn's musings about Greg to be a little off-kilter and frankly, slightly disturbing. The confounding aspect to it all was that Greg seemed unfazed by the possibility of speculation.

Perhaps that alone should have been a warning sign to her.

'No, I'll get those steaks on. I'm starving. I bet you are too, aren't you, love?'

Robert returned to the lounge carrying the large bar of chocolate and four tins of beer.

'Yeah, ravishing! I'm nipping next door. I'll be five minutes.'

The evenings were becoming noticeably milder as May began its evolution into early summer. The sky above shimmered with a deep red glow as the sun dropped below the distant horizon.

Robert rapped loudly at the front door of number forty-one.

A knock that was quickly answered by an unsmiling occupant.

'Oh. It's you. Alright, Mister Aspinall?'

Robert was a little amused by the manner of address.

Greg seemed surprised - almost disappointed in fact - that it was not Karen calling at the door.

'Hi, Greg. By the way - it's Rob! *Not* Mister Aspinall. Friends don't call each other by their surnames, I'm sure!'

Greg's eyes focused on the bounty in Robert's arms.

'The choc is from Karen. The ale is from me.'

Greg looked indifferent - almost puzzled. It was evident to Robert that he did not understand the reasoning behind the gifts. He took the items from Robert as a hand of thanks was offered his way.

'Where's Kaz?' Greg enquired, as though concerned about her absence.

'She's watching telly. Besides, I wanted to see you myself. These are to show our appreciation for being a great neighbour. You *and* your mum. It's nice to know we can count on good friends should we need to.'

There was a momentary pause as Greg carefully mulled over his response. Inside he began to churn with annoyance as Robert's arm remained outstretched in the murk of early evening.

Finally, the pair shook hands and Greg accepted the gesture.

'No worries. Any time. It was the battery wasn't it, Rob?'

'Yes, I think so. Simple enough to sort out. Karen wouldn't even know how to lift the bonnet up though! Let alone get her hands dirty in trying to solve the problem!'

Greg exhibited a smirk and glanced over Robert's shoulder towards his gleaming new company car perched on the drive behind Karen's.

'How's your motor? Looking pretty nifty, isn't it?'

'Oh yes. Goes like the clappers. And all on the company expense account!' Robert grinned.

Greg continued to peruse over the sight of Rob's car before looking at the beer and chocolate in his hands.

'Yes. Must be nice to have everything you want, Rob. You'd better look after it, hadn't you?'

'Oh, don't you worry, mate. I will. Anyway, must be off. Karen's got my dinner on. I'll see you soon, Greg. Thanks again.'

Greg stared as Robert skipped back down the driveway of number forty-one past Evelyn's black saloon. Then along the front pavement and past both cars perched on the driveway of number thirty-nine. Then on through his own front door as Greg silently continued to scrutinize him.

Then Greg's gaze fell to the front garden of number thirty-nine, with its neatly trimmed hedges that Karen had tended to over the last fortnight and to the large, front, white-painted gate that closed off the property to unwanted guests.

He sighed before closing the door on the intensely frustrating view paraded before him.

His voice carried through a low hiss as he contemplated the developing scenario involving the next-door neighbours.

'Yes. You'll be seeing me soon, alright...Robert. Very soon.'

*****

Whilst the Aspinalls embraced the onset of another blissful family weekend together, they spoke of what had happened during the previous days and made their plans for the coming Saturday and Sunday.

They could not have known that just beyond their bubble of utter contentment, the neighbours they had so recently heaped praise upon were about to enter conference, with the aim of making plans of a different, much less savoury kind.

But before commencing the latest stage of the conspiracy with his ever doting mother, Greg Chapple's first port of call was the kitchen waste bin.

Into which he forcibly deposited four cans of beer and a large bar of chocolate, before returning to the living room.

twelve

'I'm absolutely stuffed. Couldn't eat another thing.'

Karen stretched her browning legs in the beer garden as Robert placed the tray of drinks on the table. The Warrcner's Arms was a favourite haunt for the Aspinalls. Out in the countryside beyond Tenbridge and surrounded by wonderful scenery. There was a play barn for the girls to romp about in for an hour and a sumptuous Sunday carvery.

Robert positioned himself next to his wife and gave her a kiss on the lips.

'Full tums all round then! I thought it was about time we all ate out together. It's been an age. You all deserve a treat. Long overdue.'

Karen stared at the smiling face of her husband which was alarmingly pale considering the amount of sunshine that had been prominent of late.

'Yes, I think the girls enjoyed their dinner, Rob. Even Lauren ate her greens. She must have been hungry!'

Robert gazed at the top of his pint as he pondered the events of the previous few weeks.

'I still feel guilty, Kaz. Leaving it all to you. I'm making a go of things in Coventry, but I can't help feeling it may be in sacrifice of something else.'

Karen's hand reached across the table and wrapped her fingers around the wrist of the man she loved. She studied his gold watch - the one she bought him the previous Christmas. It glinted in the sunshine as a pleasant memento.

A symbol of passing time, but also of eternal longing. She was missing her husband yes, but she was not prepared to compound his obvious turmoil by saying so.

'Have they told you when you'll be entitled to any leave? We could book a summer holiday if you can get some dates together.'

Robert was evidently inflated by the suggestion.

'Brilliant, Kaz! A fortnight in the sun. Wonderful! Simon says I may be due for some time off in July. Not long now. Should coincide with the girls' school holidays as well, which is a bonus.'

Out of the corner of her eye, Karen spied Chloe and Lauren scampering toward them from the door of the play barn.

With rosy cheeks and panting breaths, they chirped in unison as they clattered into the table.

'Mummy! Can we have fifty pence each for the slot machine, please?' squealed Lauren.

'Please, Mummy, please?' pleaded Chloe.

Robert reached into his pocket and retrieved some coins.

'Guess which hand. If you guess it right, then you can have the lot!'

Chloe's trepidation was obvious as she debated the puzzle with a furrowing brow. Eventually after some deliberation, she correctly picked the fist which contained the money and the pair skipped contentedly back toward the playroom as two proud parents looked on.

'How much did you give them, Rob?'

'Oh, about a fiver, I think. They deserve it. I've neglected them. It's the least I can do, isn't it? Put a smile on their faces.'

Karen took a swig of her orange juice before nuzzling closer. At that moment she felt happy with the world. Her husband back by her side. The kids having fun and getting along with one another.

Nothing could tarnish her welcome pang of inner solace.

'You haven't neglected anyone, Rob. We knew the score before you accepted the job. We supported your decision. Everything is fine.'

A heavy sigh conveyed doubts from Robert as he stared vacantly into the distance.

'I know, but...Jesus. It's pathetic having to go to the neighbours with thank you presents. It's wrong. I should be there with all of you. Not turning up like a bloody stranger each Friday night playing catch-up with my own family's life. And talking of strangers, it's not fair to burden Greg with my responsibilities.'

Karen's heart began to beat a little faster as a tangible sense of unease encroached into the exchange. She strived for positivity.

'Greg's no stranger. The girls like him. Besides, from your point of view it must be good to know that someone is available to help out. I'm sure the Chapples understand our predicament. I bet Greg was quite touched by the gesture, anyway.'

Robert drank deeply from his glass.

'I couldn't tell, really. He didn't say much when I went round. Seemed a bit put out, to be honest. Which was weird. Perhaps he's sick of the sight of us! I reckon he's a decent chap, though. I bet his mother keeps him in line!'

Karen chuckled at the thought. It was certainly contrary to Judy's analysis of the scenario.

Still, Karen was intent on enjoying her quality time with her family. She had not come twenty miles into the sticks to discuss her neighbours.

Yet it was an indictment of current circumstances.

Every conversation she seemed to have these days centred on the occupants of number forty-one.

It was becoming uncanny. And nauseating.

The obligatory, unavoidable subject; Greg and his bloody mother.

'I wish today could last forever. It's been so nice, Rob. And you took me clothes shopping yesterday! I've been spoiled again, haven't I? Yet these weekends together seem to get shorter and shorter.'

Robert kissed Karen on her neck and reduced his voice to a whisper.

'The night is still young, my dear wench!'

Karen collapsed in hysterics as the girls re-appeared carrying two plastic balls each.

'Mummy! Look what we won!' yelped Chloe.

'Well done, girls! Come and have a drink you must be thirsty.'

Chloe and Lauren skipped across the grass to their parents' bench.

At that moment, the mutual acknowledgement of family unity could not have been more affirming.

*****

Greg Chapple paced the lounge as his mother maintained a fixed gaze on the TV set.

'For Christ's sake, will you sit down? You're getting on my nerves now!'

He moved to the front window and peered through the gap in the curtains.

'Mum. They've been gone out for almost the entire weekend. Both days! The last I saw of them was that prick with his bloody poxy presents on Friday.'

Evelyn offered her son an authoritative, maternal glare that he noticed but ignored.

Greg's sense of agitation was almost uncontrollable.

'Greg, love. He's only here until tomorrow morning. Then you've got all week to enjoy yourself. Relax. Be calm, lad. And shift out of the way of the bloody telly!'

A minute or two of silence followed as the soap omnibus edition concluded and the end credits rolled. Evelyn stood up and moved to the window. Karen's car remained unaccompanied on the drive of number thirty-nine. Her son became impatient once more.

'Are they back yet, Mum?'

His mother folded her arms and scrutinized the street up and down.

'No. Not yet. They can't be far, though. They'll be back soon. You'll see.'

Greg joined his mother at the window.

'It's not fair leaving me alone all Saturday and Sunday. They're taking the piss out of us, Mum.'

'I know they are, love. But be patient. You'll have your time. Don't worry. They've had it coming for years. Bloody snobs. Bloody *rich* snobs, to boot! That's all they are. They think they're better than us. We'll see about that, won't we lad?'

Greg cackled as his mother gestured toward the opened envelope on the dining table.

'Have you studied that letter that came yesterday? It seems that your solicitor thinks he can swing things around for you. You'd better get a reply in the post sharpish and tell him proceed. Go on! That'll take your mind off the neighbours for an hour. Get it written. I'll check it when you've done it.'

Rather disgruntled by his mother's loyalty to diplomacy, Greg fetched a pen from the kitchen draw and read the previous day's correspondence as Evelyn continued her vigil by the window.

'Don't fret, lad. I'll tell you as soon as they arrive.'

*****

The blue metallic automatic purred in the road as Karen unlatched the large white gate and swung it open for Robert's company car to crawl onto the driveway. She made her way around to his window which he lowered at the flick of a switch.

Her husband had an idea to convey.

'How's about you open a bottle of wine and I'll set the swing-ball up on the back lawn. I'll challenge you to the death.'

She giggled before giving him a peck on the nose.

'Brill idea, Rob. You can't beat trying to play swing-ball when you're drunk!'

Within minutes the sound of bat on ball was accompanied by shrieks of laughter and mild screams of pain.

Robert and Karen attempted to knock the skin off the little green tennis ball as battle was well and truly underway.

Chloe and Lauren rolled with amusement as they watched their parents play like children together for the first time since they could recall - certainly the first time that year.

'Top me up, darling. I can still see only one ball! It's easier when you can see two or three to smash!' chuckled Robert.

Once more Karen exploded with mirth as she hovered over the two wine glasses precariously perched on the grass.

'I say, hubby dear. It's bloody warm, isn't it?'

Robert smiled as he held the ball in his fingers ready to serve.

'Well don't be shy, wife. Take some clothes off if you're sweaty!'

More guffaws followed as she raised a middle finger and offered an expression of feigned enthusiasm.

'I know! We could play *strip* swing-ball! Brilliant!' declared Robert, enthusiastically.

He then duly smashed the ball narrowly avoiding Karen's nose as it orbited the pole.

'I'll apply to patent the idea tomorrow, love. Should prove a very popular pastime in the coming summer months! Though men should be advised to wear groin protection for their own safety!'

The game continued amid more wine and much laughter and gasping over near-misses. Chloe and Lauren were not accustomed to seeing their mother and father together sharing in such joviality, but this afternoon it seemed entirely natural.

The scene of domestic harmony was bathed in golden sunshine.

A scene which silently enraged Greg Chapple, as he strolled down his own garden path and approached the fence gate.

The air of jubilation on the Aspinall's rear lawn was abruptly disturbed by his snapping declaration.

'Oh…you lot decided to come home, then!'

Karen turned to view the source of the sudden commentary as Greg stood at the gate, trying desperately to eclipse his grimace with something resembling a smile.

Robert raised a hand to his apparent friend and neighbour as he swayed unsteadily with a bat in one hand and wine glass in the other.

'Hi, mate. Fancy a game? Every point you lose you have to take something off!'

Greg keenly observed Karen's perspiring form and his thoughts veered to an imaginatively sensual image of her completely de-clothed having lost the match.

'Erm…no thanks. There's a time and place for nudity.'

Not a good response.

The mocking calls from Robert and Karen only served to fuel Greg's anger at discovering the neighbourly throng having so much fun. His hands rested on the top of the gate. He placed his full weight onto the hinges as he spoke.

'Where have you been all day, then? Anywhere nice?'

Robert was puzzled by the line of enquiry and more than a little dismayed at the motive behind it.

He opted for the standard, semi-humorous reply.

'Well, for one, we didn't go out until midday, and for two, it's got bugger all to do with you!'

The statement did not draw a reaction of amusement from Greg, who continued to stare inanely at Karen.

Robert tried to fortify his previous quip.

'Greg? That was a joke? Only joking, mate! Smile! As you can see, we're a bit the worse for wear. We've just been out for Sunday lunch at a little place I know out at Woodham. And it was such a nice day we decided to play strip swing-ball to help our dinner go down!'

Karen could sense Greg's annoyance, yet she struggled to justify his possible reasons for such a standpoint. The tension in his features was obvious to her. She knew him slightly better than Robert and could tell that her husband's jollity was not being received too well.

'Mummy, the phone's ringing!' shouted Chloe from the back door.

Greg watched Karen trot up the garden path and into the house to answer the call. She looked lithe and fit in her short skirt.

He felt turned on by the image.

By the same token, he acutely resented the presence of her husband.

A reaction that he seemed unable to restrain.

An irrational response that consumed him.

'Would you like a beer, Greg? I've some cold ones in the shed fridge.'

Greg eyed Robert with barely concealed disdain.

'No thanks. I like to keep a clear head in the daytime. Where did you take Karen yesterday, then?'

The continuous line of scrutiny was unorthodox, but Robert supposed it was also harmless interest from a bored friend and neighbour.

'Oh, just into Tenbridge. Bought her some clothes. Some summer things. This and that. Bits and bobs. You know.'

Greg continued to clench the waist high wooden rim of the fence gate. His knuckles whitened and his eyes darted toward the house as if expecting Karen's return.

Chloe emerged from the back door once more now licking an ice lolly and confirmed that the caller on the phone was Judy.

Greg winced inwardly as Judy's name was mentioned.

Fucking Judy Simpson.

Always hanging around in the background like a bad smell.

At least he knew where he stood with Robert's comings and goings.

There was no chance of a surprise visit from Robert.

But fucking Judy Simpson.

Greg had decided he couldn't stand her. Or her opinions.

He had picked up on the negative vibes at her parents' house party the previous week. The dislike was apparently mutual, then. Well, he knew where he stood so far as her thoughts of him were concerned.

He didn't care about that.

It was just the unpredictable intrusions that Greg could not tolerate.

He opted to end the exchange with Robert on a cordial note.

'I'd better be going. Have a good week at work.'

'Yes…thanks, mate. You, too.'

With that, Greg Chapple was gone from the fence. Robert looked at his daughters and mockingly shrugged his shoulders as if to mimic their own perplexity at the young neighbour's sudden appearance and line of conversation.

Karen returned unsteadily to the fray carrying a fresh bottle of wine.

'Thought we might be getting a bit thirsty after all this exercise. Shall I do the honours, sir?'

Robert adopted the posh voice of a country gentlemen.

'Indeed yes, splendid. Please do. By the way, darling. What did dear Judy want?'

'We're going out for dinner one night next week. I'll have to get mum to come and baby-sit. She won't mind.'

Karen looked over to the back garden of number forty-one.

'Oh, has Greg gone so soon?'

'Yes, dear. He didn't fancy strip swing-ball. Asks some weird questions too, does that lad. Still, never mind. Top us both up. Then it's your serve, I think.'

*****

With glasses re-filled and amusement resumed, the Aspinalls continued to bathe in their sun-drenched oasis of love and contentment.

Engaged in the energetic, drink-fuelled game, they were oblivious to events next door as Greg Chapple cradled his bleeding knuckles under a soothing cold tap.

Sinking to his knees, he turned to his mother standing behind him.

She simply stared in sympathy at the indentation in the kitchen cabinet door that her only son had punched, in an attempt to quell the storm that was brewing in a confused and dangerous mind.

Some moments later as Karen patted the ball back and forth with her husband, she felt sure she caught a glimpse of Evelyn with arms folded, watching them from her back bedroom window.

Karen waved and smiled.

There was no active response.

Not even a glimmer of acknowledgement.

Then in the next instance, the indisputable vision of Evelyn Chapple was gone.

A cold and empty blackness left in her wake.

thirteen

The third week of the sixth month brought with it the hottest sunshine of the year so far. Karen sat on the sofa one morning after dropping the girls off to school. She debated which of her chores to attack first. However, it seemed such a waste to spend all day inside attending to ironing and hoovering.

Such menial tasks could surely wait until the rains came.

Should she venture into the garden, appropriate attire would need to be a consideration. Something light and airy. Perhaps short sleeve blouse and skirt? No. Not for gardening. Turning over borders would entail muck and sweat. Something more durable but less obstructive was required.

Pulling open her wardrobe doors, Karen scanned the coat hangers for something to wear. After ten minutes and much deliberation, she closed the wardrobe and moved towards her bedside underwear draw, from which she dug out her royal blue bikini.

Well, why not? It was blisteringly hot, and Karen was something of a sun worshipper. She liked the effect that strong sunlight had on her hair, usually turning it from a dark yellow into a lightly bleached hue.

Stripping and donning the two-piece outfit in the dress mirror, she felt slightly perturbed by the areas of pale flesh around her chest and upper arms. However, she was toned and taut and her legs were already tanning nicely. Now was the time to take advantage of the weather and make the most of the day.

Generally, she liked what she saw in the reflection. The bottoms were modestly revealing, and the cups seemed to fit as they always did. Perhaps her belief that she had put on weight was a personal myth.

Gardening in the bikini it was then.

The time on the kitchen clock was veering towards a quarter to ten. This would give her a good two hours' weeding before fetching Lauren. She couldn't set any plants as she hadn't had the chance to buy any, yet. Still, it was a good day to get the donkey work out of the way.

The searing heat swathed her form as she emerged tentatively from the back of the house in a pair of flip flops. Her initial embarrassment was soon eclipsed by the thought that she was possibly still wearing too many clothes. It was like walking into an oven.

Inside the shed, she uncovered her gloves, a bucket, a trowel and a cushion for her knees.

That was one of the priorities. Get the shed shifted. It was out of place where it was. If Robert could get it moved, she would be able to decide what would look good in its place. It was impossible to ascertain whilst it was still perched halfway down the garden.

It was in the way but there wasn't very much she could do about it at that moment in time.

The earth was hard and dry, and the hardier weeds seem to be rooted like trees. It had been a while since Karen had done any serious gardening. Probably nearly a year, in fact. The sweat readily began to form on her forehead and at the backs of her legs as she crouched and dug frantically.

Like most jobs around the house these days, once commenced, Karen invariably wished she hadn't bothered starting at all. But Robert had promised to buy her all the plants and shrubs she wanted so long as she sorted out preparation of the ground. Karen had little option. Tidying up was not pleasurable, but certainly necessary.

Consumed by her task, Karen did not notice Greg approach the fence gate and assume the role of silent observer. He was not about to interrupt her endeavours, particularly as it presented him with the rare chance to covertly admire her partial nakedness.

Liking what he saw he watched without word for several minutes, only to make his presence known when Karen stood to her feet, wiped her brow, and stretched her stiffened, cramping legs.

'You ought to walk round like that all the time, Kaz. I might even take up gardening with you!'

Startled, Karen spun around and was swept over by a sudden wave of embarrassment. However, any attempt to try and divert attention from her body would be in vain. Something instinctive told her that she had been under scrutiny for a while.

'Greg, you made me jump! How long have you been there?'

He smirked knowingly as he leaned on the gate.

'Oh, I've just come out to mow Mum's lawn. Growing quick now, isn't it?'

Karen felt his eyes wandering all over her, yet she felt strangely comfortable with the fact. It was almost liberating *not* be wary of his attention. It was then that she noticed Greg's own attire. A pair of skimpy shorts that barely achieved the task. The amusing thought flashed through her mind that they looked as though they had been sprayed onto him.

The mutual appreciation of one another's physical forms created a rapid sense of ease between the pair as they drew closer at the gate. Karen could acknowledge a fit man when she saw it. Her eyes rested willingly on Greg's torso.

It was noticeably different to Robert's.

The six-pack abdomen was textbook.

Greg's chest was hairless, expansive, muscled.

Almost *too* enticing.

But she would preserve her private thoughts as exactly that - private.

'What you up to, Kaz?'

She gestured around the garden as she spoke, though Karen found it difficult to maintain a focus away from his athletic arms and shoulders.

'Well, I need to sort out the flower beds. I've also been intent on shifting this bloody shed, but I haven't got round to it. Need Rob here, really.'

Greg saw his opportunity and seized it like a shark would attack stray bait.

'I'll do it. I'll do it for you. I'll do it today. Now!'

His response was lightening quick and caught Karen off guard.

'Greg, I wasn't trying to…'

'I'll do it! No problem. I'll fetch the tools and come through.'

With that, he was gone and into his father's garage.

Karen unbolted the fence gate and retreated to the kitchen to make them both a cold drink. No sooner had she turned her back, Greg reappeared with a small bag in hand and proceeded to begin unscrewing the wooden panels of the shed with his electric drill.

'Greg, this really isn't necessary. It'll take you all day, won't it?'

He did not look up as he manically attuned himself to the task.

Karen afforded herself a prime view of his physique as he worked. Placing the glasses on the patio table, she wandered down to the shed and continued to observe him in action.

'Where is it going to be moved to then, Kaz?'

She did not hear him speak; her attention centred elsewhere.

'Kaz? Where do you want me to rebuild it?'

'Oh…sorry…erm…over there, by the hedgerow at the back.'

He looked round to assess the new location.

'Okay. I see it's sitting on slabs. That's good. I'll have them up and re-laid within the hour. I'll have to re-use the roof felt, though. We haven't got any. What's already on looks in good enough nick if I'm careful taking it off.'

'There's a drink here for you. If you're hungry later, I'm sure I can rustle you something up. What's your mum doing today?'

Greg hauled himself onto the shed roof and gingerly began to peel off the felt covering.

'She's in the house. She's not one for the sun.'

Karen emptied the shed as Greg continued to dismantle it and commenced repositioning of the concrete base. She discreetly watched his arms flex as he carried each slab in turn to its new setting.

This was an unexpectedly pleasurable and productive morning.

Then another thought crossed her mind.

If only Judy could see the pair of them. She would probably explode with rage and disown Karen forever.

It seemed unjustified that Judy could pour such misgivings on Greg and his mother. How many neighbours would come and move a shed for nothing? Although she would offer him a few quid, it was expected that he would refuse.

At least, he should refuse. After all, it was his idea.

The morning passed by quickly and Karen made significant progress with her dig. There had been little conversation between the pair. Greg obviously wanted to achieve results in the shortest space of time with little or no interruption. Karen was not about to stop him in his cause. Having donned a t-shirt and shorts, she hollered down the garden.

'Greg…I'm just nipping out to fetch Lauren from nursery. Do you need anything fetching from anywhere?'

He did not face her as he shouted across the lawn to the patio where she stood with hands on hips. He would only observe her when she wasn't aware of it. Not once did she catch him looking at her body, yet whilst kneeling at the flower beds she carried the uncanny, almost enjoyable sensation of being watched.

Karen paid it no mind. It was a fleetingly brief thought. Not one that concerned her or made her feel vulnerable as it might do many women.

That was the main attraction of Greg as a friend. Karen never felt threatened by him in any way.

That he was capable of a fractious temperament, she did not doubt. But it was a side of him she had not yet witnessed.

Karen always felt assured in the company of the Chapples. This feeling had not diminished over time.

'No, Kaz. I'm all good. I've got all I need right here.'

*****

On her return from fetching Lauren, Karen was most touched by the gesture that sat filled with water on the back lawn. The girls' paddling pool had been folded up in the shed for months. Greg had obviously needed to move it as he worked.

Lauren's excitement at the spectacle overwhelmed her instantly.

'Mummy, can I put my swimming costume on? Please? Please?'

Karen continued to stare at Greg's handiwork. The slab foundation had been repositioned and the floor panel of the shed sat atop it. He had worked like a Trojan for over two hours. He was also nowhere to be seen as Lauren pulled frantically at her mother's shorts.

'Yes, love. Looks like Greg has set everything out for you, bless him.'

It was a welcome treat for Lauren to be able to splash around in the water under her mother's watchful gaze. Stripped off to her bikini once more, Karen knelt by the paddling pool and playfully threw water over her youngest daughter, resulting in the inevitable squeals of pleasure.

Karen assumed Greg must have nipped home for some tool or other, yet he said he had everything to hand. She peered through the fence gate which was wide open. There was no hint of activity at number forty-one.

Then a familiar voice echoed from behind her.

'I thought it seemed like a good idea. Hope you don't mind, Kaz!'

Greg emerged from the back door of number thirty-nine adorning an infectious smile.

Karen initially failed to see the humorous side.

'What are you doing in there?' she snapped, instantly regretting doing so.

'Why? What's the problem? Just been to the toilet, that's all! Don't worry I didn't go through your knicker drawers!'

He chuckled as he strolled manfully past her and picked up his drill from the grass.

'How's the water, Lauren?'

'Ace thanks, Greg. You're brilliant!'

Karen felt herself grinning at her little girl's sincere appreciation.

Setting up the paddling pool was such a small thing to do, but it meant so much to her daughter. It showed real thought and consideration. Her gaze fixed on Greg for a second or two before she returned to the kitchen to prepare some lunch.

She watched through the window as Lauren played happily in the pool. Within minutes, Greg had screwed all seven shed panels back together and promptly clambered onto the roof to relay the felt.

In all, the job that she had ignored for months had taken him less than three hours from start to finish.

Lathered in perspiration, Greg willingly collapsed into a chair on the patio as Karen set down a plateful of sandwiches and a glass of cold beer on the table before him.

'Wonderful, Kaz. I'm famished!'

'Lauren, come and dry yourself off and eat something, please!'

'Yes, mummy.' came the dainty reply from down the garden.

The three relaxed, ate and drank as the sun continued to beat down, bathing the scene in its sedating warmth.

'The shed is where you want it now, I take it?' asked Greg as he swigged his lager.

Karen had caught the sun already.

She felt her face glowing as she smiled in gratitude.

'Your mum was right. You might be pretty useful to have around the place. Yes, it's perfect, Greg. Thank you. It's nice to have a strapping man about the house again. I'd forgotten what it's like!'

They both reached for another sandwich. Their hands touched above the plate, causing both to quickly retract in a brief second of awkwardness.

An uncertain silence prevailed. Lauren swallowed the last of her snack as she quietly watched her mother and the man from next door exchange pleasured looks.

'This is nice, Kaz.'

'Well, the weather's playing a big part, I suppose. I don't think I'd see you at all if it was raining all the time, do you?'

Lauren continued to observe the adults before feeling it to be appropriate to contribute to the conversation.

'Chloe says you're Mummy's boyfriend when Daddy's not here.'

Greg instantly spluttered beer down his front and sat up in his chair.

Understandably, Karen stared at her little girl in shock and disbelief at what she had just heard.

'Lauren...don't be so silly! Why would she say something like that? It's not true and she knows it. Wait until I see her later! I'm sorry, Greg.'

He raised a hand as though trying to subdue her growing displeasure.

'Kaz, it's just something kids would say. Don't be too hard on her. She didn't mean anything by it, I'm sure.'

'No, Greg. I'm not happy about her saying things like that to Lauren. It's not on. I'm bloody annoyed. What if Rob heard her say it? Then what?'

Swabbing the spillage from his upper thighs, he looked Karen firmly in the eye as a sudden coldness framed his expression.

'Well...what if he *did* hear it? Would it be so disastrous? After all, we *are* good friends...aren't we?'

Karen was a little concerned about Greg's naivety in the matter.

Still, it was a falsehood after all. The opinion of an impressionable child. Nothing more; nothing less. Perhaps she shouldn't react too harshly. Children see things differently.

If they are not told the facts it stands to reason that they will make up their own minds. For this, Karen blamed herself. She would have to rectify things at the first discreet opportunity.

The early afternoon passed amid intermittent banter and playful water fights.

Lauren enjoyed Greg's company - nearly as much as her mother did.

It had been a most enjoyable and relaxing day. Karen had not spent much time playing with the girls since Robert's promotion. It was heart-warming to see her youngest so carefree.

Yet Greg seemed to have a natural aptitude for keeping things interesting for her daughters. There was little doubt as the clock signified three pm that Lauren had been completely besotted with the paddling pool idea.

'I'd better get ready to fetch Chloe from school. I might even be early for once!'

Greg watched her pull on her shorts and T-shirt once more, paying particular attention to the droplets of water that trickled down her legs.

'It's been great today, Kaz.'

'Listen, Greg. Thanks for doing the shed. You're a star.'

She had no opportunity to prevent her next act.

She wilfully leaned over and playfully kissed him on the cheek.

His response was conservative but assured.

'Any time, Kaz. I'm never far away. What are you up to tonight? Thought we might go out for a drink somewhere. Take the girls as well, of course.'

Despite her willingness to maintain their friendship, being bold enough to venture out in public together was not on the agenda.

Things could be misinterpreted very easily.

'I can't. It's Wednesday.'

'So what? What's so special about Wednesday?'

'I take the girls to my parents on Wednesdays after school. It's a family ritual. Sorry.'

Greg thought for a moment.

His anger brewing instantly.

Karen's refusal did not sit easily on his shoulders having spent most of the day working for her.

Yet he strived to quash his annoyance with an alternative suggestion.

'What about tomorrow night, then? We can do it then.'

'Sorry, Greg. I have a date.'

Greg Chapple bolted up in his chair and leaned forward.

He could no longer hide his inner frustrations, whether they were warranted or not.

'What do you mean you've got a date? Who the fuck with?'

Karen had never appreciated being sworn at.

Especially by a friend.

Especially in front of little Lauren.

'Er...can you alter your language, please. There's no need for it.'

Greg rose from his chair and walked toward her as she stood at the back door.

'I only asked you who you were going on a date with.'

'It's with Judy! Calm down! There's no need to get jealous!'

Karen studied the evidently stressed visage of her friend and neighbour and could not help but laugh out loud. Thankfully, her amusement served to calm the storm, forcing Greg into submission.

'I'm not jealous. I'm just interested. That's all.'

'Well, just consider your language before you go off on one!'

Greg sat down once again as Karen reminded him that time was now against her.

'Look, I've got to find some clean clothes for Lauren to change in to. I'm in a hurry.'

'Okay, okay. What if I baby-sit for you tomorrow night, then? Is that a good idea?'

Not for the first time, Greg's consideration regarding the girls shone through and overshadowed his momentary loss of temper.

'Brilliant, Greg. I would be very thankful. It would save me driving to and from my mum's. That would be great. If you don't mind.'

'Of course not. Tell me in the morning what time you want me. I'm sure we can entertain ourselves for a few hours. I'll order us pizza and watch a Disney movie with them.'

Lauren did not hold back in voting positively for Greg's proposal as she jumped up and down in the paddling pool.

'Yeah! Pizza and Disney! Can we Mum? Can we?'

'That sounds like a popular plan, Greg. Thank you. Come on Lauren. Time to dry off, now. We must fetch Chloe and then go to Grandma's.'

The youngster's vibrancy took a downturn as she observed the blades of grass floating on the surface of the water around her knees.

'Okay, Mummy.'

With a final wave goodbye and a blown kiss, Greg disappeared back through the fence gate, leaving Karen to reflect on a very pro-active day so far.

*****

The weekly visit to her parents' house was always a pleasure for Karen.

Yet for some reason, this week she could not truly be bothered.

She had fully expected to be berated for her slightly drunken performance at the Simpson's anniversary party - not to mention the inevitable concern over Greg's presence.

The two hours with her mother and father offered them the weekly indulgence with their granddaughters, so purpose was served. So long as they were both healthy, Karen saw no need to interest herself with her father's argument with a young plumbing apprentice at the merchants' yard, or the fact that her mother's friend Sylvia had enjoyed a successful visit to the chiropodist.

Even Lauren's ongoing battle with Long John continued unnoticed.

Once back home, she spent the rest of the evening in front of the television, watching the screen but retaining nothing that was shown.

Her concentration was elsewhere.

Even Robert's nightly phone call was ordinary in content and unstimulating. The stinging fly in the ointment was his depressing revelation that he would not be allowed to take any leave during the summer holidays.

It was as though Karen had finally accepted the map that life had drawn out for her and had now happily become wrapped up in the little diversions that interjected her daily existence.

She told Robert about the shed being moved and of her green fingered efforts. Predictably, he promised to take her to the garden centre at the coming weekend.

If the truth was known, Karen would have admitted to being bored with the chats with her long-distance husband. He was no good to her if he was two hundred miles away.

It stood to reason there was little chance for diverse interaction between man and wife if he was absent.

The nightly calls barely seemed more than a ritual check-in appointment these days.

Karen had now become fully accustomed to the Monday to Friday estrangement from her husband. Yet she still needed her man next to her. It was her natural, feminine right.

The comforting presence. The satisfaction of her wants and whims. It was a feeling that had grown in her heart over the previous few days. Maybe even during the previous weeks. The genetic desire and necessity to interact with Robert's company was beginning to eat away at her conscience.

That was why she felt pangs of guilt about declining Greg's invitation for a drink. He was a nice guy and she found she had a lot of time for him.

Though it was far too tempting an offer and would only invite the rumour mongers to divulge their conclusions.

Though, she could now tell that Greg was seriously attracted to her.

Secretly, by the same token she hoped he understood that Karen Aspinall was forbidden territory.

Yet he excited her so.

He was all man. Rough and masculine around the edges but with a soft core. She also believed Greg had a good heart and offered genuine friendship. She was not completely happy about rejecting his furtive advances. Part of her craved the alternative and the unknown.

In her view she was being deprived of attention that should be hers by right.

It was an uncomfortable situation for any wife to admit to, but life was gradually becoming far more interesting without her husband around.

fourteen

'Mummy...where are you going with Aunty Judy?'

Chloe drew her attention away from the TV set as Karen entered the lounge carrying a hairbrush and a pair of heeled leather ankle boots.

'Only to the cinema, darling. Then for a bite to eat maybe. There's a film Judy wants to see. We won't be late back, though.'

Karen checked her make-up and pulled the brush through her blond locks. She wanted to look presentable but wasn't prepared to pull out all the stops. Not for a night out with Judy, anyway. There weren't too many people to impress whilst sitting in a darkened theatre.

Chloe's interest was now fully centred on her mother.

'Who is going to look after us? Is Grandma coming?'

Karen looked at her eldest daughter and pondered a reply.

She had not spoken to either of the girls about the issue concerning her relationship with Greg. But at that moment, the subject seemed unavoidable.

'Greg is going to look after you both, darling. Just until I get back. He said he might order pizza.'

Karen waited for Chloe's reply, which was predictable, but no less awkward for the fact.

'Is Greg not taking you out again, Mummy?'

Karen crouched beside her daughter and turned the TV volume down. Her heart began to beat faster as she selected the most suitable approach to Chloe's justified curiosity.

'No, darling. Not tonight. I need to talk to you about Greg. He's not my *boyfriend*. Just a friend. That's all. Just a friend. And he volunteered to babysit you tonight so Mummy can go out.'

An air of discomfort encroached into the room. Chloe's innocent blue eyes practically bulged from their sockets. Karen tried to anticipate her reaction, but with a child aged only nine such a feat was nigh on impossible.

Chloe's only response was an expression of puzzlement.

'I *know* he's not your boyfriend, Mummy. He can't be, can he? Not while you're married to Daddy.'

Now it was Karen's turn for a sense of relieved bemusement. Her eldest daughter seemed quite assured about the situation.

A mature outlook that again caused Karen to halt her intended train of conversation.

'Have you spoken to Lauren about this?'

Chloe adamantly shook her head as she looked directly into her mother's eyes.

'No, Mummy. Why?'

'Because…oh…because nothing. It doesn't matter. Would you like the telly turning back up?'

Karen resumed putting the finishing touches to her face and hair whilst sensing that Chloe had more to say on the matter.

'Mummy…did Lauren say Greg was your boyfriend?'

It was now obvious that the girls had discussed the subject between themselves at some recent point.

'No, love. Well…yes…but she didn't mean it. But it doesn't matter. Forget about it.'

There was a substantial pause before Chloe continued.

'I know *why* she said it.'

This was an unexpected twist in the exchange.

Suddenly, Chloe was the holder of information. Kids are very adept at keeping things to themselves - until they decide the time is right to speak up.

Now it was Karen's turn to be curious and request answers.

Her nervous gaze became stern as she quizzed her eldest daughter.

'Okay. *Why* would Lauren say something like that, then? She knows I love Daddy.'

Chloe's attention rested vacantly on the screen as she hunched her knees to her chest and began to sway back and forth. Her response to the scrutiny was totally out of character and the revelation wholly unpleasant for her mother to hear.

'Lauren said that it was *Greg* who *told* her to say it.'

A sudden sense of concern caused Karen to crouch to her daughter's eye level once more.

'He told her *what*, Chloe? *What* did Greg tell her? What did he say?'

Chloe continued to fix her attentions on the television as she spoke.

'…that he is your boyfriend and that you don't love Daddy anymore…'

Karen's mind began to whirl.

She grappled for a mental foothold that only led her somewhere between panic and nausea.

The conflicting stories were at best, annoying. At worst, potentially disastrous. This boyfriend story had been dreamed up by somebody.

Whilst it rankled her conscience to admit it, Karen was prepared to ignore the entire episode and consoled herself that the whole thing was a misheard storm in a teacup.

But her daughters would surely not fabricate such a tale, would they? Just as ludicrous was the thought that Greg would possibly implant such an idea into their minds.

Not Greg.

Not Greg Chapple, the handsome friend from next door.

Certainly not.

Absolutely, certainly not?

As she attempted to placate her overloaded brain, a loud knock at the door signified the arrival of the babysitter in question, prompting Chloe to jump to her feet and play greeter.

He shimmied into the lounge with his young escort.

His affecting expression immediately eradicated any of Karen's current fears or doubts.

'Hi, Kaz. I've brought a menu round for the girls to look at. I thought I'd go with the pizza idea for them later. Have they had their tea, yet?'

Karen's attention was diverted to the unannounced figure of Greg's mother standing behind her son in the hallway. What the hell had she come round for? Evelyn held her usual authoritative position, with arms wedged up under her overhanging chest.

'You look nice, Karen.'

'Well, I'm amazed if you think so, Evelyn. I haven't tried very hard this evening.'

Greg offered a compliment of his own as he stared through and into her. Again, Karen fought the sensation of her unquenched and somewhat yet undiscovered inner desire.

'Why don't you cancel with your mate and let me take you out instead? Mum will baby-sit. She doesn't mind.'

Karen noticed Evelyn's overly eager expression, but also the enquiring glances of both her daughters standing quietly in the kitchen doorway.

'Er, no. If you don't mind, I'll stick with plan A.'

Immediately, Greg's expression and tone altered.

His attitude became tinged with disapproval, almost as though his advance had been rebuked - which of course, it had.

'You sod off out and enjoy yourself then. I'll look after your kids. Go on.'

The air turned cold.

Karen felt simultaneously offended and on the offensive.

Chloe and Lauren jumped onto the sofa and proceeded to flick through the movie channels with the remote control. Karen could not decipher whether the strange atmosphere was conducive to her departure.

'Look…if there is a problem, I'll stay with the girls myself. There's no need to get grumpy, Greg.'

Evelyn Chapple's eyes lit up at the impending crackle of friction displayed before her.

Then, as if deemed by the turn of a switch, Greg reverted to the charming, selfless character that Karen had become far more accustomed to. He winked before brushing past her and offering the pizza menu to the girls.

Karen stood with hands on hips, awaiting some reference to an apology. It begrudgingly arrived albeit in veiled, even slightly mocking tones.

'Only joking, Kaz. If you don't want me to take you out…that's fine by me. At least I know where I stand on things.'

Big Chief Crazyhorse readily took the uninvited chance to interject.

'Yes, Karen. At least he knows you won't be stringing him along. You've got to be straight with our Greg. He gets the wrong impression very easily, you know.'

Karen found herself completely at a loss for words as the sound of Judy's car horn announced her arrival outside.

She did not want Judy to see the Chapples, but Karen was not in control of events.

Kissing her daughters goodbye, Karen pledged to be back home as soon as possible. Chloe and Lauren seemed untroubled as their interest was now firmly fixed on the opening film credits on the screen.

Greg followed her out of the front door and toward Judy's car.

He grinned knowingly as Judy's evident dismay at seeing him fuelled her immediate agitation.

So much so that it caused her to restart the engine and press down on the throttle.

'Hello, again, Jude.' he sneered.

Judy did not reply and wound up her window whilst staring straight ahead.

Once more Greg enjoyed the competitive arena that he now found himself immersed in.

'Take as long as you like, Kaz. Don't feel you've got to rush your evening. I'll be here waiting when you get back.'

Offering a muffled thank you, Karen jumped into the passenger seat and the car raced off.

Evelyn strolled onto the pavement to join her son and followed the path of Judy's car as it merged with the distant trunk road traffic.

With a knowing look to her son, she returned to the front door of number forty-one.

'Right then. I'll leave you to it, lad. Well done. See you later.'

Greg continued to stare into the distance, his thoughts concentrated solely on the evening ahead.

fifteen

Judy and Karen departed arm in arm through the glass doors of the multiplex cinema and cheerfully greeted the mild evening air with a crescendo of giggles.

'That was just the best film I've seen in ages! I think I need to queue up for that again straight away!' gushed Karen.

'I've a better idea, Kaz. Let's pop to the Crown for a nightcap.'

Karen checked her watch in the growing darkness.

Her thoughts were now totally centred on what lay in wait for her at number thirty-nine.

'I ought to be getting back, Jude. It's half-nine gone.'

'Come on, Kaz. Just one drink. I'll get you back before you turn into a pumpkin. Don't worry.'

The Half Crown pub was situated on the outskirts of Church Drayton and presented a relaxing atmosphere for local villagers. Karen and Judy tucked themselves away in the corner snug as they sipped their drinks.

As expected, Judy was keen to discuss the one topic that seemed to have persistently infiltrated their friendship lately.

'Did you notice I kept my mouth shut tonight, Kaz?'

'About what?'

'Him. And his mother. And your daughters. The babysitter. How cute.'

'What about it?'

'Don't keep encouraging him. Don't go and mess things up, Karen. How many times do I have to waste my breath on this issue? I don't fucking trust him. He's well dodgy.'

Karen emptied her glass and chuckled to herself.

'He's about as dangerous as a teddy bear. You just don't like him. I've learned to deal with that. But it doesn't mean *I* can't be friends with him, does it? Besides, he's useful when I need him to move sheds and stuff.'

Judy was not smiling as her friend spoke.

There was real strand of foreboding in her tone, which partially unsettled Karen.

It wasn't like Judy Simpson to be serious about anything in life.

'Robert's home tomorrow, isn't he?'

'Yes, Jude...why?'

'Does he know that Greg's babysitting instead of your mum?'

'No...I've not even told him I'm out tonight. I'll ring him later. But it's not a problem, Jude. Anyway...it's high time you got *yourself* a bloke so I can give *you* the lecture on the potential evils of men.'

Judy shook her head in disapproving amusement and drained her own glass.

'Come on, Cinders. Let's get you home.'

*****

As Karen waved goodbye to her friend and turned toward the house, she saw that the lounge lights were switched off. Peering closer through the glass at the drawn curtains, it was apparent that the television had also been turned off.

Strange.

Although the front door rightly remained unlocked as Greg had no key.

Greg assured her that he'd let the girls stay up late so she could put them to bed. Besides which, they always stood at the front window to greet their mother on her return from a night out.

Quietly entering the hallway, Karen placed her handbag on the console table and eased the door shut behind her. Flicking on the hall lamp, she crept upstairs.

The house was silent. The girls must have been tired if they've gone to bed this early.

All seemed well as Karen peaked around each bedroom door in turn to see Chloe and Lauren snoozing away with the fairies. She felt a little easier knowing that her daughters must have been ready for sleep.

But Greg's current whereabouts was more disconcerting.

Surely, he wouldn't have just gone home and left them without being able to secure the premises?

The hall lamp guided her creaking descent back down the stairs and into the lounge. Illuminating the living room, Karen's eyes glanced at the clock on the mantelpiece.

Nearly ten-thirty.

Her anger was now beginning to arrest her conscience.

Karen could not believe the irresponsible attitude of the friend she had trusted to guard her babies. Well, it would be the first and last time. If she could not rely on him, it was futile him volunteering.

Entering the unlit kitchen, Karen pulled open the fridge door for the carton of orange juice, in turn casting a shaft of white light across the kitchen floor. She drank deeply, knowing that if the girls caught her drinking straight from the carton they would not be impressed. After all, Karen always insists that they use a beaker for drinks.

Karen's mind raced with the unthinkable.

Her darling little girls.

Alone in the house.

Whilst she was sat in the pub, indeed.

If Rob found out he would go absolutely nuts. Karen opted to wait until morning to confront her deserting babysitter.

Then at that precise moment, the decision was taken from her.

'Took your time, didn't you?'

The resoundingly deep tone of Greg's voice emanated from the back wall of the kitchen, shocking Karen into dropping the carton of juice to the floor.

Slamming the light on, Karen struggled to believe her eyes as Greg stood leaning against her sink with one of Robert's beer cans in his hand. Three more empty cans lay crushed on the worktop next to him.

Karen squinted in disbelief at the figure stood before her.

'What the bloody hell do you think you're doing? Why are you standing in the dark? You scared the shit out of me, you prat!'

Greg's expression remained unmoved as he took a swig from the can. He placed his free hand in his pocket and continued to stare at her.

'I've been waiting here for two hours. Where have you been?'

Karen was now gradually beginning to lose her temper.

Whatever game Greg thought he was playing was not acceptable.

Her confusion matched the growing antagonism.

'You *know* where I've been. The cinema. There's no way I'd have been back for half-eight. Stop being silly. Why was the house in darkness?'

Greg placed his beer on the worktop and moved toward her.

Karen's heart instinctively began to beat faster, and it crossed her mind to retreat. Yet something stopped her. Her own will rooted her to the spot as Greg now stood at arm's length.

Then suddenly, his scowl evolved into a smile as he placed both hands on Karen's shoulders.

She was still wary as he moved his face within inches of her own. Her chest felt like it was about to burst, but not with fear or anger. More in anticipation that something forbidden was about to occur.

The danger was intoxicating. Yet this was all wrong. The entire situation was completely inappropriate. The silence seemed to go on forever before Greg finally released the tension.

'Only joking, Kaz. Rob's phoned earlier. I said you were out on the piss.'

Karen's renewed reaction of horror induced a loud guffaw from her friend.

'Look at your face! Don't take me so seriously, Kaz. I'm joking again!'

Finally, she felt calmed enough to be able to contribute to the conversation.

'What did Rob say?'

'Oh, he was fine about me sitting the girls. Glad in fact. Said he loves you and he'll see you tomorrow. That sort of stuff. Just a quick call, you know.'

Karen felt suddenly weary and expressed a wish to get to bed. What came next was uninvited and certainly unprecedented. Greg bid her sweet dreams as he passed her in the kitchen doorway, before leaning across and planting a firm kiss on her lips.

In her stomach, she felt a warm sensation tinged with ice.

In the reality of the moment, Karen was dumbstruck.

Rigid with shock and amid a titanic struggle to register what had just happened.

By the time she had rapidly gathered her thoughts on the matter Greg had closed the front door behind him and returned home.

Swishing a damp tea towel across the floor, she mopped up the puddle of orange juice and placed the towel in the empty washing machine. Opting for cocoa as an alternative, Karen heated a pan of milk and emptied chocolate powder into a large mug. Then finally it was time to head upstairs for the sanctity of the bedroom. Not that the adrenaline coursing through her blood stream would allow much sleep for a while.

Checking the girls once again, she entered her own room and switched on the bedside lamp.

Setting down the mug, Karen became overwhelmed by the instinctive feeling that something was amiss.

The bedclothes were a mess. She had made the bed herself every day for as long as she could remember. Each morning it was neatly arranged into the same order. She could do it blindfolded these days. She observed her collection of stuffed teddy bears on the duvet. They were definitely not how she liked to position them.

Certainly not how she had left them that morning.

The thought came and went through her head that the girls may have been jumping on the bed to tease Greg before they went to sleep. A practise they often employed on their own beds to annoy their grandmother at bedtime.

Yes. That must be the explanation.

After all, there was no likely alternative.

Stripping off in front of the pine dress mirror, Karen noticed another anomaly in the reflection. Her gaze rested on the chest of drawers under the windowsill. The middle drawer - the drawer containing her underwear - was half open. The contents had evidently been disturbed.

But not by her.

And it was also most unlikely that it would have been the girls.

Perhaps she had not closed it properly before leaving earlier. That was a possibility - however untypical it might be.

But Karen was nothing if not house proud. Especially since Robert was working away. Karen never left anything untidy.

Particularly something as personal as a bedroom drawer.

Too tired to contemplate the puzzle further, Karen pushed the garments together and shut the drawer before closing the curtains. Changing into her nightdress she found herself diving under the ruffled duvet. Her head hit the pillow and sank into its downy embrace.

Only when her head settled and her concentration on the world around her lessened, did she notice the folded piece of paper on the adjacent pillow.

Weary eyes struggled to re-focus in the half light as she stretched an arm across to switch on Robert's bedside lamp and retrieve the item.

She leaned on one elbow as curiosity abounded.

Unfolding it revealed a hand-written message.

It soon became obvious that it was from the person who had been in her bed.

No doubt the same person who had rummaged in her drawer.

She read it again and again as her mind reawakened to the combatting prospects of the uncertain and the certain.

Karen continued to hold the note between finger and thumb, re-reading the scrawl inscribed in red felt tip pen.

Dear Kaz. Hope the bed was warmed up enough. Love G x

Resisting the stirring will to rise from the duvet and confront the self-pronounced intruder, Karen laid down her head once more as thoughts raced and clashed around her mind.

The mental roller coaster eventually subsided until the manacle of sleep finally claimed her.

sixteen

The alarm clock did not sound, because the alarm clock had not been set. Sunlight streamed through the narrow gap in Karen's bedroom curtains. The first signal that a new day had begun and notification that she was very late in greeting its arrival.

Pushing herself off the mattress, Karen cut a very unsteady path onto the landing and pushed open the girls' bedroom doors simultaneously.

'Chloe! Lauren! Hurry up! We're running very late! It's gone eight! Move yourselves!'

Despite a head that had yet to catch up with the fact that her body had decided to move, Karen's thoughts immediately transferred to those of the previous night.

Sleeping on the matter had provided little in the way of a solution in what to do next.

On the one hand, Greg had seemingly stepped over the boundary of trust. On the other hand, he was probably bored whilst doing her a favour. If the girls had gone to bed early, it would have been a pretty dull night for him. Maybe he needed to lay his head down for a while.

Karen could not decide how she felt about it all.

Had Greg actually done anything wrong?

Karen's inner debate was tempered by the need to set the breakfast table. The clatter of cereal, bowls and spoons was accompanied by her further shouts in response to the lack of activity upstairs.

'Oy! You two! Shift it!'

Switching on the kettle and radio helped bring the house to life. It was a home of noises. Karen wasn't used to silence and didn't like it. Music was the basic requirement to any day, whether in the car, in the bath or first thing in a morning.

The taste of coffee injected new life into tired bones.

Eventually after a couple more echoing demands for her daughters to leave their beds and with the time approaching half past eight, two pairs of bare feet padded their way into the kitchen as the owners slumped into their chairs.

'I wanted to sit there, Chloe!'

'Tough luck. Too slow.'

Lauren threw daggers at her elder sister before catching the weary eye of her mother.

'Mummy…tell her.'

'Lauren, it doesn't matter where you sit. Crispies or Wheaties?' sighed Karen, holding a cereal box in each hand.

'I want to pour mine out, Mummy. Let me.'

The four-year-old reached out for one of the boxes of cereal.

'We haven't time to mess about this morning, Lauren. I'll pour for both of you otherwise we'll all still be here at dinnertime.'

Lauren threw both her sister and mother a look of defeated scorn.

A reaction that did not go down well with Karen.

'I don't know why *you're* so grumpy this morning. You've had plenty of sleep. Had an early night last night, didn't you? What happened to the usual game of being naughty like you are when Grandma comes to baby-sit?'

Immediately, Lauren's thoughts turned to the previous evening's entertainment and forced her grimace into a grin of delight.

'It was brill last night, Mummy!' Chloe interjected. 'We watched The Lion King! And we had pizza from a man at the door!'

Karen laughed as she drained her mug ready for a refill.

'Oh, you did, eh? Properly spoiled weren't you, then?'

Lauren took a mouthful of cereal before re-joining the conversation.

'Can we have pizza tonight, Mummy? From the same man?'

'Maybe. If you hurry up with your breakfast and then get ready for school.'

Karen turned up the radio as the girls crunched their breakfast in the background. Judging by the view through the window, it looked like being another beautiful day. A minute or two passed before Karen's mental solitude was interrupted by Chloe.

'Greg's funny. He was making us laugh. Can he baby-sit for us all the time, Mummy?'

Karen turned to her daughters as she cradled her fresh mug of coffee.

'Perhaps. We'll see. Now eat up and then get your faces washed and clean your teeth, please. Your uniforms are on the sofa.'

As she got dressed upstairs, Karen's mind toiled once more with the correct way to respond to Greg's supposed trawl through her bedroom.

Her reactions seemed to alter by the minute.

She was peeved that he had been so presumptuous and invasive. Yet the girls evidently had a wonderful time with him. Telling him he was no longer required seemed inappropriate.

Twenty minutes later after a frantic process of dressing, brushing of hair and locating shoes, the Aspinall ladies spilled from the front door of number thirty-nine and clambered into Karen's car for the journey to school. The radio pounded the door speakers as they veered through the village.

'I've just thought…we can't have pizza tonight, girls. Sorry.'

A united chorus of disapproval sounded from the back seat.

Karen eyed the rear-view mirror which reflected two cherubic if miserable faces.

'Why not, mummy?' asked a gutted Lauren.

'Cos Daddy is home tonight. He'll want something else. Probably steak. Perhaps he'll order pizza for us all tomorrow.'

'But we don't like steak.' added a perturbed Chloe.

'Yes, but Daddy won't order pizza for just you two. It's not worth it.'

'Greg did! Greg's nice to us!' argued Chloe.

Karen talked into the mirror as she drove through the back lanes of Church Drayton.

'Daddy's nice to you too, Chloe.'

The eldest daughter presented some solid reasoning.

'Yes, but he's never here. He should do what *we* want when he comes home. It's not fair.'

It was the first time that either of the girls had expressed an opinion on their father's absence. Three months had passed without them mentioning any hint of dismay about Robert's stay-away role.

Karen initially thought Chloe's outburst disrespectful, yet as she steered the car into the school grounds and pulled on the handbrake, pangs of guilt countered her initial aversion to the point that had just been made.

Karen suddenly felt sorry for her daughters.

Maybe Robert's absence had begun to affect the family without her even realising.

Perhaps now the cracks were beginning to show.

They were missing their father.

Of course, it would only be natural they were missing him.

And only recently, Robert himself had alluded to the possibility that he was effectively becoming a stranger to his own household.

Moreover, it was only to be expected that Greg would be incurring some kind of positive influence over the lives of Chloe and Lauren. After all, he saw them far more often than Robert did these days.

Perhaps she ought to listen to her children occasionally.

Then suddenly, with one phrase, Chloe eradicated all her mother's sympathy as she pulled herself from the rear passenger seat and kissed her mother through the open window.

'Greg says that Daddy can't love us very much anymore as he's never home. And I think Greg fancies you, Mummy! See ya later!'

Karen sat motionless behind the wheel.

Literally stuck for words.

Gobsmacked by her own offspring.

Chloe spoke with unwelcome honesty. She was growing up. Her views were forthright and justified, if painful to hear at first hand. Lauren sat in the seat behind watching her elder sister enter the main school door.

A mother's emotions lurched from one extreme to the other.

Karen did not know how she was supposed to feel in such circumstances. The message was now clear that Greg was playing a furtive game in trying to make himself attractive as a potential boyfriend. He had obviously mentioned this to the girls - or at very least, they had picked up on the signs over the past few weeks.

Karen gripped the wheel and stared blankly ahead over the car bonnet. Perhaps she ought to begin taking things rather more seriously.

Judy may have been right all along.

The whole thing was a powder keg just waiting for the fuse to be lit.

A bubble that was waiting to be burst.

Yet had anybody actually done anything to be reproached for?

Friendship with Greg was as far as it had got or would ever get for that matter. But the perception of the scenario was a different issue altogether.

Vivid imaginations and exaggerated rumours could incur great problems into what was basically a very happy existence for the Aspinalls. Yet the situation and any consequences would not affect the Chapples one way or the other.

And they knew it.

This line of thought shored up the concerns that Judy had conveyed.

That the Chapples were not to be trusted.

But Karen did not want to believe that.

She did not want to burn any bridges or isolate people.

There was no good reason to.

At least, not yet.

*****

Karen took Lauren to nursery and made her weekly trudge around the local supermarket. Selecting suitable items for the trolley seemed to take an age. Karen could not focus on where she was or what she was doing. Her mind was in a fog of uncertainty. There was no guiding light to show her the way.

An hour later as she emptied the carrier bags in the kitchen cupboards, the front door rattled with the knock of an uninvited visitor. Begrudgingly, Karen shuffled through to the hall to answer it. If only she had a spy hole in the door. It would be far more convenient not to bother acknowledging the visitor at all. She was in no mood for frivolity.

Especially on revealing the identity of the caller.

'Hi Evelyn. What's up?'

Big Chief Crazyhorse crossed her baggy arms and offered an inciteful smirk.

'You look tired, Kaz. Well, come on. Get that kettle on. I'm gagging!'

Karen's lack of enthusiasm must have been on display for her friend to see.

'You okay, love? Late night, was it?'

'No. Late morning. The alarm didn't go off. I've had a bit of a rush start. Come in, Evelyn.'

Across the kitchen table, the neighbours eyed each other with mutual concern. But motives for that concern could not have been more different.

Coffee was quickly made. Karen cradled her mug in expectation of the subject at hand.

She almost predicted the exact content of Evelyn's opening lines.

Greg, Greg, and more bloody Greg.

'He enjoyed himself last night. Says he'll do it more often if you want. Though, I think he'd prefer to be the one going out *with* you!'

Evelyn emitted a chuckle that echoed into her coffee.

'Not an option is it, Evelyn? Not really.' replied Karen, bluntly.

Evelyn seemed almost shocked by the reply.

'Well, I told you he gets the wrong messages, Kaz.'

'I haven't knowingly *given* him any messages. He seems to decide things in his own head, regardless of my input.'

Silence resumed for a few awkward seconds.

'He was tired last night. Did he tell you?'

'Not in so many words. But I think he took a quick nap in my bed. Not part of a normal babysitting arrangement, is it?'

'Well, he did tell me about that when he got in. I thought it was a bit cheeky myself! But it's all harmless, isn't it?'

Karen felt her reservations beginning to fade once again.

Any trepidation or doubt seemed to vanish once she discussed things about the Chapples that bothered her.

Perhaps she was weak-minded.

Perhaps not.

Nonetheless, Evelyn managed to assuage her fears as the conversation developed.

'Greg's not out to annoy you, Karen. He's really taken to you and the kids. He'd do anything for you. You must know that by now.'

'Yes, but he makes it obvious he might expect more at times.'

Again, Evelyn displayed an unreadable grin.

'Well, you are a looker, Karen. And he's a fit healthy young man. It's inevitable that attraction will come into things.'

'Not when I'm married, Evelyn! Impossible.'

Evelyn lowered her tone and leaned across the table.

'Forgive me for saying so, Karen, but at times you don't *act* very married. Sometimes you act as though you might fancy a bit of danger in your life. Like I keep saying…wrong impressions…'

Once more, dual emotions simmered away inside Karen's conscience. Was Evelyn being serious or just teasing again? It was becoming more difficult to distinguish the difference these days.

Like her son, she was quite adept at not saying what she meant. The true implications of her words were hard to decipher. Karen was becoming tired of the game as the Chapple Matriarch spoke again.

'Did Greg remind you about his birthday?'

Another invitation forthcoming.

Another chance for speculation.

Another shroud of dread engulfed Karen.

'No. Not last night. Why?'

'Well…he's twenty-six next week. He wondered if you might like to go out with him into Tenbridge. Perhaps for a few drinks?'

Karen grappled for a rapid response.

Pinned to the target board, she stalled for an answer.

As per usual, Evelyn had everything worked out.

'I'll stay with the girls for the night. You two will have fun together. He was a little shy to ask you himself. He knows that you think he's trying to put pressure on you. So, I said I'd ask you for him.'

Suddenly, Greg was bathed in a different kind of light.

The kind that portrayed him as a shy, bashful, modest creature. These qualities appealed to Karen. She understood them.

She felt safer with the quiet, withdrawn types.

Then she hit Evelyn with the perfect reply.

'That sounds good. I'll pass on the invite to Robert. We'll look forward to it.'

Evelyn's quickfire reply conveyed a sense of desperation.

'Oh no! Robert can't come…well…I mean…he'll be at work. Greg wants to go out on his actual birthday. On Thursday.'

Whilst smacking of pre-planning, the day mentioned afforded Karen a chance to intervene with a minor condition of her own.

'If it's on a Thursday, the girls will be able to stay at my parents' house. They go there every week on Wednesdays after school, anyway. My mum can get them up the next morning and take them to school with Dad. So, there'll be no need for a sitter after all.'

Evelyn Chapple's disgruntled features forced themselves into a reluctant half-smile.

'It's sorted then. You and Greg. Next Thursday.'

Karen continued to submit another her own specifications.

'And…Judy…and I reckon she'll bring somebody along to make up the foursome. Sounds great!'

Karen's inner sense of victory comforted her.

Yes, Greg could take her out. But not alone.

Karen would try a subtle way of throwing him off the scent.

He would not refuse the chance of an evening out with her. But he'd have to accommodate the others as well.

He could like it or lump it.

His choice entirely.

Evelyn did not outstay her welcome for once and bid Karen a hasty goodbye after finishing her drink.

'I'll be sure to let Greg know you've accepted his invite.'

'What about another coffee?'

'Another time.'

Karen simply nodded as she closed the front door after her friend.

She was not in any position to say no to the offer of a date, but Greg wasn't going to have it all his own way.

Not this time.

This time, Karen would call some shots.

*****

Some minutes later, Karen had put away the remainder of the shopping and emptied and refilled the washing machine.

The kitchen radio was brought to life once more, vibrating the room with its energetic pop beat.

Concentrating on the task as she sang along, her attention was not drawn to the back garden, where a certain neighbour and her only son were watching Karen sternly over the fence gate.

As his teeth ground together, Greg tightly gripped the top of the gate, contemplating his own fury.

When Karen finally emerged to erect the rotary washing line in her own back garden, she was alone, but for the lingering presence of unruly minds.

seventeen

'Daddy! Daddy!'

Robert waited contentedly in the company's metallic-blue automatic as he watched his wife swing open the front gate to allow him access on to the drive. The calls of his daughters were music to his ears. Settling in behind Karen's car, he secured the hand brake as Chloe and Lauren bounded toward his open window.

'Hi, darlings. You both good? Okay, Lauren. Let me get out then I'll carry you!'

With a girl cradled in each arm, Robert kissed his wife as she relieved him of his briefcase and led the group inside. She was glad to shut the rest of the world out. For it was at these moments on a Friday night, she realised just how much she loved her husband, and how much his absence was truly hurting.

Laughter accompanied the family through the hallway and into the lounge. Squeals of delight resonated as Chloe and Lauren exchanged kisses, hugs and playful tickles with their father. Karen placed Robert's briefcase on the kitchen table and pulled a beer can from the fridge door.

'Drink, love? I'm sure you're ready!'

'Wonderful. Ready isn't the word!'

Man and wife embraced tightly in the kitchen as their daughters stood patiently by, awaiting their next turn.

Karen held her husband close.

Closer than she felt she had done in an age.

Robert sensed her eagerness to touch him.

He had no idea of her true motives, suspecting only that it must be because of a fonder heart.

Karen eventually drew away as the girls competed for their father's attention once again.

'So, how's life in Coventry treating you?' she enquired, handing him his beer.

'Good. Good. No complaints. Not as good as life here, but then nothing is as good as coming home. No, work is fine. Dealt with my first disciplinary today. Didn't sack him though! He's too good to give to anyone else!'

Karen nodded in admiration of her executive, caring husband.

'He'd been using company credit for domestic use. He won't be anymore, though. I confiscated his card!'

Robert collapsed onto a dining chair as Lauren fought to clamber onto his knee. Offering a helping hand, he pulled her close as he sampled from the beer can.

Karen placed herself across the kitchen table. She wanted to see the face of the man she married. The will to familiarise herself with him once more was overpowering.

She needed to recognise Robert Aspinall all over again.

It was a most pleasurable task.

Especially as it served to eclipse her anxieties regarding current, external relationships.

'I could bore you all weekend about computers, Karen. Tell me about *your* week. How's things this end?'

'Oh, fine. Nothing drastic to report. Mum and Dad are fine. Asked how you were. School seems quiet at the moment, thankfully. Nothing dramatic happening there. Erm...went to the pictures with Judy last night. Sorry I missed your call.'

Robert took another swig from the can and smiled at Lauren.

His attention was only half-focused on what Karen had just said.

'Oh yes...the pictures. Anything good?'

'Yes, bit of a tearjerker. Can't remember the actor's name but I think I now love him nearly as much as I love you! Like I say, that's why I couldn't take your call. Sorry, love.'

Chloe forced her head underneath her father's free arm, nearly causing him to spill the contents of the can.

Robert then looked at Karen, slightly confused.

'Call? I didn't call last night. I couldn't get to a phone. I was out myself. Stuck at this bloody evening seminar with some bigwigs of the sister company. I could have done with phoning you to get me away from the damned place for half an hour!'

Karen's temporarily suppressed misgivings about her neighbour suddenly honed back into view.

'But...I came in at gone ten...and...'

Robert stared at her in bemusement, anticipating some sense might accompany her continuing response.

'...well, you know Evelyn's son, Greg, from next door? He baby-sat the girls for me, which I thought very kind. I'm sure he'd said you had phoned...'

Her husband simply smiled back in her direction and tickled his daughters who simultaneously shrieked with excitement.

'Must be age, love. Your memory's going. Can't remember the night before? I don't know. Losing your marbles at thirty! What hope is there?'

She watched her husband chuckle to himself. She was not losing her mind or her memory.

Greg had definitely claimed to have spoken to Robert. She recalled it as though it was only a minute ago.

Why would he make it up? Why concoct such a silly story?

Was he expecting to cause trouble if the truth came out about him being the nominated babysitter?

Perversely enough, it was the only conclusion that Karen could determine. Greg evidently expected Robert to express some displeasure about the scenario. A prediction he had gotten totally wrong. Served him right.

Inventing stupid stories.

Making things up to create an argument.

It was the kind of thing that children did.

Yet worryingly, Greg was no child.

Robert's response to the revelation could not have been more placating.

'Good lad, that Greg. A local super-hero. Top bloke.'

*****

As they sat to dinner later that night, Karen's mind was struggling to attune to the fact that her husband was back at home with her once again. Her concentration wavered to and from the business with the Chapples.

The situation was confusing at best.

Very disconcerting at worst.

Karen was unsure whether to trust her own judgment at that moment, yet it felt impossible to go and talk to anyone about how she felt.

Least of all to the man who sat across the dining table from her.

Opting to broach the subject of her latest invitation, she held her breath as she spoke.

'It's Greg's birthday next week. He's asked me and Judy out for a few drinks. What do you think about it?'

Robert stopped chewing his steak and looked vacantly at his wife.

'I…I don't understand what you mean, Kaz.'

'Do you think I should go? It's on Thursday. Just going into town, I think. Would you mind if I went…with Judy…I meant?'

He offered a look of distinct puzzlement.

'Of course I don't mind! Why would I mind? Have a drink for me. I'll offer my apologies for not being able to make it when I see him over the weekend.'

Robert placed another morsel of rump into his mouth as Karen continued to play idly with her own food.

He stopped chewing again and watched her for a second or two.

'Are you alright, love? You seem a bit pre-occupied. Nothing bothering you, is there?'

Shocked into a reply, she directed her attention back to the table and swallowed a lump of trepidation.

'Yes, I'm fine, Rob. Why? Do I not seem okay, to you?'

'Yeah…a bit quiet perhaps…but still gorgeous as ever!'

Karen smiled at her man and flashed her blue eyes.

Eyes that were training themselves to disguise the torment she was beginning to feel in her soul.

eighteen

The elements had adopted a greyer hue the following morning. Church Drayton had become accustomed to a canopy of brilliant blue sky for weeks.

But not today.

As Karen pulled herself upwards from the mattress and squinted into the facing dressing table mirror, the absence of familiar sunlight streaming into the bedroom had been notably replaced by a fearful dullness.

And by a silence.

A numbing, unyielding silence.

As was customary for any Saturday morning in the life of the Aspinalls, Karen yawned her way downstairs to hear the hushed volume of the TV set become gradually louder as she reached the closed lounge door.

Pushing it open with one finger she then poked her head through the gap to see her two beloved daughters sat cross-legged on the hearth rug, totally enraptured in the chaotic activity on the screen.

Two empty cereal dishes were place in front of them. Karen smirked as she stood unannounced behind Chloe and Lauren. Still in their nightdresses, they looked like two little orphans with begging bowls.

'Morning ladies.' Karen croaked.

'Mummy! Mummy!' came the instant dual reply

Lauren jumped to her feet and rushed across to her mother before offering her the tightest and most heartfelt of embraces around her legs.

'You two are quiet as mice. What time did you get up?'

Lauren engaged her mother's gaze and presented her most bizarre cross-eyed face.

'You must stop doing that. I've told you if the wind changes, you'll stay like it!'

'That's what Grandad says as well.' concurred Chloe, whose attention had also temporarily diverted from the screen.

'I need coffee. Where's your dad? Has he gone out already?'

Both girls resumed their former positions four feet from the television screen and replied in harmony.

'Don't know, Mummy.'

The kitchen was almost in darkness with the slate shroud that passed for sky framing a rather dank looking view through the window.

In turn flicking on the lamp and the radio, Karen intended to try and bring some much-needed atmosphere to the situation. She then visually located Robert as he prowled around the back garden like some lion guarding his territory.

It was difficult to establish what her husband was actually doing, but at that precise moment, Karen' priority was for an intake of caffeine as she bellowed beyond the back door.

'Rob...do you want a drink, love?'

His thumbs-up affirmed his thanks for her offer as he gradually made his way along the garden path back to the patio.

'Morning, my sweet. Sleep well?'

'Yes, love. You?'

His attention drew back through the window to the dimness of the rear yard.

'No...not really. Something woke me in the middle of the night. About three-ish. I couldn't get off after that. I was up and at the paper shop for six!'

Karen reheated the kettle.

Robert's words took their time to register as she pulled mugs from the cupboard.

'What do you mean...*something* woke you?'

Robert continued to stare at the back lawn and scratched his chin.

'A noise. Well...a series of noises, actually. Sounded like it was coming from the back. I've just been out looking for evidence.'

She couldn't explain her reasoning, but something instinctive told Karen that Robert's imagination was not working overtime.

She too had stirred in the dead of night with the thought she had heard activity outside, but at that moment declined to say so.

'There's a lot of things it could have been, Rob. A fox? A dog? A hedgehog...anything.'

Robert laughed without restraint.

'A *hedgehog*? What...sounding like a frigging Jack-hammer? Come of it, Kaz! Bloody big hedgehog!'

Karen mirrored her husband's smirk as she poured hot water into his mug and stirred it.

'Here then, smart-arse! I don't know what it was, do I? Perhaps Big Chief next door was out riding her bloody horse!'

Man and wife immediately burst into a fit of the giggles as the image simultaneously formed in their minds of Evelyn Chapple astride a trusty mount.

'Jesus, Kaz! I bet the banging was the horse's belly dragging on the ground under the strain!'

More laughter echoed from the open kitchen doorway.

The echo of which travelled down the garden, just as Greg emerged from the shadows next door to survey the arena.

'There's our neighbour. I'll go and ask him if he heard anything last night.'

Before Karen could respond, Robert was gone and at the fence gate in a flash.

Again, the unwarranted anxiety returned as she observed the scene unfolding before her in the rear garden.

Greg was so kind in some ways, yet underneath there was something elusive about him that Karen could not quite grasp.

He seemed regularly intent on being economical with the truth when it suited.

Not out and out lies. Just silly bouts of misinformation that seemed to be deliberately confusing.

The thought had occurred to Karen more than once that at times it seemed Greg was enjoying the uncertainty he created.

A game he wanted to play, yet only he knew the rules.

None of it made sense.

She watched him in conversation with Robert. She saw that Greg was far more interested in looking elsewhere.

His stare fixed itself on the house as he eventually spotted Karen watching at the kitchen window, cradling her coffee.

Both men waved toward her.

She did not respond.

'Bet she hasn't seen us, Greg. She's a bit vacant this early in a morning.'

'Yeah, Rob…I know what you mean…'

Karen studied the soundless movement of lips as if to ascertain the subject of their conversation. Then suddenly, Robert gestured toward the shed. Greg shrugged his shoulders as they continued the dialogue.

A teasing glimpse of sunshine split the blanket of blackened cloud to temporarily bathe the garden in golden rays.

But the treat from the heavens did not last long.

Karen watched her husband as he reached over the gate and shook Greg's hand before retrieving his wallet from his back pocket and giving him money. One, single note. Impossible to determine the value.

The men continued to chat.

Greg glanced at intervals toward the back door of number thirty-nine, directly at Karen's curious form.

Then, no sooner had Robert turned his back, Greg was gone.

Like a phantom visiting his playground of disturbance.

One moment there; the next…nothing.

Robert carried a smile and an empty coffee mug back to the kitchen.

'I could do with another one of those, Kaz. Thirsty work this pottering about, lark!'

Karen felt herself becoming quietly aggrieved, not only at what had just transpired over the fence, but also the fact that Robert did not seem intent on offering any kind of explanation. She re-boiled the kettle before opening her line of angered enquiry.

'Rob, what did you give Greg money for?'

He husband sat down at the table and unfolded his newspaper.

'For moving the shed, of course. I think I ought to show some gratitude for the job he's done…don't you?'

Karen's surprised tone left Robert in no doubt that he had done the wrong thing in her eyes. She reinforced her standpoint.

'But if I had *wanted* him to do it, I would have paid him at the time *myself*.'

Robert offered his wife a look of bemusement as he peered over the top of the paper.

'Do you mean he *volunteered* to shift the shed?'

'Yes, I bloody do! That's *exactly* what I mean! I couldn't have stopped him if I'd have wanted to! He was like a man possessed as soon as I mentioned the bloody thing!'

Robert chuckled as his eyes scanned the day's headlines which did not serve to lighten Karen's overview on the matter.

'What's so bloody funny about it? More to the point, how much did you just give him?'

'Only twenty quid, love. Just twenty.'

'Twenty bloody quid! That could have helped buy Lauren some new shoes!'

Again, Robert looked to his wife, now more than a little stupefied by her attitude.

'But he's done us a favour, Kaz. You wanted the shed moving, didn't you? Greg's moved it. Problem solved. I'm showing our gratitude, that's all. No big deal? Now then… where's my drink?'

Karen was now beginning to fume inwardly.

Why would Greg refuse money off her when he initially did the job, yet take payment from Robert a few weeks later?

'It's not your gesture that's annoyed me, Rob. It's the fact that he's took the money. I don't get it.'

Robert did not divert his attention from between the pages of his paper.

'Forget it, love. Don't let it ruin your day. Get my bacon on, there's a good little wife.'

Half smiling, Karen turned to face him and placed her hands defiantly on her hips.'

'Erm…Mister Aspinall…'

'Yes, Mrs. Aspinall?'

'Up which particular orifice of your anatomy would you like me to ram the frying pan?'

*****

The unfolding hours brought the eventual welcome return of warm sunshine and a resumption of the garden inspection. Karen joined her husband as they stood next to the shed deciding on the next task.

'Well, I started to dig the borders a couple of weeks ago. But I got bored because you haven't bought me any plants to plant in them yet, have you, sweetie?

Robert offered her a sly yet expectant glare of amusement.

'Garden centre? I've got the hint. Don't panic. We'll go now if you want.'

Karen squealed with delight and offered her man a playful embrace.

The scene of childish romance was interrupted by a new presence on the other side of the fence.

'Look at you two…love's young dream all over again.'

The voice was instantly recognisable.

'Morning, Evelyn…' sighed Karen. '…you okay?'

Entwining her thick forearms, Evelyn Chapple edged nearer to the gate as she whispered.

'Just like to thank you for the money you gave our Greg. Like I said, he wants to feel appreciated.'

The Aspinalls were still arm in arm as Evelyn spoke.

Their neighbour struggled to disguise her abject distaste at the loving display.

'Good friends like you and Greg should be appreciated. You're hard to come by.' gushed Robert in reply. 'Greg's a fine son. He does you credit…as well as keeping an eye on things for me during the week. He's been a godsend over these past few months.'

Evelyn's blank expression did not alter.

'Well, yes…he likes to do his bit…you know…play his part in events…when he gets the chance.'

Karen remained silent as Robert continued heaping the praise.

'I hope he gets many more chances. I'm glad I can rely on you both. I really am. This new job is testing enough without having to worry about what I'm missing at home.'

Evelyn began to walk toward her own house.

She didn't look back as she offered a parting comment.

'So long as he isn't taken for granted. Don't forget his birthday on Thursday, Karen. Greg can't wait.'

Karen did not reply as she watched her friend venture through the back door of number forty-one.

Robert had noticed his wife's minimal contribution to the exchange.

'You alright, love? You really do seem very quiet since I came home last night.'

The mention of the imminent date with Greg had sent shivers down Karen's spine.

Her vulnerability had been exposed once more.

Next week she would be alone once again. On a supposedly friendly date with the man from next door who she did not really know.

No doubt in some place that she knew she would not wish to be.

And without the wonderful husband she truly loved to comfort her as he did so readily at that moment.

Her fears seemed so unfounded, yet nonetheless, they were present and unrelenting.

She steered her thoughts away from the daunting future and accompanied Robert's stride back to the kitchen.

'Come on, husband. You promised to take me to the garden centre. I've got plants to buy.'

nineteen

It was Wednesday before the hot sunshine returned in earnest, encouraging Karen to brave her own territory once again in her bikini top but this time complimented by shorts. Despite Robert's insistence that Karen pick whatever she wanted from the garden centre, just a few trays of small bedding plants was the result of an entire Saturday afternoon's browsing.

Something unseen yet tangible had previously prevented her from exposing herself openly to the ardent sun during the previous forty-eight hours. But Karen's resistance had finally been broken.

Today, she was out to plant her plants.

No ifs or buts.

It was her garden.

Her right.

The sweat trickled down her back and cleavage as she forked away and set down splashes of pink, white and yellow. With the green foliage and soil base, a couple of hours of artistic and practical application had brought the back yard into very effective bloom.

Checking that Lauren was happily occupied in her Wendy house, Karen enjoyed the tranquillity of the early afternoon as she patiently worked through the borders.

But, as was becoming the custom of late, her immersion in solitude was not granted for long.

Greg announced his appearance at the fence gate with a low bark that made Karen jump. She stood to her feet and flexed the muscles in her stiff legs. Whereas before, she would have been under Greg's admiring gaze, his attitude now seemed different.

He did not even glance at her browning form.

His eyes bored into hers as she faced him.

'Hi, Greg. Alright?'

His pause in response was purposed and somewhat agonised.

His mood was difficult for her to judge.

Karen now realised why she had stayed indoors for the past couple of days. Greg's demeanour was becoming unsettling.

There was little in the way of friendship emitting from her neighbour.

His expression was one of suppressed frustration, finally borne out by his manner of address.

'Why haven't I seen you all week?'

'What are you talking about?'

'Don't piss me about. Have you been avoiding me?'

Karen's heart pumped instinctively faster in her chest. How she wished that Robert was there with her at that moment. Greg was noticeably reticent when her husband was around.

Yet there and then, Karen felt defenceless and isolated.

Like a slave in the lion's den.

'I beg your pardon. I haven't been avoiding anyone. Stop being so childish, Greg! Rob's been home…as if you hadn't noticed.'

Greg gripped the top of the gate as if preparing to tear it from its hinges. Karen nurtured a sudden sense of defiance. If Greg wanted to act with such immaturity, then she would only be obliged to point out the fact.

'Are they the plants he bought you at the weekend?'

'Yes. I couldn't be bothered to set them until today. Besides, it's a good chance to top up my tan.'

Only then did his eyes wander down to her womanly form, as Karen felt the irritation at the interruption begin to rise within her.

She was also still annoyed about the issue of the money he took from Robert on Saturday morning.

Her inner will began pushing for an argument.

'Did you actually want to talk to me about something, Greg?'

'Not really. Just came out for some air. And to check you're still alright for tomorrow night.'

She slowly walked towards him. He held his position.

'I wasn't going to ask you, Greg, but being as you're here, I'm going to.'

Greg's eyes widened and a half-smirk finally emerged through the fierce grimace.

'What? If I'll marry you? Like a shot! Just ask!'

Karen was not distracted by his subsequent laughter. It only served to give her confidence in broaching the subject that had bothered her for several days.

'Greg…were you in my bedroom the other night…when I went out with Judy?'

His guilt did not need to be confirmed vocally.

Karen saw by his suddenly sheepish expression.

That he had been in her bed.

That he had opened her underwear drawer.

That he had left the note.

In her own mind, Karen's suspicions were vindicated.

'I don't know what you mean, Kaz? What…in *your* actual bedroom, you mean?'

Despite now being convinced, she decided to defer with a feigned defensive approach.

'I'm sorry…it must have been the girls. If you let them out of your sight for a minute, then they get up to mischief. It doesn't matter.'

It wasn't fair to render her daughters with any level of blame, but the mind trick had worked. Greg had been suckered.

A woman could spot a liar from a mile away.

Even without knowing it, Greg had effectively ended his unsteady friendship with Karen.

She decided in her own mind there and then that Thursday's date would be the final time she would associate herself with Greg Chapple.

The other anomaly regarding Robert's non-existent phone call and the issue surrounding the 'boyfriend' rumours did not warrant further discussion.

Evidently Greg found some degree of pleasure in tormenting people that valued his companionship.

Karen could no longer trust him. That much was obvious.

Judy was correct all along.

'Did your mum tell you about tomorrow?'

A look of expectant horror befell Greg's features.

'What? You're still coming, aren't you?'

'Yes. My mum's having the girls. I'm going to pick up Judy and her friend Josh about six. We can walk into town if it's a nice evening.'

Karen had now visibly aggrieved Greg.

The mere mention of Judy's name was enough to induce a scowl.

He stood back from the gate and folded his arms.

Very reminiscent of his mother, Karen thought.

'Judy? But she's not invited. You are.'

'Yes, well, I've asked her to join us with one of her male friends from work. He's not her boyfriend, so don't ask him if he is.'

Greg moved back toward Karen and hissed his disapproval as he leaned further over the gate.

'You don't need a fucking bodyguard, you know. I'll look after you.'

His suddenly altered temperament completely countered his statement.

Karen felt that she did indeed need someone with her on the night as back up.

'Well, I'm sorry, Greg, but if she doesn't come, then nor do I. It's your choice. Take it or leave it.'

Karen held all the cards as Greg huffed to himself and relented.

'Okay…If that's what you want then…whatever. I'll be round for seven tomorrow night.'

Greg struggled to muster any reasoned excuse for further debate and sauntered off with a begrudging nod.

Karen had seemingly attained the upper hand in the situation.

And it was amusingly obvious that her supposed friend did not like it one bit.

Greg Chapple was not used to being told to play by anything other than his own rules. Karen Aspinall was slowly proving herself to be an opponent of worth.

After tomorrow night, she hoped that the game would come to an end.

Once and for all.

twenty

‘Belts on girls, time to visit Grandma.’

‘Yeahhy!’

With Chloe astounding her mother by emerging from school at the same time as everyone else, Karen steered her way through the throng of parents and pupils and navigated an exit from the school car park. She checked the view behind before climbing through the gearbox at unwarranted speed.

‘Help Lauren with her belt please, Chloe. And don’t pull a face! I can see everything you know, even if I am driving.’

Without the customary accompaniment of a booming stereo, the car cruised in silence through the tree-lined avenues of Church Drayton and on towards Goltham.

The welcoming sight of Jean Hope standing at her front door was a timely reminder of some stability that remained in Karen’s life. She waved to her mother whilst bringing the car to a stop on the driveway behind her father’s trusty old van. In a flash, the girls were unbelted, out of their seats and hanging off each of their grandmother’s arms.

‘Hello, my darlings. Good day at school? Hello Kaz. You okay, love?’

Jean immediately noticed that her daughter appeared strained. Mothers have an instinct for spotting such things about their offspring. Quite often over the years Jean would suspect that her daughter was carrying something on her mind but would not broach the subject unless the symptoms were particularly worrying.

As it was, Karen looked preoccupied and tired, but nothing more. Jean welcomed her family inside.

Brian Hope put his hand inside the wire cage to allow Long John to clamber back onto his perch. The bird acknowledged the entrance of Chloe and Lauren with a hearty squawk and a flap of his wings.

‘Ayup, Long John! Here comes trouble! Got you back in there just in time by the look of it!’

With a kiss for each of his granddaughters, Brian reclined into his armchair as Lauren climbed onto his knee for a cuddle.

‘Hello, tiny. You been a good girl for your mum? Yes of course you have.’

Lauren's squeals of laughter were the result of some serious tickling at the hands of her grandfather. She wriggled and screamed with delight, which in turn encouraged Long John to contribute to the noise.

Whilst her mother performed the task of preparing a pot of tea, Karen slumped into the chair opposite her father and smiled at the playful exchange.

'Don't get her over excited, Dad. She's a bloody nightmare at bedtimes when she's hyper.'

'This little one? A nightmare? I can well believe it! Better keep tickling her then, hadn't I?'

Lauren writhed about as Brian continued to torment her. Finally, she succumbed to her mother's wishes and joined her sister in front of the television. Peace was restored once more.

Brian Hope looked at his daughter and smiled.

'How's things, then?'

Karen averted her gaze and sighed heavily.

'Oh...you know...the usual.'

'And Rob? Coping okay with work?'

'Yes. He seems happy enough.'

Jean set down the tray of teacups on the lounge table and perched herself on a stool between the pair. An uneasy silence ensued.

Brian was not so reserved in assessing his daughter's appearance.

'You look bushed, Karen. You've seemed a bit quiet to me the last couple of times we've seen you. Not your usual self at all. Is something troubling you?'

Karen looked at her parents in turn before answering. She didn't have any problems to confess as such. Aside from a weirdly temperamental neighbour, his obsessive mother, and a husband who she could only see at weekends.

It was very consoling for Karen to think that the former little problem would be dealt with soon enough.

'I'm fine. Honestly. Perhaps I have felt a bit run down of late. I don't know. But I don't feel unwell.'

They weren't convinced. Karen could tell.

But then again, parents were never very good at being kidded.

And Karen was never very good at being a kidder.

'Are you pouring that tea, Jean? I'm parched.'

Karen allowed her weary gaze to rest on her father.

'You been at work today, Dad?'

'No...no. Can't be bothered with it just lately. If people ring up for me, I just pass them on to Charlie or one of the other lads. My knees aren't behaving. I think the end is nigh, my girl!'

Karen chuckled at her father's expression. She was pleased that he had seen some sense. No point working through pain. At last, he was heeding his body's signals.

'Have you been anywhere, Kaz?' asked Jean as she stirred the teapot.

'Oh, only to the garden centre with Rob on Saturday. I set some pansies earlier this afternoon. Look nice. You'd be proud of my expertise with a trowel!'

Karen's father sat up in his seat and grasped his cup and saucer.

'Yes, it's been ideal gardening weather, lately It's given you a good colour too, my girl! Mind...you've always got on with the sun, haven't you? Always had good skin, hasn't she, Jean?'

The trio sipped their tea as Chloe and Lauren quietly gawked at the TV. Karen felt it appropriate to broach the subject there and then.

'Mum...I need to ask a little favour.'

'Yes, love?'

'Can the girls sleep here tomorrow night? I've got to go out. There's no need to get them up for school the next day. They can have it off. They break up soon, anyway. I know they play you up sometimes. I'll pick them up Friday lunchtime.'

Jean responded instantly with an expression of pleasure.

'Of course they can come and sleep, love. But I thought your friend Greg did a good job of baby-sitting last time you went out. Have you sacked him? I thought the girls got along with him.'

Karen only wished it were so and smiled along with her mother's innocent inquiry.

'No. They do get on with him. He's very good with them. But it's Greg I'm going out with. It's his birthday tomorrow. He wants us to go for a drink in town. Judy's coming, I hope. I can't really be bothered, but I said I would.'

Brian watched his daughter as she spoke.

Her discomfort was evident, but he didn't feel it correct to probe for good reason.

Instead, positivity came to the fore.

'He seems a decent lad, that Greg. Helped you out quite a bit lately, hasn't he?'

It felt crazy to be in support of her father's appraisal.

'Yes, Dad. Yes. He's…he's always on hand if I need him.'

Jean blew on her tea as another concern arose.

'Does Rob know that you're going out with him again? This is the second or third time in a few weeks, isn't it? Some people might get the wrong idea, you know!'

'Don't worry about that, Mum! Rob thinks he's the bees' knees. He gave him twenty quid the other day for shifting our shed! Rob knows I'm being looked after if I'm with Greg. There's no problem on that score. I'd just rather the girls came here for the night. That's all.'

*****

Within the hour Karen was headed back home. Brian and Jean watched her red motor car pull away and waved it out of sight before making their way back to the house.

Jean shut the front door as her husband hovered in contemplation.

It seemed inevitable that the next exchange needed ironing out.

'Do you think she's alright, Brian? Very subdued, isn't she? Not her usual buzzing self at all. Do you think Rob's job is beginning to wear her down?'

Brian scratched the back of his head as he entered the lounge.

'I've no doubt it's tiring her out. It was always going to, wasn't it? But she's a big girl. They've made their decision as a family, and we must stay out of it. Besides, if Karen had any real difficulties, I'm sure she'd tell us. She knows she can come to us about anything. Don't you go worrying yourself, Jean Hope.'

'That's what mothers are for Brian. It's our job to worry.'

'Look. Leave it be. She needs to talk it out with Rob if she's not coping. It's nothing to do with us. Besides, she's got good friends as well. There's no problem. Don't interfere.'

Brian placed both hands on his wife's shoulders and smirked.

'I tell you what you can do, though.'

Jean looked at her husband in expectation of some wise prophecy.

'You can tell me what you're cooking me for my tea.'

*****

Karen turned the volume down on the television set as she held the telephone to her ear. The ring tone engaged with its connection.

'It's seven-thirty, girls. Come on. You can watch your programme for an hour if you get your pyjamas on now.'

Eventually, the call was answered, distracting Karen from her intention to get the girls ready for bed. They duly ignored their mother's request anyway and repositioned themselves on the hearth rug listening to Karen's side of the telephone dialogue.

'Hi, Jude. Only me! Still on for tomorrow night?'

'What do mean you forgot?'

'Don't you dare do that to me, girl!'

'Is he coming? Great! Be good company for Greg!'

'Okay. I'll fetch you about six to six-thirty. Okay?'

'Yeah...probably a cab...unless you want to stay here overnight. Be just like old times!'

'Okay, Jude. See you tomorrow night, girly!'

Karen replaced the receiver and turned the volume back up as the shouting from the soap opera echoed around the lounge.

Chloe swivelled position on the rug and engaged her mother with a hopeful wide-eyed smile.

'Mummy...can we watch this first and then put our pyjamas on? Please?'

'Okay...but bed at eight! No messing!'

*****

Darkness encroached outside as light rapidly conceded to shadow.

The rear garden of number thirty-nine, Benton Road, lay still. Not a breath of wind disturbed the scene as nocturnal residents of the area considered their routine pursuits.

A time for the hardy hedgehog to snuffle and scour.

It was the hour for the family of mice that had recently set up home under the shed to race across the lawn and hopefully avoid any feline interest.

And of course, this was also the arena of the wily fox.

Stealth, silence and speed were the attributes of this rarely observed creature as it scavenged for scraps in and around the estate on its regular evening trek.

Of course, the fox takes no interest in flowers.

Neither for food nor for pleasure.

Yet Karen Aspinall will readily accuse this sacred animal of wanton destruction when she awakens the next morning to find most of her bedding plants pulled from their housings and carelessly strewn across the back lawn.

Of course, it must have been a fox, she will claim.

What else could have been so furtively callous and cruel?

Besides, which other beasts would be stalking the gardens of Benton Road in the dead of night?

twenty-one

The day was Thursday. Greg Chapple's twenty-sixth birthday.

A day that would mark the beginning of a new chapter.

The supposed commencement of a different direction for friendship.

The onset of a cold realisation that ignoring one's instinct was an act of folly.

Yet Karen Aspinall thought it best to try and conform to another's wishes, rather than obey her own. She had purposely remained out of the house for most of the day. A visit to the hair salon; a walk along the river. Then on to nursery to collect Lauren and a trip into town.

Anywhere but exhibiting herself under the watchful eye of the Chapples.

She did not relish the prospect of her final night in the company of Greg, but it was seen as the last generous act of a kind-hearted woman who couldn't say no.

The last thing Karen wanted to achieve was upset. Especially not on this day of all days. As his mother would readily remind her, Greg liked to be appreciated. Not taken for granted.

So, it was with this dictum in mind that Karen set about the task of selecting a suitable birthday card for her friend and neighbour.

Lauren crouched at the other end of the greeting card shop playing with the assortment of stuffed toys and immersing herself into a world of playful fantasy. At times, Karen too wished she could join her youngest and forget about the sometime-harsh realities of life.

But of course as a parent and a wife, harsh reality was the only option available most of the time.

Lauren's tiny voice carried down the aisle to Karen's ear.

'Mummy…are you buying Greg a present?'

The thought had already passed through her mind, but Karen had no idea as to what kind of gift Greg would like. A card was enough, surely? She didn't want to encourage his interest again by lavishing him with some expensive trinket.

The evening was destined to be a gentle exercise in disconnecting herself from the situation once and for all.

As cleanly and politely as possible.

'I don't think so, love. Come on. I've picked his card. We've got time to go on the swings before we fetch Chloe from school. Then I've got to get you to Grandma's.'

Karen queued at the cash till pondering the potential turn of the evening's events. She glanced at the card briefly.

On the front was a cartoon drawing of a hunter pointing a large rifle at a little mouse, which quivered in fear.

The caption read, *Hands Up! Where's My Birthday Present?*

It was only on reflection of this image that she decided to return to the selection of teddy bears with Lauren and pick out a small stuffed baby elephant with a red ribbon bow around its neck.

It made Lauren giggle and seemed to suit the intended recipient down to the ground.

'We'll take this as well, shall we? Should manage to raise a smile from him…hopefully!'

Having packed the car with the girls' things earlier that morning there was no need to return home before depositing Chloe and Lauren at her mother's.

A mildly doleful half-hour watching Lauren play on the swings at Greenacres was followed by the journey back to school. Chloe was out of the gates on time once again and in a good mood to boot.

As the car crawled on towards Goltham, Karen's attitude toward the evening ahead was becoming gradually tempered with dread.

The sight of her mother did little to ease her growing reluctance in the matter.

'I don't think I've forgotten anything, Mum. Change of clothes for them both. Pyjamas, toothbrushes, reading books…should do for one night, shouldn't it?'

Karen handed her mother the carrier bag on the front drive and kissed her on the cheek.

'Your dad said he'll take them for a burger later. Give them a nice change, won't it?'

'Yes, lovely idea, Mum. Where is Dad?'

Jean offered her daughter a knowing glance.

'Not working surely, Mum? After all that he said yesterday?'

'I know…I know! But it's a favour for a dear friend, apparently. Your dad doesn't like to let people down. He's promised me it would be a half-hour job. That was three and-a-half hours ago!'

Karen shook her head as a resounding squawk capably echoed from the living room.

'I bet Lauren's poking that blessed bird again. I've told her keep away.'

'It doesn't matter, Kaz. It doesn't matter. Where are you going now?'

'Well, I've got to get in the bath and change, then fetch Judy and her friend. Then we're off out into Tenbridge, I think.'

Jean studied her daughter's expression.

It was guarded and distant.

Difficult to assess.

'We're always here for you, Karen, for anything. Just ask. Don't bottle things up. I know you're troubled about something. Your father has noticed as well. Even if it might be a small and insignificant thing, get it out in the open. Don't fester on it. Have a good time, tonight.'

Karen just wanted to get the impending evening out of the way.

Hopefully then, her whirring mind would placate itself.

She kissed the girls goodbye and embraced her mother.

It was almost hurting inside as she put the car into first gear and trundled along the road. Her thoughts turned to an absent husband and then in turn to her two happy, smiling daughters.

One more night.

Just one more night.

*****

There was no sign of activity from next door as Karen pushed open the big white gate at number thirty-nine before positioning the car on the drive.

Nevertheless, on closing the gate behind her again, she sensed prying eyes watching her.

On further inspection, she was partially satisfied there was nobody around to view her return home.

The knot in her stomach was becoming larger and tighter by the minute. The trepidation was beginning to encroach into Karen's every thought. She felt unable to gain any sensible perspective on the situation. Yet ironically, the cause of her concern was not even strictly genuine.

Greg was a friend whose motives were dubious.

It was suspected that he had broken Karen's trust.

Yet the question repeated itself in her mind on an hourly basis.

Was she overreacting?

Was she overthinking?

Had Greg actually done anything wrong?

Not really.

He had just displayed a potential to upset the Aspinall applecart. The only person that was able to nip things in the bud was Karen herself. She hoped it would be a smooth ride.

Flicking on the kettle she opened the back door and looked at the flowers strewn across the grass as the high early evening sun highlighted the colour of the now limp petals.

Her flowers, that she had spent time and had pleasure in setting.

Her upset, at seeing the mess that greeted her first thing that morning.

Damn those pesky foxes.

As the bubbles formed in a hot steaming tub, Karen thought of her little girls and their undoubted pleasure at being taken for a burger by their grandfather.

How Karen wished she was there to share that moment with them.

Her father was a good, strong man. He had set the benchmark for all men in Karen's life. Maybe that was why she couldn't be excited about the upcoming evening.

Other men rarely made their mark.

Aside from Robert, of course. That went without saying.

Immersing herself into the embracing, aromatic hot water, Karen made the most of the spare hour she had available.

*****

'Sorry I'm late, Jude! Jesus! I nodded off in the bath!'

'Don't worry about it, Kaz. Come in a minute. I'm afraid we've started without you though!'

Judy escorted Karen through her flat to the kitchenette where a vaguely familiar face stood with a glass of wine in his hand.

'Kaz...you remember Josh, don't you? My friend from university! We graduated together...among other things! We're at the Infirmary together now! Small world, eh?'

The chuckles echoed around the room as Karen offered a hand of greeting.

'Pleased to meet you again, Josh. I'm sure we have met before somewhere but can't think where it was. Yes, I'm pretty sure we have.'

The tall, slender man smiled and presented a bony hand of welcome. Karen observed his floppy fringe and wire-framed spectacles as he replied warmly.

'Probably one of Jude's crazy raves. I've met hundreds of people through her and forgotten all their names. The nature of the beast, isn't it? Parties…I mean.'

'Well, yes. I suppose so.' stuttered Karen. 'To be honest it's been a while since I went to a *proper* party…about ten years, maybe!'

Judy checked her handbag and passed a final make-up inspection in the hall mirror.

'Come on then Joshua. Drink up! The birthday boy is waiting!' giggled Judy as she set the flat's burglar alarm.

More laughter abounded as the trio clambered into Karen's car. It was past seven o'clock as they swung into Benton Road. No doubt Greg would be wondering what had happened to his prospective throng.

As Karen pulled onto the drive, she immediately saw Evelyn Chapple's grimacing stare decorating the lounge window of number forty-one.

'Oh God, guys! We're late and we've been spotted!'

Judy tried to calm her friend down with a slightly alcohol-fuelled tirade.

'Oh fuck 'em, Kaz! Big deal! It's only a drink for that knob-head of a son. None of us even want to bloody go! She ought to be thankful that anyone wants to even associate with him!'

Josh found himself intrigued by Judy's outburst.

'He doesn't sound terribly popular, this Greg fellow.'

'That's because he isn't!' snapped Judy.

Karen's anxiety had been steadily eased since collecting her friends. Their sharp quips and ready wit were a welcome change from the banality she had become accustomed to of late.

In truth, Karen's mood regarding the evening ahead had lightened considerably due to her jovial companions in the back seat. They laughed about most things in life. Thoughts begun to encroach in Karen's mind that maybe *she* should have gone to university as well.

She had definitely decided it was time for a catch-up drink or two as she pushed open the front door.

'Open that bottle of white in the fridge, Jude. Just going upstairs to make some final adjustments.'

Josh followed his friend into the kitchen whilst having a quick scan around Karen's abode.

'Karen's kids look cute, Jude!'

Josh held a framed picture of Chloe and Lauren in his hand taken a year earlier at school.

'Oh, they're simply adorable. Bloody great, those girls! Shame they aren't here to meet you. You'd love 'em!'

His gaze rose to meet that of Judy's.

'Remember when you said you wanted my children?'

The prevailing silence gave no indication of whether such a memory was pleasant for her recollection.

'Yes, Josh…I remember…like it was yesterday…'

Replacing the photo-frame back on the lounge shelf, Josh took a big swig from his wine glass that Judy had graciously filled to the brim.

His mind became occupied by other pressing matters.

'So, what's the story with this Greg fellow next door, then? Not flavour of the month with you from what I can gather?'

'Er…not really…no…I just dislike him.' replied Judy.

'So, forgive my naivety but what the fuck are we *doing* here, then?'

Judy pulled her friend closer and checked that Karen was out of earshot.

Her whisper caused Josh to strain as he listened.

'Look. Greg came back to live with his mum next door about three months ago. He's made a play for Karen from the start. He fancies the pants off her! But of course, it's completely forbidden territory but he's not getting the message! She's hoping to shake him off tonight for good.'

Josh gulped a good sample of his drink.

'The elbow? On his birthday? Should go down well!'

Judy smiled as she beckoned Josh's ear even closer.

'Well…this guy's a bit, well, dense. I mean, who in their right mind would chase a married woman who lives right next door?'

Her friend displayed a knowing yet cute grin from ear to ear.

'Well, of course, apart from *you*! But you've never been in your right mind, have you, Josh Garton?'

He emptied his glass and continued to smirk mischievously.

'I bloody well hope not! I've tried bleeding hard to remain detached from sanity all these years!'

Karen retuned to the fray in her man-eater dress and black heels.

The welcome sound of giggling escorted her re-entry into the kitchen.

'Wow...you look *too* good, girly!'

'Thank you, Jude. Right, where's my drink then?'

Judy watched aghast as Karen downed an entire glass in three gulps.

'Jesus, Kaz. Steady on! Refill? I've taken the liberty of opening two bottles. Shame to let them go to waste!'

'Brilliant idea!' chuckled Karen.

The minutes passed as the group readied themselves for the night ahead. Josh's light-hearted inquisition about Greg was answered in the same jovial manner.

'So then, Kaz. The birthday boy. Bit of a nuisance, eh? Doesn't get the hint, eh? Have you thought of any extreme tactic to throw him off the scent?'

Karen looked puzzled by the suggestion.

'Such as?'

'Grow a moustache? Buy a tractor! Tell him you're a raving lesbo!'

Booming laughter resonated throughout the lower floor of number thirty-nine.

A soulful, uplifting noise that was to be abruptly halted by the sound of three loud knocks on the front door.

The occupants of the kitchen were stunted into temporary silence, promptly followed by nervous giggles.

Karen's latent sense of trepidation instantly returned.

'I'd better get that. Must be Greg.'

'Oh, fuck it! We're better off without him now, surely?' argued a wine-fuelled Josh.

Judy playfully slapped Josh on the behind as further laughter emitted from the trio. Karen wavered before braving the emptiness of the hallway and the unknown quantity that awaited her behind the door.

As she fully expected, Greg's expression comprised a concoction of inner frustration and forced patience.

'Hi, Kaz. Are you ready, yet?'

'Yes, nearly. Come in, Greg. Come and meet Josh.'

It was with some considered hesitancy that Greg made his way into the kitchen, but the welcome from Judy and Josh was warm if well performed.

'Happy Birthday, Greg!' burst Judy as she produced a card from behind her back. A single nod of reluctant thanks was the only reply.

Josh extended a hand of congratulations.

'Many happy returns, old man. Drink?'

Greg eyed the pair with suspicion for a few moments, unsure whether to be pleased about their presence or not.

'Yes, please. Beer.' he grunted.

'Where's your mum? Thought she might pop in as well before we went.' enquired Karen, politely.

'Bit out of sorts. Not feeling too good. She doesn't have to hold my hand everywhere, you know.'

'Oh, okay. I bought you a little present as well as this card. It reminded me of you!'

Greg fumbled awkwardly with the wrapping before he unveiled the stuffed toy elephant. An act which eventually and thankfully produced a mild smirk of approval.

Unsheathing the card had a similar effect.

'We're just nipping out the back for a smoke, Kaz. If that's okay.' Judy announced.

Karen nodded nervously. The last thing she wanted was to be left alone with her neighbour. Greg watched as Judy and Josh shut the back door behind them. It soon became evident to Karen that he was determined to begin the night with arms drawn.

'I expected to see you this morning. What have you been doing all day? Where have you been? My mum's pissed off. She wanted to baby-sit for you tonight.'

Karen could observe his childish temper rising - exactly what she didn't anticipate at that moment.

'Oh, well, the girls are better off out of the way, what with all this boozy talk. I had things to do too, Greg. By the way. You look very nice tonight.'

The complementary approach appeared to work.

'Thanks. So do you.' he whispered. 'Good enough to eat in fact.'

'Er...don't start all that again. Behave yourself!'

At last - considering it was a day of supposed celebration - Greg offered what Karen perceived to be a genuine smile.

'That's better! What time is the taxi coming?'

'Eight. I knew you'd be late in getting ready, Kaz. You always are! Josh seems like a nice bloke. Bit stuck up, but nice.'

'Josh is lovely. I've known him years. He and Judy used to be together if you know what I mean.'

'Yes. Even *she* seems pleased to see me tonight. Must be putting it on, though.'

Karen placed a hand on Greg's arm and moved her cheek towards his. The alcohol was eroding her sense of self-preservation already.

'You are paranoid, Greg. By the way…'

'What?

'Happy Birthday, handsome!'

Lightly placing a peck near his lips, Karen turned to see Josh and Judy walking back toward the rear of the house and re-opened the back door.

'Looks like we're all ready, then!'

Judy was not reserved in pointing out the scene of destruction that was laid out in and around the flower borders.

'What's up, Kaz? Get bored of the gardening?'

'No. Bloody foxes, wasn't it? They'd only been in a day as well!'

Josh turned his gaze from the garden back to the kitchen. As his eyes met with Greg's steely glare, he offered an alternative possibility.

'Foxes? Don't think so dear! Some fucker's pulled them up by the looks of things. The mindless bastards!'

'Come off it!' argued Judy. 'Who would even consider such a dirty deed?'

'Anyone with the sad inclination and the crazy motive, my dear!' declared Josh as he clanked his empty glass on the worktop.

The sound of a taxi horn brought the debate to an end as Greg led the group to the front door and in turn to the waiting cab.

His silence was no coincidence, yet nor was it a clue as to the cause of the minor debacle in the rear garden of number thirty-nine.

Laughter soon engulfed the group once more as they slammed the taxi doors and sped off toward Tenbridge town centre.

twenty-two

The evening uncoiled quickly and surprisingly amiably. Tenbridge High Street was a typical modern drinking avenue with a mix of high-octane bars and an eager myriad of summer participants.

The warm weather encouraged and accentuated the effect of the various beverages the group sampled during their crawl along the line of pubs and clubs.

Karen, not being a habitual drinker, was pleasantly intoxicated after six drinks and enjoyed a hilarious stagger with Judy up the stairs of *Beeners*, the so-called hottest night club in town.

With the eager assistance of Greg and Josh, the foursome found themselves at the final venue of what had been a relatively enjoyable night.

Greg leaned over the balcony with beer bottle in hand and studied the two dozen or so occupants of the dance floor. Josh and Judy were engaged in a tight embrace, exchanging smiles and brief, flirtatious kisses. The intensity of flashing neon-light and rampant shadow seemed to bring out the hidden desire in them as it seemed to be doing for most others on the floor.

Yet tonight, instead of feeling happily drunk on his birthday, Greg Chapple was sober.

Stone cold sober.

And unfulfilled.

Unfulfilled and now teeming with frustration as he observed Karen laughing and dancing.

He had expressed his disapproval to her when she rang up her mother at half past nine to check on the girls. The call satisfied Karen. Yet her natural maternal considerations only served to aggravate Greg.

His demand for her to forget about her real, other life for one evening had not rested too easily with Karen, though she wasn't prepared to let it ruin her night.

Unbeknown to her, the incident had rained torrentially on the intended parade of Greg Chapple. He wanted Karen to himself, yet even he did not know for what purpose.

In truth, he didn't have the first idea of what constituted friendship.

He understood nothing of what made Karen tick.

He had little comprehension of the position he had put her in, making his advances, suggesting certain possibilities.

Wanting what he could never, ever have.

Moreover, he didn't care for these factors.

In fact, Greg's idea of friendship was a one-way scenario.

He got what he desired.

The other person concerned mattered precious little.

To the point where he would even wilfully cause her emotional distress if only to exert his self-imposed superiority over her.

And as already proven, he would consciously intrude on her sacred domestic privacy.

He was quite prepared to orchestrate wilful, slaughtered sacrilege of all that Karen held dear.

In her garden.

In her bedroom.

In her home.

In her mind.

Yet coincidentally, Greg's game had only just begun in earnest.

Just as Karen secretly anticipated its conclusion.

Yet her focus at that moment remained set for the dance floor as she took Greg's hand and pulled him down the steps to join Josh and Judy for the final track of the evening.

A supposed celebration of a twenty-sixth birthday.

For those few furtive minutes in the flitting darkness, Greg was in his own twisted idea of heaven. As hand and eye wandered freely, he convinced himself that the woman in his arms was his.

Yet whilst achieving this futile, aimless ambition, he still could not quantify his motives. Greg Chapple had no incentive to make Karen his target. All that he knew was that his target…she unwittingly was.

Affection, attraction, covetousness, even…love.

These were not the currencies at the bargaining table.

Obsession, jealousy, resentment, distaste.

This was the combined foundation for Greg Chapple's need for acquaintance.

Yet such emotions were being summoned without justification.

And as the final song ended and the friends exited the dance floor, Greg awaited the signal that would surely come.

The signal for him to fully open the game.

The signal that Karen Aspinall had intended not to send him all evening.

Judy staggered toward her friend and planted a stabilising hand on her shoulder.

'Look, Kaz…Josh and I are pissed…as you can probably tell…so we're jumping in a cab back to my flat. You two coming with us or what?'

Karen's booze-diluted and confused mind struggled to concentrate as the surrounding chatter of departing nightclub patrons drew to a level of crescendo.

'No, Jude…I need to walk…Greg will get me home in one piece…'

Through the semi-darkness of the club, Judy scanned the nearby crowds.

'Where is he, then?'

Karen searched the crowd of unfamiliar faces but could not see Greg. She had held his hand only a moment ago but had lost sight and touch of his whereabouts in the throng of inebriated clubbers.

'Must be waiting downstairs.' giggled Karen.

Judy still had some wits about her and repeated the offer.

'Come on, Kaz. Me and Josh will get you home in our cab. Please.'

'No, its fine, Jude. I'll be fine.'

As the trio descended the steps toward the nightclub foyer, Greg could be clearly seen leaning up against the glass frontage.

Judy disguised her misgivings to uphold the jollity.

'Ah yes! There he is, Kaz! Waiting to take you home, bless him. He's not such a bad sort after all! Will you be okay? Josh and I have got some catching up to do!'

Karen shook her head in mock disapproval.

'You're a very naughty girl, Judy Simpson.'

'And I'm a very naughty boy!' Josh chuckled.

The four members of the party embraced and bade farewell before Josh and Judy disappeared into the night to claim a taxi.

Karen shivered and stared at her friend's vacant expression in the murk of the club entrance. Her head spun as her legs buckled slightly.

'Come on, Greg. We'll walk. I need the air. I'm going to feel so bad in the morning. I just know it!'

Greg did not answer as he brushed passed Karen and strode off in front with his hands in his pockets.

He was yards ahead before Karen could summon a response to his strange action.

'Hang on a moment, Greg! I'm not sure of the way. Wait a minute.'

Karen removed her heels and skipped after him barefoot.

Quickly out of breath, she managed to identify his form in the shadowed distance.

'Greg…fucking wait a minute! What's up with you? Slow down!'

With that abrupt command in mind, Greg stopped and turned to face her as she caught him up.

Grabbing on to his shoulders with both hands, Karen leaned into him very unsteadily and replace her shoes using her feet.

'Really Greg…you must stop throwing these fucking strops. Fucking grow up! What's the matter?'

'Nothing's up. I've just had a crappy birthday, that's all!'

He began to walk away once more as Karen again gave chase in the early summer moonlight. It was at this juncture that she realised she had no idea where she was. And that she was far more drunk than she initially suspected.

'Greg. Stop racing off! I'm lost. I need you to get me home! Why was your birthday crappy? I thought it was a good night.'

He stopped again and forcefully grasped her upper arms.

His stony glare induced Karen's sobriety to begin early.

Suddenly, her supposedly unwarranted fears of the previous few days returned to haunt her.

'I didn't invite those twats! I only wanted *you,* tonight. Not *them*! They can't stand me!'

Karen's arms were now beginning to feel the pain of Greg's incessant grip.

'Let go, you're hurting me. Thank you. What about your present? Did you like that?'

'What? A fucking toy elephant? Are you taking the piss or something?'

Karen's emotions began to well as she considered her response.

'Lauren helped me pick it for you! We thought it was cute.'

The atmosphere instantly turned hostile.

'FUCKING RUBBISH PRESENT! FUCKING CRAP! YOU TAKE FUCKING LIBERTIES!'

With his vocal explosion released, Greg began to up his pace and disappeared ahead once more.

Once more removing her shoes, Karen followed at jogging pace.

How she wished at that moment she had gone home with Judy.

Or at least got into a taxi alone.

She now found herself under the influence of far too much alcohol, lost in the city and with a man who was slowly but surely proving to be more of a foe than a friend.

She continued to trot along the blackened pavement as tears began to fall onto her cheeks. She whimpered as her wrenched craving for the comfort of home and the love for her family pierced her conscience.

What on Earth was she doing in the middle of town in the middle of the night?

What had ever possessed her to think it might be a good idea?

Her bare feet were now hurting. As were her mind and heart.

Karen strained to see through tear-strewn eyes as she ran faster.

Panic began to set in, and her emotions took an even stronger hold.

The orange glow of the streetlamps gave little guidance as to Greg's location.

Then out of nowhere, he appeared.

From behind her.

Two hands placed themselves around her waist and pulled her into a side alley.

The next she knew they were around her neck.

Then onto her buttocks; then under her dress.

Karen struggled desperately to fend off his assault.

She cried, screamed and kicked whilst unleashing blows on his head with her shoes.

The fight seemed to go on for an age.

Then no sooner had her plight begun, it was over, and she was alone once more in the darkness of the alleyway.

Sinking to her knees, still clutching her stiletto heels, Karen Aspinall wheezed, wept and physically pulsed under the night sky.

Her ultimate dread had now become a frightening reality.

Greg was no friend.

He was indeed as dangerous as Judy had insisted all these weeks.

Why had she not listened to those warnings or indeed, countered her own instinct that he might possess a positive nature?

What was it about the man that had compelled her to indulge him?

She had persuaded herself to trust him.

With herself, her home and her young children.

She concluded that she was losing her mind.

It was the only feasible explanation for her poor judgement.

More tears flowed freely as she held her head in her hands and under the cover of that stinking alleyway she hid from the world in an emotional retreat.

Her skull began to thump vigorously with the combined force of inebriation and mental stress.

How she longed for her husband at that moment. How she wished to be with her loved ones. Her beautiful, smiling, loving daughters.

For the next few minutes Karen allowed herself to fall into the void of wanton, unattainable whim until the storm finally passed and the uncontrolled release eventually subsided.

The solitude around her was suddenly soothing.

Momentary peace surrounded Karen Aspinall.

But it endured for only a few short seconds.

Until approaching footsteps disturbed the temporary tranquillity of her gradually relenting distress.

Then, opening her eyes to identify the oncoming figure, Greg Chapple was revealed once again.

A defiant, despondent, desperate man.

A man who had evidently not completed his session of torment.

It took an eternity for Karen to summon the words.

When she did, it was obstructed by a choking throat, crammed with regret.

'Why, Greg? Why? What have I done? I thought we were mates?'

Silhouetted against the alley wall and framed by an amber hue, Greg Chapple spoke softly under his convenient yet terrifying shroud.

She could not see his face. She did not wish to.

'You led me on. Mum said you would. I love you, Karen. But I'm not good enough, am I? Now you're going to pay. You've left me no choice.'

Anger returned to fuel Karen's response as she arose to her full, barefooted height.

'What the *hell* made you think I would be interested in you, Greg? You are a neighbour. You *were* a friend. No more. No less. Why do you feel so let down?'

He did not move from his position.

His tone was assured and threatening.

'You're nothing but a cheap slapper. Well, bitch…you fucked with the wrong marine today! You'd better watch out for your family when they're all asleep in bed. Because I'm going to burn your fucking house down with you all inside!'

Again, the tears flowed unrestrained causing Karen to cover her face in an attempt to compress the sound of her wailing. Her stomach knotted sharply with regret and her spine chilled with the coldest of fears.

Another minute passed before Karen dared peek through her closed fingers. Her breathing was heavy and irregular as she warily scrutinised the alleyway.

But Greg Chapple was gone once more.

Nowhere to be seen.

Vanished into the night air like the phantom he seemed to be.

His work done.

His victim greeted, impaled, and left with a sinister calling card.

Then she ran.

Karen Aspinall ran like she had never run before. She ran until the blisters on her toes gave way to blood and her heel bones baulked with bruising pain.

Eventually, the renewed familiarity of her location gathered around her rapidly, and she set her sights for home.

The miles clocked as she continued her desperate sprint.

Into Church Drayton. Those beautiful tree-lined avenues.

Onward to Benton Road. Along Benton Road.

Toward the home she loved.

And the neighbours she now hated.

Clambering over the large, white wooden gate, Karen collided with her own car as she dropped her shoes and fumbled for a key in her handbag.

The darkness exaggerated her frantic search, but finally brought success. Locating the keyhole, she let herself in to the sanctity of the house, being sure to secure herself inside.

Back to the peace, solace and protection that number thirty-nine, Benton Road had offered for so long.

Yet there was no longer that instantaneous feeling of safety.

There was no longer the obliging sensation that her personal fortress would deter the demons outside.

Because now it was way too late.

Because those same demons were now *inside*…and in truth, had been for some time.

They were within her mind and body.

They had already begun eroding her mental and physical resistance.

The rot had set in.

The decay now flourishing in earnest.

Crying herself to sleep on the settee as her head pounded relentlessly, Karen Aspinall slowly acknowledged that the menace she had tried to elude and even exorcise that evening had regained full advantage.

Greg Chapple had easily broken her feeble guard and penetrated her soul.

He had worked his dubious charm and seemingly claimed control of her existence.

Yet hope stirred deep in her heart as she relaxed into creeping dormancy.

Surely her current sufferance would ease as she lay supposedly protected within the walls of her own home.

Maybe tomorrow…just maybe…things would be different.

twenty-three

A desolate silence had invaded number thirty-nine, Benton Road. An uninvited, ailing emptiness only matched in its torturous presence by the aching pit of Karen Aspinall's stomach.

The hangover was particularly intrusive. She had stood to her full height only twice during the morning.

Once to visit the toilet and once to make a pot of black coffee. Hunched on the settee, she observed the surroundings in the lounge. Her scuffed and scratched heels lay strewn on the carpet where she had discarded them nearly twelve hours earlier.

The rest of the room seemed untouched from the previous evening.

All looked to be in its place.

Unlike her head at that moment, the memory of what happened after leaving the nightclub was all too clear.

The frenetic upset. The perverse anxiety.

The absolute fear that had been induced at the mere sight - now the mere thought - of her so-called friend.

Who, unfortunately, still retained his status as her neighbour.

Reasonable comprehension of his actions was beyond her.

In truth, it mattered little now, anyway. He had crossed the forbidden boundary and laid a hand upon someone who he should rightly have been cossetting if he truly had any affection for her.

Instead of reliable companionship he had deserted her as she cowered pathetically in the wake of his temper.

The very mention of his name was now a signal for Karen to be instantly afraid.

Afraid of what she now knew about him.

And even worse, afraid of what she was yet to discover.

She felt justified in assessing his irrationality; his lack of humility; even his questionable sanity.

No longer was Greg Chapple the friendly face from next door.

No longer was he the handsome son of her long-time associate and confidante.

What would his mother make of such conduct; the conduct of a son she claimed to hold in such high esteem?

If only she knew what despicable acts he had played out under the protective shadow of night.

If only she knew of the terrifying true face that lay concealed beneath his mask of sociability.

If only she knew what her son was truly capable of.

Then a disturbingly brief thought flashed through Karen's mind.

Perhaps Evelyn Chapple *did* know.

Perhaps she was already fully aware of everything that had transpired.

Maybe she was perfectly well acquainted with his dubious mindset and all he might wish to incur.

Evelyn's attitude to Karen and her family had certainly altered since Greg's return home.

She was colder; more distant.

More critical.

Openly scornful; maybe even resentful of the supposed happiness of Karen Aspinall.

Things had changed so much in the past months.

The people Karen thought she knew so well seemingly no longer existed. Two homes and their occupants once stood as a united front. Now, at least as far as Karen was concerned, they stood irreparably divided.

No trust. No faith. No reliance.

The previously accepted status quo was now shattered.

And all Karen Aspinall possessed at that moment curled up on the settee, was a sense of total, utter incredulity.

She had sat and stared at the voiceless, blank television screen for hours as her beating head gradually subsided and sobriety strived for a return.

The phone had rung at least four times that morning, possibly five or six. Karen did not even look at the caller display screen. She knew it would either be her mother or Judy.

Or school to find out where Chloe was.

Yet Karen felt somehow ashamed to be sitting alone with her upset. She did not wish to confess to the previous evening's episode. It filled her with disgust that a grown woman, an upstanding parent of two children and a loving wife, should even be mentioned in the same context as a drunken assault.

But that was the most confounding aspect to the whole damning scenario.

So far as Karen could recall, Greg had hardly touched a drop of alcohol all night.

He was fully aware of his actions.

His intent was all too clear from the outset.

He had been in full manipulation of events.

And if starkest truth be known, he still was.

The early afternoon sunshine tried beat a path through the closed curtains of the living room.

Karen could not remember shutting them before she collapsed on the sofa in the darkness in the early hours. Then she remembered closing them before going out last night.

Some small relief that at least some aspect of her memory bank was still intact.

A loud knock at the door shook Karen's from her docility.

Upstanding albeit unsteadily, she moved to the slight gap in the curtains and squinted to identify the caller.

The postman. She would not answer. He could wait.

A minute of inaction followed before the letterbox clattered and a missed delivery slip floated onto the doormat. Karen observed it from the lounge doorway. She didn't even bother to retrieve it from the floor such was the effort and the inconsequence.

The telephone echoed its shrill tone around the corners of the room once more as Karen reluctantly glanced at its display reading.

Judy.

She should answer, if only out of courtesy. Besides, a lack of response would only serve to increase Judy's curiosity.

A lump of trepidation formed in Karen's throat as she lifted the receiver. She listened to the sound of her own voice as she spoke her replies to the questioning from her true friend.

It was a battle to retain composure, but Karen Aspinall was adamant she would not admit to the previous evening's events.

'Hi, Jude.'

'A bit green around the gills.'

'Yeah…walked home.'

'About one-ish, I think.'

'I think so…he didn't say an awful lot.'

'Yes, I did notice!'

'Yes…I think the whole nightclub saw that you were both up for it, you dirty girl!'

'Is Josh still with you?'

'Yes, I'm fine…why?'

'No, I'm fine…just in recovery phase at the moment.'

'Yes…I'm sure…don't worry…'

'A couple of weeks…perhaps the cinema again, yes?'

'Okay, Judy…see you soon…bye.'

The emotion took full hold once more as Karen returned the receiver to its cradle.

She had lied to her friend out of some unwarranted shame.

Yet should she have told the truth about her journey home with Greg?

What could Judy have done about it now?

Aside from serving an intensive, unrelenting portion of *I told you so!*

Karen felt scarred inside her mind as the ramifications of Greg's attack became gradually clearer by the minute.

Should Karen tell her parents? Did the girls need to know? What about Robert's reaction? Would he go to the police?

Indeed, should *she* go to the police?

And what would Greg's reply entail should the spotlight be cast his way? Complete denial? Would he claim he was encouraged to drag her into an unlit alleyway and force himself upon her?

Or could he claim to be out of his mind with drink and totally oblivious to his actions on the night in question?

As Karen shuddered at the fruitless, unenviable possibilities, she knew she needed her husband back by her side there and then. She wanted him like never before and cursed herself for ever believing that his absence was something she could ever accommodate.

Never mind positively endorse.

Especially not now.

Not now. Not ever.

Consolation came in the knowledge that he usually came home a little early on Fridays to avoid the traffic.

She would wait. Wait for his return and fall helplessly into his warm embrace. Yet could she summon the courage to confess to him the cause of her obvious trauma?

Or should she put the entire episode to the back of her mind as a dark, climactic remnant of a once promising relationship with the lunatic from next door?

She would have most of the afternoon to ponder her position.

Reaching for the cooled coffee pot on the lounge table, Karen poured another and hunched her knees to her chest as she cradled her mug.

The sunshine outside, whilst high and proud, could not lighten the expanding gloom that had infested the realm of number thirty-nine, Benton Road.

*****

The next Karen Aspinall knew she was being gently prodded on the shoulder.

A gesture that slowly roused her from slumber on the sofa.

'Kaz...Kaz...wakey-wakey...rise and shine...it's nearly five p.m.!'

Through blurred vision and a thankfully calmer head, Karen gradually ascertained that her unannounced companion looked vaguely, lovingly familiar.

'Rob? Rob! Oh Rob...I'm sorry. I nodded off again. I've done no shopping and...'

Robert began to laugh at his wife's bedraggled appearance.

'Good night last night I take it? You've been hiding all day, haven't you? Poor little drunken sleepy flea can't get up!'

She watched him place his briefcase onto the armchair before making his way to the kitchen. Rising to her feet, Karen followed scratching her head as Rob filled the kettle.

'The girls still at your mum's I take it?'

'Er...yes...I was in no state to drive this morning. Coppers would have taken me in!'

'Yes...Greg says you looked like you'd had too much when you got home last night.'

That name.

That fucking name.

The last fucking name on earth she wanted to fucking hear.

Especially when spoken by her husband.

'When did you see him?'

'As I pulled the car up...just now. He opened the front gate for me, bless him. I thanked him for taking you out last night. He said he enjoyed himself.'

As Karen watched her husband pull two mugs from the cupboard, she almost vomited as his words registered in her mind.

Greg Chapple.

That lying, scheming, demented bastard.

Greg Chapple.

That vindictive, evil, manipulating bully.

Greg Chapple.

That fucking, fucking, brave actor.

Karen quickly composed herself as Robert brushed passed her and collapsed on the settee.

'The four of you had a good night, then?'

Greg must have reminded Rob that Judy and Josh came along for the ride.

'Y-yes…it was okay…I suppose I was a bit over the top with the drink!'

'Well, once in a while does no harm, does it?'

Never again, thought Karen.

Never again.

Never.

'How's the rest of your week been, darling? Pretty quiet?' asked Rob as he reached for the TV remote.

The change of subject effectively dispersed Karen's renewed anger.

'Erm, yes. Quiet, really. Nothing doing. Rob…would you mind fetching the girls for me from Mum's before you settle? I must still be over the limit.'

'Of course, love. I'll go now. I'm shattered too so I won't hang about. Any message for your mother?'

'No…other than thanks, of course. Tell her I'll give her a ring tomorrow.'

Robert stood to his feet and gave his wife a tight, comforting hug.

She revelled in the security it offered, and the embrace became immediately mutual.

They kissed before looking into each other's eyes.

'You okay, Karen? You don't seem with it at all. The morning after the night before, eh? I don't know. What are we going to do with you?'

Karen smiled before retreating into his cover once more and whispering into his chest.

'Rob.'

'Yes, love?'

'I've missed you this week. Missed you so badly.'

'Okay, darling. Okay. I'm home now. I'm sorry. I'm going to try and sort out some leave, okay? I know it's taking its toll on us. I'll enquire first thing Monday.'

Holiday entitlement was not what Karen wanted from her husband.

She needed him back…permanently.

Not for a weekend. Not for a fortnight.

Permanently.

She held the thought for a few silent seconds.

'Okay, love. Do you want to come with me to get the girls?'

Karen needed little time to debate the response.

'No! No. You go. I'm going to get in the bath. Tell my parents I'll see them soon. Tell Mum I will definitely ring her. I don't feel like indulging them tonight. You go on your own. You'll be far quicker than me, anyway! Besides…I think we're overdue an early night. If I go to Mum's with you, it'll be tomorrow by the time we get back.'

Karen watched through the gap in the curtains as her husband reversed and sped off in his automatic company car, leaving the gate open for his return.

In tandem with his departure, the maelstrom of her mind became eclipsed once more by gnawing worry.

And her far reaching thoughts regarding the very recent past.

twenty-four

'Girls, are you ready yet? Hurry up, then!'

Dressed and made-up unusually early for a Saturday morning, Karen inspected her features in the bathroom mirror. Once again prepared to face the world, she took a deep breath and adjusted her blouse as she traipsed downstairs.

Robert sat dozily at the kitchen table debating whether to finish a soggy bowl of cereal.

'You sure you don't want to come to town with us, Rob? I thought I'd try and get the girls some new clothes for the summer break.'

'Er…no thanks, love. I'll be fine. I can entertain myself for a few hours. Might even cut the lawn. You okay this morning?'

Karen tried and failed in her attempts to avoid her husband's gaze, which in itself was a worrying state of affairs.

'Yes…I'm wonderful…why do you ask?'

'Well, you seemed very huggy-feely last night. Almost as though something had frightened you. Like you were really glad I was back home. I don't know…ignore me. I'm going for a shower. Oh, I'd better shift the car first to let you out.'

Man and wife exchanged a long stare as Chloe and Lauren entered the room ready for the shopping trip.

'Okay, girls. Kiss Daddy. We won't be long. It's too hot to shop really but they desperately need some new gear.'

On the front drive, Karen made tentative steps after her daughters. She could not bring herself to look towards number forty-one. She made straight for the gate and unlatched it for Robert to reverse out.

'Morning Karen!'

Lyndsey Robinson's unexpected holler from across the road made Karen jump.

Calming herself, she turned, smiled and waved. She did not dare to raise her voice, should she attract unwanted attention from the occupants next door. Lyndsey returned the gesture and promptly disappeared indoors, much to Karen's silent relief.

Robert, still clad in pyjamas and slippers, sat in the road with the engine purring anticipating Karen's imminent reversal. The seconds passed as he observed his wife over the top of the hedge, as she stared bemusedly at the rear end of her car.

Detecting that something was amiss he switched off the ignition and re-joined her on the drive.

'I don't believe it, Rob. Flat. Look! Flat! As a bloody pancake! Chloe noticed it straight away. I'm glad she did because I wouldn't have.'

Robert opted to intercede with a humorous quip as he studied the driver's side rear tyre.

'You'll be alright. It's only flat at the bottom!'

Karen's look of disdain prompted a change of approach as he knelt in his pyjamas to inspect more closely.

'Well, I can't see what it is. I'll just change it. Be quicker. Let me put some clothes on first though.'

Karen's trepidation regarding venturing outside had eased in the five minutes since she departed the front door. In fact, the potential spectacle of her husband changing a wheel in his dressing gown brought a welcome smirk to her face.

Within a minute, he was back out on the drive attired in shorts and t-shirt and proceeded to rummage in the back of Karen's car for the spare wheel and jack.

'That much bloody crap in this boot…surprised I can even see the spare to get at it!' he mumbled, again making Karen smile to herself.

'You may as well watch telly for a while, girls. Looks like we're stuck for a bit…unless of course Daddy lets me take *his* car for a spin into town!'

'No bloody chance!' came the immediate if muffled reply from behind the boot lid.

Needing little further encouragement, Chloe and Lauren scampered back into the house. It looked like being another very warm day in Church Drayton. Karen ideally wanted to be back at home for dinner time to enjoy the rest of Saturday with Robert.

So much for best laid plans.

'Okay…now we can change the wheel.' exclaimed her husband, as he clanked and scraped his way to the scene of the crime.

'Oy…watch my paintwork, you!'

Robert offered a glance of mock scorn and pointed to the array of dints and scrapes that peppered all sides of his wife's car.

The uninvited diversion, whilst an inconvenience for all, at least brought with it some long overdue amusement.

Karen felt a sense of mild contentment for the first time in an age.

Even the sight of her husband's head bobbing up and down at the back of the car raised her spirits.

It was just like old times for the Aspinalls.

Doing things together as families should do.

Such a simple thing, a flat tyre. But it united them for a few minutes. Karen realised how little they had laughed together in the previous weeks…even months.

However, Karen's re-immersion into domestic bliss was short-lived.

Her conscience suddenly became aware of an unwelcome, detracting force nearby.

Then her eyes focused on the vision of Greg Chapple in the short distance as he strutted defiantly towards home.

A mild panic enveloped Karen's mind.

Sudden indecision coupled with nervous, clawing dread.

A woman in fear.

Without further thought she retreated indoors.

Up her stairs. Into her bedroom. To her vantage point behind the closed curtains. Hidden behind the slightest gap to enable her to observe in private.

She waited and watched as Greg got closer and closer still to Robert, whose measured attempts to prise loose the wheel nuts were proving unsuccessful.

Karen's heart now beat like a bass drum. Her own pulse echoed in her ear. Her palms became clammy as she surveyed the developments below.

Finally, the men met under her covert gaze.

She observed Greg with an unforced grimace. She had quickly become disgusted by his appearance, never mind his presence. Yet her recently acquired distrust of him did not affect her recognition of his well-honed act.

The jovial stance. The ready script.

The line of cheeky humour.

His crocodile smiles.

His twisted, treacherous mind.

In painful turn she watched Robert's oblivious, innocent reaction.

His instinctive, natural response to seeing his neighbour.

Passing the time of day.

Rob shaking Greg's hand.

The very same hand that had unleashed pain on his wife's weakened form only two days earlier.

Greg must have been laughing inside.

Congratulating himself on convincing the world that he was the good guy.

In effect, he had succeeded.

After all, who was around to question the fact? Karen had not divulged any detail from Thursday evening.

Only two people knew of the incident.

And so far, both obviously felt compelled to say nothing more on the matter for their own individual reasons.

Yet Karen had tried to convince herself that what happened did not matter. It seemed irrelevant. Unnecessary for anyone to hear, let alone concern themselves with.

It was no more than a memory. Not distant; not forgotten; yet seemingly compelled to the annals of history for eternity.

Karen watched unnoticed as Robert finally lifted the deflated wheel from the axle and slid on the spare. Greg took the faulty tyre and began to inspect its surface. He rotated the rubber in his able grasp, supposedly checking carefully for foreign bodies that had become accidentally imbedded into the tread.

Karen was confused. The tyre was only replaced after Christmas at the last MOT. It hadn't done nearly enough mileage to be vulnerable to a puncture. She eyed Greg as he unscrewed the dust cap, checked the valve, and affixed the foot-pump.

Within minutes, the offending tyre was inflated once again, by which time Robert had secured its replacement and released the jack.

More words were exchanged as both men scrutinised the once-flattened tyre.

Expressions of mutual puzzlement brought proceedings to an end.

With his typically gallant style, Robert offered a thumbs-up of appreciation to his neighbour before disappearing into the garage.

Karen held her position and continued to study Greg as he furtively shifted position at the end of the Aspinall's driveway.

He looked towards the gate which remained open, and it held his attention for a few mysterious seconds.

Greg then began to scan the floor around his fect and around the car.

He seemed to check toward the garage before crouching down and picking up some unidentifiable object from the concrete.

Seemingly satisfied with his find, he straightened up.

Again, Greg glanced up and down the road.

Then he honed his gaze directly toward the bedroom window, making Karen physically withdraw in a reflexive reaction.

His stare fixed itself on the glass behind which Karen stood.

Where she was supposedly hidden by closed curtains.

Surely he couldn't have seen her?

Greg smirked in her direction before throwing something up toward the window.

Nothing visible left his grasp.

Then, with another smile and a loosely directed wave, he was gone.

Back along Benton Road.

Karen watched his departure until he disappeared around the corner.

Karen could not know whether she had been spotted in her stake out position, but Greg was pretty astute in his guess work.

Her own suspicions were accurate also.

The object launched from his hand was indeed a small stone.

The very same small stone that had been purposely placed in the valve of her rear tyre, causing gradual, undetectable deflation once the dust cap had been re-attached.

Nobody would have been aware such a devilish deed had been administered.

Until, of course, the evidence spoke for itself the next day.

A silent act of malice completed in the dead of night.

No witness; no suspicion; no proof.

'It's sorted Karen. You're good to go, wife.'

Troubling thoughts flashed through Karen's head as Robert's voice carried up the stairs.

'Okay, love…thank you.'

Karen rounded up the girls and headed into town.

Agitation now being her constant accomplice.

*****

Tenbridge was a busy place to be on a Saturday. Like any other city centre, shoppers blocked every which way, and the heat was not making things easier.

Having finally found a parking spot, Karen, Chloe and Lauren had trudged through several clothes stores with considered enthusiasm though had made little in the way of a purchase.

A temporary respite from the melee was required, which came in the form of a relaxing bench in the market square and a soothing ice cream apiece.

The bedlam around them was far less troublesome whilst seated. The trio simply watched and licked at their cones as hundreds of people passed in and around them from all directions.

'Watch your cornet, Lauren. Don't let it melt all over you. Eat it quicker.'

Karen smiled adoringly at her youngest who turned and offered her mother the cross-eyed stare, her face nigh on smothered with ice cream.

'Look at you. Mucky pup!'

Staring up at the cloudless azure sky, Karen felt blessed in the company of her daughters. The highly unpleasant feelings she had nurtured for the past couple of days seemed to have dissipated of their own accord since hitting Tenbridge.

She felt a gradual wave of inner maternal happiness.

The sensation was most welcome.

If only short-lived.

'Mummy…there's Greg!'

Her heart plummeted like a stone once more as Chloe's announcement struck into her like a dagger.

She watched despairingly as Chloe frantically waved towards an unseen figure among the labyrinth of shoppers.

'Where is he, Chloe? Are you sure it's him?'

'Yes…he's over there, by the bus stop.'

Karen glanced toward the area which was the focus of her elder daughter's attention. She saw somebody that looked like Greg Chapple. It was difficult to identify him positively. The distant form lurched from one spot to another. He did not respond to Chloe's friendly gesture.

Karen satisfied herself with the wilful thought that her daughter had most likely been mistaken. Relief washed over her.

'Come on you two. I think this hot sun is making you see things!'

Chloe looked up at her mother as Karen wiped Lauren's face with a tissue.

'Do you think I've just seen a mirage, Mummy? Like what they get in the desert?'

'Most likely, darling. Don't worry about it. Time to shop again. Hold my hand, Lauren. There's a bin just there for your ice cream if you don't want it.'

The trio departed their position at the bench and gradually mingled with the crowd before vanishing altogether.

But Chloe had been quite correct.

From a partially concealed location, Greg Chapple watched excitedly in the knowledge that his presence had been noted by at least one of the trio.

He moved from behind the bus stop, before walking in the opposite direction.

*****

Robert adjusted the dial on the kitchen radio before returning to the garden. Mowing the lawn was not a favoured occupation but Karen seemed to have left things go astray of late judging by the length of the grass.

Evelyn Chapple wasted little time in interrupting his progress as she appeared at the gate in the fence with a cheery hello and an unusually broad smile.

'You can come and do mine as well while you're at it!' she squawked over the hedge as Robert fought to untangle the mower flex.

'Hello, Evelyn. Just tidying things up for when the women return. By the way, thank your lad for me. He seemed quite concerned earlier about the flat tyre.'

Folding her swollen forearms, Evelyn removed the smile and replaced it with a mask of feigned curiosity.

'Did it have a puncture, then?'

'Well, he pumped it up over an hour ago and I've just checked and it's still up, so you tell me. Puzzling to say the least.'

Robert was not Evelyn Chapple's greatest fan, but surprisingly he found himself tolerating her as they stood at the fence. Then the thought struck. Perhaps Karen might like to go out tonight.

A meal. The pictures.

Something simple. Something romantic.

Quality time together.

A luxury that didn't seem to exist for them anymore.

Robert eagerly pounced on the opportunity.

'Would Greg mind babysitting tonight? I'll pay him, obviously. I know he's reliable…and convenient!'

Evelyn did not seem overtly surprised by Robert's query.

In fact, she was positively enthusiastic about the idea.

'Well now, I'm sure he'd *love* to. It shouldn't be a problem. I'll ask him when I see him later.'

'No…wait…I'll talk to Karen first. See where she'd like to go. Sort a time out and stuff. Then I'll give you a knock.'

Big Chief Crazyhorse spun on her heel with a gleeful nod.

'Okay, Rob. See you later, then.'

*****

Karen, Chloe and Lauren finally made their return in the middle of the afternoon. The sun was at its highest and hottest, as they found the man of the house trimming the edges of the back lawn.

'Hi love! Hi girls! Good shopping trip?'

Karen collapsed into a patio chair and squinted toward her husband.

'Wow, sexy shorts, darling! Could do dangerous things to a girl!'

Throwing the cutters down, Robert wandered to the patio and planted a kiss on his wife's lips.

'Buy anything?'

'No. Too busy. Too hot. And I need a cold drink!'

Rattling in the kitchen cupboards for a glass, Robert decided to divulge Karen with good news and shouted through the open back door.

'Guess what?'

'What?'

'I'm taking you out tonight! Just me and you! Anywhere you want to go. You name it. We're going!'

Karen sat up in her chair and stared wide-eyed.

'Wow. What's all this in aid of then? Are you feeling guilty about something, Mister Aspinall?' she teased.

Robert handed over the glass of iced orange cordial and took a seat opposite.

'Yes...I am. Guilty of negligence. I want to take you somewhere and enjoy your company...because it's been bloody ages since I did. Okay? Any arguments?'

'No...brilliant idea, Rob.'

There was a pause before Karen broached the ultimately destructive question.

The answer to which would immediately leave their plans in tatters.

'Rob...what about the girls?'

'What do you mean?'

'Well. Mum and Dad are out tonight. A bowling club function or something. So...who's sitting the girls?'

Robert threw Karen a justified look of bemusement.

'Well, who do you think? Greg, of course!'

Karen's instant and evident change of heart regarding the suggestion of a romantic night out was completely baffling to Robert.

Her look became stern as she raised a defensive hand.

'No...no way. I don't want that family anywhere near this house.'

Robert curiously examined his wife's demeanour as complete confusion descended on the arena.

'What? What are you talking about?'

Karen showed total assurance in her responses.

'Rob...just forget it. Forget the whole stupid idea.'

'*Stupid*? You just said it was a brilliant idea. Make your bloody mind up, woman!'

Her adamance was unflinching.

'Rob. Drop it. We'll stop in. I'm not bothered.'

Initially puzzled and now reasonably annoyed, Robert stood to his feet and cast a shadow across Karen's inflamed, perspiring features.

'I don't understand. What's the problem, Kaz?'

'Look, they're *my* girls and I'll choose who sits them? Okay?'

Robert was totally unaccustomed to such a dismissive attitude from the woman he married.

'No, actually. It's not fucking okay, Karen! Don't I get a say in this? Are they no longer my girls as well, then?'

Karen angled her face away and focused her gaze down toward the garden.

'Please, Rob. Don't swear. Just drop it. We'll stay in tonight. It doesn't matter.'

Her husband's volume justifiably increased with every word.

'Well, it fucking matters to me! I don't know why I bother coming home at weekends these days. I may as well stay in fucking Coventry, hadn't I?'

'You can do as you like, Rob. But tonight, I'm staying with my daughters.'

'Well, so long as *you're* okay...that's all that matters, isn't it! Excuse me for caring!'

The concluding slam of the back door announced Robert Aspinall's departure from the patio and into the house.

Karen sat silently, thankful that she had averted a potential nightmare.

Yet the quandary remained unresolved.

It wasn't fair to Rob to keep him in the dark about events regarding the Chapples.

But would it be any fairer to plague his mind with the truth whilst he was helplessly distant all week?

Looking vacantly around the rear lawn, Karen observed the gateway in the fence. It had been there since they had moved in and had proved to be a useful and convenient method of access to both properties.

But now, as the tide was determinedly turning, Karen decided that the gate was now a little too convenient.

Indeed, it had evolved into a potential liability.

She did not want access to the Chapple's property any longer.

And it was a cast-iron certainty that she no longer wished for the Chapples to be intruding on the grounds of number thirty-nine, either.

Her plan to eradicate them from her life would begin soon enough. She needed a little more thought on the matter before embarking on any positive, remedial action.

However, the first job at hand was to go and sooth her husband's steaming temper.

As Karen entered the kitchen to find him, she did not notice the furtive figure that had been listening to every word of the heated exchange between Mister and Mrs. Robert Aspinall.

Nor would she have observed the strangely satisfied smile on the face of her former best friend and once trusted neighbour.

twenty-five

The subsequent seven days had been a solely uncomfortable period for Karen Aspinall. Saturday had made its entrance once again as she stood checking the bacon under the grill.

She had finalised her decision regarding the fence gate.

Her eyes averted from the cooker and out through the kitchen window. She had witnessed both Evelyn and Greg over the past week in and around the area of the gate. They weren't specifically up to mischief, but the spectacle of her neighbours in such proximity only served Karen's inner belief that she would need to make a concrete move.

The Chapples needed to be given the message that they were no longer welcome visitors to number thirty-nine.

To casual observers, it may have been a drastic conclusion and particularly harsh on Evelyn. After all, on the face of it she had done little to offend.

Yet subtleties regarding her demeanour of late suggested to Karen that Greg's mother may be more involved in events than first suspected.

It was an instinctive inclination.

There was no tangible proof that Evelyn had contributed to her son's behaviour, but it wasn't exactly a subject that Karen herself was willing to discuss with anyone.

Let alone the perpetrator's mother.

That is, until today.

She poked her head into the lounge on a mission to convey a plan.

'Rob…'

'Yes, dear?' he murmured from behind his newspaper.

'…I've been thinking…'

'Really, dear. Did it hurt?'

'Old joke. Not funny. No…I've been considering blocking off the fence gate in the back garden…'

Robert looked up from the newspaper and studied his wife's profile as she gazed at him.

'Dare I ask the question…*why*?'

In hesitation, Karen checked the spitting rashers once more.

It was as though she did not want to make eye contact with him to avoid witnessing his reaction.

'Well…it's hardly used, is it? And I think we ought to replace it with some other wooden panel. Something to plug the gap. What do you think?'

Robert Aspinall closed the newspaper and glared at Karen.

Finally, she turned to face him through the lounge doorway once more.

'I just don't understand *why*, Kaz. It's not doing any harm. It's always been there. Sounds to me like you're just creating a job for the sake of it. Don't let that bacon burn.'

She turned the grill to low before sitting next to him. Her face expressed anxiety, which understandably puzzled Robert.

'I ask again, Kaz. What's the point?'

'Because…because I'm not happy that next door can get through if they want to.'

'But that's why it's there for lord's sake!'

'No, Rob. It's got to go. Today.'

'What the hell are you talking about? Why today?'

'Because I said so!'

Karen ventured back to the cooker. Her emotions were now beginning to take a hold. Robert was being unwittingly obstructive. Of course, he didn't understand. And she hoped in her heart that he would never need to. This was Karen's way of presenting a practical and psychological message to her neighbours.

Keep out …and stay away.

Robert maintained his opposing and baffled stance and set his folded newspaper on the settee.

'Firstly, it doesn't need taking out because you'll be left with an eyesore. Secondly, you'll need permission from the Chapple's because it's on their border, not ours. We can't touch it, Kaz. Sorry. Though I really don't see what the fuss is about, myself.'

The tension of the previous fortnight began to raise its head once again as Karen sensed her temper becoming inflamed.

'It's not much to ask, Rob, is it? One little job. For my peace of mind.'

Now her husband was veering very near to a revelation she didn't want to sustain.

'I'm sorry? Your *peace of mind*? Am I missing a chapter here? What is the problem, Kaz? It's only Big Chief next door. Is she giving you nightmares? Are you scared she's going to creep out of the shadows on her horse and get you?'

Robert's final statement was too much for Karen.

Her tears streamed unrestrained as she slumped on the seat next to her husband. Hiding her face in her hands, Karen wept into Robert's bewildered embrace.

His tone was comforting yet now deeply concerned.

'Jesus Christ, Kaz! What on earth is the matter? Tell me! Please tell me, now! Why the upset?'

She fought to stem the flow of pent-up frustration. A battle that was won within a few seconds. Yet with all the will in the world, Karen could not confide. The memory was too painful for her to recollect and would certainly be too incredulous for Robert to digest.

'Please, Rob. Can we just seal the gate off, then? Plant some trees in front of it…or something…anything.'

There was severe distraction in his wife's wondrous blue eyes. Her inflammatory reaction had been an incredibly powerful influence.

She, really, desperately wanted him to make her feel more secure.

Robert had never seen such vulnerability in Karen before.

But the cause of her sudden distress remained undisclosed. It was obvious that he should comply with her wishes and hope that the mysterious source of her troubles subsided. Yet the privacy she upheld over the issue was equally confusing to him.

He felt excluded from something important.

Something that had evidently occurred in his absence.

Certainly nothing he could directly relate to at that moment as he held his wife's quivering form.

'Yes, Karen. I'll plant some trees. We'll get them today. Okay? We'll do it together. If that's what you really want. I'll do it.'

Her solace seemed to return on his acceptance of her wishes. Her stunning smile warmed his heart once more. He sought to make that smile grow ever larger.

The woman he loved was weeping before him and he did not know why. It was possibly the most excruciating sensation of helplessness he had ever experienced.

Especially during his relationship with Karen.

Mrs. Robert Aspinall.

It was his job as her man to make her happy and contented.

It was with this in mind that he offered a little quip to restore the mood.

'Darling…you know now that I'm buying you your trees…'

'Yes, Rob? Thank you, darling.'

'…you'd better not have burned that bloody bacon!'

*****

Robert opened both rear passenger doors of Karen's car to reveal Chloe and Lauren perched in and around half a dozen junior conifer plants. Their smiling faces peered from between the feathery foliage, yet surprisingly to their father, neither had asked what the trees were intended for.

'Don't get out just yet, girls. Let Daddy take the trees out of the car first. Okay?' instructed Karen.

Being careful not to break the cane stakes as he wriggled them one at a time from the back seat, the line of young firs was placed in front of the garage door. Karen opted to enter the hallway to evade possible scrutiny from the occupants of number forty-one.

However, in her heart she knew that such a confrontation would occur soon enough.

Yet Karen was feeling sufficiently strong today. She was no longer fearful whilst Robert was at home. She needed his firm leadership in dealing with this issue, even if it was at her request.

Carrying a large bag of compost along the path between the house and garage led Robert to the back garden and onward to the fence gate. Within minutes he had retrieved a hammer and four-inch nails from the shed and secured the gate firmly shut. Karen supervised where she wanted the trees to be positioned and handed her husband the spade.

In anticipation of an un-neighbourly response from the Chapples, Karen returned quickly to the security of the back door.

'I'll make you a coffee, Rob. You've earned it, love.'

Nearly an hour had passed as Robert set the last conifer into the sixth and final hole. Padding down the compost around the root base, the sweat began to form in large beads on his forehead as the two-p.m. sun beat ferociously above.

Checking their alignment, the thought entered his mind that despite initial reservations, the new plants did not look overtly out of place.

The gate in the fence was now rendered unusable.

Blocked off and closed forever.

A job well done, thought Karen as she attained a pleasing view of her husband's handiwork through the kitchen window.

Yet the sensation of slight relief was soon tempered by an unwelcome presence at the fence as Evelyn Chapple made her inevitable entrance.

She wasted little time engaging in confrontation.

'What the hell do you think you're playing at, Rob?'

Looking across the boundary to his neighbour, he immediately sensed Evelyn's anger at seeing the display of new evergreens that had been laid before her.

'What does it look like?' he smiled.

'It looks like a bloody mess, that's what it looks like!'

Robert sniggered as he tried to placate Evelyn's aggression.

An act that only served to infuriate the debate. Greg was not long in joining his mother at the gate and adopted a similar attitude in response to what he saw.

'Jesus, Rob! What's all this in aid of, then?'

'We've decided to make the gate obsolete. That's all. There's no need for any argument. We haven't touched your border. Everything's on my property.'

Mother and son offered Robert their frigid grimaces of disapproval.

'I suppose this was *her* idea?' spat Greg.

'If you mean my wife…we both decided. It was a joint decision.'

Greg was not convinced.

'Bullshit! You're hardly fucking here these days! What difference does it make to you?'

Robert was not particularly comfortable with being left to fight the good cause alone.

He glanced to the back face of the house, where Karen's convenient absence added to his dismayed confusion.

He was certainly not happy about having to wilfully upset the neighbours that had been so good to his family.

Particularly when he was without any explanation or indeed any personal motive.

'Look. We didn't want the girls bothering you and wandering through. We thought it best.'

Evelyn was rapid with her retort.

'Those girls are welcome *anytime* into my garden. Well, at least, they *were*. But not now it seems. What do you reckon to this then, Greg? I tell you, lad, I'm lost for words. Hurt is how I feel. Hurt and annoyed.'

The gnarled expression on her son's face issued a conclusive tirade toward Robert as he stood with spade still in hand.

'You think this will do the trick do you? Keep us out of your life? Out of sight, out of mind? Is that what she wants, is it? Well, it won't work. I can promise you that much! Fuck your gate and fuck you! Come on, Mum!'

Robert was left rightfully speechless as the Chapples returned through their back door and slammed it behind them. This was not a good situation.

The message from the Aspinalls had certainly been conveyed successfully, but why things should have come to a head like this, Robert could not fathom for the life of him.

Lack of knowledge was Robert's chief source of frustration at that moment as he remained alone in the back garden. He felt almost as though he had been set up. His wife appeared to have loaded the gun and left him to fire it.

As the conflicting thoughts piled on top of one another he started to become annoyed himself. As he threw the spade into the shed Karen finally appeared onto the patio.

'Thank you, love. They look great!' she beamed.

Robert stomped toward her across the lawn to avoid having to raise his voice.

'How can you stand there and say you're happy about this, Karen? Well, if it makes you feel any better, I think you've achieved your aims. The neighbours are well pissed off! And so am I for that matter!'

Karen placed a hand on Robert's shoulder as he removed his trainers and kicked them across the patio.

'You've done a good thing today, Rob. Believe me.'

'I wish I *could* believe you, Kaz. But I don't even know what this is all about! You obviously don't want to speak to them again. Why, I don't know. What I do know is that after all these years it's a bloody shame. Childish and pathetic. Whatever Evelyn has done I'm sure it could have been resolved better than this. Now they hate *my* guts, too!'

Karen retained absolute composure under fire.

'Don't worry about it, Rob. I'm not going to.'

Robert looked into his wife's eyes and struggled to find a clue as to what she had been rankling with. Yet Karen's whole visage looked blank and soulless. Empty and devoid of life at that moment.

She was evidently a troubled woman.

He found it too much to try and comprehend her issue if she wasn't prepared to assist him with any reasoning.

'Evelyn has been like a mother to our children - and to *you* for that matter! Greg has been a star since he came home. Well, I hope you realise you might have burned a bridge today, Kaz. They are not happy with us. Not happy at all.'

Robert strode through the kitchen and up the stairs, mumbling to himself. Karen listened to his footsteps in the bedroom as she fingered her chin and rested her gaze on the refurbishment in the garden.

Inside her own mind, despite the animosity now emanating from number forty-one, she hoped that her days of personal consternation were now at an end.

Little did she know that her train of thought could not have been further from the truth.

Because the real nightmare was about to commence.

twenty-six

Monday morning. With arms folded and presence disguised behind her partially drawn lounge curtains, Evelyn Chapple observed Robert Aspinall's metallic blue automatic company car as it reversed out of the driveway to begin another working week.

She continued to stare intently at the scene as Karen then came into view still in her pyjamas, proceeding to swing the large front gate shut before hastily going back indoors.

Evelyn was now very familiar with the weekday habits of the Aspinalls. Moving her position to the rear upstairs bedroom, she waited patiently for a good twenty minutes until her fully dressed neighbour honed into view in the back garden with a basket of damp laundry.

Yet another blissfully warm day beckoned as Karen searched in the shed for her clothes pegs. As she emerged with the cloth bag Karen was immediately confronted with the vision of Evelyn at the back fence, standing ominously in her Big Chief pose above the line of newly planted conifers.

'No doubt this is your idea of a joke.'

Karen felt not one iota of trepidation as she considered her reply.

'It's no joke, Evelyn. A necessity, yes. But in no way a joke.'

'Who do you think you are, Karen? What game are you playing?'

Karen removed a garment from the laundry basket and shook it with a snap to remove the creases.

'The thing is, Evelyn, I don't think I can trust you anymore. Well, not you exactly, but that son of yours. He's dangerous. Un-hinged, even. I can't have any more to do with him. I'm sorry.'

Evelyn unfolded her bulging forearms and gripped the top of the fence in an uncanny imitation of her son.

Her eyes began to narrow as a mist of malice descended on the exchange.

'There's nothing wrong with my Greg. I told you he needed a good woman to keep him in line. That's all.'

'Yes, Evelyn. But he doesn't seem to understand that this particular woman is already married. He doesn't seem to take the hint. Neither do you for that matter.'

Evelyn's features contorted into a bitter mask of hissing vitriol.

'Well, you can hardly say you've discouraged him, can you?'

Karen was more than taken aback by the implication as she dropped the bag of clothes pegs at her feet.

'And what exactly is that supposed to mean?'

'Come off it, Karen. You don't exactly give him the cold shoulder, do you?'

It was difficult at that moment for Karen to believe what she was hearing.

'How dare you! Are you trying to say I've led him on?'

'That would be the way it looks to me. Gardening nearly naked. Going to parties together. Going to nightclubs together. And others in the street have seen it. They've all noticed how well you and Greg have been doing. Now you've gone and spoiled it all for him.'

'I suppose by *others* in the street you mean the Robinsons over the road?'

Evelyn Chapple suddenly looked rather sheepish.

'Well…yes. Colin and Lyndsey have shown an interest.'

Karen sensed her emotions beginning to surface once more and her voice raised a notch.

'Well for your information and any other nosey bastards that might be interested, Greg *attacked* me on the night when we went out for his birthday. *That's* why I don't trust him anymore.'

An uncomfortable silence engulfed the debate. Karen felt a lump of courage develop in her throat as she checked back to the kitchen to see that Chloe and Lauren were still having breakfast.

Evelyn mentally chewed over her next line and dismissively folded her arms once more as a gesture of defiance.

'I don't believe you. Neither would anyone else. You're making it up.'

'What you or anyone else would *believe* doesn't matter, Evelyn. You weren't there. I was. Besides, you're always going to side with your own son, aren't you? Your little angel that can do no wrong.'

Karen could tell that her one-time friend had been rocked by the starkness of the revelation, although Evelyn was trying her level best to conceal her reaction.

'But Greg hasn't said anything to me about this.'

'No? What a surprise! I wonder why that might be?' remarked Karen as she resumed with hanging the laundry.

'Look, I've nothing more to say, Evelyn. Besides, there've been one or two other things as well. Little puzzling episodes that I suspect he's been behind.'

Evelyn's tone grew louder in defence of her son.

'Full of your accusations this morning, aren't you! Does Robert know about these so-called little episodes, then?'

Karen was now the one stuck for a response.

Her heartbeat rapidly increased at the mention of her husband.

The one chink in Karen's armour.

Evelyn didn't know it, but she was now holding the ace in the pack.

She had unknowingly exposed Karen's weak spot.

In turn, Karen remained resolutely calm as she spoke.

'Robert sympathises entirely. That's why he's put the trees down rather than have a row about it all. It's a peaceful solution to the problem.'

Evelyn's sly smile conveyed her thoughts adequately.

Karen instinctively knew what was coming next.

'You haven't told Robert about this mystery attack, have you? You can't have. Or he'd be trying to plant our Greg, not bloody conifers!'

'Please, Evelyn. I've nothing more to say on the matter.'

'Well, Karen. I'm gob-smacked! I thought we were friends! You're nothing but a stuck-up snob with a dangerous imagination. You don't deserve friends like me and Greg. The way I see it, you're shutting us out of your life for no good reason. And what about your girls?'

Karen didn't appreciate the uninvited change of subject.

As far as she was concerned, Chloe and Lauren should not even be brought into the conversation.

'I don't know what you mean, Evelyn. What about my daughters? What have they got to do with any of this?'

'Well, *they're* losing two friends as well. Don't they get a say in things? Or do they have to take orders from you like your bloody weed of a husband?'

From the corner of her eye, Karen saw Chloe and Lauren standing on the patio understandably shrouded in confusion at what was transpiring down the garden. She turned to them but could tell that they had both witnessed the ensuing argument.

'Go back inside girls, please and get ready for school. Go on!'

Chloe wavered and ventured to enquire.

'Why are you fighting with Aunty Evelyn, Mummy?'

In a mild state of panic, Karen raised a forefinger to emphasise her command.

'Back inside, Chloe! Now! Lauren! You too, please!'

Casting her attention back to her former friend, Karen could sense Evelyn's inner satisfaction brewing.

'You've some explaining to do, haven't you, Karen? You're out of your depth with this. You've got no right! Greg is very upset about the way you've treated him. Let me warn you now…he won't forget this. Neither will I for that matter.'

Karen retrieved the nearly full laundry basket from the grass.

'Well, I don't appreciate being man-handled and assaulted by someone I thought I could trust. I won't forget *that* in a hurry, either!'

Evelyn turned away and slowly headed for her back door as Karen watched her with a simmering temper.

The parting shot was telling.

'I suggest you keep that accusation to yourself if you have no proof, Karen Aspinall!'

Karen could no longer control her desire to shout.

'Why don't you fucking ask him yourself then, Evelyn? You might be surprised by his fucking confession! Then again, maybe not surprised at all!'

Nothing more was uttered by Evelyn Chapple as she entered the domain of number forty-one and quietly closed the back door behind her.

Dropping the laundry basket onto the patio, Karen once again urged her loitering daughters to get dressed for school. Whilst her heart felt ready to burst from her chest under the strain of a pulsing dose of adrenaline, Karen also felt a certain sense of victory.

It was almost as though a large hurdle had been successfully navigated.

Karen felt strangely inflated.

As though she had faced the dragon in its lair and escaped unscathed.

Yet little did she know that the recent negative downturn in her relationship with the Chapples was merely the tip of a crumbling iceberg.

Far worse was to come.

Karen's sense of triumph was woefully misplaced.

She may have struck the opponents cold and with a degree of success, but their plan for redress was well in preparation.

twenty-seven

Two days later. Seven-fifty-two a.m. Two young daughters observed their mother on the telephone. They listened intently to her side of the conversation.

The tone of voice was laced with apprehension.

'Judy…it's Karen. I'm sorry to phone you.'

'When does your shift at hospital start?'

'You're on day off? Great!'

'No…no, I'm not…not really…'

'I need to speak to you…face to face…'

'Yes…I'm a bit upset…'

'No…Robert's fine…'

'No…it's not the girls…'

'Today? Lunch? Great!'

'Yes. In the square at twelve-thirty.'

'Thanks, Jude. See you later.'

Chloe and Lauren looked at their mother forlornly as she gently replaced the receiver in the cradle. They were told to stay in bed that morning and that they could have the day off school. Yet neither daughter wanted to stay in bed. And neither had been informed as to why their school routine had suddenly been altered. Something which had become a regular occurrence of late.

All they could decipher was that their mother was not a happy woman.

That something was tangibly wrong.

That their strong, beautiful mother seemed sad.

Scared.

Unsure.

Unsettled.

Not how mothers are supposed to be at all. Their mum had always been in charge and given out the orders. She had always organised everything. She had always led the team in a morning.

But not today, it seemed.

Not today.

Securing her daughters into the back of the car, Karen jumped in the front seat and crunched the gear box into reverse. She did not bother to shut the front gate behind her as the trio embarked on the familiar cruise along Benton Road.

The swinging front gate being left open. Another foregone daily ritual that further bemused Chloe and Lauren as they sat silently behind their mother.

Chloe glanced over to her younger sister as the curiosity became too much to bear.

'Mummy…why didn't we go to school again today?'

Karen checked the rear-view mirror as she approached the T junction. She felt certain that Greg had appeared at the end of his driveway as she promptly guided the car towards town.

The look on his face was not pleasant to behold.

A scornful guise that teemed with rage.

It was the same look that he had been repeatedly offering Karen on his rare appearances for the past couple of weeks.

A knowing yet playful mask of foreboding.

Maybe a warning of things to come. Perhaps a signal for danger.

Whilst not able to interpret the message being sent, it was nevertheless a sign that Karen could not help but heed.

Her focus returned to respond to the query from the back seat.

'Because I couldn't be bothered, Chloe. Don't worry, though. I'll write you a note to take tomorrow. You won't get into trouble. I promise.'

Quietly placated by her mother's assurances, Chloe smiled half-heartedly and looked through the window as the sun-drenched Church Drayton raced past.

However, another answer was soon required.

Chloe's next question was inevitable.

'Where are we going now, Mummy?'

Karen heard her daughter's voice but wasn't really listening.

She scanned the scenery as the car groaned through the gears.

The query was repeated.

'Mummy…where are we going?'

Finally, Karen answered.

'Oh…just to meet Aunty Judy in Tenbridge for lunch.'

The mention of food alerted Lauren to the conversation.

'Can we go for a burger meal, Mummy?'

'Yes…I suppose so. Are you both belted up? Don't forget about Mister Policeman! He might be watching.'

*****

Twelve-thirty-four p.m. It was not very often that Judy Simpson found herself unduly concerned about her friend. Karen was inherently headstrong and sensible. She rarely made mistakes in life. She had done everything to plan - the right way.

Moreover, the successful way.

Whereas Judy was not so well attuned to adult responsibility.

Judy seemed to fall at every fence due to some oversight or other.

But she wasn't envious of her best mate. Far from it.

Judy loved Karen Aspinall like a sister. She loved her for all the things that she was.

Because Karen was all the things that Judy wasn't.

And she had loved her for most of her life.

That was why today's phone call had bothered her so.

Her friend sounded desperate.

Afraid.

Uncertain.

Not the Karen she had known for nearly thirty years.

Yet Judy had been given no clue as to what the underlying cause of her dearest friend's supposed distress could be. All she could do was comply with Karen's request to meet in the market square.

Since the phone call four hours earlier Judy had tried in vain to turn over the possibilities. If it wasn't family trouble, husband trouble or car trouble, what could it be?

Financial trouble was no longer part of Karen's life since Robert's promotion. Besides, Judy was certainly the last person to be offering advice on money management.

On seeing Karen and the girls appearing across the square in front of the council house, Judy instantly knew that something was seriously out of place. Karen stood staring vacantly into the distance. Chloe was one side. Lauren the other. Both holding their mother's hands.

The trio looked lost. As though they had just been stranded off a distant sea ship and left on some undiscovered desert island. Judy approached without announcement. Instinct suggested that merriment seemed somewhat inappropriate as a greeting.

The first thing Judy noticed was that Karen's deep blue eyes looked glazed and colourless, as though she were on another planet, in another time.

The girls hugged their Aunty Judy enthusiastically as she held Karen's hands in her own.

So as not to overly engage the children, she attempted to maintain a hushed tone.

'You've worried me, Kaz. I hope this isn't going to be serious.'

Karen kissed her best friend on the cheek and embraced her tightly.

'Me too, Jude. Me too.'

*****

Chloe and Lauren were completely engrossed in their cheeseburgers until they looked up to ascertain the cause of a strange whining sound which was accompanied by a slight rocking of the table.

A low, stirring wheeze of pained release.

The tears of their mother were adequately contained, yet not sufficiently concealed as she relayed recent events to Judy across the table.

The youngsters exchanged worried glances before resuming their food and studying the puzzle game that came with their free toys.

In turn, Judy tried desperately to convey her responses to what she had heard in a controlled whisper of unsheathed despair.

'I fucking *told* you, Kaz! He's a crank! Fucking screw loose! But Jesus! Do you think he would have gone further if he'd had time? Fucking hell! The possibilities are frightening. You might not even be sitting here now! You are a stupid, stupid cow! If only you'd come home with me and Josh. Jesus!'

Karen continued to weep quietly into her sleeve without attracting too much attention to the table.

Judy's venomous reaction continued to spill forth.

'I can't believe it, Kaz. That bastard! Wait 'til I get my fucking hands on him! The fucking lousy perverted bastard! Who the fuck does he think he is?'

Karen wiped her eyes as her girls hesitantly continued with their meals.

'I'm sorry to burden you with this, Jude. Obviously, I can't talk to Robert. But the strain is beginning to tell. I don't know what Greg will do next. I keep catching him staring at me. In the street. In the garden. I don't feel my house belongs to me anymore. It's like he's taken over everything. He gives me the real creeps.'

Judy squeezed her friend's quivering hands and looked her sternly in the eye.

'Listen, Kaz. You've *got* to tell Rob. I can't believe he hasn't worked it out for himself, but I suppose if he's not around...that fucking job of his...*that* is where this all started!'

'I don't know *how* to tell him, Jude. How's it going to look? Evelyn even says I've been leading Greg on. Can you believe that?'

All too sadly for Judy, she saw the signs long before anybody else. She could see the potential peril. But it really wasn't her business.

Yet Karen had made little secret of her brief friendship with Greg and the fact that she felt it to be a positive thing. Even so, sexual assault was not something anyone could define as remotely excusable.

'I don't think he *needs* leading on, Kaz. He's mental. He's not right in the head. You can tell by just looking at him. His eyes are always everywhere, and he can't sit still. A bag of pent-up nerves.'

Judy was surprised to see her friend smile at such words.

'You're not much comfort, Jude. Telling me I live next door to a certified maniac!'

Judy herself was drawn to chuckle about the scenario.

'Don't worry, Kaz. He might feel like he's got the upper hand over you. But he knows what he did. He needs to toe the line to stay out of trouble.'

Karen took a large swig of coke through her straw and smiled at the concerned faces of her daughters.

Judy's hand touched each little girl on the cheek.

'It's okay. Mummy's fine. Don't worry.'

Judy's expression lightened as she proposed a solution.

'There is one other possibility, of course. Action that could sort him out good and proper. If you wanted.'

Karen's eyes flickered with false hope.

'What? Tell me! Anything!'

'I could get my brother Daniel to pay him a visit. Teach him some manners. Know what I mean? I'm sure he's a black belt in something.'

'No, Jude! Definitely not! No. That would only lead to more trouble. Hopefully things will die down now. I feel better just for speaking to someone about it. Hopefully he'll get bored and find some other interest. I just wish I didn't live next door. It's like it's in my face every waking hour.'

Judy placed her hands over Karen's clasped fingers and drew her face closer to her friend across the table.

'I'll tell you what to do. Go home. Set the paddling pool up. Get your sunbathing gear on and relax with a book. Forget the twat. I bet he hasn't given you another thought. Don't let him know he's scaring you. Face him off!'

Karen did not fully adhere to her friend's faith in such a policy.

'Really? Do you reckon, Jude?'

'Yes. I do reckon! Do it! Now! When you get home. Listen, I'm back to work tomorrow. I'll stay in touch. I hope I've helped. Ring me tonight if you need to, won't you?'

With lunch concluded, the four gathered outside the restaurant. Judy hugged and kissed Chloe and Lauren before turning to embrace Karen. She pecked her on the cheek before whispering a further piece of advice.

'Be big, Kaz. He'll lose interest quickly. That's if he hasn't already. I'll bet he's secretly very relieved you've kept your mouth shut. I bet he's been bricking it this last couple of weeks.'

Exchanging smiles and farewells, friends went in opposite directions. Karen felt a little happier having heaped some of the problem onto Judy.

Returning to the multi-storey car park, she concluded that her friend was probably correct.

Karen was a mere plaything to Greg Chapple.

A novelty that would quickly wear off.

He was most likely out somewhere at that moment finding someone else to torment. His attention would soon be diverted by another distraction.

Consolation gradually began to wash over Karen Aspinall as her family exited the city centre and headed back to Church Drayton.

*****

Greg watched from his mother's upstairs bedroom window as the familiar sight of the red motor car honed into view and pulled to a stop on the road outside number thirty-nine.

His mind stirred with anticipation as Karen vacated the car and opened the gate.

The thought flickered through her mind that she had purposely not closed it when she left the house that morning, but she couldn't be totally certain. Positioning the car onto the driveway, she decided to adopt Judy's plan.

Summer was being very generous and again the sun beat a high arc, bathing the back garden in tropical warmth that was now almost being taken for granted.

Following Judy's advice to the letter, Karen re-filled the paddling pool for the girls, who proceeded to play and splash with vigour. Reclining on her sun-lounger in her bikini with magazine in hand, Karen's fine figure was in need of some renewed exposure and gladly soaked up the warming rays.

Yet Karen could not relax. She read and re-read the same line over and over.

Her attention was regularly diverted to the scene of the girls in the pool, or to the line of new conifers next to the gate in the fence, or beyond that sacred border, to the potentially subversive activity in the Chapple household.

Her thoughts were constantly clouded with darkness.

Visions of the unknown; the unseen.

Expectation of the unexpected.

Awaiting the return of the phantom to the empty theatre.

'These sweets don't taste very nice, Mummy!'

Karen's attempt at concentration was once again broken by the sound of Lauren's tiny voice in the short distance.

'What did you say, love? Mummy can't quite hear.'

Lauren stood up in the paddling pool and held up an object in her little fingers for Karen to see. It wasn't easy to identify what her daughter was displaying.

'These sweets, Mummy! They're horrid!'

Karen stood up and made her way down to the pool. She smiled at the sight of Lauren in her bright yellow swimming costume and matted hair that framed her impish features.

Then the smile was suddenly eroded by shock as she saw that Lauren was holding a used cigarette butt.

Then her concern turned to mild panic as she noticed that her youngest daughter was in the process of chewing another. Then horror eclipsed the golden scenario. Beside the paddling pool on the grass were strewn the contents of an ash tray. Two dozen or so cigarette ends lay among the smattering of dirty, grey powder.

'Spit it out. Lauren! Spit it out! Now! Quick!'

Lauren did as her mother requested with an expression of sincere revulsion.

'I don't like them, Mummy.'

'They're not sweets, darling. Go and have a drink of water, quickly. Chloe, can you take her for a drink, please.'

Karen watched her daughters walk hand in hand back to the kitchen before scrutinising the mess on the grass.

It was most odd. Robert had quit smoking two years ago. She knew for a fact that he hated the very idea of it nowadays.

Karen bent down and picked the dirty filters off the lawn before brushing the ash into the grass with her hand. Moving toward the patio, her attention was briefly attuned to a figure next door.

In the rear upstairs bedroom of number forty-one, Karen exchanged stares with Greg, who stood defiantly in the window.

He carried an expression of sordid pleasure that only served to confirm him as the owner of the ash tray.

Yet, Karen had never seen him smoke.

Nor his mother for that matter.

But the deviant grin that he displayed for her benefit was all the evidence she needed.

Greg was not bored with the game.

He was anything but bored with Karen Aspinall.

Casting the stubs into the kitchen dustbin, she checked Lauren was okay and washed her hands.

'The taste's gone now. Can we go back outside, Mummy?' asked her youngest.

For the first time in their lives, Karen did not want her children to play in their own garden. It was twenty-seven degrees. Not a cloud in the sky. Yet the garden did not seem to be the haven it once was.

It was now deemed open to attack.

Defenceless against intrusion.

Perhaps her girls would be at risk in this once-idyllic setting where they had played together since infancy?

Karen was doused with returning anxiety and the dawning realisation that Judy's optimistic forecast may not become true after all.

Her mind tossed around indecision and insecurity as the droning bell of the nearby ice cream van echoed around the estate.

Chloe and Lauren's excitement at the fact turned to tears as again their hopes and desires were quickly dampened.

It was also another first-time occurrence in the life of Karen Aspinall. With trembling hands, she peaked through the gap in the lounge curtains and saw the ice cream van parked directly outside.

Then she saw Greg in the queue.

The shrieks of abject disappointment from her little girls jolted her maternal senses.

'Why can't we have one, Mummy? Why?'

Chloe's tears were unrelenting as she screamed her displeasure and frustration.

'Chloe…please calm down…I haven't got any money. Not today. Okay?'

Karen did not see the full flood of emotion from her eldest daughter who retreated up to her bedroom in a confused, juvenile state of distress.

Lauren merely stood confused in silence.

These little girls could not understand the fear that their mother was steadily nurturing in her soul.

Similarly, Karen did not fully acknowledge her own daughters, who were wracked with sorrow at the thought of missing their rightful summertime treat.

She would never know the grief that young Chloe felt at that moment as she screamed into her pillow until her throat became raw.

Karen would never know.

Because she did not see how things were changing before her very eyes.

All Karen Aspinall could see these days was the face of a reaper.

A vision that induced greater dread with each passing day.

A force that had invaded the fabric of her existence like a virus.

At that moment as she studied the cause of her inner misery through the gap in the curtains, Karen wondered if a cure might ever arrive.

twenty-eight

A relatively peaceful following day had endured for the Aspinall family. The girls had attended school and nursery. Chloe with a letter of apology to her teacher. Karen had spoken to the nursery supervisor in person.

There had been no contact with the outside world aside from the journeys in the car.

Almost a prisoner in her own home. But not quite.

Yet the demons were gathering around number thirty-nine.

Karen now felt to be under the authority of some unseen entity.

Her mind had toiled with endless possibility all day. The phone had rung three times. Each time being her mother, Jean, who no doubt wondered why Karen and the girls hadn't made their customary visit yesterday.

Yet Karen was in no mood for explanations. Besides which, it had not even occurred to her that yesterday was Wednesday.

The evening call from Robert did nothing to improve her disposition, either.

In fact, his opinions could not have come as a worse time.

Yet again Chloe and Lauren were in earshot of their mother's side of the tense dialogue with their father.

'Well, yes, Rob. She has spoken to me about the trees.'

'Monday…just after you left.'

'No…it didn't go well.'

'What did you expect?''

'Well…Rob…its tough luck. I want to keep them, now.'

'I know she has been a good friend.'

'Things change though, Rob. People change.'

'So, you don't understand. Live with it. You don't understand very much these days.'

'Cos you're never fucking here, that's why!'

'No, if I'm honest. I don't like you being away all week.'

'It's fucking crap, Rob.'

'It's not like we're even married anymore.'

'No…we're like strangers.'

'I know I said I'd support you, but it's getting difficult. You need to be here for us.'

'*You* feel let down? I feel fucking let down!'

'I'm sorry but I'm pissed off. And I know I shouldn't swear.'

'I *do* try and keep things organised.'

'It's alright for you pissing of all week and leaving me to it!'

'No, I'm not happy. Not at all.'

'Well, if you could get Fridays off maybe it would be a start.'

'I am trying to understand your side of things.'

'Oh, fuck the neighbours. Why are you so bothered about them, anyway?'

'*We* should be your priority, or have you forgotten that little thing in your life called your family?'

'Yes, I am totally fed up with it all!'

'Well fucking hang up, then!'

On that terse note, Robert obliged his wife's blunt suggestion.

Karen threw the receiver to the floor and slumped onto the sofa.

Holding her knotted stomach, she let her gaze wander to the view beyond the front window. Red deposits of early dusk flecked the skyline.

For a few blissful moments, she was on another planet, flying with the stars. Her daydream was disturbed by a familiar yet welcome voice.

'Mummy...we're hungry!'

Chloe and Lauren stood in the lounge doorway in their nightdresses. Crumpled ponytails and bare feet were the trademark bedtime signs. Karen smiled and held out her arms for them both to fall into. She held them long and tight, before Chloe ventured to sate her curiosity.

'Mummy?'

'Yes, darling?'

'Why were you and Daddy fighting on the phone?'

It was becoming difficult to keep her daughters' eager ears from detecting certain aspects of the situation. Honesty with her little girls was long overdue, if only in edited form.

'Adults argue now and again, love. But we'll be fine. We're just a bit grumpy with each other. That's all.'

Karen kissed Chloe on top of the head as Lauren opted to volunteer a query of her own.

'Mummy?'

'Yes, darling?'

'Can I have toast and jam for supper?'

*****

With Chloe and Lauren fed, watered and finally into bed, Karen ran herself a luxurious bath with bubbles and candles.

Supposedly the best antidote to encroaching stress.

The kitchen clock showed the time to be just after eleven. Karen felt dog tired, despite having done little physical activity during the day. Inspecting her face in the bathroom mirror, she pushed and pulled at the skin around her forehead and nose, before puffing out her cheeks to check for blemishes.

She didn't feel good, and her skin was showing signs of strain. Dryness; tautness; colourless. This was not the face she liked to see in the mirror. Grey shadows were growing under her eyes.

In all, not a pretty picture to behold. At least in her view.

The telephone interrupted her process of facial inspection.

She knew instantly who the caller would be and rushed into the lounge to answer.

It was time to make amends with her husband.

'I'm sorry, too, darling.'

'Yes. I'm okay really. Just miss you. That's all.'

'Just running myself a lovely hot bath.'

'Well, there's room for two but isn't life a bitch!'

'Yes…I know the next line, you cheeky git!'

'I don't know. Perhaps a change of scene for a few days.'

'I'll talk to Mum tomorrow.'

'Perhaps stay with her next week or something.'

'Yes, they've been in bed half an hour or so.'

'Of course, they miss you, silly.'

'Okay. As soon as you can tomorrow, then?'

'Tell him you've got a desperate housewife to see to! Can't wait!'

'Okay, love. See you tomorrow. Bye.'

A rush of contentment reigned temporarily in Karen's soul as she checked her bath. With a few minutes to spare before it would be ready, she ventured to the kitchen and proceeded to tidy up the few pots and paraphernalia that lay about the worktops.

Robert always used to mock her for her principle that she preferred to wake up to a tidy kitchen in a morning but rarely felt the inclination to clean up the night before.

Moving some ironing that was definitely not urgent, Karen's attention was diverted by a strange tapping noise emanating from somewhere in the room.

It was akin to a clicking sound.

Though not like a dripping tap.

More a hardened echo.

She stopped what she was doing and remained still to strain her ear.

The noise persisted. It was impossible to tell where it was originating from.

For nearly a full five minutes she listened, scrutinised, and second guessed its source. All to no avail.

Then the tapping stopped.

Silence resumed around the kitchen once more.

Concluding that it must have been air in the water pipes, Karen conceded defeat to the tidying up before switching off the kitchen light and getting undressed upstairs in the bathroom.

Bath time. Welcome respite from the aches and pains of another idyllic day in Church Drayton.

The welcome immersion into soapy oblivion soon encouraged the onset of sleep. In one instance, lovely, soothing heat enshrouded her form.

Then the eyes and limbs became heavy and the head light as slumber took control.

Then came the explosive bang at the bottom of the stairs.

A split-second impact that resonated around the hallway. It jolted Karen from her watery doze and forced her to sit up in the bath.

Water dripped from her nose and ears as she listened intently for a repetition of the sound.

It could have a boot against the front door.

It could have been Karen's overactive imagination.

As with the tapping in the water pipes, she concluded the noise to be a figment of mental invention.

Nevertheless, she had heard the bang.

Just as she had heard the tapping in the kitchen.

It roused her.

Her mind and body had reacted, so therefore it surely could not have been imagined.

Could it?

Pulling herself from the now tepid water, she pulled out the plug. Karen wrapped towels around her head and body before over coating the arrangement with a dressing gown.

Her descent down the stairs was rapid if wary.

The hall remained still and dark.

Seemingly undisturbed.

Apparently untouched.

Unlike her mind, which had now recoiled from its temporary solace in the bathroom to become once again plagued with undue thoughts and prevailing doubts.

Karen tentatively eased ajar the front door and peered through the gap into the shadows of midnight.

She saw nothing but the silent vision of her car and the closed gate behind it. All around was tainted with an orange hue from the nearby streetlamp.

Placated to a degree, Karen closed the front door once more and hastily applied the lock and chain.

Inside her bed, she wrapped herself in warm, positive, comforting distraction.

Yet outside in those same shadows she had just inspected, a phantom did stir.

twenty-nine

Karen had hardly slept during the night. Her eyes had closed at intervals, yet any temporary submersion into slumber was soon disrupted by an unseen, unforgiving presence.

An unrelenting gremlin in her brain that had left her feeling decidedly fatigued as the seven-a.m. alarm droned from across the other side of the bedroom.

Dragging herself from beneath the bedclothes, Karen was surprised to hear voices coming from downstairs. Retrieving her dressing gown from the floor, she squinted into the shafts of sunlight on the landing before confirming that her daughters were indeed up and awake before she was.

Another first-time experience in the life of the Aspinalls.

A school day where the pupils were out of bed first.

Karen entered the lounge and crouched down to hug her little girls as they sat watching television.

'What are you two doing up? It normally takes me ages to get you to open your eyes, never mind move!'

Chloe ventured an explanation.

'Someone was throwing things at our bedroom windows, Mummy. We got scared.'

The trinity of love was rocked in its nest once more as Karen stood unsteadily to her feet with a worried heart pumping in her chest.

She did not even need to ask herself the question.

The answers were brutally evident.

Greg Chapple had been on the prowl last night.

Under cover of darkness.

His deeds supplying a total absence of proof and no witness.

Yet it was definitely him. The nocturnal menace.

Karen attempted to eclipse the haunting conclusion with talk of breakfast.

'Would you like cereal or toast, girls? Come on. Get to the table, please. We look like being on time this morning for once.'

It was the only credible response Karen felt able to give.

What more could she do? Aside from let her quashed emotions rage into her straining gut and terrorise her already vulnerable psyche.

That was not the side of their mother that Chloe and Lauren ever needed to see.

Karen Aspinall hoped that the wavering concealment of her abounding torture was sufficient to maintain an even keel.

With her daughters munching happily to the accompaniment of the kitchen radio, Karen traipsed back upstairs to face the bathroom mirror.

Again, she examined her features in expectancy of discovering some tell-tale sign of her inner havoc.

The sign she was looking for, she found.

But not in her own reflection.

She turned; observed; became slowly dismayed; then resigned herself to further possibility and speculation.

The bath remained half full of water. The plug hanging between the taps; exactly where she had left it after getting out last night.

Just after hearing the thud of a boot against the front door.

Karen adopted a logical process of elimination. It must be something lying in the drain grate. She quickly remembered that as a plumber of repute and experience, her father told her that water backs up in down-pipes if the drain grate is not regularly cleared. Blockages will inevitably occur over time.

It could be a few leaves, maybe. Wastepaper, perhaps. The odd stray crisp packet, no doubt. Anything could have blown into the grate.

This was most certainly a solvable problem.

One that Karen would contentedly deal with alone.

'You two finish your cereal. I'm just nipping outside for a moment.'

Neither daughter responded as they wearily chomped.

Karen retrieved the back door keys from the side of the kitchen cupboard. The place they were always kept for security.

Inserting the key; she proceeded to unlock the latch.

Without further thought, Karen pressed the handle down.

No sooner had she achieved this, a crescendo of shattering glass erupted from the other side of the door, giving cause for the three occupants of the kitchen to jump out of their skin. Chloe sensed a need for urgent inquiry as she watched her mother warily peering through the gap to ascertain the cause.

'Mummy! What was that?'

Karen pushed the door open to reveal the problem.

'It looks like a broken beer bottle, darling. No, correction, it looks like *two* broken beer bottles. Looks like they've been placed on the outside handle. I'll clean it up. Do *not* come out here. You two finish your breakfast and get ready for school, please.'

Anger was now the primary emotion cursing Karen's veins.

Outwardly frothing fury that she should ever be subjected to such treatment.

Inward frustration that she should stand by and continue to allow it to progress untamed.

As she swept the jagged trap into her dustpan, a distinctly unwelcome voice echoed from across the fence in the back garden.

It was a vaguely familiar tone. Recognisable as belonging to someone that Karen once considered to be an amiable companion. Crouching amongst the sharp debris in her dressing gown and slippers, Karen glanced upward to the source of the call.

She was in no mood for pretence.

Evelyn Chapple had picked the wrong moment to display her feigned concern.

'Whatever was that crash, Karen?'

The anger felt moments earlier had now been fuelled into incessant rage by the sound of Evelyn's voice.

'MIND YOUR OWN FUCKING BUSINESS!'

'No need to speak to me like that! I was just asking.'

Karen stood upright and pointed her hand brush in the direction of the inquisitor.

'You know all about it, Evelyn. Don't you dare fucking pretend you don't! You and your fucking nutcase of a son! I've had enough, Evelyn. I've had enough of him! You'd better tell him!'

With practiced charm, Evelyn folded her meaty arms and smirked. Karen had seen the gesture employed by her neighbour on many occasions over the years.

It was usually exhibited in response to somebody or something she took a particular aversion to.

'More accusations, eh? You're paranoid, Karen Aspinall! Bloody paranoid!'

With that, Karen's one-time friend disappeared back into her lair.

A retreat behind enemy lines that would be a significant episode in the relationship between two people that once considered each other as completely trustworthy.

Once upon a time, as close as mother and daughter.

Indeed, a relationship that Karen once claimed to be a pivotal asset in her life.

A reliable confidante.

A sacred shoulder to cry on.

A friend in need, whenever she was needed.

She didn't know it during that precise moment of heated release, but Karen Aspinall would never exchange words with Evelyn Chapple again.

*****

Yet again, there would be neither school nor nursery for Chloe and Lauren. The red car pulled to a stop outside the home of Brian and Jean Hope.

For once there was no welcoming wave from Karen's mother.

This was an unannounced visit to Cobden Terrace in Goltham.

Karen peered through the driver's window as her mother offered a reserved and curious smile from her position at the front door.

In an instant, the girls were out of the car and hanging on their grandmothers' apron.

Jean's rehearsed expression of joviality briefly masked her instinctive, maternal concerns.

'Karen! Oh, it's wonderful to see you! We missed you so on Wednesday! I've been ringing you.'

Her daughter maintained the act of stoicism with a forced grin.

'I'm really sorry, Mum. Just lost track of time this week.'

'Well, no mind. You're all here now. Come on in. You've caught me just right. I'm baking. Are the girls off school today, then?'

'Not really. But I've got a bit of a problem. Can the girls stay with you for an hour?'

Karen was pleased to see her father's van on the front drive.

'I'm glad Dad's in. I need a favour.'

*****

The white transit van inscribed with the name *B.G. Hope Plumbing and Heating* pulled onto the drive of number thirty-nine, Benton Road.

Karen sat nervously in the passenger seat beside her father. The intense, overriding dismay she carried at that moment was disguised by a stream of trivial chatter between the pair.

Karen was thankful of the fact. She did not want awkward pauses.

But she knew that her father was very adept at sensing trouble given the chance.

'You say it's the down pipe from the bath? Lucky I've got the ladders on then, isn't it?'

After inspection of the half-full tub of water upstairs, Brian Hope duly went to remove his ladder from the roof rack of the van. His reassuring tone echoed up the stairs as Karen sat on her bed in expectant fear.

Despite her father's authoritative presence, she was petrified of the whole damning scenario he had willingly if unwittingly entered.

Her heart raced quietly. Breaking point was not far away.

'If I find the cause, I'll try and shift it while I'm up there. It can't be anything permanent, I'm sure. You stay in the bathroom and check the water for me. Okay, love?'

'Okay, Dad.' Karen choked, as a hard cyst of wrenching emotion formed in her gullet.

She sat in silence on the side of the bath for what seemed like only seconds. A sudden gurgle from the plug hole was followed by the swift exit of water from the tub.

Good old Dad, she thought. Always handy in any crisis.

Bounding down the stairs with a mildly diverting feeling of glee, her pleasure at the successful outcome of the operation was instantly eroded by the sight of her father standing outside the back door holding the cause of the blockage.

She vaguely recognised the object in her father's hand.

A toy elephant with a red ribbon bow around its neck.

Then realisation dawned.

Her gift to Greg on his birthday.

Karen's father chuckled as he held the toy aloft.

'He's a bit drenched but should survive with a bit of tender loving care. Perhaps a run in the washing machine wouldn't be a bad idea. Strange thing is it was rammed in the bottom of the pipe. A tight fit.'

It was only her father's smile that prevented Karen from collapsing in front of him there and then. Her stomach cramped. Her vision blurred. Her legs began to shake.

She held desperately onto a semblance of sanity as he re-loaded the ladders onto the van.

'No, Dad…bin it. Please. Get rid of it. I don't want it.'

Karen could not even bear to glance across to the possible spectating scenario at number forty-one. No doubt the neighbours had watched and drawn great mirth from Karen's moment of realised agony.

It was time for Karen to make her decision.

Desperately fighting a frothing mix of sensations, she followed her father to the van.

'Dad. I need to talk to you and Mum. Today. Now. It's serious.'

Brian Hope looked wide-eyed as his little girl clung to his side. He placed a reassuring hand on her shoulder as Karen slowly calmed herself down. He could see she was on the verge of dreadful upset.

Escape from Benton Road was now a necessity.

An immediate and vital step. If only on a temporary basis.

She secured the house and front gate before turning to her father who waited patiently in the road behind the wheel of the van.

'Hop in, love. Come on, cheer up. It can't be all that bad. Let's go and talk about it with your mum.'

*****

Father, mother and daughter sat opposite one another in the relative safety of the lounge at Cobden Terrace. Unrestrained emotion flooded the room, as Jean and Brian Hope listened patiently and sympathetically to every single, torrid detail of the chronicle of torment that had unfolded in recent weeks.

Brian was partially confused; partially enraged.

He sat on the sofa with an arm around each of his granddaughters, gently squeezing their tiny arms as their mother convulsed with distress in her chair.

The innocent tears of Chloe and Lauren were a natural reaction to seeing their mother's sorrow. Quite rightly, they grasped very little of what was revealed in that room.

Yet Karen Aspinall recalled absolutely everything.

The recollections were frighteningly vivid and barbed with toxic afterthought.

Her memory banks had carefully filed each and every aspect of the campaign that the Chapples had begun to wage.

Mother and father could only watch in helpless despair as their only child crumbled before them.

Just as two sisters could only watch as their mother crumbled before them.

Once the full, sorry tale had been conveyed, that secure living room in Goltham had become infested with an atmosphere of unrelenting fury.

A combination of mental trauma ensued.

The guilt felt by uninitiated parents.

The gut-wrenching remorse of a loving wife and mother.

The bewilderment of two oblivious little girls.

Finally sensing an easing of his daughter's anguish, Brian Hope spoke.

The rest of the family listened as he addressed Karen.

'You must tell Robert. You can't keep him in the dark. Too much has happened, Karen. And I think you must consider telling the police. We'll support you all the way. But you can't keep this quiet any longer. You've become sport for them. Nothing more. It's a game they are enjoying by the look of things.'

Karen covered her mouth with a shaking hand, straining her vision to focus on her father.

'But Dad, telling people would make them think I asked for it. Robert would be mortified. Don't you see the situation I've put myself in? I'm trapped by my own stupidity.'

Her father continued with his judgment.

'Only you can decide, love. But being at that house is doing you no good. You look pale and gaunt. Your eyes are filled with fear. You're making yourself ill. Your mother knew something was up a good while back. But we never, ever guessed it would be something this unseemly.'

'Mum…Dad…please…let me speak to Rob when I'm ready. Please can we stay with you here next week? Just while Rob's away. I can't stand being at home alone. It's like a haunted house these days.'

Her father drew his face closer to Karen's.

Their eyes met in a bond of sincerity and intrinsic love.

'This door is open as long as you need it to be. You know that. We'll expect you first thing Monday morning. Stop here as long as you like. That's what we're here for.'

The Hope's telephone echoed from the hallway into the lounge, causing Jean to jump to her feet in anticipation.

Karen listened as her mother picked up the receiver.

'Hello, Robert.'

'Yes, fine thanks, love. You?'

'Oh, right. Yes, she's here now with the girls. Do you want her?'

'Oh…you're home already!'

'Oh good…she will be pleased. Yes.'

'Yes, I'll tell her you're waiting, then.'

'See you soon, love. Bye.'

*****

Karen tightly embraced both parents before getting into the car. She wound the window down as her father offered a parting word with his voice carrying a distinct trace of authority.

'Our thoughts are with you, Karen. It's your choice how you deal with it, but you've made it our business as well as your own, now. If you need us, then we are here for you all. I hope things die down. But I still think that bastard deserves a lesson.'

Karen looked at the inevitably worried figure of her mother at the front door.

'Tell Mum I love her, Dad. I'll see you both Monday morning. And thanks.'

Brian Hope strained a smile at his young family and blew the fondest of kisses to the two innocents in the back seat.

And as he did so, he silently pledged to himself they would never have cause to glimpse the black hole that had formed in his heart.

thirty

Jean Hope had herself succumbed to immense worry. Whilst Karen had decided to forgo further involvement in the ills surrounding Benton Road, the situation remained unresolved.

She had carefully observed the abrupt changes in her daughter's manner. Karen was not her natural, carefree self. She was carrying a burden that was taking a psychological and physical toll. The strain was very evident. But Jean had suspected a problem for at least a month or more.

A mother knows instantly.

Whilst Karen was content to be away from her source of torment, revealing the arrangement had incurred diverse reaction in Robert and the girls. The weekend flashed by in a mix of unnecessary petty arguments and subsequent prevailing silence.

Robert knew something was amiss but maintained a careful distance from his wife and her sudden prickly mood swings. Yet he had no apparent qualms about his wife and daughters staying with the Hopes.

Nor did he harbour any suspicions regarding the motives for the arrangement. The girls revealed nothing of what had occurred previously. They were happy to be in the company of their mother and father once again - albeit under a cloud of growing animosity.

Karen herself could not wait for Monday morning.

To flee the arena of insidious scheming.

To feel safe once again.

To indulge herself and her young in the protective fold of her parents' abode.

A full week had now passed since Karen Aspinall had set eyes on the Chapples. Possibly the longest she had ever gone without witnessing or hearing any activity from the territory of number forty-one.

Yet the personal struggle had eased only mildly.

Friday came around all too soon for her to return home.

It was now only a crumb of comfort that Robert would also be home that evening. The past few days had been wonderful respite, but all too rapid in passing.

It was not a pleasant feeling for Karen to pack her car boot in readiness for resumed weekend residency at number thirty-nine.

The dark shroud of the unknown blocked out the sun as she waited in the car for Lauren to emerge from the nursery building on that particular Friday dinner time.

Karen sat in impatient, dreadful silence, chewing at the flesh near the nails on her forefingers until she winced in pain and drew blood.

When her youngest finally emerged under supervision from the class leader, she was carrying a windmill she had made from coloured paper.

Lauren smiled avidly at her mother as she skipped into the golden light of day.

As Karen belted her youngest into the back seat, a thought hit her like a thunderbolt.

She really did not want to go home.

There was now a revulsion that stirred within her at the very thought of even driving along Benton Road, let alone pitting herself against the unseen monsters that inhabited, slept, and played in and around number thirty-nine.

Her daughter's first request only compounded the quandary.

'Mummy…can I have the paddling pool out again today?'

The sunlight crashed through the windscreen and the temperature outside must have been pushing the thirty-degree mark. The hottest summer day so far. Yet Lauren's natural wish to cool herself and play with water was not answered.

Karen was very reluctant to say yes.

But similarly, she should not willingly refuse her daughter the opportunity for fun.

The conundrum ricocheted around her mind as the car navigated the T junction leading to Benton Road. The profile of the house came ever nearer.

Karen's heart thudded ever faster in expectant recoil of what lay beyond the threshold.

The large white gate was shut - just as she had left it on Monday morning. On first inspection from the relative safety of the car, the house looked untouched.

It appeared that no one had tried to disturb the scene in her absence, which placated her only for the duration it took to leave the car, open the gate, reposition behind the steering wheel, navigate the driveway, and tentatively close the gate behind her.

She could see from Lauren's reaction that her youngest was more than pleased to be back in familiar surroundings. Her excitement manifested itself in intermittent giggles and mutterings.

Thankfully, Karen detected no sign of any presence next door as she fumbled in her handbag for the house key.

Had she identified Greg Chapple reliably in position at the front bedroom window of number forty-one, she may not have dealt with the return home so capably.

Karen selected the front door key and placed the tip inside the lock.

It would not enter fully.

Believing herself to have erroneously selected the wrong key, she scanned the others on her brown leather fob.

Yet, Karen knew full well that the first key chosen was the correct one.

In her second attempt, she sensed an obstruction in the lock mechanism. Something inside the barrel was preventing insertion. Removing the key once more, she peered into the small, dark slot.

A futile act that revealed nothing conclusive.

Yet it was obvious that the lock had been tampered with in some way.

Similarly, Karen did not need to second guess the culprit.

As her mind toiled with the problem of getting into the house, a shriek of horror from the side of the garage diverted her attention.

Lauren came running to her mother carrying an expression of disgust on her face as Karen swept her into her arms.

'Mummy! Mummy!'

'Whatever is the matter, love? What is it?'

She watched as Lauren pointed toward the scene with a tiny forefinger.

'There's a dead bird next to the side gate, mummy! Its head is gone!'

Sure enough, a quick inspection of the offending article confirmed Lauren's sorry story.

Although the size of the lifeless blackbird made Karen wonder about her initial theory on the cause of its demise.

'It's okay, Lauren. I bet a cat's killed it. That's what cats do you know! They sometimes eat birds for their dinner!'

'It's horrible, mummy!'

Karen comforted her sniffling daughter with a warm embrace before putting her back down to the floor. Lauren's distress at seeing the helpless feathered quarry was minimal compared to the intensive alarm Karen was now weighed down with.

'Well, I suppose we'd better get Grandad to come and look at this door, hadn't we? Come on, darling. Back in the car.'

Lauren's attention was suddenly attracted elsewhere.

To another area near the garage.

She seemed transfixed by something up toward the side of the house hanging above the garage roof. Again, she pointed avidly whilst looking to her mother for some explanation.

The head of the dead bird swung from the toilet overflow pipe. Attached by a length of string, the lifeless black eyes seemed to stare straight into her. It was like an image from a cheap suspense movie. As though the severance of the animal represented a warning of some terrible event to come.

A shiver cursed its way down Karen's spine.

The cat theory was evidently way off the mark.

*****

An hour later Brian Hope had followed Karen's car and parked his van outside number thirty-nine, Benton Road. With the aid of his trusty ladder, he scaled the side of the house and disentangled the peering head of the blackbird.

Reunited with its carcass once more, the whole thing was bagged up and duly placed in the dustbin.

Minutes later, he had inspected the lock, removed it from the door, checked its mechanisms and finally located the blockage.

Her father delicately unpicked the broken matchstick from the barrel with the end of a paper clip.

Karen watched her father intently as he then screwed the brass latch back into the wooden recess.

His concentration was matched by an inner turmoil.

He could not stand back and accept that the Chapples had stooped so low as to perform such a deed.

Karen watched over his shoulder as he turned the screwdriver and shook his head slowly.

'This is not good, Kaz. Are you sure its them next door?'

'No doubt, Dad. No doubt at all.'

'But why? What have you done to deserve to be treated like this? It's barbaric, what with that bird being strung up. It's the work of lunatics!'

Karen glanced over her shoulder to scan the apparently vacant territory of number forty-one.

'Looks like staying away only makes matters worse, Dad.'

Tightening the last screw, her father closed his toolbox and looked Karen in the eye.

His daughter looked frightfully worn.

Dejected and fatigued.

'Are you staying here next week? It's up to you, my girl. It's up to you. Our door is open. You know that.'

'I ought to stop here, Dad. I don't think Robert's overly impressed with the idea of me leaving our home for another week. In fact, I suspect he thinks I'm going a bit nuts myself!'

Her father retrieved his toolbox from the floor and offered his daughter a word of sincerity.

'That is why you must *speak* to him, love. *Tell* him for Christ's sake! You can't go on living like this. He's home tonight, yes?'

Karen nodded without answering.

'Right. No excuses. Fill him in on what's going on…or *I* will!'

Waving to her father as he drove away, Karen's thoughts turned to the imminent arrival of her husband.

And the horrendous revelations he would be greeted with.

As Brian Hope's transit van steered out of view, another figure stood out of view in studious observation.

The face on the figure displayed a malevolent smile.

Smugly appeased by his accomplishments.

Distinctly unmoved by the untold sufferance he was now engineering.

thirty-one

Friday evening evolved relatively painlessly into Saturday morning, but tensions were still in evidence.

'Okay. So, my job is putting pressure on us as a family. You don't like me being away all week. I accept these things, Kaz. But I'm in no position to do much about it at this moment. I need more time. I need more patience from you, as well.'

Robert and Karen sat facing one another at the breakfast table. The recent frosty atmosphere between them had showed little signs of thawing.

Both had adopted full justification for feeling the way they did about the current domestic situation.

Karen was now at a total loss on how to deal with the neighbour problem. The wise words of her father hung around her conscience.

Karen did not like the fact that she seemed to be in control of so little in her life at that moment. It thwarted any possibility of genuine intimacy of communication with the man she so dearly loved.

Quite rightly, Robert's oblivious, blissful ignorance regarding the bigger picture was becoming an insurmountable problem for him as well as his wife.

'I suppose you'll be packing off to Goltham all next week again, then? I don't get it, Karen. I know the days can be a bit long, but we've got everything we need here. Plus, while the weather's good the girls are going to appreciate being in their own garden I would have thought. And you can't stay cooped up at your mum's for the school holidays surely? I'm surprised you don't see it yourself.'

Karen picked at her bacon sandwich.

'Karen…are you listening to me?'

'Yes…yes, I'm listening…there's no need to shout, Rob! I'm only here!'

Throwing his cutlery onto the plate, Robert stood to his feet.

'Well, it's obviously going to be another bleeding lovely weekend under the same roof. I'll be cleaning the cars if you decide you might need me for anything before I go back to Coventry on Monday morning.'

Karen sat trembling as she listened to her husband clattering outside and then returning to the kitchen to rummage under the sink.

The silence between man and wife was unbearable and unhealthy.

The situation could not be allowed to continue.

Emerging from the side of the house with a full bucket of soapy water, the welcoming sunshine instantly relaxed Robert as he mopped down the dusted metal of Karen's car with a large sponge.

Judging by the grime and dirt encrusted around the bumpers and front grill, it was obvious that Karen hadn't cleaned it all summer. Still, even more reason to get stuck into the task as a welcome if laborious distraction. The water splashed over his sandaled feet as he lightly scrubbed.

Engrossed in his chore, Robert did not hear the approach of a car from the other end of the road.

Only as it reached the frontage of number thirty-nine did he then acknowledge its presence and look up. The racing green three-door had stopped outside the front gate with the engine running.

At the wheel was a young man that seemed familiar. He was definitely from the local area. Something of a renowned trouble causer as far as Robert could recall.

He stared intently at the figure in the driving seat, who returned the glare through heavy black shades and grimaced through a goatee beard.

There was little expression in the driver's face aside indifference.

Not a flicker of emotion was emitted.

Robert noticed the front passenger window was open and felt duly obliged to enquire as to the reason for his stop.

'Hi, there! You okay, mate? Can I help you? Are you lost?'

The driver seemed to let his focus wander over the Aspinall house.

As though he were studying it for some reason.

Having been ignored once, Robert's repeated offer of assistance was somewhat less cordial as he moved closer to the gate.

'Are you deaf, pal? If you don't want anything…hop it!'

Yet again, the only response was silence and a steely glare through the blackest of lenses.

Robert's confusion was interrupted by the sound of someone emerging from the front door of number forty-one.

Greg Chapple bounded out of the house and along the pavement.

'Hey. Greg! How are you?' shouted Robert.

Greg turned to his neighbour and seemed to look right through him.

Rob repeated the query.

Again, there was no reaction.

It was though he was looking at a stranger.

Greg got into the front passenger seat of the racing green car as his friend - who Robert now identified as one Jason Steel - began to rev the engine furiously.

In an instant, the car then sped off into the distance and turned out of sight.

Robert felt a sense of dismay at Greg's uncharacteristically ignorant display but opted to continue with his task.

It must be the day for silences, he mused to himself as he sloshed more soapy water over the rear windscreen of Karen's motor.

*****

It was sometime later that he opted to try and break the ice with his wife as he broached the subject with Karen over a drink on the patio.

They were communicating betwixt the unwelcome periods of friction, but as he spoke, Robert could tell that his wife was barely interested in his observations or the incident with Greg and his mysterious friend.

Robert sat peacefully and sipped his lager as he became aware another possible issue down the garden.

'Are some of those new trees turning brown, Kaz, or is it my eyes?'

Karen rested her gaze on the line of young conifers.

It was difficult to determine whether Robert's assessment was accurate.

But at least it forced a glib response to her husband's claim.

'I don't think so. It must be your eyes. You never see what's in front of them these days.'

Opting to retreat indoors, Robert quietly surrendered any hope of amiable communication with Karen for the remainder of the weekend.

thirty-two

Departing for work after yet another pointless Monday morning argument with Karen, Robert Aspinall selected the drive mode in the automatic gearbox and cruised away from Church Drayton with a mind plagued by utter despondency.

He was not in the habit of leaving his family behind without so much as a word of goodbye but felt it to be the preferable option today.

The situation, whilst giving Karen cause for serious consternation, had also conveniently eclipsed any immediate worries regarding the neighbours. Her relationship with her husband was the priority and it was under considerable strain.

That was rightly the sole focus in her life at that moment.

She was by no means fearful for their future as man and wife, but nevertheless upheld earnest doubt as to her ability to continue with the current domestic arrangement.

Karen had secretly succumbed to Robert's wish for her remain at home instead of going her parents for the week ahead.

Unfortunately for her completely bemused and moderately fuming husband, he was not aware of Karen's compliance in the matter.

Besides, Robert was not the chief influence in the decision.

Over the course of the weekend, Chloe and Lauren had both expressed their disapproval at being forced to reside with their grandparents for the entire week. As Karen suspected, her daughters liked being at home with their own bedrooms, their own garden, and the familiar comfort that they felt in the environment.

The irony of the scenario was crucifying.

Lodging at her parents' house brought its own complications. Long John was a persistent temptation for Lauren and inevitably brought short shrift from Karen's father should the squawking begin.

Karen and the girls were crammed in the one spare bedroom and sleeping was nigh on impossible with at least one of the girls wanting to get in bed with their mother as opposed to reclining on the makeshift camp-bed that Jean had set up.

Whilst temporary re-location to Goltham partially removed the phantoms of Benton Road from Karen's daily routine, the practical cons of the arrangement admittedly outweighed the pros.

Robert was quite correct.

His family should be at home.

But Karen was also fully convinced that her standpoint was justified in motive. Of course, the details of such motives were yet to be revealed to him.

Yet again, he had spent two days within spitting distance of the undisclosed protagonists but had still not suspected anything was wrong. She had not even discussed the incidents with the be-headed bird or the mysterious tampering with the front door lock.

Aside the minor incident with Greg as Robert washed the car on Saturday, Karen was happy that he remained blissfully unaware of the summer's chronicle of increasing misery.

A book that she sincerely hoped had now been closed to further entries for good.

In her sympathy for the girls' vested opinion, Karen decided to keep them off school for the week. The six-week holidays loomed in a few days anyhow. It was high time she bonded closely with them once again in the Aspinall residence.

Not elsewhere, evading detection from an as-yet elusive enemy.

It was time to re-assert their presence at number thirty-nine. The weathermen had predicted a searing heatwave for the impending month, and it looked on current evidence that they were pretty accurate.

The paddling pool was filled, and the garden echoed once again with the sound of squealing laughter and splashing water.

Karen's thoughts had turned full circle. She was pleased to have remained at home and not continued to flee as hunted prey. She was suddenly happy to sit in the sunshine with her book, her long cool drink and her daughters.

This was family life, wasn't it?

This was what it was all about, wasn't it?

Not dwelling on the childish antics of the bored idiots over the fence.

Reclining in a bright, white bikini, Karen felt momentarily inflated to be back on her own territory. She felt like announcing to the whole street that the Aspinalls were back and determined to stay put.

'Hello, girls. You both okay?'

Greg Chapple's voice carried over the fence toward the intended recipients in the paddling pool.

Aggressively pushing the lawn mower, he glanced across and smiled at them in anticipation of a reply.

Chloe and Lauren simply looked with vacancy at their neighbour before both smiled and continued to play in the water.

Karen stared covertly through her sunglasses at the man she once called a friend. His wild grin and jerky movement made him look decidedly agitated. She continued to study his head and shoulders for a few minutes.

Not once did he look in her direction.

This empowered Karen. She felt as though her battle was slowly coming to a victorious conclusion.

Judy's forecast that he would get bored if she didn't play his game seemed to be finally bearing some truth.

Karen wanted to smile as she lay in the sun watching her daughters. Yet something held her back from such a gesture. Her focus lowered a little to the line of new conifers that Robert had planted. As her husband had suggested at the weekend, there did appear to be some discolouration in the foliage. Even through her dark lenses, it stood out a mile.

Karen slid her shades up to rest on her forehead. She scrutinised the young trees and how they did indeed appear to be heavily flecked with a light shade of brown.

Finally, she stood up and walked over to the fence to get a closer look. Greg had conveniently disappeared from sight, leaving the lawn mower unattended.

Karen studied the grass at the base of the trees where the lower branches spanned wider. The lawn underneath was also patched with brown.

As though the area had been burned or scorched.

But the sun had not been that hot. Not enough to erode an evergreen.

Karen's instincts were screaming the obvious conclusion to her as she stood brazenly by the fence in her bikini.

Her new trees had been poisoned.

Whatever had been poured or thrown over the baby conifers had splashed onto the surrounding area.

Robert was spot on in his observation of two days earlier.

The new trees were changing colour at a rapid rate.

The new trees were dying.

Her despondency returned in an instant.

After days away from her home and a relatively peaceful weekend, it appeared that the game had now been raised to another level.

Destruction of property was now the aim, it seemed. But again, despite her overwhelming belief as to the guilty party, there were no witnesses and therefore no proof of any wrongdoing.

All Karen could do was watch as the dogged symptoms tormented by the hour.

Soon her newly planted baby trees would be rotten.

Soon Greg would be in control once again.

And Karen Aspinall had no mode of defence - or retaliation.

*****

The hot afternoon evolved into balmy early evening. Karen was no longer enjoying her day. Her return to so-called domestic comfort had fallen flat on its face. Her daily life in general was now a sham as far as she was concerned.

With the girls having been in the sun most of the day, she called them in for tea and ran a tepid bath before rubbing moisturising cream into their shoulders and backs. The air was still close and humid.

Karen hoped to calm them down, yet in effect, Chloe and Lauren simply moved venue from the garden to the bathroom. The squealing, splashing and laughter continued as Karen descended the stairs.

At least her daughters were happy.

A soft rap on the front door made Karen suspicious.

It was a strange time to get callers unless they were expected. She glanced into the living room to check the clock on the mantelpiece. Nearly half past seven.

The knock sounded once more, this time with increased assertion.

Karen really did not want to open it, but it seemed rude to ignore the visitor. Unpicking the security chain and peeling back the door from the frame, Karen was shocked to see a face that she had not seen for months. His kind, smiling features and smoothly combed brownish-grey hair had not altered at all.

The man produced a bunch of flowers from behind his back and offered a hand of greeting. Karen automatically responded in kind as she shook his hand and then in turn accepted the bouquet.

'You look as lovely as ever, my dear Karen! How are you? Thought I'd give you a quick hello. I've just got back. About an hour since.'

Unbelievably for Karen, she reacted as she always did on seeing Nigel Chapple. He was a warm and gentle type and exuded an air of comradeship.

'Wow! Nigel – hello! What a lovely surprise! I wasn't expecting to see you! Come in! Come in!'

'It's nearly as hot here as where I've just flown in from!'

'Where might that have been? Somewhere exotic no doubt!' Karen smirked as she closed the front door.

'Well…yes…Dubai, actually. It's the fastest growing area in the world you know. Plenty of rich people want to build there. Amazing place!'

Karen presented Nigel with a can of beer as they both perched on the patio chairs among the lengthening shadows of early dusk.

'So, how is life for the family? Rob okay, is he?'

'Yes, thanks. He's just been promoted, you know. Well, a few months back now. He's based in Coventry during the week.'

'Brilliant. Good for him. Evelyn never said anything. Probably forgot.'

Realisation quickly dawned on Karen as she watched Nigel speak.

Judging by his manner and tone of voice, he evidently had no idea of the friction that had ensued between the families in recent times.

She probed for further confirmation of her suspicions.

'I suppose you were quite surprised to see Greg at home when you got back.'

'Well…yes and know. I knew it might be a possibility before I left. Hope he's keeping his nose clean. Although, I haven't actually set eyes on him yet. Probably up to mischief somewhere. Honestly, he's like a teenager at times. You wouldn't think he was a man of twenty-five.'

'Twenty-six. You missed his birthday.'

'Ah…of course. Yes. Bet that was a night to remember.'

Karen did not answer. She did not wish to spoil Nigel's joyous return. He was obviously pleased to back in the family fold. The negative business with his wife and son did not warrant mention at that point.

'Evelyn says she hasn't seen much of you lately. Have you been hibernating?'

Karen observed his eyes as he spoke.

Nigel Chapple wasn't fishing. His scrutiny seemed genuine. His motives appeared earnest.

'No. I think it's just one of those things. You can go for ages without really talking to people. Even if they do only live next door.'

Nigel drank from the can and peered around the back lawn.

'Garden's looking nice. Have you shifted the shed or is it me losing my marbles?'

'No. It's moved alright. Your Greg did it for me.'

'I hope you didn't pay the lazy bleeder! What's with those trees? Strange place to put them, isn't it? In front of the gate?'

Karen felt the searing heat of the spotlight.

Struggling for an answer, her mind raced as her pulse noticeably quickened.

'Er…well…they were going cheap at the garden centre. I fancied a few, that's all.'

She continued to watch Nigel as his eyes squinted into the late afternoon sun.

'Looks like they could do with a drop of water. They're browning off, girl! Better get the hose pipe on them! Anyway…I'll be getting back. Evelyn's got my tea on! Thanks for the drink.'

Karen escorted Nigel to the side gate and out past the garage.

His sudden decision to make an exit struck her as very odd.

It was the same procedure that his wife had been employing of late.

Perhaps he had been dispatched to observe the state of play in camp.

Perhaps Karen was becoming neurotic.

'Nice to talk to you, Nigel. Thanks for the flowers. Perhaps see you again soon?'

'Yes, love. I might pop back at the weekend when Rob's back. He can tell me all about his new executive status! See you then, perhaps!'

Nigel Chapple's chuckles followed him around the corner of the garage as Karen closed the side gate behind him.

He was the last person she expected to see that day.

Yet his ignorance of the more pressing circumstances was of some comfort. At least he would not be joining sides with his wife and son.

Perhaps the return home of the father figure might signify the beginning of the end of the unruly game.

Karen secretly and sincerely hoped it to be so.

thirty-three

There was no phone call from Robert that day. Karen felt deeply hurt that the situation should have ever come between them. She also now felt guilty that her husband was having to commute and perform at work with this unresolved mess hanging in the air.

The following evening, she took the girls to her mother's house to collect the remains of their laundry. She was quietly thankful for once that her father was out working late.

Unavoidably, Jean Hope threw unwanted light on the issue in Benton Road.

'Are you sure you want to stay at home, Karen? I'm concerned that you're placing yourself and the girls at risk. Even if his father is back home, it doesn't necessarily mean the problem will stop.'

Karen placed the carrier bag of clean clothes into the boot of her car.

'To be honest staying here has caused more problems that it has solved, Mum. Rob's decided he's not happy about us leaving the house unattended.'

Chloe and Lauren were perched quietly in the back seats. Jean stared at her daughter and lowered her voice so as not to draw the girls' attention.

'Yes, but he doesn't understand why you did it in the first place, does he, Karen? It's terribly unfair to leave him unawares like this.'

Karen gently closed the boot lid.

The conversation was already at the point of tedium for her.

'But what can he do from Coventry, Mum? More to the point, what would he try and do if he ever found out? I'll just have to keep my fingers crossed that all this mess blows over now. I won't have any more to do with them. Simple as that.'

'But that attitude is going to raise Rob's suspicions even more, Karen. Can't you see it?'

'Yes, Mum. Of course, I'm aware of that! It's difficult. I know. But neither option appeals. Telling him will create just as much fuss as not.'

The youngsters continued to sit contentedly in the car as they observed their grandmother's rueful expression through the side window.

Karen also saw how worried her mother was becoming but felt helpless to appease her concerns.

'And you think that Nigel knows nothing about this?'

'Well, he was nice as pie to me yesterday. But he's only just back from working abroad. He's been away most of the year. If I know Evelyn, she'll probably tell him a pack of lies anyway if he gets suspicious. I know something, though...Greg's dad won't stand for any nonsense. So, as I say, it's hopefully all over and done with now.'

Karen smiled and jokingly raised crossed fingers before leaning toward her mother and kissing her on the cheek.

'Thanks for everything, Mum. And tell Dad we're okay when you see him later.'

Jean's expression adorned itself with lines of maternal tension as she reached over to lightly touch Karen's face with her thumb.

'What's that, Karen?'

'What's what, Mum?'

'That mark, there. On your cheek. It looks painful.'

'Oh...that...I don't know...I noticed it over the weekend. It's probably because it's the time of the month. I sometimes get a bit spotty.'

'Keep your eye on it. I don't think it's a spot. Doesn't look like one, anyway. It looks like...well I don't know. Drive safely, love.'

'Bye, Mum. We'll perhaps pop round tomorrow as normal for tea, okay?'

'Okay darling just let me know.'

Jean watched as her family vanished around the corner.

She had never felt more helpless as a mother than she did at that moment in the resuming silence of Cobden Terrace.

*****

The girls had requested pizza for supper and were rightly treated to such. It was nearly nine p.m. when the reluctant return journey through Church Drayton became a dreaded reality.

A red sun dropped below darkened rooftops as the car pulled to a stop on Benton Road. Karen applied the handbrake, never averting her attention from the frontage of number forty-one.

'Stay in here, girls. I'm just going to open the gate.'

No sooner had she lifted the latch and gripped the top slat to gauge the weight of the gate, Karen noticed it felt unusually light in her grasp.

In a split second of confusion, Karen grappled in the semi-darkness.

The trap had been sprung.

In the next instance the gate had seemingly vanished from between her fingers.

There was a resounding clatter that vibrated the ground around her feet as the gate slammed over onto its side, instinctively shocking Karen into jumping a step backward.

She looked down before glancing back to Chloe and Lauren who peered from the back seat of the car to uncover the source of the noise.

Clambering over the obstruction, it soon became evident that it had been lifted completely off its hinges and left perilously in wait for the family's return.

A purposed exercise that could have done serious injury to two unsuspecting little girls.

A sick, wilful prank incurring such risk that it could have only been performed by one person.

She would never be able to re-align it with the hinges on her own. It would take two pairs of hands. As Karen strained to heave the gate back up and lean it out of the way, pure anger began to course through her veins.

An all-encompassing rage that grew internally as she eventually parked the car and quickly ushered the girls into the house.

'Mummy…why did the gate fall over?' enquired an ever-curious Chloe.

Karen did not respond to the question.

Instructing her daughters to get ready for bed, Karen's vexation was rising to the fore and rapidly taking control of her thoughts and actions.

Her enraged mind flashed through other recent incidents.

The tampered lock; the dead bird; the poisoned trees; the blocked drain; the smashed bottles; the flat tyre.

The list of despicable occurrences went on and on.

And now it seemed the game had been notched up to the next level in the most potentially dangerous way.

He obviously now intended to cause innocent people harm.

The briefly mild consolation that her youngsters had narrowly avoided a hospital visit was countered by erupting rancour as Karen stomped up the stairs and straight into her bedroom.

With fingers firmly clenched, she stood at the interior wall that adjoined with number forty-one.

Chloe and Lauren were dumbstruck to hear the commotion from their mother's room as she ferociously and repeatedly hammered the wall with her fists.

In all their young lives they had never heard their mother unleash herself in such a fashion.

'HAVEN'T YOU DONE ENOUGH TO US? YOU FUCKING MENTAL BASTARDS! WHY DON'T YOU FUCKING LEAVE US ALONE! I OUGHT TO GET THE FUCKING POLICE DOWN HERE TO SORT YOU FUCKING BASTARDS OUT. ARE YOU FUCKING LISTENING? ARE YOU?'

Now hearing the subsequent flood of tears echoing along the landing, Chloe and Lauren rushed to console their mother as she sobbed unrestrained into their hopeful and desperate embrace.

Karen's resolve had finally been broken. Her previously controlled resistance to the vitriolic campaign of her neighbours had now conceded to an unrelenting and undiluted hatred.

She fully intended to rouse the Chapples into an immediate response. To throw light on the devious mother; the menacing son; and the seemingly oblivious father.

With Karen's assault on the bedroom wall having subsided as swiftly as it occurred, her ambition to provoke had been realised.

The occupants of number forty-one had heard the crescendo of abuse. But two members of the Chapple clan had been quietly expecting Karen's highly audible outburst.

It took less than a minute.

Loud raps on her front door brought Karen back to a semblance of composure as she sat in deeply contemplative mood on her bed with her two young daughters.

The forceful knocking resonated up the stairwell, encouraging Karen to her feet and to an unsteady descent to confront the caller. Pulling back the front door revealed the supposedly concerned features of Nigel Chapple.

He engaged with Karen's fearfully defiant expression glaring back at him in the porchlight.

He gestured to the gate that leaned against the garage wall.

'Karen…what on earth is the problem? What's the matter?'

Chloe and Lauren hid behind their mother in the semi-lit hallway as they listened to the frantic exchange.

Karen's voice trembled with declaration as she imparted her statement through gritted teeth.

'I've fucking had enough, Nigel. Your son. Your wife. I am not going to take anymore. The gate is the last straw. It all ends. Now.'

Completely bemused by her statement, Nigel Chapple withdrew toward the driveway and hoisted the gate back onto its hinges before returning to the open doorway of number thirty-nine.

'I hope you realise that I was in bed. I don't know what you're accusing people of but there are ways and means, Karen. We're not cave men, you know! Come and talk to us if you have an issue.'

Karen felt her daughters tug gently on her skirt. It was neither the time nor the arena to try and justify her actions or explain her motives.

Karen was dog tired.

Her fire had been doused sufficiently for one day.

'Just…tell them…Nigel. Please. Tell *him*…to stop…'

His features exhibited the response of a man completely uninitiated about recent history.

'Karen…tell *who* to stop? And to stop *what*, exactly?'

'YOUR FUCKING SON!'

Nigel Chapple shook his head in disbelief and gestured with a thumb.

'I can assure you that Greg's been home all night. He's not been anywhere. So, I suggest before you start slinging mud, that you get your facts in order. I also suggest you get some sleep, girl. You look bushed.'

There was little ambiguity in Karen's reply.

The line in the sand was now well and truly drawn.

'And I suggest you all fucking DROP DEAD! You and the rest of your fucking hideous excuse of a family!'

With her parting shot, Karen slammed the front door shut and trooped back upstairs with Chloe and Lauren in tow. Cradling her little girls in the bedroom once again, Karen whispered softly to try and appease their alarm.

'Listen girls. Mummy needs her sleep, so I need you to be good for me. Get in bed and read for a while, okay?'

Chloe was not convinced of her mother's disposition.

'Why were you shouting at Aunty Evelyn's husband, Mummy?'

Karen stroked her eldest's blond hair to try and bring some calm to troubled waters.

‘Don’t you worry about that, darling. Now go at get your pyjamas on for me, please.’

Without further word of argument or protest, both daughters obliged their mother’s wishes.

Karen ventured into the bathroom to wash.

Removing the last of her make-up, she examined the visible blemish that had been present on her left cheek for the past two or three days.

It had become dark in colour, almost like a small bruise. It was also painful to the touch, like a blister. She ran her fingertips over areas of dried skin around her forehead and ears. Her body was beginning to reveal symptoms of trauma.

Physically, Karen looked and felt a wreck. She prodded and poked the small lump again. This was not the face Karen Aspinall was accustomed to seeing.

Finally opting to leave the cosmetic analysis to another day, she retired gratefully to bed.

*****

It was well past midnight when the electronic drone of the lounge telephone carried up the stairwell and sufficiently penetrated Karen’s slumber enough to cause disturbance.

She rubbed her dry eyes in the darkness and reluctantly hauled herself from among the bedclothes.

Thankfully the girls remained asleep.

The phone had been ringing for minutes on end.

It must be urgent.

It must be Robert.

Once into the lounge she reached for the receiver and placed it gently to her ear.

She checked the caller display.

The incoming number had been withheld.

‘Hello, Rob? Is that you?’

Silence prevailed from the other end of the line.

A presence was detectable yet remained unannounced and unidentified.

Karen could barely hear the caller breathe as she strained to listen.

'Hello, who is this, please?'

Again, there was no response.

Karen gradually realised that she was the victim once again.

The game had moved forward into ever more menacing territory.

Replacing the handset into its cradle, inevitability placed a hand on Karen's shoulder.

She examined the caller history for the entire previous day.

For the second night in a row, Robert had not phoned.

The situation had become completely untenable now.

She could no longer face the monster alone.

Karen needed her husband back beside her more than ever.

And on his return, she would tell him everything.

thirty-four

Squinting against the early morning sunshine, Karen opened the back door to deposit some kitchen refuse into the main dustbin which was situated in its usual position at the side of the house.

Dropping the bag of rubbish, she closed the lid down before turning back toward the garden.

It was at that moment that her heart lurched.

Her legs began to shake beneath her.

At first, she thought it must have been some curious accident.

Garage windows break easily. The glass could have been missing for weeks. She may not have spotted it until now.

Her attempts to avoid the obvious conclusion were foiled as her glance dropped to the floor. The putty around the side garage window had been carefully chipped off piece by piece, and the pane of glass - still intact - had been positioned on the floor leaning against the wall.

This was no accident.

The phantom had struck again.

Greg Chapple's devious crusade was gathering momentum.

It was evident that he was still not yet dissuaded from his mission.

Now in a state of enveloping nausea, Karen retreated to the kitchen and through to the lounge.

Picking up the telephone, there was only one person she felt inclined to call at that moment.

*****

Robert Aspinall's emotions rocked as he listened to his weeping wife from the hotel bedroom. What she had told him in between bouts of open wailing had left him empty inside. His heart transformed into a hollow cauldron of wanton vengeance and the blood raced through his veins like acid.

His loved ones were at great risk, and he had to go to them.

The centre of his world was about to implode.

Time was against him.

He needed to be back in Tenbridge as soon as possible.

Robert dressed quickly and grabbed necessities from around the room.

Thankfully, the hotel car park was quiet, and his departure was unhindered.

Engaging the motorway allowed him to concentrate his mind on what lay ahead.

He privately cursed his blinkered ambition and wilful ignorance.

He inwardly berated Karen's stupid reluctance to tell him of her sufferance and the vulnerability of their daughters.

Yet currently he was aware of only a handful of the facts.

He would also have to be prepared to listen.

His wife had only outlined her grief over the telephone, yet it needed unearthing fully if she were to rid herself of the decay that had begun inside her.

*****

Three hours later, it was approaching Midday when Robert Aspinall was finally standing in his own hallway, embracing his wife and children as their plight echoed from the foundations to the roof.

He held them long and tightly as they quivered, united in the grip of long-standing turmoil and temporary relief.

Robert stood strong and defiant. It was time for him to absorb the abhorrent decline that his family had endured in his continuing absence.

It took little longer than an hour.

The kitchen table became the arena for a family conference that shook Robert to his core. Karen bravely enlightened her husband as to each and every episode of the Chapple's campaign.

He interjected with requests for fuller explanation and expansion as his toiling mind fought to digest the tale.

Yet as the woman he loved finally begged for his assistance, Robert did not fold. Something instinctive had suggested to him that circumstances at home were not agreeable many weeks earlier.

Finally, he could now attach his previously unspoken misgivings to Karen's awful sufferance.

Their relationship had been under strain for a while. Karen had been acting as the sole keeper and defender of the family and had understandably buckled under immense pressure.

In reality, their marriage had very few issues.

Any bumps along that road were easily navigable.

The family unit would remain intact.

However, the ensuing and yet surreal situation with the neighbours now needed professional intervention.

A nervous silence descended as Karen concluded her account with the events of the previous evening and that morning's discovery of the damage to the garage.

Robert observed Chloe and Lauren's angelic yet perturbed faces.

He visualised them being crushed under the weight of the falling gate. Nervously, two daughters watched their father as without further word he defiantly rose to his feet and moved toward the telephone.

'I'm contacting work. I need to be here.'

Karen remained gratefully calm as Robert dialled and then she listened carefully to her husband's commanding tone.

'David. It's Robert.'

'Yes. I had to come back home.'

'Yes, I'm sorry. Short notice for me too.'

'Thanks. The journey was fine.'

'Look, I don't think I'll be back for the rest of the week.'

'Possibly not next week, either.'

'Yes, I know about that. Okay.'

'Can you clear it with Mike for me?'

'Tell him to give me a buzz at home today, will you?'

'Thank you, my friend.'

There was an uneasy pause as Robert listened to his colleague's concerned enquiry.

'No. It's not the company's problem.'

'I've got major issues at home to sort out.'

'No, they're all fine. It's personal…very delicate.'

'No…look, David, I'll give you a ring later in the week.'

'Bye. And thanks again.'

Karen watched intently as Robert put down the handset.

He glanced to the most important people in his world before retrieving it once more.

Now dialling a different number, he turned to his family again and smiled resiliently.

Karen's psychological trauma was suddenly being soothed by a growing consolation.

Her man was finally back and in control of events.

‘Hello? Yes. Police, please.’

‘I need to speak to an officer about our neighbours.’

‘Possibly an attempted break-in aside many other things.’

‘No, there’s no immediate emergency.’

‘Okay, fine. Yes.’

A pause ensued as Robert’s enquiry was transferred to the local constabulary station.

‘Hello…is that Tenbridge Police?’

‘Yes, please.’

‘A house visit?’

‘Yes…yes that’s absolutely fine.’

‘Robert Aspinall.’

‘Thirty-nine, Benton Road. Church Drayton.’

‘Okay, yes. Thank you.’

With the telephone redundant once more, Robert resumed his seat at the kitchen table and enclosed his hands around Karen’s.

He studied her fraught features and hollow eyes.

He noticed the flaking skin around her ears and neck.

The mark of stress that was now evident on her cheek.

Her beautiful, yet damaged face.

She could not summon herself to speak any more about the situation. It was an all-encompassing relief for her to know that Robert had now taken over the reins.

Her emotional release at eventual disclosure to him was overwhelming. Yet she suddenly felt liberated from the strife and trepidation that had plagued her for so long.

But Robert’s struggle was only just beginning.

His anxieties for a form of retribution were charged with simultaneous bolts of guilt. It was only a crumb of comfort to see his family safely together, knowing that he had unwittingly allowed them to suffer without him for so long.

‘The police will be here sometime this afternoon, Kaz. We’ll get this sorted out once and for all. I’m so sorry. I’ll never leave you and the girls here again. Don’t worry. I’m staying until this mess is cleared up.’

*****

t was nearly six p.m. when the knock at the door arrested the Aspinalls rom their partial solace in the lounge.

Peering through the front room curtains, Robert confirmed the resence of the police vehicle outside.

'Okay, love. They're here. I'll go. Just be calm. Everything will be ine. We are doing the right thing. Trust me.'

Robert shuffled to the front door in his slippers and pulled it open evealing a rather diminutive looking man in a florescent green jacket. A hin moustache sat above a practised smile.

Robert immediately gained placation from the silver insignia on the fficer's hat and shoulder patches. The panda car perched at the front of he house would also issue a pertinent message to the neighbours.

'Good evening. Mister Robert Aspinall? I'm PC Lottinger. You nade a complaint this morning about your neighbours?'

'Yes. That's correct. You'd better come in.'

The officer introduced himself to Karen before sitting next to her n the settee and removing his headwear. A small notebook was xtracted from his inside pocket. Chloe and Lauren shifted uneasily to he kitchen. Their first ever contact with a policeman was giving both irls cause for curious concern.

PC Lottinger repeated the exhibition of his smirking expression.

'Okay, Mister and Mrs. Aspinall. I'm all ears.'

Robert said nothing as he positioned himself in the armchair pposite Karen. She calmly and concisely relayed relevant events to the upposed figure of authority beside her. She sounded confident and in ontrol whilst Chloe and Lauren played contentedly out of earshot at the itchen table.

Yet within only minutes of observing and listening, Robert sensed omething was amiss.

Severe misgivings regarding the responses of the officer served to uel his renewed annoyance.

The policeman's painted smile did not diminish, despite the npleasant nature of what was being revealed.

The officer did not write down one single aspect of what he was earing. Karen's detailed recollections had currently endured for nearly alf an hour.

The constable listened without offering any obvious reaction to the nventory of incidents that Greg Chapple had allegedly instigated.

As the minutes continued to pass, Robert Aspinall had convincingly gleaned the distinct impression that his wife was wasting her breath.

PC Lottinger finally displayed a mask of albeit mild compassion as he digested Karen's conclusive wishes.

'All I want you to do is tell him to stop. Not to press any charges. It's making me ill. Just warn him off. Just bring it to an end.'

Robert felt his torment beginning to surface as he perceived the dismissive summary by the policeman.

'I'm afraid it's not as simple as that, Mrs. Aspinall. There is no proof to link Mister Chapple to any of these allegations. Subsequently, I can't caution him…as in the eyes of the law…he's done nothing wrong.'

Robert was now becoming furious.

It was a struggle to cage his frustration as the officer continued.

Robert felt it high time to interject.

'What about the garage window? There must be prints on the glass?!'

The officer sighed heavily before emitting his disinterested reply.

'You are alleging he's done this, and you say he's done that. Well why wasn't it reported at the time?'

Karen was now beginning to reach the same conclusion as her husband, yet PC Lottinger displayed precious little empathy as he pressed on with his sermon.

'A physical assault is a serious offence, I agree. As is vandalism. But I'm afraid the time lapse separating these events places doubt on the issue. A lack of a witness is a fundamental obstruction to any of your claims. It's your word against his.'

Karen looked forlornly to her husband who finally felt it appropriate to let his temper fray through grinding teeth and clenched fists.

'Listen, mate! My wife is bloody terrified of this guy! She can't even go out into the bloody street in case he's around! My kids can't play in their own bastard back garden! Are you saying that's justified? Is this truly acceptable? The bloke's a fucking menace!'

The officer simply glanced up to engage with Robert and again offered an unconvincing standpoint.

'If you could curb your language, please sir. I'll go and get his side of the story, certainly. But without any substantial evidence, he's fully entitled to deny everything. And at this juncture, I - and the both of you - must accept that.'

‘So that’s it?’ barked Robert. ‘Your hands are tied unless we catch the evil fucker red-handed? He can continue to terrorise my family unless we get a photograph of him actually doing it?’

PC Lottinger stood to his feet and grinned without restraint once more.

‘Mister Aspinall. I’ve known Greg since he was a youngster. He can be a handful, sure. But he’s not evil.’

Quickly engulfed by disbelief, Robert leaned forward and looked the policeman in the eye.

‘*What* did you just say? You *know* him? YOU FUCKING *KNOW* HIM?’

Karen placed her face in her hands and completely relinquished matters to Robert. PC Lottinger continued to perform with an inanimate, unwavering expression.

Robert now stood and placed his furious form only inches from of that of the law.

‘What do you keep fucking smiling about, mate? Listen to me P.C. Plod! My family is under threat and in great danger from those bastards next door, and all you can do is fucking smirk about it? Call yourself a fucking copper? You’re fucking useless! Absolutely fucking useless!’

Karen’s tears began to fall once more as she tried to contain her husband’s raging release.

‘Please, Rob. He’s going next door to talk to them. It might do the trick. Let him do his job. Please calm down.’

‘It’s alright saying calm down, love! But you and our babies are being victimised and this dickhead here obviously doesn’t give a fucking shit!’

The officer raised a hand as a signal of address.

‘I strongly suggest you do as your wife advises, Mister Aspinall. I sympathise, but verbally abusing an officer of the law is an offence, you know.’

Robert was not about to stand down.

‘Oh…you *sympathise*, do you? Officer of the law my fucking arsehole! He’s laughing at you, Karen! Fucking laughing at you! One of these days it might be too late! Someone might get hurt. *Then* I’ll come looking for you! You wait and see! Talking to the wankers is no good. They want fucking hanging!’

PC Lottinger turned to Karen as Robert stormed upstairs in an explosive fit of emotion.

Replacing his unused notebook into his pocket, the policeman then re-positioned his hat. As he entered the hallway, he seemed neither flustered nor impressed by the tirade just administered. The pane of glass from the garage awaited him by his feet. He lifted it without even giving it a second glance.

The officer barely forced himself to look Karen in the eye as he offered a perfunctory goodbye.

'I'm now going to visit the occupants next door. I'll see what reaction I get, Mrs. Aspinall. I will get the pane of glass checked for matches. But this is effectively a domestic issue at this point. We are reluctant to get involved unless a criminal offence has actually occurred. If you want some sound advice based on what you've told me, though, I'd keep your car locked in the garage. Just in case. Prevention is better than cure. I'll see myself out. Good night.'

*****

It was over an hour before PC Lottinger emerged from the driveway of number forty-one, slid behind the wheel of the panda car, and cruised away from the falling debris of Benton Road.

Karen had expected him to at least indicate how his meeting with the Chapples had transpired.

Yet her vain hopes were evidently not to be met.

As she watched through the gap in the lounge curtains, Karen still felt somewhat appeased that she had at last involved an officiator. The whole affair was now on record, even though it had seemingly had little obvious impact at that moment.

She had laid her cards on the table for all to see. In her heart, Karen believed that the issue may just be reaching a peaceful conclusion.

But she has succumbed to this false mindset before.

No more than five minutes had passed since the departure of the police before the knock at the front door came.

Now in a moderately calmer frame of mind, Robert joined his wife downstairs in the hallway as she opened the door.

Nigel Chapple stood in the shadows of early evening.

His demeanour had evidently been altered since his previous call.

A shroud of disapproval seemed to envelope his appearance.

Standing next to him was the equally unsettled figure of Colin Robinson from across the road.

The Aspinalls stood hand in hand and stared disparagingly at the pair of visitors as they visibly grappled for the appropriate words.

It would have appeared that Nigel was in a similar boat of confused desperation.

'Good evening, Robert. Good evening, Karen. I would just like to make a statement on behalf of my family considering the visit of the police that you felt necessary to arrange. I have asked Colin to witness events for the benefit of all concerned.'

'This had better be good. You've had fucking long enough to think about it. And I don't trust your so-called witness as far I as I can throw him. So, let's hear it then.' Robert sneered.

Colin Robinson's eyes widened at the insinuation, but he said nothing in response.

Nigel Chapple was not distracted as he looked both subjects in the eye.

'I wish to assure you that at no stage will any member of your family be under threat from any soul residing at number forty-one. The police have informed us of your allegations but have also decided not to proceed further. I hope this can bring an end to matters. I am eternally sorry for any upset that has transpired in my absence and extremely disappointed that the police have been brought to my door. I will now leave you in peace. Goodnight, all.'

Robert and Karen offered no further comment, with Robert simply shutting the door on the two messengers.

Man and wife embraced each other tightly in the hallway as they attempted to allay their mutual exhaustion.

They could now only pray that Nigel Chapple was as good as his word and that the hostility was finally over.

thirty-five

Monday morning. It was with immense reluctance that Robert Aspinall departed the family home at four-thirty a.m. He had tried desperately to secure a contingency to allow him the week off work, but the company supposedly had pressing matters that unavoidably required his attention.

His wife and children slept soundly as he reversed his company motor car into Benton Road and shut the gate behind him. A red sun crept slowly above the horizon. The absolute peace of another early summer morning was temporarily placating.

Back behind the wheel of his car, he glanced toward the garage door which was still securely locked. Inside was parked Karen's run-around. The one piece of intelligent advice that the police felt obliged to supply had been duly followed.

Another deliberate message for the seemingly demented inmates of number forty-one.

Chloe and Lauren had now officially begun their six-week holiday from school. It was a wrench for their father to potentially miss so much of it.

As he drove toward and then on through Tenbridge, Robert hoped to be re-joining his wife and daughters as soon as humanly possible. But an important meeting in Coventry beckoned. There was no justifiable excuse to miss it so far as his superiors were concerned.

Thankfully, despite his great reservation and despondency on the issue, Karen was steadfast in her insistence that Robert go to work as normal if he was needed there.

In her eyes, the Chapples would now be fully aware that their actions were under scrutiny. There was effectively no longer any threat.

There had been a curious cessation of movement next door since the police visit. Not forgetting the subsequent knock on the door from Nigel and his neighbourly witness.

The Aspinalls should have been resting assured in the belief that the police were now supervising the situation.

Yet in his heart, Robert did not believe it to be the case.

In his eyes, the Chapple's game was far from over.

*****

Ten-thirty p.m. The shrill drone of the phone echoed through a darkened hallway and up into the bathroom as Karen examined the lump on her cheek.

Scurrying downstairs in her pyjamas, she hoped that it would be Robert ringing belatedly to confirm his repeated request for holiday leave had been granted.

Although the rightful course of action had been administered is tackling the problem with the Chapples, Karen's spirit was becoming increasingly deflated once again.

The deafening unholy silence inside number thirty-nine slowly cemented her gradual conviction that Benton Road was now becoming an unbearable place to reside.

Her home was now merely a house.

Her resolve for battle was all but completely vanquished.

She held the receiver gingerly and placed it quietly to her ear.

Confirmation of her fears duly arrived with this latest mystery telephone call.

Twenty seconds of threateningly loud nothingness through the handset left Karen reeling with the thought that informing the police would not be enough to discourage the demons that continued to haunt her.

It had now become nigh on impossible for her to erase from her conscience the tragic thought that tackling matters head on would not succeed.

Indeed, her mindset was now becoming accustomed to the probability that fleeing the enemy may be the only resolution to the continuing nightmare.

thirty-six

It could have been the following day when Judy arrived. Karen had lost all track of time when she made the call at some point in the previous twenty-four hours. But to see her best friend standing at the front door in the early afternoon sunshine gave her a flicker of hope that all was not yet lost.

'I'm on mornings. I left work early on purpose, Kaz. I wanted to see you as soon as possible. Jesus…look at you. You're a mess, girl.'

Soul mates sat at the pine table in the kitchen of number thirty-nine, Benton Road.

Once such a happy and secure place to exist.

Now rendered nothing more than a scene of perpetual torment in the eyes and minds of its occupants.

Karen Aspinall stared into her coffee mug.

Emotionally spent.

Mentally confounded.

Physically ailing.

'I can't stay here, Jude. I don't want to live here anymore. I'm breaking up. It's killing me by the day.'

Judy looked helplessly at her most cherished chum. The pained figure across the table did not look like Karen Aspinall anymore. Even to the casual observer, she had evolved into a withered victim.

Consenting to her fate; accepting to her punishment.

'I don't blame Robert for being angry. He knows everything, now. He believes me. We've told the police. They don't want to know. They took the pane of glass for fingerprints. But my hopes aren't high.'

Karen held her head in her hands as Judy listened to her friend's plea for explanation.

'I can't believe this mess, Jude. I just can't get my head around the entire thing. What have we done wrong? Can anyone tell me? What have my family done to deserve such hate?'

Judy felt her friend's deep anguish. She was witnessing Karen's deconstruction first-hand. It was enough to evoke an emotional release of her own. Not tears induced by loathing; but out of frustrated concern for someone she cared deeply about.

Judy looked through to the lounge to observe Chloe and Lauren in front of the television.

Those two beautiful little girls, who thus far had been protected from the oppressive campaign from beyond the fading solace of home, but nonetheless had seen their parents fighting the odds, fighting with one another, and haplessly dealing with their plight.

'When is Rob home?' Judy asked.

'Tonight. He's swung tomorrow off.'

It was at this juncture that Karen remembered it was Thursday - not Wednesday.

'You need to sit down together and look to end this for your own sakes. For the sake of the girls. If moving out is really what you want, maybe it will cure things. Maybe that's the answer. You can't go on like this, Kaz. Look at your face. You should see a doctor about that lump.'

Karen's forefinger tentatively caressed the blackening blemish on her cheek.

'It's only a spot, Jude. I get them from time to time. It was bleeding this morning, though. Very painful.'

Judy moved closer across the table.

'That is no spot. It needs attention. It looks infected to me. It's like a boil or bruise. It feels hard. It's not normal, Kaz. Get it looked at.'

Karen suddenly emitted a weary chuckle before blowing her nose into a tissue.

'For Christ's sake, Jude! I haven't got much going for me at the moment, have I?'

'Let me know what you and Rob decide. I'm here to help, whenever.'

The parting embrace was long and emotional as one friend attempted to console another. The union was intimate and profound. Judy Simpson did not want to exit number thirty-nine that day. She wished for a magical cure to appear and wipe out the ebony clouds that currently shrouded the Aspinall's one-time blue-sky existence.

Driving away from Church Drayton, Judy stopped her car in a wooded lay-by, bathed in shafts of golden sunlight.

Cradling her face from any passing onlookers, she opened her heart and wept alone.

Accompanying her spiralling exhaustion was a prayer.

A heartfelt plea for the hurting to end.

*****

Robert's return home that evening did little to ease the brewing tension. He was restless and unwilling to try and relax. He declared it time for a drink and pulled a bottle from the fridge.

He stared vacantly through the kitchen window as he un-corked it.

Daylight was dissipating from the tranquil scene in the rear garden.

The girls were happily engaged with the offerings on television as he made his way upstairs to the bathroom.

'I've just rung the cop shop. They haven't had time to study the glass. They said they'll come round and set up a phone tracer if we want. To try and find the mystery caller…as if we didn't know.'

Robert Aspinall placed a glass of wine on the side of the bathtub as Karen soaked her weary form in the warm scented bubbles.

'Rob…I can't stay here any longer. I've decided I want to leave. We need to go. As soon as possible. I don't care where to. Just not here. I'm losing it, Rob. My mind is frazzled.'

Robert crouched to his wife's side and scrutinised the evidence on her face. He looked at the woman he loved. He knew she was adamant and earnest in her statement. Secretly, he had also adopted the belief that Benton Road was no longer the estate they thought they knew.

It had become ravaged by a disease.

Infested by an evil plague.

Inhabited by betrayers.

Robert felt for Karen's hand under the surface of the water.

'I'm going to talk to Mike. I'll explain fully that I need to be here and that we need relocation. Perhaps even to Coventry. If that's what you want, then I'm with you, Karen. We will stand together. If I can get us out of this mess…I will.'

The momentary peace was interrupted by the shriek of the lounge telephone.

'I'll get that, Kaz. It might be work. They know we've got a problem.'

Trotting downstairs and into the lounge, Robert tensed as he lifted the receiver and placed it cautiously to his ear.

Glancing at the caller display revealed yet another withheld number.

He waited a few seconds for the caller to speak.

They did not utter a sound.

Robert opted to open the conversation.

'Hello?'

Silence prevailed.

It was evident that the call was perhaps not of a social nature.

Then a female voice suddenly responded.

'Hello, Karen? Can I speak to Karen please?'

'Yes. Who is calling?'

A slight pause was broken by comforting words.

'It's…Judy.'

'She's just in the bath, Judy. I'll get her to ring you back.'

'It's very important. It can't wait.'

'Okay, Judy. Hang on.'

Having hauled herself from the tub and sheathed her wet form in towels, Karen took the receiver from the table as Robert poured himself another glass of wine in the kitchen.

He listened with suspicion as she responded to the caller.

Karen's instantaneous reaction confirmed his inkling that it wasn't Judy on the line at all.

Chloe and Lauren immediately forgot about the programme on the screen as they observed their mother's despair unfurl once again.

'You fucking bastards! Wait till we find you! You fucking sick bastards! Fucking leave me alone! LEAVE ME ALONE!'

Wrenching the handset from Karen's grasp, Robert continued the tirade…to a deadened line.

'They've hung up. What did they say, Karen?'

'That my life's in danger. That my kids' lives are in danger. We're going Rob. We're leaving here. I'm packing tomorrow. I'm going to Goltham. We're going to Mum's!'

The fragile embrace of man and wife was the last remaining link in their completely crumbled world.

Fragments of their life together continued to fall around them as they shielded one another from the final swells of the unrelenting storm.

thirty-seven

Cobden Terrace in Goltham became the last-gasp, soul-saving refuge for the ailing Aspinalls. With most possessions temporarily abandoned in Church Drayton, it was a very crowded situation at the home of Brian and Jean Hope, but a very necessary course of action in retaining any semblance of sanity.

Karen completely ensconced herself in the company of her parents and daughters. The feminine bond would remain solid. Authentic, mutual dependability was now the welcome remedy.

Over the weekend, Robert had braved in-depth talks with his father-in-law as to a way forward in escaping the predators that lay waiting in Benton Road. All were in avid agreement. A long-term future in that once idyllic place was no longer an option.

Sunday lunch was homely and filling. Appetites were satisfied and nerves had been calmed to a degree. Jean pulled out all the stops to sate her wish for the family to at least remember something of domestic happiness as it once was. And as it might be again in the near or distant future.

Securing short term arrangements were the priority amid the sudden upheaval. Practical solutions to everyday issues. In truth, nobody in the Hope household could seriously consider any plan for their future until the present debacle was over.

It was an unusually wet mid-August afternoon. Sunshine had disappeared behind a belt of slate cloud for a good while, which had dampened hopes for a visit to Greenacres. The girls had seemingly been cooped up indoors for weeks and despite their incredible displays of cooperation considering recent events, they were in dire need of a change of scenery.

Entering the cramped spare bedroom which accommodated the Aspinall clan just about adequately, Robert's offer of a ride in the company motor car was greeted with sincere enthusiasm by Chloe and Lauren.

Karen poked her head around the bedroom door as she observed her daughters slipping on their shoes.

'I'm only nipping to the supermarket in Tenbridge. We need a few bits. Anybody coming?'

'We are Daddy!' shouted the girls in unison.

'We won't be long. Do you need anything, Kaz?'

'We could do with some toothpaste, love.'

He lovingly observed his wife as she swung lazily from the door frame

Finally sheltered from harm. Safe from intrusion.

Kissing her softly on the lips was apt confirmation of his devotion.

'Don't be long, Rob.'

'We won't!'

Jean gave her granddaughters five pounds each in spending money as she waved them off at the front door with a request.

'Don't spend it all on sweets, now, do you hear, darlings? Get a magazine or something.'

*****

The sheeting rain battered the windscreen as Robert eased the purring automatic through the moderate volume of Sunday afternoon traffic. He watched his daughters' reflections in the rear-view mirror in between scanning the drab scene out front.

Judging by the lack of parking space the supermarket looked like it might be very crowded. Probably because of the weather. Evidently the idea of doing some shopping with his bored offspring was not an original one.

Robert slowly guided the car whilst scrutinising for a vacant space. Chloe and Lauren eagerly helped their father in the quest, resulting in an increasing crescendo of squeals and shouts as they aimed to beat one another to a successful discovery.

Robert's mirth at the commotion in the back seat was coupled with an inner satisfaction. It had been a long time since he had taken the girls anywhere. The excursion - albeit local and inherently simple - offered a welcome sense of paternal contribution.

He continued to observe the dank, miserable vista beyond the windscreen.

Then without warning, he halted the car by instinctively stamping on the brake pedal. Transfixed by the haunting vision only yards away.

In amongst the brightly coloured mosaic of rain-splashed roofs was a vehicle he recognised instantly through the intermittent swish of his wiper blades.

A large, imposing beast which dwarfed those around it.

A five-door saloon in jet black.

With a registration plate that beckoned his undivided attention.

The last three letters of the plate piercing his conscience like a poisoned dagger.

S…C…R.

Robert's heart started to race as his palms became clammy. The steering wheel slipped through his fingers as he continued to quickly navigate for somewhere to position his own vehicle.

The inner rage that had gradually subsided over the previous days now returned in an instant. It rapidly enveloped his form, ordaining him to respond in kind.

Unspoken desire fuelled his bloodstream as he finally occupied a vacant space and applied the handbrake.

He was no longer the Robert Aspinall of moments earlier.

He was now a man consumed by aspiration.

A need to assert his presence and a burning will to confront.

An appetite perhaps, for destruction.

Letting the girls out of the car, his mind was a swirling torrent of options as he engaged the central locking. Walking towards the sliding glass doors of the shop, his original motive for being there was now eclipsed by a desperate desire to seek out the enemy.

Firmly grasping the hand of his daughters, they struggling to keep up with their pacing father as he unwittingly dragged them along.

Chloe and Lauren could not have detected the inner turmoil that their father was experiencing at that moment. The speed of his stride was the only clue to what was coming.

Yet, Robert suddenly felt devoid of all confusion as he entered the store. Only blinkered ambition remained.

He had waited for this moment for many, many days.

The path of fate had now been inadvertently placed before him and he would willingly and consciously walk that line.

Through the clothing department. Scanning the crowds.

Beyond the newspapers, greetings cards and confectionary.

Between the fresh and the fridge aisles he continued to hunt and continued to tug his little girls toward the uncertain scenario.

Transfixed by rabid intent, his concentration was only partially disturbed by a tiny voice at his side.

‘Daddy…pick me up…I’m tired…’

Stopping his advance, he cradled his youngest daughter into his arms, leaving Chloe to walk unaided beside them.

Still the voyage into the unknown continued.

Now halfway through the store.

Scrutinising the movements between shoppers and trolleys.

His mental radar activated and fully operable.

And finally, the sensor locked on to its pre-meditated target.

In the distance, queuing to pay for her groceries like dozens of other oblivious customers, stood the self-preserving, disgraceful article of human reproduction that was Evelyn Chapple.

Big Chief Crazyhorse herself.

In the flesh. In all her despicable glory.

Defiant; dishonoured; now destined to meet with consequence.

Robert squeezed Lauren tighter into him and re-affirmed a grasp on Chloe as he stepped up the march.

Only yards away from the quarry now, his advance continued unhindered and undetected.

Then, as she glanced along the conveyor belt, she saw them.

The approaching Aspinall trinity.

Her innocent victims, suddenly bearing down on her unsuspecting vulnerability.

Her eyes widened as mild panic set in.

Yet she would not openly display her trepidation.

Evelyn Chapple looked around for some semblance of assistance, but she was alone.

Out in the open and ripe for attack.

To finally perish for her actions.

A wonderful demise for all around to behold.

The arena awaited the combatants.

Something instinctive halted Robert’s stride no more than ten yards from his subject. His daughters remained uninformed.

Their father and Evelyn Chapple exchanged loathsome glares for a few seconds.

No one in proximity would have expected the exchange that followed.

Pure animosity poured from Robert Aspinall as he eventually unleashed his restrained vexation in an unseemly yet controlled manner.

'You...fucking...bitch! Not so fucking big and full of yourself now, eh? Not so nasty and mean away from the pigsty, are we? And where's the runt of the litter, today? In hiding, no doubt!?'

Robert was suddenly the cause of intrigued attention from all around as his acidic tone brought the area to a standstill.

Yet his tirade was nowhere near complete.

'And to think you were supposed to be her friend. How can you ever live with yourself knowing what you have done to us all?'

The cashier sensed trouble brewing and pressed her emergency assistance button.

'Look at these little girls! They've doted on you all their lives. And you've betrayed them with sheer poison. Well at least we all now know what you and that retarded cunt of a son of yours are capable of.'

Throughout, Evelyn Chapple stood and listened without reply, seemingly unmoved by the verbal assault she had succumbed to.

Two security guards emerged through the expanding melee, but they would not prevent Robert's broadside.

'You don't look very fucking worried to me, but you should be! One final warning, bitch! If any of you or your inbred relatives comes anywhere near my family again I will personally... fucking...*kill* you! That's not a threat, either. That's a fucking *promise*!'

A bemused Lauren buried her face into her father's shoulder as dozens of shocked passers-by cleared the area.

Sensing the approach of the security guards, Robert decided he had issued his full message and slowly retreated into the aisles.

He had exorcised his vitriol. The task was accomplished.

Borne out of pure necessity, the deed was done.

His anxious desperation of moments earlier was now consciously displaced by somewhat deflating relief.

And yet still he remained with eyes fixed firmly on his nemesis.

Evelyn Chapple stepped back from the immediate vicinity and carefully pushed her trolley to one side.

Her eventual and departing words to Robert Aspinall were softly spoken yet laced with the premise of consequence.

'Thank you, Rob. That's all I needed to hear.'

With that, she turned on her heel, left her trolley half-loaded and promptly vacated the store.

Robert watched her exit and felt victory flush through him.

He then engaged with his daughters, who had been left wide-eyed and speechless by their father's highly uncharacteristic performance.

He lowered Lauren to the floor and with a much calmer manner of address, told them everything was okay.

'Come on girls. She's gone now. Let's do our shopping.'

Yes. Evelyn Chapple had indeed gone.

But not for the reason Robert Aspinall surmised.

She was no wilting opponent.

No shrinking violet.

Robert had been played to a tee.

Bringing her large, black saloon to a halt in the car park of Tenbridge police station, Evelyn Chapple smiled to herself.

The next level of unwarranted immoral affliction was solely hers to administer.

And she would do so with utter glee.

thirty-eight

The following week passed without further incident. Robert had been granted unconditional and indefinite leave from work. It was a time to regroup and close ranks as a family.

Everyone was made fully aware of what had transpired in the supermarket and predictably all supported Robert's motive and actions.

There was little more to be said on the issue.

Efforts were focused to absorb the past and consider the future.

Yet still the demons would not abate.

Even within the comparative, supposed refuge in Goltham.

Even the protective blessing of Karen's parents could not shield the Aspinalls from their thoughts.

The days were dissected with over-zealous imaginings.

Would the family's haven be discovered?

What awaited them should they return to number thirty-nine?

If indeed, they ever did return.

The full move to Cobden Terrace was achieved relatively quickly and most of the important and valuable items had eventually been retrieved from Benton Road by Robert and Brian in his van.

The Chapples remained noticeably hidden from view throughout the day-long operation.

Robert still made brief visits every few days to tend to any mail deliveries or other miscellaneous tasks that may have arisen.

Any hope of identifying the fingerprints on the garage windowpane was laid to rest during one such visit. As was his preference, Robert made the journey to Benton Road under cover of darkness so as not to arouse any unwarranted attention.

As he stealthily approached the front door to number thirty-nine, he could not fail to notice the large package wrapped in postal paper leaning against the brickwork under the bay window.

The police had evidently called at some point during the previous forty-eight hours and had considerately left their gift on full display.

Unattended for all and sundry to pass by and spectate over.

Inscribed on the wrapping in felt tip was a message from the local constabulary which only further exemplified the ineptitude that was exhibited when PC Lottinger made his initial house call some weeks ago.

Evidently his tardy standards were not specific to him alone.

Mr and Mrs Aspinall - Sorry we missed you.

No matches for these prints.

The sheer lack of professionalism from the local police force left Robert speechless for days afterwards.

It was of course another deflating blow to Karen when she was told of their actions, but not totally unexpected.

If there was no link to a possible suspect, then that was the end of the matter as far as the law was concerned.

Yet those caught up in the eye of the storm knew full well that an end to the heartache was not yet in sight.

*****

It was Saturday. Late August in the afternoon. Robert heard Karen shout from her parents' bathroom. Brian and Jean had gone into Tenbridge with the girls to meet some old friends for lunch.

The Aspinalls were alone as a couple once more, yet seemingly unable to shake off the persistent shadow of peril that pursued them.

'What is it, Kaz?'

The look of sheer terror on Karen's face adequately detracted from the fact that she was stood in front of the mirror, naked but for a towel.

'Rob…'

Staring mournfully at her own reflection, Karen looked like a child.

A lost, confused, desperate infant.

Emotion gripped her as she struggled to speak.

'Rob…I've found a lump…here…when I was in the shower…'

Embracing his wife with one arm, Robert followed his wife's guiding hand to a hardened area underneath the skin of her left breast.

'Can you feel it, Rob? Can you feel it?' she quaked.

Robert concentrated without response. He massaged the area through the skin, desperately trying to find absolutely nothing in his attempt to allay her deepest fears.

But he could feel the lump.

It most certainly was there.

Large enough to detect, yet not small enough to ignore.

He looked deeply into the eyes of the woman he cherished. Her reaction to the discovery was all too evident.

How much more was this woman going to suffer?

How much more could this family take?

'Is it something, Rob? Be honest. Tell me. Or is it me?'

'Yes…there is something.'

The truth scythed through Karen like a bolt of lightning as she crumpled to the floor in ensuing hysteria.

'Jesus, Rob. No! It can't be! It can't be! Not me! No more, please God!'

Straining to try and even up her severely wavering keel, Robert sat beside his wife's broken form and whispered words of hopeful encouragement.

'Kaz, listen to me. It might be nothing. It could be anything. Listen to me. Stay calm!'

He wiped the cascading tears from her face and cradled his wife's bruised features in his hands. Karen's torture was unavoidably his. Her wilting spirit was laid bare for him to see as she stared back into her husband's eyes with the heartfelt wish for an end to the never-ending struggle.

'Karen, I'll call the surgery first thing Monday morning. They will see you straight away, I'm sure. We will go together. This will be sorted…okay? We will get through this *together*. Okay?'

'But what about work?' she whimpered.

'Work is not a consideration. I'm on leave, remember?'

Man and wife consoled one another tightly as the moment passed.

Again, Karen looked to her man for affirmation.

'What about my babies, Rob? I don't want to die.'

'Nobody needs to be told anything yet. Stop jumping to conclusions. I'll phone the doctor Monday morning. I promise, darling. Let me make you a drink while you dress.'

Downstairs in the kitchen Robert Aspinall leaned over the sink to gaze through the window at the Hope's rear garden.

He studied the serenity outside as the kettle boiled.

Summer sunshine bathed the manicured greenery.

Nature's beauteous endurance lay in abundance all around.

Yet such an inspiring vision could not sever the link with the relentless despair that now cursed him every second of every single day.

thirty-nine

'Karen Aspinall, please.'

Grasping for the guidance of Robert's hand, Karen rose unsteadily to her feet and followed the nurse along the wooden panelled corridors of the surgery. The unfamiliar sterile scent of the building's interior was overwhelming and of little comfort.

Fear was the main player in the morning's agenda.

Fear of the unknown.

Fear of what may only be assumed.

In only a matter of a few minutes, Karen would be at the mercy of a professional verdict. Entering the consultation room with her husband at her side, she felt petrified.

And so incredibly fatigued by events.

Following her brief explanation of background and possible contributing circumstances, the male doctor examined the symptoms. He said nothing as he gently prodded and poked at the area under Karen's breast.

It was perhaps expected that his attention would trace upward to the mark on her cheek and the areas of drying skin around her forehead.

He looked Karen in the eye and offered a warm half-smile.

Seated in the chair against the wall, Robert waited silently in excruciating anticipation.

Finally, the dreaded sentence was bestowed as the GP resumed his seat and spoke with soothing authority.

'Well, Karen…I don't think you've anything serious to concern yourself with. I am pretty sure that stress is the underlying cause for these reactions.'

The weight of dread lifted from the room in an instant as the doctor continued with his diagnosis.

'I'm going to make you an appointment for a mammogram. Sounds alarming, I know, but is merely procedural. I am certain that they will find nothing untoward. I believe it to be nothing more than a benign cyst.'

Karen wiped a solitary tear from her eye as she absorbed the doctor's words.

'The mark on your cheek is an Epidermoid. It looks to be latent at the moment, but the darkness indicates some blood content. The bruising will disperse in time. It's just the body's way of giving you the signs of its struggle. I'm also going to refer you to the dermatologist - just for reassurance that there is no other underlying cause and to eliminate risk of infection. It should remedy of its own accord.'

The doctor squinted as he leaned across the desk once again to examine Karen's forehead.

'Prescription steroid cream should replenish the skin around your eyes and hairline. You need to try and relax. You say these all these symptoms have appeared within the past two months or so. They will dissipate with time, but if the pressure you're experiencing is not eased then you will continue to suffer with some severity.'

Resting his elbows on the desk and clasping his hands, the doctor peered at his patient over black-framed spectacles.

'Have I helped appease your worries, Karen?'

'Yes. Thank you, doctor.'

'Good. The hospital appointments will be processed swiftly. I estimate the wait will be little longer than a month or two, but rest assured that if I had any real concerns then I would be sending you today. Here's your steroid prescription. Apply very sparingly. This stuff is incredibly strong and can cause damage if over-used. Please don't hesitate to see me again if you've any further concerns.'

*****

A welcome if unfamiliar feeling of contentment enveloped the Aspinalls as they drove away from the town centre. Statements of loving and reassuring comfort were exchanged between man and wife as they returned to their waiting family.

Yet, further heavy rain was about to douse the welcome parade of placation. As Robert's company car came to a stop in Cobden Terrace, Karen developed an uncanny sensation.

Something awaited their arrival. Entering the hallway, she instantly observed the expression of concern on her mother's face.

Brian peered around the lounge doorway to greet his daughter.

'How did it go, love? Okay by the judge of the smile on your face.'

'Yes. All okay. Nothing to worry about. I'll be fine. There are some hospital tests to be done, but the doctor is happy that it's nothing serious.'

Chloe and Lauren bounced from the lounge and showered their mother and father in welcoming hugs.

Cradling Lauren up from the floor, her father kissed her on the nose as his gaze was met sternly by Brian's.

'What is it? You both look worried?' enquired a curious Robert.

Brian looked to Jean before offering his son-in-law a sigh of resignation.

'While you were both out, we took a phone call.'

'Not the bloody cranks again.' spat Karen, angrily. 'How the bloody hell have they got this number?'

Brian Hope shook his head and closed his eyes.

'Not this time. It was the police. PC Smalley, to be precise. He wants to talk to *you*, Rob. You've got to phone the station today and make an appointment.'

forty

Tuesday morning. The twenty-seventh of August. Robert locked the metallic blue automatic in the cramped car park at Tenbridge police station and nervously made his way to the front entrance. Checking his watch to see that he wasn't late for the eleven o'clock appointment, Robert spoke into the intercom unit attached to the wall.

Upon confirming his name and reason for the visit, the glass door unlocked itself and allowed Robert access to the reception area. The desk sergeant made the necessary phone call and Robert was asked to take a seat.

Looking around the grey walls of the station interior was an altogether uninspiring diversion. He wasn't even sure why he was there. Possibilities ran through his mind as he casually observed posters about bicycle theft, drug abuse and fly-tipping.

He was inwardly hoping that his summons was positive in nature.

Perhaps there had been some leads on the garage window after all.

Maybe the identity of the nuisance caller had been discovered.

It was about time fortune shone on the Aspinall family. The odds had been firmly against them for too long.

Robert stood to his feet as a bearded young policeman approached, introduced himself with a handshake as PC Smalley and confirmed Robert's identity.

'Please come through here, Mister Aspinall.'

Having been led into a room at the end of a short corridor, Robert was asked to take a seat at the other side of a large black table. He immediately noticed the recording device on a shelf and two unused cassette tapes on the tabletop.

Robert quickly sensed that something was amiss as Officer Smalley and then another unnamed colleague entered the room and sat opposite.

Now mildly perplexed, he felt duty bound to enquire as to the reason his presence had been requested.

PC Smalley took little time in relaying the brutal truth.

'Mister Aspinall. Do you know a lady by the name of Mrs. Evelyn Chapple?'

Robert paused and looked into the constable's piercing blue eyes.

'Yes. She's my next-door neighbour. Why do you ask?'

'Do you recall an encounter with her in the supermarket a week last Sunday - the eighteenth of August - at approximately three p.m.?'

Now the reason for Robert's visit was becoming all too apparent.

'Yes. Yes…I do. Why?'

PC Smalley did not avert his gaze from Robert for a second as he continued.

'She is alleging in a formal complaint that you approached her in an intimidating manner before verbally threatening to kill her in front of several other witnesses. Can you confirm or deny these allegations Mister Aspinall?'

Robert's heart pounded in his chest as an awful, twisted clarity descended on the arena.

'I…I did say that. Yes. I admit it. I said it to her. I was…upset, but I didn't mean it.'

The officer of the law paid little more attention as his hands reached for an electronic switch underneath the table.

Within seconds another policeman entered the interview room and closed the door before standing at ease against the wall. He did not acknowledge Robert, instead apparently awaiting instruction from PC Smalley.

Three on to one.

Robert absorbed the scenario and weighed up the odds.

A distinctly unlevel playing field.

Next to be issued from the officer were words of such deflating emphasis, that on hearing them in earnest for the first time in his entire life, Robert suddenly felt incredibly scared.

'Mister Robert Aspinall. I am arresting you under the charge of making threats to kill, which comes under the legal term of affray. This is an offence under the Public Order Act Section Three. You may not wish to say anything at this time, but should you wish to do so it may be used as evidence in any potential court hearing.'

Robert's stomach lurched as the gravity of the constable's announcement hit home like a bullet straight between the eyes.

Words could not produce a sufficiently appropriate reaction.

Robert simply stared into space and stuttered a breathless reply.

'Jesus! I didn't know this would happen.'

Disbelief quickly encompassed his every strand of concentration.

He looked to the aloof vision of the conferring policemen across the table.

Flashes of his wife and daughters appeared at the forefront of his mind. Images that were all too quickly eclipsed by the unexpected distress of his emerging predicament.

If only he could have Karen by his side at that moment.

But Robert Aspinall was completely alone in his plight.

He would be facing the immediate future unaccompanied.

PC Smalley issued instruction to the colleague seated beside him.

'He's given it the nod. We're booking him. We may as well stay in here for the initial statement. Tell the duty sergeant, please.'

Authority effortlessly commenced the destruction of Robert's remaining zest as he sat awaiting further direction in a pained, soundless void of hopelessness.

But PC Smalley did not waver. He had evidently performed this ritual many times before. He was callous and calculating in delivering the procedure.

'If you wish, Mister Aspinall, you may have your solicitor present to witness this statement being recorded. If you haven't got one, we can appoint you one.'

Robert looked vacantly to the surface of the table in front and shook his head without word.

The second officer quickly returned with a selection of forms before reclaiming his seat. Scribbling furiously as he flicked through page after page, PC Smalley did not speak as he hurriedly wrote in relevant areas, ticked boxes in others, and intermittently crossed out printed sections.

Finally, he asked for a list of Robert's vital details.

Compliance was the only option as Robert answered promptly and efficiently, albeit through a taut and unyielding veil of melancholy.

Unwrapping the cassette tapes, the officer then placed them both into the recording machine on the shelf and pressed two buttons to activate the device.

'Initial interview statement. Robert Aspinall. Time is eleven-twelve a.m. Present are arresting officer PC Smalley, witness officer PC James and guarding officer PC Andrews.'

Credibly outnumbered and cast adrift from all chance of respite from his woeful penance, Robert sat and watched as the arresting officer finally looked to him and offered a knowing, satisfied smile.

'Okay, Mister Aspinall. Would you like to try and explain your actions? Starting from the very beginning. Wherever you deem that beginning to bc.'

*****

Robert completed his full statement in less than fifty minutes. A cautiously memorised, harrowing journey all the way to Hell and back. A monologue containing so many agonised junctures of recollection.

And those police officers did not recoil once during that hour as they silently observed their suspect unravel.

The shredding of his every emotion.

The uncontrolled outbursts of anger.

The pleading words of remorse.

The self-conviction of his actions that he ultimately refused to conceal.

Yet, despite the vehemence exhibited, Robert's pitiful chronicle of sufferance was met with complete indifference by the representatives of the law.

PC Smalley did not interrupt, nor did he react to anything that was said. No sympathy was expressed either visually or verbally.

Perversely, no questions were asked, either.

The arresting officer's only movement was to stand up after twelve minutes and check the spools of the turning cassette tapes.

Upon conclusion of his recounted plight, Robert surrendered to his breaking heart and with shaking hands buried his weeping eyes from view.

'Interview terminated…eleven-fifty-nine a.m. Would you like a tea or coffee, Mister Aspinall?'

Robert shook his head as he attempted to regain composure.

A drink would certainly not have ridded his mouth of a very bitter aftertaste.

Things were now all too clear.

He had made himself a very easy target for the police. Although admission was his only option, it was obvious that they intended to take things further.

PC Smalley's conveyance of professional arrogance only served to inflame Robert's inner despondency.

‘Okay, Robert. We will take you to records for processing a photograph and prints. Shouldn’t take long. Do I need to cuff you, or are we still in a good mood?’

Robert glared back at the officer of the law at that moment with nothing less than abject contempt. The sudden and uninvited use of his Christian name was salt in the wound, as though the officer was addressing an old friend.

But he would retain his dignity.

He would comply with the law and its dubious practice.

Any negative reaction would only make things far worse for himself. And the officers present were seemingly waiting to pounce on such any such display like vultures.

That much was a now cast-iron certainty.

*****

Perched on a high stool with a plaque in his hands displaying the station case number, Robert felt quietly inconsolable at the outcome of the morning’s events.

The photograph was taken.

And then a second one was taken - for nostalgia, no doubt.

Robert Aspinall had now inhabited the identity of the criminal he was purported to be.

He was requested to get off the stool and move over to the desk.

Placing each of his digits onto the ink pad was like being on some corny TV detective show. He never thought in his wildest dreams that he would ever be performing such a degrading task for real.

Filling in the court appointment form, the duty sergeant sneered as he asked the pending defendant a few personal questions.

The fury was now boiling within Robert’s core.

Of all the people in the world that deserved to be standing at that desk at that moment, Robert felt the greatest injustice that it was he.

Tearing away the carbon copy of the court form, the sergeant handed it over with the subtlest glint of pleasure in his eye.

‘Not long to wait, sir. There’s the taped copy of your interview, as well. Just in case you want a solicitor to hear it. Wait here. PC Smalley will return to escort you out of the station.’

Robert studied the form in his hand and searched for the date of the summons.

Confirming it to be the first week of October, he was surprised at how soon his appearance would be.

Clutching the cassette, he made his mind up there and then to find himself a lawyer and defend himself against the charge.

A guiding hand in his lower back ushered him through the dismal corridors, out through reception and to the front entrance.

PC Smalley activated the electronic locking mechanism and stood by the open the door waiting for Robert to leave. His words of farewell were delivered with aloof insincerity.

'If you need anything Mister Aspinall…you know where to find me. I'm here to help. Okay?'

Robert glared at the officer but did not respond as he exited the station and made his way slowly back to the car.

His rage was now all consuming.

The incredulity of the moment…calamitous

Slamming the door as he slumped behind the steering wheel, Robert was only mildly placated by the welcome silence of the car's interior.

A silence that was soon banished.

To be eclipsed by the futile whimpers that symptomized a grown man's ultimate desolation.

*****

Entering the front door of the Hopes house in Cobden Terrace, Robert was greeted by the infinitely pleasurable sight of his wife, parents' in-law, and children.

He initially presented a mask of courage, but within seconds the curious convention of inherent concern was too much for him to withstand.

Succumbing once more to uncontrolled wailing, Robert sank to his knees as the family embraced his pain.

Swaying on the emotional storm, Robert Aspinall explained all that had transpired to his family.

Wondering where or if their annal of misfortune would ever end, Karen whispered into her husband's ear as he huddled before her.

Her voice trembled with pangs of guilt as she admired the quivering form of the man she loved.

The man that had willingly defended his cherished ones against the enemy.

'I'm so sorry, Robert. This is not fair. I said everything would be alright...but it's not. This all my fault. All of it. Things couldn't be worse for you. I'm so sorry. Forgive me. I'm so sorry.'

Her husband had nothing to offer in reply.

He could only hope that the givers of fate might just possess a remaining iota of mercy for his cause.

forty-one

It was Karen and Robert's first ever visit to a legal representative's office. The aura of officialdom made them distinctly nervous as they stepped over the unfamiliar threshold and entered the daunting arena.

Holding hands, they approached the elderly receptionist as she peered over the top of a typewriter and displayed a welcoming smile.

'Good morning. Can I help you?'

Robert took a deep breath before commencing his introduction.

'Hello. We are Mister and Mrs. Aspinall. We have an appointment with David Williams at Midday.'

Suffering a sudden attack of nerves, Karen turned to gaze through the large glass frontage of the office and let her eyes absorb the passing traffic outside. The receptionist flicked through the diary and looked up with another earnest expression of pleasure.

'If you'll both take a seat, please. I'll inform David that you're here. Would you like tea or coffee?'

Robert confirmed his wife's wishes with a brief glance before responding to the kind gesture.

'Erm…no, no thanks. We're fine.'

After a few minutes of unforgiving silence, a short man in a grey suit with a thick mop of curly brown hair emerged from a side doorway and instantly thrust forth a warm hand of greeting.

'Robert Aspinall? Please come through.'

Robert insisted that Karen stay in the reception area.

An option she found to be to her preference.

Robert suggested that her suffering had been prolonged enough without listening to another rendition of her own tale of distress.

Robert kissed her lightly on the lips before venturing into the solicitor's office.

'Okay, sit yourself down Robert. Make yourself comfortable. What can I try and do for you today?'

It seemed like the umpteenth time he had explained the situation in the past few days.

Briefly outlining the background to the offence, Robert handed the cassette of his statement and court summons across the large, leather lined desk.

‘All the details are on the tape, Mister Williams. That is a copy of my statement to the police. And a copy of the form they issued me with.’

Studying the piece of paper through reading spectacles, the solicitor raised his eyebrows and glanced toward Robert.

‘Mmm…Magistrates Court? October? Didn’t hang about, did they? Soft option for them, weren’t you methinks? From what you’ve already told my secretary on the phone, the extreme mitigation should sway opinion of those on high. I might even get it thrown out if I’m lucky with the magistrates on the day. I am assuming you have no criminal record?’

Robert was still rather confused by events.

‘I’ve never been in trouble before if that’s what you mean. I didn’t realise that threatening to kill someone was an offence. People say it all the time, don’t they?’

David Williams removed his glasses and clasped his hands.

His tone was friendly and assuring which gratified Robert.

It had been a long time since he felt like anybody had presented him with a supportive standpoint.

‘The issue comes not with the words spoken, Robert, but with the recipient’s *perception* of the words. If she felt in danger, indeed if others around felt themselves to be in danger, then I’m afraid it is rightly classified as a section three public order offence. But its low end on the scale. Physical aggravation or fighting is top end of the section. As it says on the form, “giving those in the close vicinity immediate cause for concern regarding their safety and welfare.” The police are making an example of you, Robert. On paper it’s an easy win for them. But don’t take things too personally. The police certainly don’t.’

The solicitor’s refreshingly positive overview of the situation was soothing for Robert to hear, as were the disdainful references to the police.

Although he was still in the dark as to the seriousness of the charge.

‘What does the Public Order act entail, then, Mister Williams?’

‘Please, call me David. Well, put simply, it’s a grading of public behavioural levels, all the way from shouting in the street, which is termed under section three, through to section one which is basically inciting and partaking in a violent riot. Apparently, the police are placing your case somewhere in the middle.’

Robert sat forward in his chair and slammed a fist on the table.

‘But that’s ridiculous! I was carrying my young daughter! No one was in any *danger*. It was just stupid words. That’s all!’

The solicitor was not perturbed by Robert's obvious anger.

'I totally agree. Hopefully the judges will too if they sympathise! Considering your motive, the whole thing is ridiculous. But unfortunately, it's the police that are pushing it through court - not the complainant. It's now up to me to apply and try and get the charge dismissed. I can't make an argument for this until I've heard the tape and presented my own case on your behalf. I might be able to make a motion for dismissal before the hearing date which would save us all the inconvenience of having to attend.'

Robert sighed and looked upward to the ceiling for inspiration.

Teeming frustration was now coupled up alongside his initial fear.

'If the original charge stands, what then? Now that I've admitted doing it. What could they do?'

The solicitor sat back in his chair and began cleaning his spectacles with a small cloth.

'Well, your immediate admission of guilt will be looked on favourably. Not that you have much choice in the matter.'

Robert leaned forward again and looked the solicitor sternly in the eye.

'What will happen to me?' he trembled.

A merest glint of foreboding shone through the demeanour of David Williams as he spoke.

'I have known the odd cases of affray lead to small custodial sentences. But this was only with previous offenders breaching live court injunctions, however. In your position, the usual maximum response to this level of charge is a community service order. But again, that scenario is highly unlikely as you are a first-time offender.'

Robert was now quaking in his chair as he grasped for some positivity.

'And what if you can get it reduced, David? What's the worst that could happen to me, then?'

'I won't be able to get it reduced, Robert. The charge will stand as is. But with your clean record they may throw it out. You'll possibly be fined and issued with the bill for court costs. No worse.'

Robert rubbed his weary eyes as he considered the minimal options.

David Williams could see the strain showing in his potential client.

'If you leave this with me, I will get back to you by the end of next week with my thoughts. I can't believe they're wasting taxpayers' money on such a trifling thing. But I do need time to examine your statement. If

I can flex my muscles with the detail you have submitted on tape, things will look far more positive for you than they seem at this current time. I hope you didn't pull any punches. The truth will out, you know. Always has done and always will. That's of course if you wish for me to represent you. You aren't committed to anything yet. This chat is on me. No charge today.'

Within Robert there suddenly dawned a modicum of optimism.

'Okay, David. Yes, please. I want you to try. What about the final cost?'

Scribbling onto a note pad, the solicitor muttered to himself before revealing the potential expense.

'Well, as I say, today's consultation is free as standard. My input next week will put you to two hundred pounds - whatever the outcome regarding the court date. If you want me to represent you at the proposed court hearing - which I'm more than willing to do - you can perhaps add another four hundred to that if we can get this case closed to our satisfaction.'

For Robert Aspinall, there was no decision to make.

'Yes, David. Please carry on. Do what you must. You have my full backing. You can contact me at the number on the form. We're staying with my wife's parents for the time being.'

David Williams rose to his feet and made to show Robert the door.

Another firm handshake and expression of confidence from the solicitor was a most welcome sight.

'Okay, Robert. I'll call you in a few days and we can have another chat. And remember something. I'm on *your* side. You're not backing *me*! It's me that's backing *you*. Speak soon. Goodbye for now.'

forty-two

The postman's error had caused immediate interest when Robert picked up the mail from the doormat of number thirty-nine, Benton Road.

He had not visited the family home for three days.

Of the five items retrieved from the floor, three were junk mail addressed to Karen.

One was an electric bill with Robert's name attached.

The other item was something of an anomaly.

Back at the Hopes, he handed his wife her post in Jean's kitchen and placed the electric bill onto the worktop. His resulting smile made Karen curious.

Even more enticing was the white envelope that he waved in front of her.

'I think we should open this one together, Kaz.'

A look of sheer puzzlement befell her features.

'I don't get you, Rob. What is it?'

'A letter…'

Karen was still baffled.

'Yeah…so why do we have to open it together?'

'It's ended up at ours by mistake. It's addressed to number forty-one…for a Mister Greg Chapple esquire…'

An unbridled excitement descended on the room.

Karen herself smirked with intrigue at the enticing thought of what might be inside. Rob erred on the side of caution.

'Where are the girls?'

'They're both watching TV. They're ready for bed though. Mum and Dad are in the front room with them.'

Moving closer to Karen, Robert turned the envelope over as she scrutinised over his shoulder.

'Don't recognise that style of postmark, Rob. Looks like it could be foreign.'

'Hopefully a warrant for his arrest, fingers crossed. Or something equally satisfying.'

Chuckling with anticipation, Robert and Karen looked at one another before bursting into fits of laughter once again.

'Come on then, slowcoach! Let's see what's in it!' she giggled.

Robert began to prise open the seal with his thumb.

Removing the single sheet of beige coloured paper, he proceeded to unfold it as Karen's eyes widened.

'Let me read it first. Being as I found it!' insisted Rob.

'God, you're just like a kid at times. Okay. You go first. Then me!'

Karen observed Robert's eyes as he studiously began to scan the content of the correspondence. His anticipation of finding something scandalous was evident in his face as he traced down the page. Yet his enthusiasm visibly flickered away as his features gradually adopted a mask of contempt.

Just sixty seconds earlier, Robert was overcome with curiosity as to the content of the mislaid letter.

Now, as he handed the piece of printed paper to Karen, he issued a stark warning.

'I don't think you should, Kaz. You seriously won't believe your fucking eyes.'

Now, Karen automatically shared her husband's despondency. Holding the letter between shaking fingers, her eyes fell to the header at the top of the page.

'B.T.E. Solicitors Limited. Looks rather important.'

Karen then read out the subject reference.

'European Court of Human Rights? What is *that* then, Rob?'

Robert sighed heavily and turned away to the view beyond the kitchen window. The sun was dropping quickly as advancing darkness chased its retreat.

'It's a large governmental body that deals with legal disputes on behalf of the countries within Europe.'

'I…don't understand. It's from Strasbourg in France?'

'You *will* understand…you will. You won't *want* to, though. Just read on, Kaz. Read it aloud, please. I need to hear it again.'

Still confused, Karen reverted to the page and commenced with Robert's wishes.

'Dear Mister Chapple. With reference to your claim for compensation, case number GB129873, representatives acting on your behalf have investigated the circumstances surrounding the period in question and the subsequent compensatory offer.'

Karen looked at her husband, whose white-knuckled hands gripped the rim of the sink.

She continued somewhat warily.

'Having accepted that illegal incarceration prematurely ended your career in the British Armed Forces and having assessed all aspects of your previous and current situation, we feel that we should pursue a secondary, increased offer of compensation for the personal losses incurred to yourself. The British Military are undoubtedly guilty of your unwarranted imprisonment whilst stationed in Cyprus and we believe that your case should come under revue again before the annual claimant deadline is enforced.

I am informed that the current settlement offer will stand at one hundred and eighty thousand pounds Sterling should you decide to accept. We strongly advise you to reconsider acceptance of this offer, with a view to outright refusal. We believe that the sum for damages could be dramatically improved should persistence be applied.

Please consider our proposal and respond with your decision by the date shown above in red. This is our deadline to submit an application for a review of the monies offered. Should you feel inclined to instruct us to this effect, we will make a further attempt to resolve matters on your notification. We await your prompt response. Yours faithfully, Jeremy Boston. B. T. E. Solicitors Limited.'

Karen looked open-mouthed at her husband who continued to hold his gaze toward the blackening landscape outside. She thought she understood its message.

Yet Karen wasn't yet in total possession of the overall picture.

'What the hell is this about then, Rob? Am I right in thinking that Greg is due some money for something?'

Robert finally turned to his wife and took the letter from her weakened grasp. Once more he scanned the words in silence before screwing up the sheet of paper and dropping it into the washing up bowl.

Taking a box of matches from the kitchen drawer, he offered further conclusion.

'I'm only guessing from what we have just read, Kaz, but our friend Greg looks to have been in some trouble during his little army stint. That's why he came home early.'

'What kind of trouble?'

'Serious enough to get him court martialled. No doubt he's inflicted some harm on somebody. The army doesn't send people to prison for nothing. Now he's obviously had a solicitor on the case and taken it right to the top.'

Karen gestured to the letter which was now moistening in her mother's kitchen sink.

'The top? You mean this European court thing?'

'Yes, Kaz. It doesn't get any grander than that! Big mean judges with the biggest wigs on. Of all the fucking undeserving bastards in the world and all the stuff he's done to us, he's destined to become pretty bloody wealthy if this letter is anything to go buy.'

'What are we going to do? He obviously needs to see this letter, then?'

Robert opened the box of matches and lit one.

'Yeah…shame he never will…eh? I'm amazed this didn't end up back at the mail depot. I would have thought correspondence this heavy would need signing for. But never mind. What a tragedy we got to it first.'

The Aspinalls observed studiously as the piece of paper ignited and became engulfed in flames of partial retribution.

Within seconds, the only remnant of the letter was a small pile of sodden congealing ash in and around the plug hole.

Silence prevailed as the room began to accommodate the fragrance of smoke.

Karen placed a tentative hand on her husband's shoulder.

She could sense his rage burning.

'Rob…I don't know whether we should have done that.'

He did not return Karen's gaze, again preferring to stare into the evolving cloak of dusk that now descended on Cobden Terrace.

'Fuck him! And fuck his money. Fuck the lot of them! I'm in court because of those bastards. I hope he gets nothing.'

forty-three

Despite the lack of available space at the Hope's home, life for the Aspinalls had regained some much-needed stability whilst under the protective haven of Karen's mother and father. Chloe and Lauren had returned to routine as normal in the first week of September.

Lauren, now being classed as an infant, would be spending full days at school. Yet Karen had barely acknowledged such a pivotal moment in her young daughter's life, such was the preoccupation with other matters.

Robert had returned to his duties with work. His indefinite absence was causing some consternation with his superiors. The solution to re-embrace the weekly commute seemed the only amicable one.

Karen had tried to make the best of the situation at Cobden Terrace and transform her family's enforced relocation into something resembling habitable.

Whilst her husband had braved the uncertain territory of Benton Road on a regular basis to overlook the estate of number thirty-nine, Karen had not returned there since the early weeks of summer.

She had privately nurtured an all-encompassing fear of the place. Even the mere mention of the name of the road left her cold. In her heart, she understood that resumption of the life she once knew and loved was now highly improbable.

On a positive note, there had not been a single encounter with the Chapples since the conflict in the supermarket. Even on Robert's weekly check-ups, there was no visual evidence that the neighbours even lived next door.

Number thirty-nine remained as it had been left.

No more damage.

No more interference.

No more occupants.

It was incredibly hard to digest that fact that the house was so very recently a domain of contented family unity. Without the inhabiting warmth of its owners, it was now merely a bleak, meaningless shell.

Mere bricks and mortar.

A monument to a past life.

Over several visits Robert had retrieved various items from the house working off lists that Karen had compiled from memory.

Cardboard boxes of possessions were slowly occupying more space in Brian Hope's garage and loft.

But it was viewed by all concerned as a very necessary if tardy process of evacuation.

Gradually, number thirty-nine was losing identity as the former residence of the Aspinalls, although Karen's car still lay slumbering in the garage.

It was incredibly painful for Robert to recognise so very little of the place he once loved.

The house had succumbed to a rapid onset of spiritual depravation due to the events of the spring and summer.

Robert had rankled with crushing sorrow as he considered what was no longer his outright. He had unwillingly languished in the prolonged and continuing aftermath of his family's ordeal.

And looming on the horizon, just to add insult to injury, was the date with the administers of law and order. Where he had to face the possible consequences of his actions.

Actions undertaken as his family's defender.

A few careless words that had landed him with the first court appearance of his life.

A man of moral grounding, reduced to indulging in silly playground exchanges. He did not yet know whether he would be made to rue his moment of angered release.

Thursday the third of October would be a day of reckoning for Robert Aspinall. A day which had overshadowed his family's future for the preceding month. Sleepless nights were now part and parcel of his existence.

The only contact with his solicitor since their initial meeting had been a quick phone call to confirm when to convene in the court foyer.

There had been little clue given from David Williams regarding his response to Robert's emotional account of a life now in fracture.

Nearly three weeks on from their initial introduction, Robert still had no idea of how his day in court would transpire or indeed conclude.

Two weeks ago, a scheduled intermediate session with David had been cancelled due to an unforeseen hindrance in the solicitor's itinerary.

Without a guiding hand to speak of, he could only pray that the gods of fate would ultimately bless him.

forty-four

'What time is it, Kaz?'

His wife's voice carried through from the bedroom.

'Nine-thirty, love.'

'You've taken the kids to school, haven't you?'

'Yes, darling. Dad and I have just got back.'

Karen entered the bathroom where Robert was struggling to put final touches to his attire.

'Can you help me, darling? I'm all fingers and thumbs. I must have done it thousands of times over the years. Can't do it today, though.'

Knotting and straightening his tie, Karen looked into the eyes of the man she loved with all her heart.

'Rob…don't be nervous. It'll be alright. I promise.'

Wiping a tear from his eye with the tip of her index finger, she cradled her husband in her arms as he succumbed to his emotions for the umpteenth time that week.

Karen found words of strength.

'Come on, Rob. We are going to stand up for ourselves today. To prove to everyone that we're the good guys, yes?'

Robert simply nodded before dousing his face with cold water.

'Okay. If you say so, love. I've got to meet David at ten inside the court entrance, haven't I? Are your mum and dad ready? We'd better go.'

*****

Robert had opted to drive to the courthouse in his company car as opposed to booking a taxi. With Jean and Brian in the backseat and his wife by his side, his anxieties were temporarily deflected by the need to concentrate on the road - albeit for an all too short while.

With the court car park already over-spilling, it took a minute or two to position the metallic blue automatic down a side street. Locking the doors, Robert observed his wife and her parents as they stood waiting for him on the pavement. Their support had been unwavering.

Sadly, the determination they felt in meeting fate head on was not transferring to him too successfully.

He opted for humour and smirked at the trio.

'Not on double yellows, am I? That's all I bloody need today!'

All three chuckled nervously.

Robert was appreciative that his quip found a laugh.

If only they knew how so very frightened he was at that moment.

Taking Karen's hand in his, the four marched back toward the red brick magistrates' courthouse. It was a modern building. All tinted glass and landscaped gardens. Not in tandem with the traditional designs for such places.

Yet it still succeeded in emitting an air of unerring dread for those entering its hallowed arches.

Robert's attempts to remain calm were partially thwarted by the movement of a car in the distance as they crossed the road. Nobody else in the group seemed to notice the large black saloon as it pulled out of its parking space and disappeared slowly around the corner. Robert thought he recognised it for a split second. Then the thought was gone as quickly as it had arrived.

The courthouse foyer was veritably brimming with defendants and their loved ones. Legal representatives and court ushers peppered the crowd. The judges evidently had a busy day scheduled. Couples sat huddled on benches. Men and women in suits stood conferring whilst holding large bundles of files. The atmosphere was laced with expectancy and the backdrop was provided by the persistent murmur of covert conversation.

This was indeed humbling territory for Robert Aspinall. Today he was a potential criminal. Nobody noticed him or his family as they reluctantly entered the large, automated glass doors and found a spare hub of seats in the corner.

This was to be where Robert would await his call. Now overcome with nervous tension, he positioned himself across from his wife. He wanted to keep her in his eyeline at all times. He needed to know that she was there for him when his bell eventually tolled.

The minutes ticked on past ten o' clock. Despite a coarse throat, he refused Karen's offer to fetch coffee for fear of inducing a thankfully sedate bladder into action. He watched the dozens of other entrants awaiting their appointment times.

Flicking idly through a boating magazine did little by way of transporting his mind away from the scene. It felt like he was embarking on a hundred dental appointments rolled into one.

Robert's imagination spun simultaneously with anticipation, optimism, and dread.

The wait for destiny's ordainment seemed eternal.

Then, at last, the hiatus was over.

'Robert! Good morning! Good morning, everyone! There you are! Would you like to follow me through here, please?'

David Williams approach to the family was polite and concise. There was no time for Robert to acknowledge his wife's empathy with even the briefest of farewells. He observed the briefcase under his solicitor's arm as he trailed behind and was led into a small consultation office.

'Please…take a seat, Robert. I'm sorry we haven't had chance to convene before today, but it will have little detrimental effect on my plans.'

Robert placed himself on the chair in silence. His thumping heart signified an eagerness for proceedings to begin as the solicitor produced an A4 file.

'Now then, we are apparently due in house at ten past eleven. I'm hoping that things won't come to that, however.'

'What do you mean, David?'

Mr. Williams opened the file on the table and revealed several pages of typed notes.

'This is my reading for you should we have to stand. I am now going to meet with the three magistrates and persuade them to get this whole charade thrown out before it incurs procedural cost upon your good self.'

Robert was distinctly baffled and rubbed his eyes in response.

'Do you mean that I might not have to enter court after all?'

'That is my hope, Robert. But the police are really trying it on. Sometimes the CPS likes to make example. Easy pickings, I call it. But your statement is irrefutable and overwhelmingly powerful mitigation. They are reading through the case notes as I speak. I need to intercept quickly if you are going to avoid a defence play. Please remain here.'

David Williams closed his file and was gone in an instant. The relentless mumblings of the adjacent foyer were no longer audible as Robert was left sitting behind the closed door of the beige-walled briefing room.

The absence of sound felt threatening, as Robert sat alone with his myriad of thoughts.

*****

Karen looked to her mother and father. They simultaneously displayed hopeful expressions. She in turn forced a smile for them. But her sole concentration centred on what her husband was possibly being told at that moment by his brief.

Jean had noticed her daughter's attempts to cosmetically mask the cyst which was now in obvious residence on her cheek, and the perished skin of her face which was now thankfully in a stage of replenishment.

The ghastly symbols of her body's fight against enduring such incredible strain left Jean Hope with a heavy heart.

Her beautiful daughter had suffered so. It had been nothing less than heart-breaking for the Hopes to watch their young family crumble.

Their only wish was that the plight of the Aspinalls would today be ended once and for all.

*****

David Williams returned to the briefing room to disturb Robert's uneasy solace.

'Well, I tried, Robert. But they are unusually intrigued by this one. They want to hear your story. I'm sorry. They're wanting to see us now. They've pulled us in early.'

Emerging tentatively from the consultation room, Robert was led back to his seat next to Karen and her parents.

All four listened carefully as they were instructed by the solicitor.

'I've tried to get it dismissed. No good. We must enter house. Follow me, please.'

It was only a distance of twenty-five yards, little more. But it seemed to Robert Aspinall to be the longest walk he had ever taken in his life.

Clutching Karen's hand in a vice-like grip of anxiety, he was led through to the main chamber and taken forward to two rows of black leather seats positioned some way forward from those of the public gallery.

Robert looked around to observe the various officiously attired dignitaries around the outer walls of the room. It didn't seem as regal as Crown Court, but that was a small crumb of comfort as David Williams now donned in wig and mantle, conferred with the Clerk before taking his seat in front of Robert.

David looked over his shoulder to address his client.

'How do you feel, Robert?'

'Terrible, David. Very scared. Very worried. What do I do now?'

'The Clerk will await the arrival of the magistrates which is when we will all stand. You remain standing. You will be asked to confirm your name and take an oath. Then you sit down. That's it. Leave the rest to me.'

'But what about *her* lawyer? Will you have to argue with him?'

David Williams glanced left and right before lowering his voice to a soft whisper.

'Mrs. Chapple isn't the plaintiff bringing this to court. It's the police that have caused this today. It's classed as misdemeanour. They will hear my defence for you and make a judgement on that. You are not on trial, Robert. You will walk away a free man, today. Have no fear.'

Robert's gaze fell toward the large raised wooden bench at the head of the chamber and the three empty chairs.

Thoughts of his precious daughters flashed through his mind. Thank goodness they were at school, completely oblivious of their father's disturbing quandary.

Robert clasped his sweating hands and stared vacantly around the room.

This was unreal.

It could not be happening to him.

Not to Robert Aspinall.

David turned round to Robert once again and gestured for him to move closer.

'Just one more thing, Robert. In a moment if you look very briefly behind you, to your left. The man on the back row in the corner. Brown jacket. Do you see him?'

Robert quickly glanced in the direction given.

He instantly recognised the unforgiving features of Jason Steel.

'Yes…I see him.'

'Do you know him?'

'Of sorts…why?'

David leaned closer and again whispered into Robert's ear.

The tension was now unbearable.

'I have been informed that he is acting as an enquiry agent on behalf of the complainant. In other words - he's a nosy sod. Do not *look* at him again. Do not *speak* to him. If he approaches you, do *not* acknowledge his presence. Certainly, answer *none* of his questions without consulting me first. Okay? Robert? Robert…are you listening?'

Robert could not believe his eyes.

A spy placed in the audience.

Even at the gallows Robert found his enemies spectating.

The cowardice of the Chapples was beyond despicable.

So, it *was* their car he had glimpsed earlier outside the courthouse.

'Yes. Okay, David. Thanks for the warning. I don't intend communicating with anyone to be honest.'

All conversation abruptly halted as the three gowned officiators entered the arena to an uneasy hush.

The clerk's bark of command declared procedure to be underway.

'ALL RISE.'

Robert moved unsteadily to his feet.

He instinctively turned to view Karen who sat three rows behind.

Her beaming smile was etched through a mask of raw desperation.

The moment of reckoning was now upon Robert as he confirmed his name and took his oath. He resumed his seat and sensed perspiration moistening the shirt on his back.

The three magistrates looked at Robert, no doubt looking for some signs of reaction to his current predicament. The middle of the three was a kindly looking lady, maybe with potential for sympathy. Flanking her, two gruff-faced men in spectacles. It was impossible to ascertain their combined mood.

The chamber waited with bated breath before the female magistrate began proceedings.

'For the benefit of the house, could we hear the original complainant's allegations, please?'

An officer of the court positioned at the front of the room stood and turned to the gallery, reading aloud from a sheet of paper in his hand.

'Statement from Mrs. Evelyn Chapple. Dated Sunday August Eighteenth, Nineteen-ninety-six:

Whilst in the middle of my weekly shopping, I recognised my long-time friend and neighbour Robert Aspinall approaching with his daughters. He was carrying his youngest, Lauren, in his arms. As I was about to politely greet them, he unleashed a torrent of abuse and continued to walk towards me, giving me serious concern for my position.

I immediately felt alarmed, harassed, and distressed. He was angry about something, and I couldn't get a word in. I thought at one stage he was intending to assault me such was his demeanour and language.

His concluding statement was that he would kill me should I ever go near him or his family again.

That is when I left the store in a state of shock, upset and disbelief. I have no idea what could have caused this behaviour from someone I thought I was a friend to.

I did not antagonise the situation in any way, shape or form.

I felt I had little other option but to recount the episode to the police in the form of an official criminal complaint. This is my statement in its entirety.'

Robert sat in total amazement and yet also enlightenment.

It was all so simple for her wasn't it.

No reference to anything aside the ten second exchange in the supermarket.

A no frills, straight to the point account of Robert's behaviour.

A casually frank and persuasive statement of condemnation.

She was just playing the game.

Using the mechanics of the law that were in place.

Robert eyed the three judges as they turned their direct attention to him. His heart lurched as the lady magistrate then offered a subtle nod of the head to each of her colleagues.

Her features conveyed little of her opinion at that moment.

The following seconds of silence were agonising as the spotlight finally fell on Robert Aspinall.

It was time for the truth.

It was time for justice.

It was time for a saviour.

The lady magistrate gestured to David Williams.

'Would the representative of the defendant please feel free, in your own time, to legislate on your client's behalf.'

*****

For over half an hour the courtroom swayed between responses of cautious disbelief and swelling sympathy as David Williams convincingly and professionally relayed the events of the previous months in full, unbridled, harrowing detail.

He had trans-scripted Robert's statement to the police and presented an incredibly emotive and damning portrayal of how four people's vulnerability had been gradually engineered by their neighbours next door.

Not to mention the wanton and nigh-on complete destruction of their once contented existence.

Every salient twist and turn in the story was accentuated to potent effect, leaving the magistrates visibly shaking their heads on more than one occasion, perhaps in utter contempt of what they were listening to.

Robert studiously observed the judges' reactions as his solicitor conveyed so convincingly the torrid diary of wrongdoings. Behind his seat, he could hear Karen stemming her tears as the milestones of torment were spot lit for public and lawful examination.

The vandalism; the assault; the lack of police interest; the endless parade of cruelty and abuse that had been administered by the Chapples.

Robert wiped his eyes as David Williams closed his unflinchingly powerful defence.

The solicitor thanked the magistrates for their undivided attention and courteously resumed his seat.

Discussion then ensued between the three officials as absolute quiet prevailed among the transfixed throng.

Whilst the delegation discussed their thoughts, David Williams swiftly repositioned himself next to his client, nudged him shoulder to shoulder, and smiled.

'There you are, Robert. Blinded them with facts and truth. They may adjourn if there is further need for debate. But I wouldn't have thought so, would you? I think we were pretty convincing, myself.'

Robert remained in a stupor of gratitude to his representative as he watched the judges swap responses in their ongoing debate.

'By the way, Robert. That mysterious enquiry agent we spotted earlier has conveniently vanished. Just thought you might like to know!'

Robert stared behind him and smirked at the vacant chair which Jason Steel had occupied. Evidently, the advantage had successfully switched hands sufficiently for the imposter to go and report the defeat.

The growing sense of ease was then harshly broken by the commanding tone of the female judge.

'Mister Aspinall…rise, please.'

Robert's legs again shook almost uncontrollably as he became the sole focus of attention in the house. He glanced back toward Karen once more, who managed to catch his eye and display another hopeful smile.

The forthcoming verdict was as much for his wife as for himself.

He grasped the wooden panelling in front to steady his balance.

A deathly stillness descended in the chamber as the decision was delivered.

The female magistrate sternly observed the defendant and began to relay her conclusions.

'Your behaviour, as I am sure you are now fully aware, is completely unacceptable in the public domain. Your actions may have incited real concern amongst several innocent people in the vicinity. Disruption of the public peace - however quantified - is something that we as a court can never condone.

Threats of violence made directly to another person are taken extremely seriously when brought to our attention.

Under no circumstances do we feel such conduct should be tolerated. This must be clear to you, already.

However, it is quite evident from your given statement that as a responsible family man and upstanding, law-abiding citizen, you were acting completely out of character, and that you were under extreme duress. Your threshold had finally broken. That much is obvious.

And with you having no previous involvement in such activity on record, I firmly believe that your actions were borne out of a sustained period of incredible, upsetting frustration.

And in similar vein, despite the threatening nature of the altercation, I do not believe that your choice of words was a premeditated conveyance of promise.

I trust that this initial foray into such realms will also be your last. It is with this in mind, that I bestow upon you the following orders.

There will be no fixed penalty on this occasion.

However, you will leave this court under the terms of a twelve-month conditional discharge. Needless to say, that any subsequent recurrence of such behaviour will alter my thinking on this judgement should it lead you back before this bench.

Your sole financial bearing today will be the cost of these proceedings.

Mister Aspinall…you are free to go. Chamber dismissed.'

*****

Despite the sudden movement all around him, Robert was transfixed by the view in front.

His eyes stared forward, following the magistrates as they left the room.

He could detect familiar voices from behind his seat.

Then he sensed the fragrant aroma of his wife's perfume, and the welcome reassurance of her voice in his ear.

'You were incredible, Rob. I'm so proud of you. I love you.'

Finally, Robert Aspinall turned to face his family. Entering the warmth of Karen's embrace, he breathed deeply to saturate himself in the moment.

Brian shook his hand in congratulations. Jean's stoic act of maternal concern that had for so long been in place had now given way to sincere pleasure at the thought of Robert's absolute vindication.

For the first time in months, Robert Aspinall felt an inner happiness that was both consoling and relieving.

The dreaded moment of reckoning had arrived and had now passed.

The truth had been heard; the brilliant light of correctness had overpowered the creeping shadow of injustice.

Out in the foyer, David Williams waited for his client with a hand outstretched.

Triumphant smiles were exhibited by all.

'Thank you, David. You were immense. In fact, you were magnificent.'

The solicitor expressed his delight at the outcome as he handed over an envelope containing his invoice.

'Well done, Robert. Never in doubt. There's really no rush for payment. Go and celebrate.'

Robert's solicitor bid farewell to the family, strode through the glass exit doors of the foyer, and disappeared toward the car park.

A job well and truly done.

All in a day's work, for Mr. David Williams.

With business at the court remittance counter swiftly and generously taken care of by Brian and Jean, Robert finally took Karen's hand and walked proudly into the early autumn sunshine.

The air was laced with a chilling breeze, but the blue skies above brought promise of a brighter future at long last.

Joy was with the Aspinalls once more.

Today, victory was theirs to savour.

forty-five

Wednesday. The ninth of October. The euphoria generated by the previous week's triumph in court had been heavily tempered by Karen's imminent appointment at Tenbridge Infirmary.

The dermatology department was positioned at the end of a maze of white and pale green corridors that left Karen and her father struggling for clues as to their eventual destination.

'Bloody hell, Kaz. I hope they're going to replace my shoe leather after all this walking!'

Karen smiled at Brian's quip before recognising the number of the ward that she required. Confirming the appointment time with the receptionist, she sat next to her father in contemplation of her symptoms.

'It feels like I've got another face growing, Dad. It's rock hard.'

Brian leaned over and examined the area where the cyst had been caked in make-up and foundation.

'Be gone soon enough, love. They'll sort you out. Now you've put the past behind you. It'll clear up quickly.'

Unexpectedly, their conversation was interrupted by a female voice from behind the reception desk.

'Mrs. Aspinall…you can go through, now.'

Kissing her father on the cheek, Karen strode uneasily across the room towards the smiling male specialist who opened the door to a private consultation area and requested she relax and take a seat.

Commencing with procedural questions whilst donning a pair of rubber gloves, he began to press gently on her cheek.

'Have you had any treatment for this cyst, Karen?'

Karen's inner nerves were betrayed by her croaking voice.

'No. My doctor suggested it might go away on its own.'

'Has your GP administered a prescription for steroid cream for the damage to the skin around the eyes and forehead?'

'Yes.'

'The cream appears to be working effectively. But I think I need to sample some fluid. Just as a precaution.'

'Precaution against what?'

'Against infection…Karen.'

'Can't you just cut the damn thing out?'

‘No…we can’t…not without a considerable risk of scarring.’

‘Do you mean I’m stuck with it?’

‘No…not at all. This is symptomatic of a traumatic bodily reaction to stress. When the stress eases, the symptoms will ease, hence the swelling will reduce. I just want to ensure that there are no nasties in there, that’s all.’

The consultant smiled as he discarded his gloves into a medical bin.

Karen felt mildly placated by his light-hearted approach.

‘There’s very little we can do at this time. Your body has created the cyst for a reason. Your body must remove it again. I will send you to the duty nurse for the department. She is here today. You can see her immediately’

The waiting endured for less than ten minutes.

Having secured a sample from the cyst for testing, the consultant emerged from his office and gave Karen permission to leave.

‘What? That’s it, then? All done? What about the lump on my breast? What about the scan for that?’

‘All in good time. All these symptoms on your file are indicative of your physical reaction to circumstance. However, we only deal in skin condition, not breasts. Sorry. But I’m sure your GP has organised everything. It looks to me like you’re very run down. You need rest. Your body needs to recover. I will send this for analysis and if we need to see you again…we will do, I promise. If you don’t hear from this clinic again, then you must not worry. The best thing you can do is go home and try to forget it. The symptoms *will* disappear…trust me.’

*****

It was late evening when Robert called from his hotel room in Coventry and Karen relayed the details of the morning’s hospital visit. Both sensed that they had moved forward significantly in only the days few since the appointment in court.

Their relationship was already shifting to a positive new plane.

The past was seemingly, thankfully, in the past.

The trepidation of many weeks had slowly vanished along with the demons that encouraged it.

The future was now uppermost in the mind of Karen Aspinall as she confessed her wishes to her distant husband over the lounge telephone.

With her grandchildren sat either side of her, Jean Hope listened to her daughter's side of the dialogue. She had been made aware of Karen's train of thought regarding the family's longer-term plan.

It was secretly upsetting for Jean to accept, but as a doting mother and grandmother she would willingly sacrifice her selfish whims in exchange for her family securing happier times ahead.

'I've decided I want us to move house, Rob.'

'To be together again as a family.'

'To Coventry.'

'So that I can see you every day.'

'So that Chloe and Lauren can see you every day.'

'It's the only way forward.'

'Yes…I know I've surprised you by saying this.'

'Yes…I know my parents are here.'

'Mum and Dad know how I feel.'

'They are one hundred percent behind us.'

'Yes, I've thought about the schooling issue. Of course, I have.'

'But it doesn't matter. Our marriage matters. Our family matters.'

'That's why I want to make a clean break.'

'As soon as possible.'

'Well, if your work can help with the relocation, then brilliant.'

'I just want things to move quickly, now.'

'I'm tired of sitting around dwelling on history.'

'I want to feel like me again. I want to play a part again.'

'We can't live like this forever. It's not fair on anyone.'

'The girls will be fine about it. They always are.'

'Rob…I'm sick of thinking. I need to *act* on this.'

'See what you can organise. We'll go house-hunting.'

'Come and fetch me. I need to do this for my own sanity.'

'I want to make a new home for us. In a new place.'

'Somewhere safe. To start our life again.'

forty-six

It had taken Karen three full weekend visits around the suburbs of Coventry to find the location that suited. Her affections centred on an ideally situated house in a small yet welcoming market town. Mostly urbanised but with a hint of the rural setting that Karen had a natural affinity for.

Kenilworth was little more than five miles from the city centre. A fifteen-minute drive for Robert to get to work. A short walk for Karen to escort the girls to their new primary and infant schools which they would commence before the end of the month.

After some vital and time saving input from Robert's employer, the quest for permanent relocation was an accomplished and problem-free experience.

On the plot of number seventy-seven, Seedling Road, an eighty-four-year-old semi-detached, three-bedroomed abode awaited its new occupants. It needed some attention inside and out, but Karen was more than willing to rise to the challenge.

Most importantly, this was to be the wonderful new setting for the next phase in the lives of the Aspinalls.

Yet before Karen could indulge herself in the pleasures of creating her new surroundings to taste, a final shadow still loomed over proceedings.

Tomorrow was the day that Karen had feared most.

The closing of the previous chapter in their lives.

Successful departure from the ashes of the past entailed one more unavoidable, dispiriting task.

The last ever visit to number thirty-nine, Benton Road.

*****

Saturday. The twenty-third of November. Robert glanced across to his wife as they turned the corner of the T junction and entered Benton Road for the very final time.

Sitting beside them behind the wheel of the removal van was Geoff Smart - a trusted former colleague of Robert's from the local branch.

The plan was simple.

Load the van until the house was empty.

Then leave.

Forever.

Having risen with the larks to accommodate the arrival of Geoff and the van, dawn was barely in its infancy when the trio came to a stop outside the house.

Benton Road lay dark, silent, and still.

The day was not yet begun here.

No children playing. No cars shooting through over the speed limit.

No nosey neighbours peering over hedgerows.

And as Karen quickly confirmed to herself with a wary check beyond the windscreen, no sign of life from number forty-one.

Robert had insisted they start early to give them the best chance of offloading before sunset that afternoon, but it was a very tall order. Daylight was now at a premium. Time was already verging against the operation.

Besides, Karen thought it might be quite romantic to spread the job out over a weekend. She was relishing the prospect of spending the first night in her new home - albeit mostly unfurnished.

With a degree of stealth and consideration for a street still in slumber, the trio quietly approached the front door and let themselves inside. The hallway was dank and unwelcoming.

Several items of mail lay scattered on the doormat which Karen forcibly thrust into her handbag. All relevant addressees had already been notified of the change.

There would be no more misplaced postings at *this* house.

Robert and Geoff looked around upstairs to ascertain what to shift first. Karen found herself alone with her thoughts in the empty, echoing kitchen.

So often a place of thriving activity.

A hive of bustle and noise.

So many times, the setting for wonderful, organised family chaos.

The pine dining table had acquired a layer of dust. Karen pictured Emily and Lauren playing board games either side of it, or hurriedly eating their breakfast because their mother couldn't get them up for school early enough.

Her attention moved to beyond the kitchen window to the back garden and its varying landmarks.

She unlocked the back door and wandered onto the overgrown lawn.

The paddling pool; still sat half full of water.

The baby conifers had long since lost any will to strive and merely resembled six twisted, brittle branches standing in the ground.

That blasted shed that she had finally managed to get moved.

There was nothing in there that carried any fond memory.

The carefully weeded borders were now weed-strewn once again.

The dried stems of her raided border plants still lay on display.

The scattered remnants of illicit intrusion.

Foxes indeed.

The sun was now creeping above the roofline and intent on clearing the mist, hopefully leading to a fine late autumn day for uprooting one's life once and for all.

The scene was set for evacuation.

Yet Karen felt strangely compelled to hang fire.

Despite her determination to leave Church Drayton, she could not combat a gnawing sense of deep sorrow at the occasion.

So many memories.

So many good times.

Why must it all be cast aside?

Why was it that the Aspinalls were having to vacate the place they had nurtured for so long as their own?

Karen had accommodated and resisted many turns of emotion in the previous months.

Yet today, on her last day within the walls of number thirty-nine, she was overcome by the torrential injustice of it all.

There was no longer the fear.

No longer the anger.

No longer the hatred or the anticipation.

Thankfully, there was no longer the relentless, unyielding stress.

Just a lingering, unrelenting conviction that the game had been far from fair.

The losers did not deserve to lose.

She wondered if this feeling would ever leave her side.

'We had a look around, Kaz. We'll make a start loading if you want o begin boxing up the remaining small stuff.'

Karen did not hear her husband's call from the back door.

Her mind had ventured into other realms. Only when he joined her in the garden and kissed her on the side of her head did she become alerted to her present surroundings again.

'Sorry, Rob? What did you say?'

Robert gazed into her blue eyes that had suffered so much pain.

They were not lifeless, but the spark had long been absent.

It suddenly occurred to him that for Karen, moving away was a very necessary yet terminally agonising wrench.

'I just said, me and Geoff…we'll make a start. You stay indoors and pack up the rest of the smaller stuff you want, darling. Take your time. The boxes and tape are in the hallway.'

With those words, her husband and his friend bounded up the stairs to begin the move in earnest.

*****

It was mid-morning when Robert entered one of the now-emptied bedrooms to find Karen picking through a selection of old photographs.

'Hi, love.' she smiled. 'Just reviving a bit of the past. I shouldn't but I can't help it. I feel so sad.'

Robert crouched beside his wife in complete sympathy.

'Of course, you do. I do too, Kaz. It's a crap situation, isn't it? Fucking crap. Erm…by the way…somebody's here to see you. She thought you might try and sneak off without saying goodbye. So, she's come to find you.'

Karen looked at her husband bemusedly before he disappeared back down the stairs.

Rising wearily to her feet, Karen scanned the vacant space where Robert had been standing.

'Hello? Who's there?'

'Thought you might need some help, girly.'

There was no face visible at that moment, but the voice was instantly recognisable from behind the adjacent bedroom door.

'Judy? JUDY!' screamed Karen in delight.

Lifelong friends giggled and embraced on the landing.

But kisses and smiles were soon eclipsed by the forceful onset o mutually drawn emotion as they held each other tightly.

Neither wanting to let the other go.

Karen buried her weeping eyes into the shoulder of one her true soul mate and confidante.

It was the release that Karen needed.

Pulling away, she looked at Judy, whose similar upset at the outcome of events was painfully evident.

'Kaz…Jesus…did things really get so bad?'

Karen dried her moistened cheeks on her sleeve.

'Too bad, Jude. Unbelievable. I can't even begin to tell you.'

'You don't look good, Kaz.'

'I'm fine. I've seen doctors and stuff. I'm getting there. The lump in my breast is nothing. I'm sorry for not telling you, Jude…it's just that with all…'

Judy Simpson placed a forefinger to her own pursed lips and slowly shook her head.

'It doesn't matter. I know all about it. We're together, now. You're going to be fine. I understand, Kaz. I totally understand why you've got to start again.'

Offering her friend another hug, Karen conveyed a cold truth through a trembling whisper.

'You saw it all coming, didn't you, Jude? You *knew*, didn't you? I…I didn't listen, did I?'

Judy drew back and held Karen's gaze.

'Nobody could have known, Kaz. Anyway, it's all in the past, now. I've just been to your mum's. They are on their way. They are bringing the girls. You're not alone in this. She told me about court and all that business. It's all over, Kaz. You drive away from here today and then it's all over. Do you hear?'

Karen rubbed her eyes once more and allowed her features to display her most convincing smile.

'Come on then, Jude…let's get on with it. I'm a bit sick of the bloody place now, anyway.'

*****

By mid-afternoon the daunting yet surprisingly organised task of filling the removal van had been achieved.

Number thirty-nine was now rendered an empty vessel.

A vortex from history where happy memories had succumbed.

The demons had long since moved in to destroy loving harmony.

Haunting jeopardy lingered in every pore of every brick, in every pane of glass and in every blade of grass.

No more the family home.

This was no longer a safe place for the children to play.

Much as it crucified their mother to concede such a fact.

With six pairs of adult hands to help complete the job and two excited little girls to obstruct proceedings, the operation was finished.

The band of volunteers stood in the vacant lounge to reflect for just a fleeting moment.

Karen felt the need to offer her unwavering gratitude.

'I would just like to say, on behalf of myself and Rob…thank you to you all. You've been brilliant. All of you. I never thought we'd get done so quick.'

Geoff Smart highlighted one oversight Karen may have been guilty of.

'We've emptied the garage of what was salvageable. But what about the motor? I bet the battery's flat as a pancake!'

Karen followed Robert, her father and Geoff out front and stared at the back end of her red car.

She looked at her husband, who shrugged his shoulders.

'It's been stood for months. Do you actually still want it, Kaz? To be honest, you aren't going to need a car in the interim.'

Then a little voice carried through the indecision.

'I want you to take it, Mummy. I like it.'

Picking Lauren from the floor, Karen spoke softly to relay her personal verdict.

'But its old, darling. It's time for Daddy to buy us a new one, I think. Don't you?'

There was a pause for thought before Lauren eagerly nodded her head and jumped from her mother's grasp.

'Okay. New car then Daddy, please.'

Karen's father offered a welcome suggestion which placated all at the scene.

'Leave me the keys, Kaz. I'll get one or two of my lads to take a look in the week. They like to tinker with motors. Though it might be worth more at the scrappers than it is sat there. Mind you, if you leave the garage doors open some little shit might come and pinch it if we're lucky!'

The rare sound of laughter echoed around the driveway.

It was an unusual resonance in the vicinity.

One not heard there for many weeks.

It was also a signal for movement in the shadows.

Somebody had detected the audible air of accomplishment emanating from the driveway of number thirty-nine.

And they had slyly moved into position behind closed curtains to gain a better view.

'Right then, come on!' ordered Robert. 'Let's leave this cursed town behind!'

Jean secured Chloe and Lauren into the front of Brian's van before embracing her daughter with the words of a loving mother.

'Have a good weekend, Karen. Drive safely to Coventry. Don't worry about the girls. I'm very sorry for all you've been through. But I also want you to know how proud I am for the way you've dealt with it. Today is a new start. For all of us.'

Karen gave the only correct response.

'I love you, Mum. I love you, Dad. Me and Rob will be back for the girls early next week, hopefully.'

Brian Hope winked and waved to his daughter before jumping in behind the wheel of the van.

With the Hopes taking Chloe and Lauren back off to Goltham, Judy now optioned her turn to bid her friend farewell.

'Keep in touch. I've got your new address and phone number. I'll come and get on your nerves very soon. I promise! I'm really gonna miss you, Kaz!'

Through a watery gaze, Karen mouthed words of thanks and squeezed her friend tightly in an effort to hide more tears.

As Judy drove away into the distance, Geoff and Robert stood waiting next to the removal van.

'We've locked everywhere up, love. Your dad took all the keys. Ready when you are.'

Karen turned to Robert and smiled half-heartedly as she took one last peek through her old lounge window.

Bare floors; bare walls; a lifeless hovel of a former dwelling.

It required a considerable amount of will power to even begin the final walk across the driveway of number thirty-nine.

Flashes of a happy history pierced Karen's mind.

As she pulled the large white, wooden gate behind her and slipped on the latch, her mind was still in turmoil over what had transpired, yet the future already looked prosperous.

She scanned the front wall of the house one final time in readiness to face the new stage of her family's life.

Regret and remorse jabbed at her conscience.

But then, right on cue, came the moment of unquestionable affirmation.

From the corner of her eye Karen identified an observing presence in the adjacent residence.

Focusing fully on the area in question, she watched as the lounge curtains of number forty-one were pushed open, fully revealing Evelyn Chapple's crooked, callous form.

The women stared at one another, separated by distance, by glass and by time.

A chill went through Karen as Evelyn gradually adopted a sneering, almost haunting smirk.

She then began to wave at her ex-friend and neighbour in a mocking enactment of sympathy.

Karen stood, rooted to the spot beyond the gate.

She found herself saddened by the finality of the gesture.

And shocked by Evelyn Chapple's misguided but conveniently timed bravery.

Karen withstood the spectacle for a few seconds but could not summon any form of response.

The exaggerated waving did not yield as Karen eventually turned on her heel and joined her husband and Geoff in the removal van that now contained her life's possessions.

Erasing the unpleasant vision of wickedness from her mind, Karen closed the van door, buckled her seat belt, and looked firmly to the road ahead.

forty-seven

December the ninth. Monday. Eight-twenty-seven a.m.

'Hi, Karen. First day for them today, is it? Are they excited?'

'Oh…I'm not so sure about that, Gillian.' replied Karen, shivering in the sharp winter air as she guided her daughters out of the house onto the front path.

'Lauren looks a bit frightened. Here. This will cheer her up. One for Chloe, too.'

Lauren and Chloe took the chocolate bars from Gillian Jones, the widowed, elderly lady who lived next door to the Aspinall family at number seventy-five, Seedling Road.

'What do you say, girls?' insisted Karen as she nodded in gratitude to her new neighbour.

The acknowledgements of the gift were audible and earnest as Chloe and Lauren put the treats into their school bags for break time.

'I must say, Karen. You snapped this place up quickly. It had only been for sale a month or so. But its lovely to have such a nice family living next door.'

Karen was appreciative of the compliment. From the very limited time spent in her company, Karen believed Gillian to be a genuine character.

'Well, hopefully our old house won't take long to shift, either. We've accepted an offer. Shouldn't be long before the ball is rolling with our sale.'

Karen was nervous as she locked up and commenced her first journey with the girls to their new schools.

The air was armed with a biting breeze, but the neighbourly warmth was a fine antidote.

'Do you have to go into town afterwards or are you coming straight home again?' enquired Gillian.

Karen adjusted Lauren's scarf as she contemplated the question.

'Erm…well I was going to come straight back. I've a lot of work to do! Though I might get stuck at school if these two decide to play me up!'

Gillian smiled and clasped her hands as she retreated to her own front door.

'Just fine Karen, my dear…I'll have a pot of tea waiting for your return. About half hour, okay?'

'Okay. Thank you, Gillian. That would be lovely.'

*****

'Oh, hello Rob. Come in. Please sit down. Just a brief chat about things at home. That's all.'

David Marsden perched opposite Robert in the personnel office of Sissons Incorporated.

'We've all been very concerned about your personal situation, Rob. How you've managed to keep abreast of things here I can't imagine. I just wondered if you might need any further assistance in any way. Is there anything that Sissons can help with?'

Robert offered a smile of complete reassurance.

'David, this company has already gone beyond the call of duty. Especially with finding the new house and all. Aside from saving my marriage, you've probably saved my sanity as well.'

David sat forward in his chair.

'Nobody can even begin to guess what happened back in Tenbridge, Rob. We respect the fact that it was private domestic business, and we appreciate the contact that you maintained with us. If you ever feel you need to talk over things, perhaps some stress counselling? It's a common problem these days.'

Robert raised his hand and shook his head.

'No need, David. Honestly. My story is not one that I want to relate to again in a hurry. I want to forget it. Put it behind me. It's finished. In the past. Well and truly. But I thank you for your consideration.'

'Sometimes the effects of personal ordeal can lie dormant for a while, Rob. Whatever you do, don't bottle things up. You're too valuable to us to be distracted elsewhere.'

Robert Aspinall looked his personnel director squarely in the eye.

'Really, David. It's all over as far as I'm concerned. Laid to rest.'

*****

That evening, Karen stood in front of her new bathroom mirror and commenced the latest inspection of her suffering physique. In truth, she had hardly thought about her ailments since arriving permanently in Kenilworth.

Her mind had been totally occupied with the agenda of decorating, rearranging, and revitalising the new environment.

She prodded and poked various areas whilst trying to scrutinise her reflection.

A wave of euphoria descended as she scanned the cyst on her cheek, now fully cleansed of masking foundation.

'ROB! ROB! Come up here!'

Hauling himself from the sanctity of the settee, he placed his beer can on the side table and trudged upstairs. It had been a long while since he had seen the natural sparkle in his wife's blue eyes.

For the first time in an age, it appeared to be back.

Literally dragging him before the mirror, she offered a close-up of her face.

'Look, Rob! Look!'

He squinted at the area under her finger.

'What, love. What am I looking at?'

'My skin. On my cheek! The lump. It's smaller. My skin's getting better, Rob! The cyst is reducing. I'm sure of it. I haven't looked properly for a week or two. But I'm sure it's receding. I can't believe it!'

Placing her lips near his, she made a statement that she once thought would never arise in discussion again.

'Rob…I'm happy again…are you?'

'Yes, love. Very happy. It's been a mad rush lately, but we did it, didn't we? We are here!'

'We are, darling. And thankfully the girls had a good first day at their new schools. You never quite know, do you?'

A weary husband held a jubilant wife in his tired arms as she led them on an improvised waltz around the landing.

However, the few seconds of silliness was interrupted by Chloe as she stood in the bedroom doorway in her pyjamas.

'Mummy…I can't sleep.'

'Well, try harder. Second day at school tomorrow! Get a drink of water then back to bed.'

'When can I have my own room, Mummy? Like at the old house?'

‘When we’ve got round to decorating it, Chloe. Its full of Mummy and Daddy’s things just now so you will have to share with your sister until the New Year. I know its cramped, but you’ll just have to wait. Now be a good girl and get a drink and then get in bed.’

As her mother and father shuffled downstairs, Chloe drank some water from a beaker in the bathroom.

She climbed back under the bedclothes as her younger sister stirred in the half light.

‘Lauren…are you awake?’

There was no verbal reply from her sibling in the bed opposite, aside a prolonged sigh of fatigue.

‘Lauren…wake up. I’ve got something to tell you.’

Begrudgingly, Lauren sat up in bed as her parents’ giggles echoed up the stairwell and beyond the girls’ open bedroom door.

Rubbing her eyes, she struggled to focus on her elder sister across the other side of the room.

‘What is it Chloe…I’m tired…’

Another pause ensued before Chloe continued.

‘Can you keep a secret?’

‘Yes.’ muttered Lauren

‘Promise me? I’ve not even told this to Mum.’

‘*Yes*. What is it?’

Lauren listened impatiently in the semi-darkness as her sister prepared to convey her findings.

When Chloe finally spoke, the revelation did not fully register with the weary four-year-old.

Nor did the implications.

‘Lauren…guess who I saw outside the school gate at home time today…’

epilogue

Tuesday. Christmas Eve. Five minutes until Midnight.

Kenilworth; Warwickshire. Such a picturesque town.

Particularly at this most special time of the year.

The jet velvet backcloth of the evening sky played host to a million silver lights.

Excitement brewed among youngsters everywhere, in readiness for the much-heralded annual visitor.

Only a smattering of amber-hued pools punctuated the darkened vista of a sleeping neighbourhood.

In one such house, a family had rejoiced in its welcome resumption of domestic routine and a long overdue recognition of familiar sights, sounds and feelings.

The pleasurable sight of joyous children.

The welcome sound of hearty laughter.

The forgotten feelings of love that had long been submerged amid tormenting, suppressing waves of perilous anxiety.

That family now looked to a new phase of prosperity.

Having vanquished the evil that plagued them for so long, they resided within the walls of their new home as it slowly grew around them and protected them.

Immersed in renewed contentment, peace was theirs to embrace once again.

*****

Outside, a curious fox shuffled between the shadows on its nightly scavenge.

Approaching the kerbside to venture onward along Seedling Road, it temporarily ceased its search and remained at the house numbered seventy-seven to sense the joy within.

Satisfied with its findings, the fox stepped into the gutter, only to be startled by the headlights of an approaching car.

Making a hasty retreat to the relative safety of the pavement, it watched in covert silence as the car slowly came to a stop, before its quietly chugging engine was disengaged.

Neither movement nor utterance was detected from within the vehicle.

Ever alert, the fox never diverted its attention from the mysterious, black saloon.

Seconds turned to minutes, yet still no murmur or motion prevailed.

It was evidently a time for simple observation.

Then without warning, the car engine found life once more and pulled away from the scene, with the occupants seemingly having concluded their study.

Subsequently, the fox twitched its ears and nose as it watched red taillights merge with the distant murk and finally disappear once more into the night.

The residents of number seventy-seven never heard the fox's departing cry as they dreamed pleasant dreams amid their comforting slumber.

It was a shrill bark that carried on the freezing air, penetrating walls and windows all around.

Then as the fox moved silently onward, thoughts of the large, black saloon remained at the forefront of its mind.

It was now wary of the car's possible, unannounced reappearance, and remained vigilante until eventually convinced it was safe from harm.

The knowledge that the fox carried, it carried alone, as the family in the house numbered seventy-seven continued to sleep soundly.

They would never know of that discreet episode in the dead of night.

All they would have possibly detected was the echoing shriek of a wily fox as it passed through the neighbourhood.

Such a secretive…cunning…rodent…

ACKNOWLEDGEMENTS

I wish to thank the following people for their invaluable expertise and support in helping this book gain wings:
Samantha Thornton; Hannah Bliss; Charlotte Wilson; Robbie Wilson; Carole Thornton, Chris Bliss; Charlotte Bliss; Jeanette Taylor Ford; Sue Hayward; Ford Wood and last but certainly not least, David Slaney for his superb cover design.
I couldn't have done it without any of you.
I am forever indebted.
RJT

Also Available on Amazon
by Richard John Thornton

DELIVER US FROM EVIL

AT HELL'S GATE

THE SWANS AT CLEARLAKE

Printed in Great Britain
by Amazon